"All the charm of a Norman Rockwell painting, but with a much more colorful cast of characters!"
—Cynthia Baxter, author of the
Reigning Cats & Dogs Mysteries

"Celebrate Shelley Freydont's new mystery series in Celebration Bay, a city of festivals where the event coordinator plans everything. Except solving murders."
—Janet Bolin, author of the Threadville Mysteries

"Event coordinator Liv Montgomery is doing her best to squash any obstacles to a successful Celebration Bay Harvest Festival, and when a body crops up, she's not going to let her plans be plowed under."
—Sheila Connolly, national bestselling author of
the Orchard Mysteries

"*Foul Play at the Fair* is a fun romp of a story. A delicious read filled with interesting characters and good times."
—Joyce Lavene, coauthor of the Missing Pieces Mysteries

"The fun first Celebration Bay Mystery is an engaging whodunit starring a burned-out protagonist who, though she fled the city, remains in a constant state of stress."
—*Genre Go Round Reviews*

"Liv Montgomery is a terrific new amateur sleuth, competent, intelligent, with a few surprising skills. *Foul Play at the Fair* just leaves me wishing to return soon for more of Liv's adventures in a community that capitalizes on its small-town atmosphere." —*Lesa's Book Critiques*

Berkley Prime Crime titles by Shelley Freydont

FOUL PLAY AT THE FAIR
SILENT KNIFE

Silent Knife

Shelley Freydont

BERKLEY PRIME CRIME, NEW YORK

THE BERKLEY PUBLISHING GROUP
Published by the Penguin Group
Penguin Group (USA)
375 Hudson Street, New York, New York 10014, USA

USA I Canada I UK I Ireland I Australia I New Zealand I India I South Africa I China

Penguin Books Ltd., Registered Offices: 80 Strand, London WC2R 0RL, England
For more information about the Penguin Group, visit penguin.com.

SILENT KNIFE

A Berkley Prime Crime Book / published by arrangement with the author

Berkley Prime Crime Books are published by The Berkley Publishing Group.
BERKLEY® PRIME CRIME and the PRIME CRIME logo are
trademarks of Penguin Group (USA).
For information, address: The Berkley Publishing Group,
a division of Penguin Group (USA),
375 Hudson Street, New York, New York 10014.

ISBN: 978-0-425-25238-3

PUBLISHING HISTORY
Berkley Prime Crime mass-market edition / September 2013

PRINTED IN THE UNITED STATES OF AMERICA

10 9 8 7 6 5 4 3 2 1

Cover art by Robert Crawford.
Cover design by Lesley Worrell.
Interior text design by Tiffany Estreicher.

ALWAYS LEARNING   **PEARSON**

Chapter One

....

"Santa's in your office and he's hopping mad."

Liv Montgomery looked from her assistant, Ted, to the closed door of her office. "He hasn't even come to town. What seems to be the problem?"

Ted shrugged. "He wouldn't say."

"That doesn't mean you don't know." Ted Driscoll was a handsome sixty-something man, tall, thin, with a shock of thick white hair. He was slightly mysterious and the fount of local gossip. Today his usual three-piece suit had been replaced with a reindeer sweater.

"No, but in this case, you'd better ask him yourself. He didn't even say hello. Just lumbered in here and demanded to talk to the town event organizer. Since that's you, I left him in your office. Where's my favorite dawg today?"

"Over at the Woofery. He had a run-in with an overturned garbage can, and Sharise took him in on short notice."

Ted shuddered. "Poor thing, and I was hoping to get him rehearsed for the *Messiah* sing-along."

"Don't you dare." Since Liv moved to Celebration Bay three months before to become the town's event coordinator,

Ted and her Westie, Whiskey, had bonded over a mutual love of singing. Both howled loudly and happily off-key whenever they got together.

"Have you had lunch?"

Liv shook her head. "I've been at the inn, double-checking on the Dickens Dinner. They're fine."

"Told you. The Andersons have been doing a version of goose and turkey for years." Ted perched one hip on his desk and reached for the phone. "I'll call Buddy's for delivery. You go deal with Santa."

Hank Ousterhout was "chubby and plump" and about six foot two. A thick white beard tumbled over his chest to the belt buckle of his jeans. His cheeks were rosy, but not with merriment. Santa was pissed.

"Mr. Ousterhout. How nice to see you." Liv stuck out her hand.

The not-so-jolly giant grumbled but took her hand and pumped it.

Liv eased her fingers from his grip.

"Have a seat."

Ousterhout pulled a chair up to her desk with one hand, sat down, and leaned forward on his elbows. His beard spread over the desktop in front of him.

She sat behind her desk. "Ted tells me you have some concerns."

"That woman," he rumbled. "That—that woman." He fairly vibrated with anger.

"Which woman?" Liv asked, though she thought she knew. The manager of the newly opened Trim a Tree shop on the square was not doing much to instill the Christmas spirit among the townspeople or her customers.

She'd moved in over the Thanksgiving weekend, and during the following two weeks, Liv had received scores of complaints by phone, mail, email, and the Celebration Bay website and Facebook page.

Liv had encountered her once and that was enough. Grace

Thornsby's attitude added insult to injury when the town's small year-round holiday store had disappeared to be replaced by Made in Taiwan.

"You're not going to let her get away with it, are you?"

"Certainly not." Liv wondered what "it" was this time. The tasteless window display? The cheap merchandise inside?

The manager of TAT, as the store was called among the locals, had offended just about everyone. She refused to adhere to the council decorating guidelines. Had refused to contribute to the Celebration Bay Toys for Tykes Christmas Party. Was rude to her customers and humiliated her employees in front of them. If Liv didn't stop this now, it would be an awful few weeks until TAT closed down in January. And she couldn't let that happen.

Mr. Ousterhout's beefy fist slammed on the table, rattling Liv's paper-clip holder. "She hired her own Santa."

"Ah," Liv said. "Maybe she wasn't aware of the one-Santa rule here." Though TAT along with every other business in town had been sent reminders of town policy.

"The heck she ain't. Why Roger Newland sold to Clarence Thornsby is beyond me. Why he sold at all is a mystery. He didn't tell nobody. We woulda helped him out if we knew he was having troubles." Hank stopped to shake his massive head.

"And we don't need no store like that Trim a Tree in Celebration Bay. And we don't need but one Santa. I've been Santa here for over ten years. We only allow one Santa in town, and that's the town Santa, since we don't want the children getting confused with a bunch of hawkers, and jarring their belief in the real Santa.

"I won't be party to some cheap-selling gimmick. When we let a bunch of outsiders take over, the town'll go to hell. And that's a fact." He wound down and took a breath that ruffled his beard.

Liv stood up. "Thanks for letting me know. I'll get over there and explain our policy more fully. She might be getting guff from her corporate office, and if that's the case, I'll speak with someone who can make the change."

"Thank you. And you can tell her for me if she makes one more nasty remark about my, um, about me, she'll be sorry."

Liv smiled tightly as she waited for him to work himself out of the chair. She was particularly sensitive to threats, whether meant or not. Since moving to Celebration Bay in the fall, she'd already been involved in a murder investigation, something that had never happened in all her years of event planning in Manhattan. Go figure.

"You just get ready for the Santa Parade. I'll take care of the other Santa." Liv hadn't regretted taking this job or moving to upstate New York for a minute. But she had to admit some jobs were easier than others, and locking horns with the manager of Trim a Tree was not one of the easy ones. Grace Thornsby was not on *any* Santa's "nice" list.

Liv gently steered her visitor through the outer office to the door. "Don't worry, Mr. Ousterhout. We'll have this sorted out in no time."

"Before tomorrow's Santa Parade and tree lighting?"

"Before the parade," Liv assured him.

"I meant what I said." He turned on his heel, nearly knocking down the deliveryman from Buddy's who had just entered carrying a large brown bag and wearing a Santa hat.

Christmas was a big season for the town, and the citizens pulled out all the stops. Even the deliverymen.

"Hey, Hank," said the young man.

"Jason." Hank nodded gruffly and struck off down the hall.

"Betcha he came to complain about the Trim a Tree lady," Jason said, handing Ted the bag. "I've been helping him out at the machine shop in my spare time, and she sure knows how to rile him. And everybody else. You should have heard them during the breakfast rush this morning."

"I bet." Ted didn't need to be on-site to know what they'd said. He was the switchboard for Celebration Bay gossip. It made him indispensable as an assistant and as a friend.

"Yeah, I hate Penny having to work for that old—they were supposed to be helping the Newlands out. That's a joke.

When we're married, Penny's not going to have to work unless she wants to, and not for the likes of Grace Thornsby."

Ted handed him a couple of dollars. "Merry Christmas, Jason."

"Thanks, Mr. Driscoll. Genny'll put it on your tab. Merry Christmas."

Liv closed the door behind him. "So the delivery boy's fiancée is working at Trim a Tree?"

"Yep. Let's eat." Ted carried food into Liv's office and placed it on her desk. "We need sustenance before we face the Harridan of the Holidays. Pastrami and split-pea soup?"

They ate lunch at Liv's desk as they did most days, since they rarely had time to take a real lunch break.

"Maybe you should bring me up to speed on the Santa, Newlands, and Trim a Tree situation."

"This is what I know," Ted said as he unwrapped his sandwich.

"The Newland family ran a holiday shop in the same location, Newland's Four Season Gifts, tasteful merchandise, friendly atmosphere. Been there for years. It closed over the summer.

"They had some family troubles; Roger got sick. Roger's youngest daughter, Penny, and her mother tried to keep the store open, but between the overhead, the medical bills, and the economy, they got behind on their rent. They took out a second mortgage on their house to keep the business alive, but they fell behind in the payments. Now they're about to lose their home."

"That's a shame."

"It is."

Liv toyed with her split-pea soup. "So how did Grace Thornsby end up selling plastic Santas on the square?"

"Clarence Thornsby and Roger Newland are cousins. Clarence offered to take over the gift shop and hire Penny to manage it until the Newlands got back on their feet. Penny is a single mother, lives at home. It was a simple case of family helping family. Or so we all thought."

Ted, consummate storyteller that he was, paused for

dramatic effect. "Clarence owns several successful boat dealerships. Don't know why he didn't just loan the Newlands the money. Instead, as soon as the lease for the store was transferred, he took down the sign, cleared out the merchandise, changed the name to Trim a Tree, and installed his wife as manager."

"Wow. No wonder everyone is upset. That poor family. The Newlands must feel so betrayed."

"Of course they do. And it doesn't help that some people are blaming them for letting this happen. Now Roger has taken a turn for the worse. Penny and his wife, Margaret, pretty much blame Clarence for all of it.

"Clarence isn't a bad man. I think he meant to help. But that wife. There's speculation that Grace talked Clarence into the new product. Cheap junk, more profit. But not for the Newlands. Next thing we know, Grace is running the show, running roughshod over Penny, and has installed an illegal Santa."

Liv sighed. "Don't we have a zoning code? How did they get away with it?"

"Three words."

Liv waited. Ted loved to build the suspense when he had information. In the few months she'd worked alongside him, she'd learned if you showed impatience, he just took longer to tell and he enjoyed it more.

"I'll give you a hint. Starts with 'real estate' and ends with 'broker.'"

Liv groaned. "Janine."

"One and the same."

"Surely she told them about the town ordinance."

Ted lifted a bushy white eyebrow. "Are you talking about"—he shifted to a nasally falsetto—"'Those silly things? They can't enforce them, dear, just sign on the dotted line' Janine?"

"What is her problem? Does she do these things just to cause trouble?"

"Just to cause *you* trouble, maybe. You did take her job after all. Other than that, she's just spiteful and clueless in general."

"I did not take her job. I answered the ad and was hired. If it hadn't been me, it would have been someone else."

Ted grinned. "Sure, and she would have made their life miserable, too." He leaned over the desk and pushed her sandwich closer to her. "Eat."

"The Santa's one thing," Liv continued. "But I don't know if we can dictate the kinds of things Grace Thornsby sells. If the store wasn't right on the town square, it wouldn't be so bad, but we need a permanent store in that location. One that is open all year. And one that doesn't try to compete with the town's Santa."

"Definitely tacky to have two Santas right across the street from each other. Unfortunately, the location makes perfect sense, considering the Newlands left all the shelves and all the display cases behind." Ted frowned slightly. "I wonder what happened to their merchandise. There was never a liquidation sale that I recall."

"Don't even think about leaving me to open a gift shop."

Ted shivered dramatically. "God, no. I have a genetically disposed aversion to froufrou of any kind."

Liv glanced at his reindeer sweater and light-up holly pin.

He gave her his blandest look.

"And what about Grace Thornsby? I've only talked to her once, when she started blaring 'Santa Baby' into the street the day after Thanksgiving while everyone else was still recovering from tryptophan overload."

"That's her in a nutshell," Ted said. "She arrived in town in November, not that anyone would notice, what with Thanksgiving and that unfortunate incident of the body at the Turkey Trot."

Liv shuddered. "Don't remind me."

Ted shrugged. "Since then she's hardly gone out of her way to make friends. A delivery truck dumped a bunch of boxes on the sidewalk, blocking the doorway of A Stitch in Time. Grace let it sit there all afternoon. I've never seen Miriam Krause so mad."

"I seem to remember that, but I was really tied up with the ill-fated Turkey Trot and the Pilgrims' Feast, which reminds me. There were twelve hundred people there. We have to start looking for a larger venue for next year."

Liv bit into her sandwich, chewed meditatively. "It's almost like she's purposely trying to anger people. Why would any businessperson do that?"

"Because . . ." Sheer mischief glinted in Ted's eyes. "There's more."

Liv cast her eyes toward the ceiling. "There always is . . . in Celebration Bay."

Ted linked his fingers and rested his hands over Rudolph's nose. "Grace is Clarence's second wife. Second time for Grace, too, and—are you ready—she used to be married to Hank Ousterhout."

"The town Santa?"

"The one and only."

Liv groaned. "You're kidding. Talk about your six degrees of separation. Please tell me this isn't going to turn out to be some vendetta: scorned ex-wife flaunts herself and her new Santa in front of her ex-husband, the real Santa? Or worse, flaunts her new husband in front of the ex-husband?"

"Or vice versa."

"She wouldn't."

"Liv, this is Celebration Bay. Anything can happen."

"And they talk about Manhattan. The Big Apple has nothing over Celebration Bay when it comes to drama, let me tell you."

"I don't guess it does. You ready to go?"

Liv wrapped the rest of her sandwich and put it in the fridge.

They muffled themselves into jackets, scarves, and hats and went outside. It was a frosty day, which kept the snow that had piled up around the town frozen and relatively clean, but if you asked Liv, it was a little too cold for standing outside at night listening to carols while waiting for Santa to arrive and for the Celebration of Lights to officially kick off the Christmas season. Hopefully, it would warm up just a few degrees before tomorrow's festivities.

Liv paused at the sidewalk just to look over the town. "Boy, it looks great."

Every store on the square, including McCready's Pub, was decked out in swags of pine boughs and white lights that would be turned on simultaneously at the Celebration of Lights ceremony. Wreaths tied with bright red bows adorned the Victorian lampposts in the square. In the center of the green a row of colorful alpine chalets had been brought in to house the town Santa as well as a gift store and a food station where the line of children and their parents would be treated to homemade donuts and apple cider compliments of Waterbury Farms.

"It's so beautiful," said Liv. "You'd think the residents of Celebration Bay would want to adhere to the traditions that keep business healthy."

"They do, but the Thornsbys aren't residents."

"You mean they're not even local?"

Ted slowly shook his head. "They live in Keeseville. However, Clarence has temporarily rented a place for Grace in town."

"Keeseville is only twenty minutes or so from here."

Ted nodded.

"Maybe he doesn't want her to have to drive the roads at night."

Ted snorted. "Or maybe she has her own reason for staying in town."

"Heavens. I don't even want to delve into that one."

"Better left buried." Ted guided her across the street to the Corner Café, where electric candles flickered from each window. They walked along the sidewalk toward Trim a Tree, just admiring the ambience. The windows of A Stitch in Time, the fabric and quilting store, displayed a hanging row of festive quilts. One was filled with a big green fir tree made of varying patterned squares; another was decorated in wreaths and bows. There were Santa-face pillows with yarn beards, scarves with jacquard reindeer, red-and-green-striped knit hats.

All the stores in the square were decked out in their

holiday best. The atmosphere was quaint and tasteful, a reminder of Christmas long ago that made Celebration Bay a favorite of families up and down the East Coast.

And then they reached the door of the Trim a Tree shop.

Ted snorted. "Somebody, please send in the bad-taste police."

It was worse than it had been that morning, when Liv passed by during her routine stops at the Apple of My Eye Bakery and the Buttercup Coffee Exchange. Granted, it had been early, and she hadn't had her first drop of caffeine. But where there had been a blank showcase window except for two LED-lit palm trees, there were now a row of plastic dancing hula girls complete with leis, coconut bras, and Santa hats. Santas with red noses and round bellies hanging over jammer shorts carried surfboards or held up coconut drinks with umbrellas sticking out of the tops. Hanging in the center back was a rectangular banner portraying a reindeer plastered, spread-eagled, to a chimney.

Liv and Ted exchanged looks.

"I enjoy a theme as much as the next person," Liv said, "but as the Upper East Side mothers say, 'This is totally inappropriate behavior.' It looks like we're advocating drunk Santas."

Just as they were about to go inside, the door opened and Edna and Ida Zimmerman bustled out, looking anything but in the Christmas spirit. Edna and Ida were retired schoolteachers who lived in a large Victorian several blocks from the square. Liv rented the carriage house behind their house.

"What on earth?" Liv said as she jumped aside so the sisters wouldn't plow into her.

"Oh, Liv, Ted," Miss Ida said. "I wouldn't go in there if I were you." She grasped the Toys for Tykes collection can to her green woolen coat. Her coat was buttoned up to her chin, and a red crocheted scarf was tied neatly around her neck. A matching red hat was pulled down over her ears, leaving just a few wisps of white hair flying from her face. "That poor little boy."

"What little boy?" Liv asked.

"Actually," said Edna, the taller and less-forgiving sister. She had taught the older grades, and she still had a way of taking control of a situation with her no-nonsense attitude. She was dressed in tweed trousers and a corduroy car coat. A scarf with a giant "Ho Ho Ho" billowed down the front. "You're just in time to see what shenanigans are going on in that store. Disgusting. What were the Newlands thinking?"

"What little boy?" Ted asked.

"Penny Newland's boy, Bobby," Miss Ida said. "That Grace Thornsby was supposed to hire Penny to work in the store. That was part of the sale agreement. And now this."

"Best-laid plans," Edna said. "She came in to get her paycheck. Bobby tried to pet that mangy cat that Grace thinks is so fancy."

"And it scratched the poor little thing," Ida added. "It was only natural that he got scared and tried to get away from that nasty creature—and you know I love animals, but not that one. He tripped and fell down. He's just a baby. He wasn't hurt, but unfortunately, he broke a few ornaments."

Edna sniffed. "You'd think it was the crown jewels instead of some cheap glass from China." She stepped away from the door. "Don't let her run roughshod over you," she told Liv.

Liv smiled. She loved both of her landladies, and they loved her dog and by association, they liked her pretty well, too.

"That's why I brought Ted," Liv said and grinned.

"Hmmph," Edna said.

"And on top of everything, I think that awful Santa has been smoking," Ida said.

"Definitely smoking," Edna confirmed. "You could smell it halfway across the room. Next thing we know he'll be taking swigs out of a bourbon bottle between kiddies. We've got to get rid of them before this goes on any longer."

Liv couldn't have agreed more.

"We'd better get going, Edna," Ida said. "I'm sure every other merchant will be more generous than that . . . that Scrooge. Merry Christmas, Ted, Liv."

Ted tipped the brim of his plaid hunter's hat. "Miss Ida, Miss Edna." He turned to Liv. "Shall we gird our metaphorical loins and confront the . . . words fail me." He opened the door and gestured Liv in.

"Coward," Liv said, and stepped ahead of him into the Trim a Tree shop. She jumped at the "Ho, ho, ho" that greeted her, then realized that it wasn't the nearly comatose Santa slumped on a PVC throne reading a newspaper, but a motion-activated plastic Santa standing by the entrance.

In the center of the room, Penny Newland, a young single mother, balanced her three-year-old son on one hip as she tried to pick up pieces of broken glass from the floor. A few feet away a thin, dark-haired woman stood with her hands planted on her nearly nonexistent hips. A mangy-looking orange cat peered from behind her ankles.

Grace Thornsby was the worst case of miscasting Liv had ever seen. Not only her name, a contradiction in terms, but her whole person. Her hair was pulled severely back from her face. She was dressed in black slacks and sweater with an array of heavy, gaudy gold jewelry. And her expression could only be called sour.

A malevolent Olive Oyl with an unfriendly cat.

The cat jerked his head toward Liv, hissed, shot out from behind the manager's feet, and disappeared beneath one of the artificial Christmas trees.

Not very customer friendly, Liv thought. And if that cat was going to attack every child that tried to pet it . . .

Ted bent down to help Penny pick up the rest of the broken pieces. She gave him a heartfelt smile. She was a pretty girl, with light brown hair pulled back in a low ponytail, and a round little face that was currently blushing furiously.

"Ms. Thornsby," Liv began.

The manager pulled her angry stare from the unfortunate Penny to Liv. And Liv had a quick déjà vu of a mother of the bride she'd once had a confrontation with over the bride's choice of color scheme.

Liv had handled her with her usual efficiency, though the MOB had taken every opportunity to make Liv's life miserable, while she could. Which, fortunately, had been only a matter of a few days.

Here, they were looking at a good month of the unfriendly atmosphere of a store that was supposed to be bubbling over with good cheer. Instead, it was imbued with bad feeling and reeked of smoke.

"Ms. Thornsby," Liv said again, and introduced herself and Ted, who finished his cleanup and came to stand beside her.

"Just a minute." Ms. Thornsby turned from Liv to Penny, who was trying to make herself and her son invisible. "You'll have to make arrangements for that child if you intend to continue working here. I can't have you bringing him to the store. I don't know why Clarence thought he owed your family any favors. He paid more than this place was worth. I'll expect you tomorrow morning at nine, without the child."

"But my paycheck," Penny ventured in a small, timid voice.

"You'll have to wait until tomorrow, after I've taken out the amount of the damages."

Penny opened her mouth but closed it without speaking.

"I want to go home," Bobby whined.

"Shh, shh." Penny deliberated for a second. It was pretty obvious that she needed the money today. But she mumbled, "I'll be here tomorrow." She turned to leave.

"Do you have a ride?" Ted asked.

"I can walk. Jason's car broke down. It isn't far."

"If you wait . . ."

Penny shook her head, clearly on the verge of tears. And with another mumbled thank-you to Ted, and avoiding looking at anyone else, she ducked out the front door to the mechanical "Ho, ho, ho" of the plastic Santa.

That did it. It was Christmas, for Pete's sake. "Ms. Thornsby, I'm Liv Montgomery, event coordinator for Celebration Bay." Getting no response, she plowed ahead. "As I'm sure you're aware, all businesses are required to read and agree to certain town-wide stipulations." She reached into her bag and pulled out the town ordinance.

"Here's the one that Trim a Trim signed, agreeing to abide by the town ordinances, specifically the one-Santa rule. . . ."

She indicated the paragraph, gave Grace a pointed look, and glanced toward the North Pole alcove, where the Santa had roused himself enough to sit up. He was watching Liv, the newspaper dropped in his lap. The fake white beard hung from a string around his neck, revealing a square jaw covered with dark stubble.

What was wrong with these people? How did they think this would appeal to customers? And it would be such a blemish on the town's festivities.

Grace Thornsby just stood there.

Liv began to lose her patience. So she cut to the chase. "Since your Santa is in direct conflict with the signed agreement, I must ask you to cease and desist. Santa and his accoutrement must be removed immediately."

For a moment, the grinning face of Chaz Bristow, the local newspaper editor, flashed before her. He always laughed at her for her use of overly formal language. But Liv had found it to be a great intimidation technique. And it usually got the job done.

"What the hell?" Santa heaved himself from the dais, pulled the beard over his chin, and slouched over to where they were standing. His belt lay by the side of the throne, and the top buttons of his Santa suit were undone, revealing polyester padding. He was a disgrace to the name of Santa, and Liv just hoped no one came in before she could get rid of him.

The manager motioned him away with a flick of her long fingers and a jangle of bracelets. He stopped but didn't retreat.

"You signed this agreement." Liv held it up for her to see.

The woman's eyes flitted over the paper and her mouth tightened. "You'll have to talk to my husband. He signed the lease agreement, and he's the one who insisted on the Santa. And as far as this ordinance, the real estate agent assured us that it was never enforced."

Ted and Liv exchanged glances. Ted had called that one.

"I'm afraid the agent misinformed you. The ordinance is enforced. Agreement is mandatory." Liv didn't actually know that it was enforceable; she'd been in town only since September. All she did know was that it was going to be enforced from now on.

"Either you discontinue your use of Santa immediately, or the town will have no recourse but to close you down." Liv smiled her don't-mess-with-me smile that had quailed bridezillas and CEOs alike. "Shall we say . . . by tomorrow morning, ten o'clock. That should give you time to remove the Santa chair and replace it with something else before the parade tomorrow evening."

"The hell you will," Santa growled. He turned on Grace. "You can't fire me. I turned down other work for this job."

"Make him an elf," Ted suggested.

"I'll do no such thing. I paid a fortune for that suit. Is the town going to reimburse me?"

"Not until her plastic hula girls grow white beards," Ted said sotto voce in Liv's ear.

"I heard that." Grace glared at Ted.

Just as Ted had intended, Liv thought.

"Lose the Santa, Grace," Ted said.

"Tomorrow morning. I'll just drop by to see how you're doing." Liv didn't wait for an answer but turned on her heel. Ted rushed to open the door for her, as if he were an office lackey instead of her right-hand man. She stepped over the threshold.

Over the mechanical greeting, Liv heard the hired Santa say, "You're crazy if you think you can get rid of me." The door shut on the rest of the sentence.

Chapter Two

....

Ted and Liv made it outside before he burst out laughing. "Have you ever? They should x-out Trim a Tree and call it Nightmare Before Christmas."

"She is the absolute worst," Liv said. "Please tell me she's going to get rid of that awful Santa without us having to call in the sheriff. If we can even do that."

Ted grinned. "I need dessert. Let's stop by Dolly's."

"We just finished lunch. Where do you put it? And how do you stay so thin?"

"Am I hearing an unspoken 'and at your age'?"

"I don't know how old you are."

"And a gentleman never tells. Shall we repair to The Apple of My Eye?" He grinned at her. Even in the heavy down jacket he wore, he was still lean and lanky. The cold brought out the color in his normally pale face. *Hmm.* Thick white hair, twinkling blue eyes . . . a hundred more pounds and a beard he'd make a great Santa—a couple of decades younger and she'd be tempted to ask him out.

"Okay. I could use another latte from the Buttercup. Maybe Dolly has something low cal and low fat."

"Dolly? Never. But I have it on good authority that she made her first batch of Christmas stollen this morning. I bet it goes great with coffee."

"I'm sure, but I'm not a real fan of candied fruitcake."

"But you haven't tasted Dolly's stollen."

As they passed the pedestrian walkway that ran between the Bookworm and Bay-Berry Candles, Ted nudged her and pointed to the far end where Santa leaned against the wall, smoking a cigarette and talking into his cell phone. Liv couldn't hear what he was saying but from his expression, she knew that Santa wasn't happy about losing his throne.

"Maybe he's looking for a new job," Liv said hopefully. As she watched, he pulled a little black book from his Santa pants pocket and opened it while he talked.

"Or looking for a date," Ted added.

Santa ended the call, returned the book to his pocket, dropped the cigarette butt to the ground, and disappeared around the corner of the candle store.

"Ugh," Liv said as they crossed the walkway. She stopped to look in the window of the Bookworm, where copies of *'Twas the Night Before Christmas*, *A Christmas Carol*, and *The Polar Express* were surrounded by miniature figures and houses portraying a Victorian village.

Behind the display, Quincy Hinks, the owner of the book-store, waved his feather duster in greeting and went back to cleaning. The atmosphere was so lovely and quaint that it made Liv even angrier at Grace Thornsby and her disregard for custom.

The Apple of My Eye Bakery was toasty, and the air swirled with good smells. The pink tablecloths that usually topped the few inside tables had been replaced with green ones for the season. The pink cupcake wall clock was topped by a pair of felt reindeer antlers sporting a red felt Santa hat, the white pom-pom jauntily covering one o'clock.

Dolly Hunnicutt, plump and friendly, looked festive in a red checked apron with a row of candy canes embroidered across the top. She smiled at them from behind a display case of all things yummy and befitting the season. Stacks of red and green cookies, cinnamon rolls with white frosty icing, cupcakes, and turnovers. Several loaves of Dolly's Christmas stollen, dusted with powdered sugar and resembling a winter landscape, sat on top of the counter. Several more trays were waiting on a rolling baker's rack.

"Knew you'd be in this afternoon." Dolly slid two thick slices of stollen dotted with raisins and candied fruit into a bag and handed them to Ted.

She added several peppermint pinwheels and almond spritzes to another bag. "Did Hank Ousterhout talk to you this morning?"

"He did," Liv said. "We just came from the Trim a Tree shop."

"I don't guess Grace Thornsby got huffy and decided to close that eyesore."

"No," said Liv. "But we did tell her she must comply with the town's ordinances."

"That's something, I guess. I know it's not very charitable of me to feel this way, but I just don't think half-naked hula girls are in keeping with the spirit of a Celebration Bay Christmas. And it's driving Fred crazy." Dolly smiled. "He's so concerned about the children growing old too soon."

Liv knew Dolly and Fred had one son who lived in New York City whom she'd never seen. He was a big corporate executive, and somehow Liv couldn't imagine that he had much in common with his parents, both good-natured, always ready to volunteer, and content with each other and with their way of life. To Liv, they were the perfect couple.

"I couldn't agree with you more." Liv took the bag of cookies. "Hopefully, we can find a permanent business, one without hula girls, to take over the space when TAT leaves."

"I just wish the Newlands could have hung on a little longer. Since you've been here, business has already started to climb."

"Thank you, Dolly. But the town just needed some organization and efficiency."

They said good-bye and stopped next door at the Buttercup Coffee Exchange.

"Saw you pass by," BeBe Ford told them. BeBe was about Liv's age, with lush curves and a dry wit, and was still considered a newcomer even after living in Celebration Bay for twelve years. If Liv had a best friend in town, it was BeBe.

"Figured you wouldn't stop by Dolly's for pastry without stopping here, too."

"Wouldn't think of it," Ted said, reaching for the cardboard tray with their tea and coffee.

"Did you get rid of the Rat from TAT yet?"

"Not completely," Liv said, trying not to laugh. "But we told her she had to deep-six the Santa."

"That's a start," BeBe said. "Why on earth would a woman like that want to run a Christmas store?"

"That's the question of the day." And Liv didn't have a clue.

"I'm not liking this situation at all," Liv said as she and Ted walked back to the office. "You don't think anything bad will happen, do you?" She fervently hoped that Christmas wouldn't be a repeat of the recent Harvest by the Bay Festival that had plunged the whole town into suspicion, intrigue, and finally, murder. Fortunately, not many people were aware of the events of the Turkey Trot.

"Nothing would surprise me," Ted said.

"That's pretty jaded coming from you."

"A side of me that only you see."

"And how did you learn to be so jaded?" she asked. "In the big city, like me?"

"In the school of life." He took her elbow as they crossed the street.

Liv knew when to quit. She'd learned what she needed to know to stay on top of the current situation, and she had to be content with that. No matter how subtly she tried, in the months she'd worked with Ted, she'd learned everything she needed to know about the town and its inhabitants, but she'd never learned much about him.

In Liv's former life as event planner to the movers and shakers of New York City, she'd gotten to know way too much about her clients and coworkers. There was something nice about working with someone whose life wasn't an open book. She had to admit, however, she'd like to get just a little peek.

They spent the rest of the afternoon finalizing plans for the parade, checking with Fred about the parking situation, and making sure the trolleys they'd hired for transporting visitors to and from perimeter parking lots were clean and properly decorated.

Ted called each store owner, including Grace Thornsby, with a reminder of the Celebration of Lights the following evening. The last week had been a flurry of activity as businesses trimmed their windows in white lights that would be turned on simultaneously with the tree lighting. Even the few empty storefronts had been decorated and would have someone to throw the lights on cue.

Liv hung up from talking to the head of the new security firm she'd hired for crowd control. "I'm getting excited," she called out to Ted, who was whistling along with Mannheim Steamroller on the radio.

"Yeah, wear something red and green tomorrow and prove it."

"I will." Now that the situation with the TAT Santa had been dealt with, Liv was ready to enjoy a little Christmas cheer herself.

She left the office at four forty-five, which would give her just enough time to pick up Whiskey at the Woofery. Sharise was just closing when Liv arrived.

"Sorry, am I late?"

"Not at all. Just getting ready to run out when the clock strikes. A million things to do before tomorrow."

Liv wrote out a check for the bath and brush-out.

Sharise took the check and slipped it into a drawer. "He looks good as new. I'll just go get him."

When she returned a few minutes later, a white and fluffy

Westie terrier was prancing alongside her, a bright red bow tie around his neck.

"Don't you look debonair," Liv said as much to Sharise as to Whiskey, who immediately began dancing at her feet. The bow tie would last two seconds after they left, Liv thought. Whiskey had hated every sweater, grooming accessory, or Halloween costume she'd attempted to put on him.

"He's just cute as a button," Sharise said. "And so handsome—yes, you are." She leaned over and adjusted the tie, which was already sitting askew in his fur.

"He is. Let's just hope he stays this way for a few days," Liv agreed and said good night.

Whiskey trotted happily next to her. Even though it was cold, he didn't seem to mind, and he absolutely stopped to preen whenever they passed someone on their way home.

"You are such a show-off," she told him.

As soon as she got home, she took off his bow tie and went into the kitchen to feed her dog and herself; then they both curled up on the couch with a doggie treat, a bowl of popcorn, and the television remote. One of the channels had started its twenty-five-days-of-Christmas movies, and Liv watched as she ate popcorn and wrote last-minute notes to herself on a yellow legal pad. She took herself to bed, feeling as excited as a kid waiting for Santa.

The sun was barely up when Liv rolled out of bed the next morning. She'd slept like a log in spite of it being her first Christmas in Celebration Bay. She planned to spend the day making final checks of everything she and Ted had checked the day before. Timing was everything in coordinating successful simultaneous events, and the citizens of Celebration Bay had packed a lot of stuff into a very few minutes.

She fed Whiskey and let him out for a run in the Zimmerman sisters' backyard. It had snowed again during the night, and she watched from the door as he disappeared into a drift of snow and reappeared a second later shaking off fresh snow and chasing his tail.

So much for his brush-out. But it didn't matter. She had one happy dog. She was pretty happy herself. "Five minutes," she said and waited until that intrepid Westie plowed a path through the snow, no doubt heading for the Zimmermans' back door, where he hoped to get a treat.

Liv quickly dressed in sweater, jacket, scarf, hat, and gloves, and after adding a pair of moccasins to her canvas carryall, she sat down to pull on her snow boots. She heard a bark at the door and hopped on one foot to open it. Whiskey shot in, shook a few times, took one look at her boots, and dashed into the bedroom.

He returned two seconds later, his red bow tie held delicately between his teeth.

"Well, this is a first," Liv told him. She really shouldn't take him to work with her. Today was bound to be hectic. But he looked so pleased with himself that she didn't have the heart to leave him at home.

He dropped the bow tie at her feet and she caved. "All right, but you have to keep a low profile today. I'm going to be very busy." She clipped the bow tie around his neck and Velcro'ed the plaid doggie sweater she'd bought him for cold weather. He immediately tried to bite it off.

"I bet if Sharise had put it on you, you'd wear it," Liv said and took it off again. She added it to her carryall in case the temperature dropped even more.

Liv liked Christmas with its music and smells and food and lights and decorations. But it was her busiest time of the year, and she spent the season juggling events and seeing they all ran smoothly, so that by the time she was ready to sit back and enjoy the festivities, they were over.

This year she planned to have some fun. After tonight's big celebration, the activities would be run individually, like the reindeer corral at Dexter's Nursery, the *Messiah* singalong at the Presbyterian church, the inn's Dickens Dinner, the Tour of Homes, and Breakfast with Santa, which was run by the Jaycees. And of course, shopping and dining from dawn until midnight.

Once the lights were lit and Santa was ensconced on his throne in the chalet on the green, Liv's job would pretty much be done.

The thought of Santa reminded her to check in at the Trim a Tree shop and make sure there was no Santa in residence.

She grabbed a banana, a nod to healthy eating since stopping by Dolly's for breakfast had become a way of life and her daily run had been seriously curtailed by several feet of snow. She gathered up her legal pad and laptop, clipped on Whiskey's leash, and headed to town.

It took Liv extra time to get to work since everybody was out shoveling or blowing snow, and they all stopped to say hello or call out holiday greetings. Dolly's, which was usually quiet this early in the morning, was crammed with people, and there was a line at the Buttercup. Everyone was talking and excited about the evening's events, discussing the best way to make sure all their lights came on at once, reminding each other not to use chasing or blinking lights.

There was a festive mood in the air even though it was way too cold for Liv's taste. Whiskey got an extra treat from Dolly, who had begun making specialty dog biscuits, which Sharise sold from the Woofery.

Liv hurried down the sidewalk, thinking of her nice double-shot latte growing cold in the frigid morning. Several times she had to slow down for Whiskey to show off his bow tie. She stopped to peer in the window of Trim a Tree. It was dark inside, and she couldn't tell if the North Pole niche had been taken down. She made a mental note to check as soon as the store opened. If Santa was still there, she'd have to call Bill Gunnison to have Grace or the Santa, or both, evicted.

Fortunately, the sheriff, who suffered from sciatica, was standing tall these days, and Liv crossed metaphorical fingers that he would stay that way through the holidays. Even with the new security force she'd hired, she depended on Bill for crowd control and safety issues.

She climbed the town hall steps, and balancing pastries, coffee, and Whiskey's leash, she opened the door and entered the building in a swirl of windblown snow. She was attempting to turn the knob of the office door when it opened.

Ted was dressed in a green button-down shirt and a Santa tie beneath a fire-engine-red vest. He leaned over and patted his knees.

Well trained by her dog and her assistant, Liv dropped Whiskey's leash.

Whiskey darted over to rest his paws on Ted's knees while Ted yodeled, "Who's my favorite daw-aw-awg?"

"Aroo-roo-roo."

"Daw-aw-awg."

"Aroo."

Ignoring this morning ritual, Liv placed the pastries and tea on Ted's desk and took her latte and laptop into her office. She sat at her desk as the noise from the outer office changed to a duet of "Aroo-roo-roo, roo-roo-roo . . ."

Ted was teaching Whiskey to sing "Jingle Bells."

The day passed in a blur, with last-minute details to attend to, disasters to be averted, and ruffled feelings to be soothed. By four o'clock, traffic had been diverted and the streets around the square were cordoned off for pedestrians. At six o'clock, Santa's wagon and two reindeer had arrived from Dexter's Nursery and Landscaping and were parked in back of the post office where Santa would begin his parade.

At six forty-five, Liv and Ted were standing with the crowd on the green waiting for the festivities to begin.

"You're sure the TAT Santa is gone," Liv said.

"Yes, I checked three times today. No Santa, no North Pole sign, no tacky throne. Stop worrying."

"Security is in place."

"Yes."

"And the—"

"Done."

"You don't know what I was going to say."

"Doesn't matter, it's done."

Liv laughed. "Sorry, but there are so many . . . amateurs involved."

"Relax, here comes the choir. I still think you should have brought Whiskey."

"And have you two burst into song at the tree lighting? I think he'll be happy with the Zimmermans. They're watching from the warmth and comfort of the bakery. I'm sure he's already stuffed with treats."

The singers filed down the park sidewalk toward the risers set up near the tree. They were dressed in red and green and striped elf hats.

Liv also spotted several members of the security team in the crowd. Feeling easier, she took a breath and turned back to the stage. Next to her, Ted was frowning.

"What?" she asked, immediately alarmed and automatically switching into action mode.

He was searching the choir as it climbed the bleachers. "I don't see Penny Newland."

"Maybe she couldn't get a babysitter."

"She lives with her parents. I hope she's not sick. The *Messiah* sing-along is next week and she's one of the soloists."

"Do you think Grace is making her work late?"

"That would be just like her. I have half a mind to—"

"Look, she's here."

Penny Newland pushed her way through the crowd and joined the end of the line where the choir director was waiting for her with a spare elf hat.

"Sorry," Penny huffed. She crammed the hat on the top of her head and hurried past the basses and tenors and altos to squeeze into her place on the risers with the other sopranos.

"Whew," Liv said. "One problem solved."

But it wasn't to be the last.

Several carols later, just as the choir ended "Here We Come A-Wassailing," Liv's walkie-talkie buzzed. She moved back in the crowd so she could hear better. "Liv here."

"It's Dex." Dexter Kent's voice came over in a burst of breath drowning out the beginning of "Hark! The Herald Angels Sing." "I'm behind the post office with the wagon and the reindeer, but Hank isn't here. And the wagon is due to start in"—another huff of breath—"three minutes."

Liv mouthed a word that was not appropriate for the festive surroundings. "I thought he checked in."

"He did. A half hour ago, then he went down to Pyne Bough Gifts where he was going to change into his Santa suit. He uses their stockroom as a base every year. He's not there and he hasn't come back here."

"I'm on my way." Liv slipped back to where Ted was standing. "Santa's AWOL."

"No way."

"I'm going over there."

"I'll tell the choir to keep singing until we give them the word and I'll follow you." Ted took off toward the stage and the unlit tree.

Liv headed down the path toward the street. She nodded to the sheriff, Bill Gunnison, who was talking to A.K. Pierce, the head of the security agency, while they kept Main Street clear of pedestrians for the parade—if Santa returned in time. She was crossing the street in front of the bookstore when her walkie-talkie crackled.

"Dex here. Hank's back. He's suited up. We're ready to go."

"Thanks. I'll tell Ted to cue the choir."

She radioed Ted the message and hurried back to his side.

"Nothing but fun and games," Ted told her as the choir broke into "Here Comes Santa Claus."

The crowd turned as one toward the street. One spotlight shone past the bakery, coffee exchange, and stores to catch Hank Ousterhout standing in the back of a wagon driven by Dexter Kent and pulled by two reindeer.

The crowd broke into applause as Santa waved and threw candy. Dexter stopped the wagon at the curb, and two of his employees ran to hold the reindeer in place while the mayor helped Hank down to the street.

"Ho, ho, ho!" Hank boomed as he was escorted to the stage where a group of children, wreathed in smiles, awaited him.

"He's perfect," Liv said.

"Uh-huh," said Ted.

Mayor Worley stepped up to the microphone. "Santa has arrived, and he and children from the Celebration Bay Community Center will now light the tree. Let the festivities begin!"

Santa leaned over the light box, and the children piled their hands on top of his. Hank pulled the switch, and the tree burst into a hundred-foot cone of light. All around the square businesses lit their windows. The choir began to sing "O Tannenbaum."

"Oohs" and "ahs" rose in a cloud of amazement. And it *was* amazing, just a perfect, glorious moment with the towering tree surrounded by a solid ring of light.

Liv looked again. Almost a solid ring. One store was dark, standing out like a missing tooth in a perfect smile.

"I'm going to kill her," Liv said and struck off toward Trim a Tree.

Chapter Three

....

By the time Liv reached the front door to the Trim a Tree shop, the choir was singing "Silent Night" as the crowd began to disperse to one of the free cider stations or into one of the many shops, restaurants, and cafés.

Liv peered in the TAT window. The store was dark and looked deserted. Only a dim light from the back helped differentiate the cones of artificial trees that clogged the space. Liv knocked on the front door.

"Anybody in there?" asked Ted, coming up behind her.

"Doesn't look like it."

"Wait, did something move?" Liv cupped her hands and peered into the window. She knocked again. "Grace, are you in there? I know you're in there. Come to the door."

"Let's try the back."

Fred Hunnicutt, as round and pleasant as his wife Dolly, was manning the crosswalk, his orange Day-Glo vest shining under the streetlamps. "Is there a problem?" he called out as Ted and Liv hurried past.

"Only that the Trim a Tree store stayed dark when everyone else turned on the lights," Ted said.

Fred shook his head. "I saw. That woman is going to make life here very uncomfortable for herself if she doesn't get a better attitude, and soon. People won't put up with someone who doesn't enter into the festivities."

"Starting with me." Liv headed down the pedestrian throughway, followed by Ted. A larger delivery alley ran behind the row of stores, where Dumpsters were shared by the businesses and emptied weekly.

Liv slid on a patch of ice as she rounded the corner. Ted grabbed her by each elbow.

"Steady now. You don't want to break something before you can give Grace Thornsby a piece of your mind."

Liv slowed down, grabbing at the edges of her temper. It wouldn't do to let her anger get the best of her. You never won a screaming match. So even though she felt like letting the manager of TAT have it with both barrels, she took a breath, mustered her killer-but-calm Manhattan power-face, and proceeded at a more dignified pace, past a Dumpster and a pile of broken-down boxes, and stopped at the back entrance of Trim a Tree.

She knocked, received no answer. Four doors down, Dolly came out of the bakery carrying a black garbage bag. "Liv, Ted, is that you? What's going on?"

"Nothing to worry about," Ted assured her. "The TAT lights stayed dark. We've come to rectify the situation."

Liv knocked harder, called out, "Ms. Thornsby, are you in there?"

Dolly dumped her trash and came hurrying down to meet them. "Do you think she did it on purpose, or is something wrong?"

An icicle shot up Liv's spine. "Ms. Thornsby. Grace!" This time she didn't knock but shook the door handle. It turned in her hand and the door opened.

She exchanged looks with Ted.

He frowned and stepped past her, pushed the door wide, and stepped into the darkness. "Anyone here?" Silence.

"What's he doing?" Dolly asked, her arms crossed over her holiday apron to ward off the cold.

Liv shrugged. Something inside the store clattered to the ground. Seconds later an orange blur shot out the door. Liv jumped back. "The cat," she said. "Good grief. Do you see him?"

Dolly stepped back into the alley and looked into the shadows cast by the parking lot fence. "There he is, over by that Dumpster, down there near the Pyne Bough."

The door of the bakery opened and Ida Zimmerman's head poked out. "Dolly, what's taking you so long? Do you need help?"

Dolly waved. "Over here. I—"

The cat darted out of the shadows and tore torn down the alley. As he passed the bakery, a sharp bark resounded from inside. Before Liv could yell to Miss Ida to stop him, Whiskey shot out of the bakery in hot pursuit.

"Don't worry, I'll get him." Miss Ida took off after the animals. Edna looked out. "Ida, what the heck are you doing?"

"Don't slip on the ice!" Dolly yelled after her. "Edna, can you watch the bakery until I get back?"

Edna nodded and went back inside and shut the door. Dolly took off after Miss Ida, Whiskey, and the cat.

"Careful," Liv yelled after her and reached for her walkie-talkie. "Fred, can you have everyone on the lookout for Whiskey and Grace Thornsby's cat? They're headed toward the south of the square. Miss Ida and Dolly have gone after them."

She stepped inside the store. "Ted?"

She passed a small storeroom, which was the source of the small patch of light, then groped through the dark into the main part of the store. "Ted."

"Just a minute I'm looking for the light switch. Ah."

The lights jumped on.

Liv blinked against the sudden brightness. Then blinked again. One of the artificial trees had toppled over and lay on its side. Broken ornaments littered the floor.

Standing over it was Penny Newland, unmoving, her mouth agape.

Liv didn't envy her. Paying for those broken ornaments would cost her more than her salary, which still didn't explain why the Christmas lights weren't on. Obviously Penny couldn't have done it, because she'd been singing at the tree lighting. Though she must have left the singing early when she saw the lights fail to come on. She'd managed to get back to the store before Ted and Liv. But where was Grace Thornsby?

Penny's mouth closed, then opened. "Shoes," she said.

"Shoes?"

"Shoes."

Ted left the light switch and went to stand by Penny's side. "Honey? What are you talking about?"

Penny jabbed her finger toward the tree.

Ted's eyes bulged. "Oh damn. Grace?"

"What?" Liv squeezed past the fallen tree and looked down. There on the ground, sticking out from beneath the tree, were two black boots. She could see glimpses of their owner through the branches. At least now they knew why no one had turned on the lights at the Trim a Tree shop.

Ted grabbed hold of the tree, lifted it off the body, and thrust it to the side.

It wasn't Grace.

It was a man, dressed in khaki pants and a long-sleeve beige shirt. Blood covered his collar and spread across his chest. His neck was covered in blood, almost hiding the slash across his throat. His eyes were partly opened, but they were long past seeing anything. And he looked familiar.

"It's Phil," Penny said quietly, sounding confused.

The TAT Santa. Liv hadn't recognized him at first without his costume.

"Ah crap," said an exasperated voice from behind them. Liv didn't have to turn around to know who it belonged to. The editor of the *Celebration Bay Clarion* sounded totally exasperated.

"What are you doing here?" Liv asked. It was the last thing she needed to know, but it was the first thing that came to her mind.

"I heard Santa lost his suit. I thought it would make a

good human interest story." Chaz Bristow stepped past her, revealing Fred Hunnicutt behind him.

"I just came to tell you they found Whiskey," Fred said. "They're still looking for—Whoa! What happened? Shouldn't somebody do CPR?"

"Too late for that," Chaz answered over his shoulder from where he squatted down to look at the body.

"Are you sure?" Liv asked.

"I'm sure. You might want to get Bill Gunnison in here."

Ted got out his walkie-talkie.

Dolly came through the door. "Fred, are you in here? Did you tell them we found—"

Fred put an arm out, stopping her from coming any closer.

"It was an accident, right?" Liv asked.

Chaz stood up and gave her a look, half-resigned, half-incredulous. "No," he said.

Fred tried to stand in front of Dolly. "Dolly, you shouldn't be seeing this. Why don't you go on back to the bakery?"

"I'm not leaving you here alone. And what about Penny? Penny, honey? Are you all right?"

The girl looked up at Dolly, then sank to the ground. Chaz just managed to catch her before she hit the floor.

"Poor thing, she's fainted," Dolly said, eluding Fred's grasp. "Here, Chaz , take her over to that chair behind the counter."

Chaz rolled his eyes but hoisted the girl into his arms and followed Dolly just as Bill Gunnison, accompanied by A.K. Pierce, the head of Bayside Security, hurried into the room.

"What's going on here? Where did all you people come from?"

Before anyone could answer, Bill saw the body. He waited while the head of security knelt down, checked for a pulse, then stood up shaking his head.

"Okay," Bill said. "Everybody, just step back and stay calm. Dare I ask if anyone touched him?"

They all shook their heads.

"Well, that's progress." Bill stepped closer to the dead

Santa. "Guess I better get the medical examiner in here. And a crime scene wagon."

"Crime scene?" exclaimed Dolly.

"I don't suppose there were any witnesses."

Everyone shook their heads again, then looked at Penny, who was slumped against Dolly's shoulder.

She shook her head spasmodically.

Liv could only stare at the body.

"Close your mouth," Chaz said. "You remind me of a fish, and then I start thinking about how long it is until the season reopens instead of wondering how you get yourself embroiled in murder all the time."

"I do not."

"And don't get all pissy, and don't step on my foot like you did the last time you were minding someone else's business. I have boots on and you might hurt yourself."

"I said I was sorry."

He grinned, a grossly inappropriate expression considering the gruesome spectacle in front of them. "You did. But I didn't believe you." His eyes were teasing. And really blue. He winked and she found herself smiling in spite of the tragedy.

"Can any of you identify the, uh, him?" the sheriff asked.

"He's the TAT Santa," Liv said. "And Grace Thornsby said he would be gone by this morning."

"And he is," Chaz said in her ear.

"Stop it." Liv stepped away. How could the man be so callous?

"Where is she?"

"That's why we're here," Ted said. Compared to Chaz, he sounded like the voice of reason. "The store remained dark during the tree lighting, and Liv and I came over to see what the problem was. Grace wasn't here. I turned on the lights. And there he was." He stopped, frowned, glanced over at Penny. "Penny was here."

"Penny, do you know what happened?"

Penny shook her head.

"You didn't see or hear anything strange?"

"I wasn't here," she said in a barely audible voice.

"She was singing in the choir," Dolly volunteered, and patted the girl's hand.

"And no one has seen Grace Thornsby?"

"No," Ted told him. "At least—we didn't look."

They all moved at once.

"Just stay put," Bill said.

"She isn't here." Penny's voice was thin and frightened. "Do you know where she is?"

"No. But she called just before she was supposed to come in so I could go sing. She said something had come up and she wouldn't be able to make it." Penny shuddered. Hiccupped.

Dolly gave her a squeeze.

"But you did sing?"

Again that jerky nod. Liv was afraid the girl might be going into shock. After all, it looked like she had discovered the body, or at least the shoes. Liv felt an insane giggle about to erupt. She coughed it away.

Bill frowned at her.

"Phil was waiting for Grace so she could give him his paycheck. Liv and Ted said he couldn't work here. I told him I was supposed to sing, everybody was counting on me, and he said to go on and he'd mind the store until I got back." She shot an anguished look at Liv. "Then . . ."

Now that she was talking, she couldn't seem to stop.

"I told him just what to do when it was time to turn on the lights. I wrote down the cue and everything. He said he would do it and not to worry. When the tree was lit and the store didn't light up, I ran back here. I didn't even wait for "Silent Night."

"So you were the first to discover the body?" Bill asked.

"Sort of. I guess I did."

The sheriff's eyes narrowed. "Penny, how did you get here before Ted and Liv?"

Penny looked around as if she wasn't sure where she was. "I came in the front. The door was unlocked because the store was supposed to be open as soon as the lights went on and Phil was here. I ran in to see why the lights weren't on and I tripped on the tree. It was on the ground. And then I could see that Phil was under it. Grace is going to fire me for sure." She burst into tears.

Dolly put her arms around the girl and glared at the sheriff. "Bill Gunnison, don't be so mean, the girl's had a fright. It's not her fault that the tree fell on the poor man."

"Now, Dolly," Fred began.

Several security people and police officers came into the store.

Chaz snorted. "How many residents of Celebration Bay does it take to contaminate a crime scene? Oops."

"What?"

"There's someone looking in the window."

Bill turned toward the window. Two faces peered in from the other side. Bill nodded, smiled, waved.

"Meese, go out there and tell those two people the store will be closed due to, um, an electrical problem."

"Yes sir." The young officer disappeared.

Bill dispatched two others to cordon off the alley and wait for the ME.

"Johnson, see if you can find something to cover the windows with."

"I've got a roll of brown butcher paper at the bakery," Dolly volunteered. "I'll show him." Dolly turned Penny over to Fred, and the young officer followed her to the back door.

Dolly let out a screech as she reached the door.

A streak of orange flew into the room and past Bill's feet. "What the—"

"Grace's cat," Liv said, hoping fervently that Ida and Edna had leashed Whiskey and taken him home.

In answer to her prayers, a white ball of fur galloped through the back door, followed by both Miss Ida and Miss Edna, who stopped to catch their breath.

"Sorry," Edna said between gasps. "Whiskey, you come here."

"Treat!" Liv screeched.

Chaz laughed quietly beside her.

Whiskey slid to a stop, twisted in the air, and galloped back to her.

Chaz leaned over and scooped him up in one graceful move. "Gotcha."

Whiskey tried to wiggle free, but without success.

"We'll take him." Miss Ida came up to Liv, saw the body on the floor. "Edna, come look at this."

Her sister joined them. Dolly and the young officer returned with scissors, tape, and the roll of paper. In the background, a siren wailed.

Bill pulled out his radio. "There's no emergency. Turn the damn siren off and try to be a little discreet." He signed off.

"Miss Ida and Miss Edna, would you two please take Whiskey home or go about shopping or whatever you were planning to do tonight. But keep him on a leash. And don't tell anyone what you've seen."

"Hmmph. We were next on the scene," Miss Edna said.

"And we might have important information," Miss Ida added.

The sheriff's nostrils flared. "And do you have information?" he asked patiently, though with some effort.

"Well, we won't know, will we, until you ask us some questions."

"I will certainly do that. But there's no reason for you to have to wait here when it's late, and I really need someone to take Whiskey out of here."

Whiskey barked at the sound of his name. The cat, who had disappeared beneath one of the trees, shot across the room.

Bill groaned. "Please."

"Come along, Edna. *We* don't want to be in the way. We'll see you first thing tomorrow morning, Bill Gunnison."

"Yes ma'am."

Edna clipped the leash on the still wriggling Whiskey, took him from Chaz, and forced Ida out the door.

"And I only came in after Liv and Ted were already here," Chaz said.

"And I came with Chaz," Fred added. "I don't mind staying, but I don't much like the idea of Dolly being alone at the bakery."

Bill rubbed his forehead. "She won't be alone, the place is packed. And we'll finish with you long before closing time.

"But you can't stay here, and I don't want the whole town to see us parading through the streets to town hall. Meese, go down to the Pyne Bough and ask Ms. Pyne if we can use her back room. Hank Ousterhout uses it to change out of his Santa suit, but he's probably home by now, and I'm sure Nancy won't mind." He turned away. "Just tell her there's been an accident and I need a few statements from the witnesses. Do not volunteer anything else."

"Yes sir, no sir. I'll go right now." The young officer practically stumbled over his own feet to get out the door.

"As for the rest of you—Chaz, where are you going?"

Chaz had been easing toward the door, but he stopped. "I didn't see anything. And I know the drill. No details in the paper. Hell, I won't even report it. I don't have room anyway what with all these highfalutin holiday goings-on. So I'll just be moseying along."

Liv made a face at him. He was always putting on some good-old-boy act that she didn't buy for a minute. She'd checked him out online. She knew how many years he'd lived in Los Angeles, which probably helped him cultivate his already developed surfer look. Tall, buff, and blond. The *LA Times* had certainly perfected his investigative skills, but the closest he'd come to "homespun" was "homeboy," and the only colloquialisms he'd heard were street slang and four-letter words.

"I don't want any of this appearing in the paper. Got it? None of it."

Chaz gave a one-fingered salute and started to leave.

"On second thought. Maybe you better stay with the others until I'm finished here."

Chapter Four

······································

Bill decided to interview Penny on the premises and send her home. The rest of them trudged down the alley to the corner, where the smell of barbecue drew them toward the Corner Café. But Officer Meese motioned them across the alley to the back door of the clapboard building that housed the Pyne Bough, Gifts from Nature.

Nancy Pyne met them at the delivery door, looking as natural as the gifts she sold. No makeup and no bling. She was a small woman, dressed in a long black skirt and red hand-knitted sweater. Her long gray hair was held back in a raffia tie. She smelled slightly of cinnamon potpourri and incense. Nancy was a latter-day hippie, serene and unruffled.

Though not incurious.

"Come on inside where it's warm." She stood back while they filed into the storeroom, then closed the door behind them.

"What's going on? Nobody will tell me anything, just asked if you could sit here for a while. Which you're welcome to do. Was there an accident? No one was hurt, were they?"

Her questions were interrupted by the sound of a truck rattling down the alley outside. They'd turned off the siren, but the telltale red light that pulsed through the closed shades of the windows pretty much announced what it was.

"Was that an ambulance that just passed?" Nancy rushed over to the window and yanked at the shade; the shade snapped out of her hand and wound itself around the top bar, flapping like a panicked bird, just as another truck rattled by, this time one belonging to the county medical examiner.

Nancy froze, then slowly turned around. "It was a crime. Where?" She looked around the room, frowning. "Where's Hank? It isn't Hank, is it?"

"No," Ted said. "It isn't Hank."

"Then who?" For the first time she seemed to notice Officer Meese. She turned on him. "Who?"

"Now, Nancy, leave the boy alone," Fred said. "We just have to answer a few questions and we'll be out of your hair."

"You've been ordered not to say anything, haven't you? Oh dear, there was a crime. Excuse me."

She disappeared behind a madras curtain. They heard the door to the store open and close. It opened and closed again, and Nancy pushed through the madras curtain, holding a bunch of dried herbs in one hand and a cigarette lighter in the other.

She held the lighter to the stalk until it began to smoke.

"Uh, ma'am?" Meese began. Ted laid a hand on his shoulder.

Ignoring everyone, she moved toward the corner of the room, swinging the burning herb in an arc much like a priest at high mass. She circled to every corner and around the windows and doors, paying particular attention to the delivery door where they'd entered.

"There, much better," she said. "There's coffee and tea in the cupboard and a coffeemaker on the counter. Help yourselves. I have to get back to the front." She disappeared behind the curtain again. A door opened and closed. This time she didn't come back.

"Whew," Fred said. "I was afraid she was gonna expect us to smoke that thing."

"Sage," Ted told him. "It drives out evil and protects those inside."

"Hmmph," Fred said. "No offense, but I'll take my sage with turkey."

"Might as well make ourselves comfortable," Ted said. "We might be here for a while. I'll make some coffee."

Ted filled the carafe from a standing water cooler; Fred pulled the shade back down; Liv sat in a straight-back chair and watched Chaz Bristow wander aimlessly around the storeroom. One wall was covered with shelving and stacks of boxes. A shipping table ran halfway across the side wall, and was set up with string and tape dispensers, brown paper, box cutters, and mailing labels. A rack of broken-down boxes sat next to the table. The rest of the room had been turned into a lounge area, with several beat-up but comfortable-looking chairs, a cot, and a counter with minifridge, hot plate, and coffeemaker.

Chaz turned back to the room, and Liv, realizing she had been staring at him, looked away, but not quick enough.

He raised a sardonic eyebrow. He'd thrown his coat on a chair and pulled off the knit hat he'd been wearing. It left his dirty blond hair spiked and incongruous in the cozy, homespun room.

Fred eased himself down into a faded wingback chair. "Well, son, aren't you going to start interviewing us?"

Meese started. "Uh, no sir. I'm just to wait here until the sheriff comes."

Fred huffed out a sigh. "Well, I hope he hurries 'cause I really need to be out overseeing traffic. And I need to check on Dolly. What's the world coming to, somebody going and murdering Santa. Even if he wasn't the real one."

Ted pulled a stool to the counter and sat. "Not Santa. He wasn't in costume. And I think we should get away from calling him Santa. That would make headlines from here to Seattle."

"I didn't think about that."

Liv, to her discredit, had. It was not because she was callous and unfeeling, she told herself. It was an ingrained response to disaster—something that every successful event planner was blessed with—the instinct to fix the problem before it got worse. The death of a person was terrible any time and worse when it was violent. She felt sorry for the dead man, but the livelihood of hundreds of people was in her hands.

She was already planning triage measures for when the news got out. Because it would. News always got out in Celebration Bay. And from there it would spread.

"What was his name?" Fred asked. "Does anybody know?"

"Penny called him Phil," Liv said.

The minutes ticked by, Nancy didn't return, and Liv just hoped she wasn't speculating with her customers about the presence of so many official cars and trucks in the alleyway.

A knock at the delivery door made them all jump. Ted went to answer it. Another young police officer, holding a cellophane-covered tray of pastries, stepped inside and put the tray down on the coffee counter. "Sent these from the bakery."

Meese shot him a desperate look. The other young officer shrugged and left.

They all had coffee, including Ted, the inveterate tea drinker, and the young Meese, who took his cup to a corner and tried to make himself invisible. Chaz was the only one of them who had any appetite, and he helped himself to a huge bear claw, which he ate while he poked around the room.

"I wonder how much longer Bill is going to be," Fred said.

Officer Meese shrugged apologetically.

"I just wish he'd hurry."

So did Liv. The night's events were going on without her. The choir had stopped singing soon after the tree lighting. But there were sleigh rides, carolers, and church services. Fred should be out managing traffic flow. The officers should be out patrolling the streets. And why was the head of the security service *she'd* hired assisting Bill? Who was running the security team while he was examining the crime scene?

The crime scene. How could this even be possible. In all her years in Manhattan, she'd never been involved in a crime scene, though knowing some of her former clients, there may have been a few she just hadn't heard about. But not here.

Chaz finished his pastry and sat down on the stool in front of the counter to peruse the bakery platter. "I wonder what's happened to Hank?" he said to no one in particular.

Liv started. "What do you mean?"

"Just that he should have ditched the ceremony and been home by now."

"How do you know he isn't?"

"There's no Santa suit." He chose a cranberry scone and gestured with it. "See, coat hangers and street clothes, but no suit."

The others looked at the hanging clothes rack, where a pair of overalls, a sweater, and a thick hunting jacket hung in a row.

"Maybe he got waylaid by children on his way," Fred said. "He usually does. Little tots can't wait for tomorrow for Santa Village to open." He smiled. "They just get so excited."

"Hmm." Chaz bit into the scone.

They fell into silence.

The back door opened. A shock of cold air preceded Hank Ousterhout still in his Santa suit. He shut the door but stopped just inside the room.

"Guess you're wondering what we're doing here," Chaz said.

Hank pulled off his Santa hat and tossed it toward the clothes rack.

"I guess you'd say I am. But nothing would surprise me tonight."

Just wait, thought Liv, but she said nothing.

"As long as you don't mind if I get out of this suit, you're welcome. I see Dolly's been here with some supplies."

"Help yourself," Fred said.

Hank reached past Chaz and took a jelly donut, which he polished off in three bites. Brushing his hands, he walked over to the clothes rack and saw the patrolman sitting on a box in the corner.

"You catch whoever stole my Santa suit?"

Meese shook his head.

Hank turned back to the group. "Then what are you all doing here? Has something happened?"

No one spoke.

"What?"

They must have all seen it at the same time, but Ted was the only one who voiced their question.

"Hank, what the hell do you have on your suit?"

Hank looked down. "Dang it, I knew better than to eat a jelly donut." He brushed at the rusty spot on his stomach. Brushed it again.

"Hank, that's not jelly," Ted told him.

"So help me—it must've got dirty in that Dumpster. When I get my hands on the kids that pulled that stunt—they almost ruined the Santa Parade, not to mention it cost me fifty bucks just to get it cleaned in the first place. It's on the sleeve, too." He raised his arm to look at the cuff.

Against the white trim, it looked suspiciously like dried blood.

Ted moved slowly toward the annoyed man. "I think you'd better get out of the coat, Hank. It might be evidence in a crime."

Hank looked at him like he was crazy. "The hell you say. What kind of crime? If some kid stole my suit to shoplift . . ."

"Not shoplifting, Hank," Ted said gently. "The TAT Santa was found dead less than an hour ago."

"The TAT Santa? I thought you were supposed to get rid of him."

"Someone did," Chaz said.

Liv glared at him.

"I don't get it." Hank rubbed his bearded cheek. Jerked his hand away and looked at the cuff. Brought it to his nose and sniffed. "That's blood."

"Let's just get you out of the suit," Chaz said, pushing himself away from the counter. "Bill will probably want to take a look."

"Why?"

"Because someone may have worn your suit to commit a murder."

"Are you saying someone killed that fella?"

"It looks like it," Ted said.

Hank shook his head. "That's sick. And I was out there talking to kiddies wearing—" He tugged the black belt off and threw it toward the clothes rack. Tore open the snaps of the jacket.

Officer Meese jumped up.

Ted got there first. "Hank, wait, just calm down." Ted began to help him out of the jacket. Chaz silently scooped the belt from the floor and laid it on the counter.

"This is not how Christmas is supposed to be," Hank said. "Not at all like it's supposed to be."

Liv couldn't agree more. She didn't know much about Hank Ousterhout, but she didn't want him to be involved in what was obviously murder. He'd seemed so jolly—except when he'd come to her office complaining about Grace Thornsby. The manager of TAT, the woman who employed the ersatz Santa, and Hank's ex-wife. The woman who was missing in action.

"This is just plum crazy." Hank sank down on the cot.

Ted reached for his cell phone.

Bill Gunnison showed up two minutes later.

He stood just inside the door and looked around the room. His eyes finally came to rest on Hank.

"Bill, they think someone wore my suit to kill that hired Santa."

"We did not say that," Chaz said quickly. "Just that it's something you should probably look at."

Bill leaned over the counter where Chaz had gingerly folded the Santa jacket. "Meese, radio Johnston and tell him to get over here with an evidence bag. Hank, we're gonna need those trousers, too."

Hank looked down at the red velvet pants, pushed himself off the cot like an old man, grabbed his overalls from the clothes rack, and stepped toward the madras curtain.

Bill jerked his head toward Meese, who hurried after Hank. When they came back, Hank was back in his coveralls and Meese was carrying the Santa pants. He added them to the jacket and belt, just as two more officers came inside. They went straight to the red suit.

"When can I get them back?" Hank asked. "I need the suit for tomorrow morning. It's Breakfast with Santa, then the official opening of Santa Village."

He looked at Bill, then Ted, then Liv, and finally Chaz, but Chaz had turned his back and was watching the officers bag the Santa suit.

"Hank, I'm afraid you're not going to get it back. It's possible evidence in a crime."

"But where the heck am I gonna get another Santa suit by tomorrow morning?"

Bill didn't answer. Neither did anyone else.

Hank looked around at each one of them. "What? Am I missing something? Ms. Montgomery? You must be able to get stuff at the last minute."

Liv swallowed.

Bill let her off the hook. "Hank, I'm afraid you're going to have to come down to the station."

"Why?"

"Just to answer some questions."

"Because someone stole my suit? Is that what it is? Someone wore my suit to commit murder?" Hank's ruddy cheeks drained of color.

Bill stepped toward him. "Now, let's not get ahead of ourselves. Right now, I just need a detailed account of your activities earlier this evening."

"I was home all day. I brought the suit in yesterday, and

when I came back tonight, it was gone. I found it in the Dumpster right out there in the alley."

"So you don't know when the suit was taken?"

"No. I told you. It was gone when I got here. You should ask Nancy. She keeps the back room locked. I have a key to let myself in."

"Hank!" Ted said so sharply that the man jumped. "I think you shouldn't say anything more without a lawyer."

Hank frowned. He wasn't catching on.

"I was getting to that," Bill said. "Officer Meese will take Nancy's statement with these others. I'm only taking you in for questioning, Hank, but I think you should have a lawyer present."

"A lawyer? You mean—you don't think I killed that man?"

"I'm not thinking anything except that your Santa suit has blood on it and it needs to be tested. But that's gonna take a few days."

"A few days? But what about tomorrow?"

Yeah, what about tomorrow? Liv wanted to ask. One Santa dead, the other possibly suspected of murder, his Santa suit bagged as evidence. Where the hell were they going to get another Santa in full regalia by tomorrow?

She looked around the room. Ted had the hair and twinkling eyes, but she needed him in the office. Bill's back would probably go out if he tried to lift a child on his knee. Besides, he had to investigate and keep the community safe. Ditto the other officers. Fred had the stomach, but he had to control traffic flow. She reluctantly looked at the only man left in the room.

Chaz Bristow looked back at her, not a care in his sleepy, unused little heart. Yet.

She smiled, grim though it was. "How soon can you get your butt into a Santa costume?"

His blank look became blanker. She was looking straight at him, but he turned to look over his shoulder at the row of boxes behind him. Slowly, he turned back to Liv. Even more slowly, he shook his head.

She nodded just as slowly.

Suddenly galvanized, Chaz sprang to his feet. "Sheriff, you can't put Santa in jail. He has to be here to talk to the kiddies tomorrow morning."

"How many times do I have to say this? I'm just taking him in for questioning."

"Yeah," Chaz said. "Great. And when it gets out that Santa is a suspected murderer, do you think anybody is going to bring their child to sit on his lap? They'll go to some other town to do their shopping. The local businesses are going to love that."

"I didn't do anything," Hank said.

"Remember what happened in *Miracle on Thirty-fourth Street*?"

Bill frowned at Chaz.

"They put Santa on trial. Parents were in an uproar. Children were brokenhearted. The judge was on the hot seat."

"I didn't do it," Hank reiterated.

Bill looked toward heaven. "If you just let me take him to the station and don't talk about what's happened, he may be back in his sleigh before anyone knows he was gone."

"Just like with Joss Waterbury?"

Low blow, Chaz, thought Liv.

"I wasn't the one who arrested Joss."

"Do you think people are going to remember that it was those jerks from the state? No. They'll just remember that you're trigger-happy when it comes to arresting local citizens. And that you arrested Santa Claus."

"That's not fair, Chaz." Fred hoisted himself out of the easy chair. "But he may be right, Bill. Hank has been the town Santa for over a decade. Do you think he would go off and kill someone right before the Santa Parade? He'd have to be nuts."

Everybody looked at Hank.

"I'm not. I didn't."

Liv had seen him jolly and seen him angry, but now he just looked tired, resigned, defeated. His round cheeks had lost their roundness, his eyes were dull. His shoulders stooped like an old man's. Even his beard seemed to droop.

"I'm not saying you did, but the sooner we get out to the station, the sooner you'll be back looking for a new Santa suit."

"I'll get on it right away," Liv said. There had to be a costume shop she could rouse at nine o'clock on a Friday night. Sure. And reindeer could fly.

"Come on Hank. Get your coat. We'll call your lawyer once we get there."

"I don't have a lawyer."

"I'll call Silas Lark," Ted said. "But don't say anything until he gets there." Ted was already scrolling through his cell phone for Silas's number.

"Can't afford no lawyer."

Bill took Hank's coat off the hanger and helped him into it.

"Officer Meese will stay and take your statements here and then you'll be allowed to leave. I don't have to ask that you not talk about this situation."

He escorted Hank toward the door.

Chaz jumped up and grabbed his jacket. "I think I'll make my statement at the station if that's okay with you." Without waiting for an answer, he headed for the door.

"I know where you live," Liv said sotto voce as he passed by.

"Chaz was sure in a hurry to leave," Fred said. "Do you suppose he knows something he didn't want to share?"

Liv sighed. "No. I think he was afraid of me tagging him for the job of Santa tomorrow."

She looked up to find Nancy Pyne standing in the doorway to the shop. Her face was as gray as her hair, her lips colorless.

"Where are they taking Hank? Did they just arrest him for murder? They can't do that. You heard him. He didn't do anything."

They had heard him, Liv thought, and evidently so had Nancy Pyne. She must have been listening at the door.

"Someone stole his suit," Nancy said. "He found it in the Dumpster behind A Stitch in Time. I helped him look."

"Just a sec." Officer Meese fumbled in his pocket. "I'll just turn on this tape recorder. Would you mind repeating that and answering a few questions, ma'am?"

"I would. But in the spirit of the season, I will." Nancy sat down on the stool, and the policeman turned on the mini-recorder.

"I'll just move these pastries out of your way." Ted caught Liv's eye, and they moved to the far side of the room where Fred was sitting.

"Your name is?"

"Nancy Pyne."

And you're the owner of this store?"

"Yes."

Nancy answered his questions in a calm, almost disinterested voice, and Liv only half listened. At the moment, she had bigger problems to deal with. Like where to find a Santa suit. And then find someone to wear it. Or get Hank Ousterhout out of jail. But first, she had to move this interview process along before it got any later.

"What now?" she whispered to Ted.

"As soon as we're through here, I'm going to take a drive out to the station. See what the score is there and try to get Hank out of there tonight."

"Why wouldn't you be able to? Someone stole his suit. There were witnesses."

Ted gave her a look. "Hanks *says* someone stole it. Hank *told* Nancy someone stole it. So far, no witness."

Liv shivered. "I can't believe this. Do you think he'll be back in time for the pancake breakfast tomorrow?"

"Bill will make sure everything is done by the book. And they won't charge him until he's been fingerprinted—"

"He's been fingerprinted along with the rest of us. It's part of the our new policy. Bill knows that."

"Sure he does. But they'll want to do it again. Along with some other tests. It just depends on what they've got and what Silas can do to get him out."

Fred leaned forward in his chair. "Even if they let Hank go, and if Liv can find a suit by tomorrow, can we allow Hank to be Santa? Would it be responsible to allow a suspect to be that close to children? What if the news gets out?"

"Oh Lord." Liv slumped against the wall.

Ted shrugged. "Hank has been Santa for ten years. I don't think he suddenly snapped tonight. If they don't arrest him, we'll be okay. If they do . . . that's a problem we'll have to take up with the town council."

"Nonetheless, I think I'll put a security person on the premises, just to be safe," Liv said.

"Good idea," Ted said. "Santa's helper."

Liv held up a finger. She'd been listening with one ear to Nancy's interview. Now it had her full attention.

"When was the last time you saw the suit?"

Nancy shrugged. "I didn't really pay attention. Hank uses my back room every year so he can have a place to relax between shifts. It was hanging over there." She pointed to the now empty clothes rack.

"Did you see it today?"

"I don't recall seeing it this morning, though I wasn't back here much," Nancy said. "The door is usually locked except when I'm accepting deliveries. Then we leave it open until everything is unloaded. There were several deliveries this afternoon."

"So it's possible someone could have sneaked in and taken the suit without being seen?"

Nancy deliberated, then slowly nodded. "There was a misunderstanding with one of the craftsmen. We had to recount the order before it off-loaded. Someone could have sneaked in then. I don't know. I didn't know someone was going to steal the suit. I didn't notice. The order was from a craftsman over in Lake Placid. If you'd like to talk to *him*, too."

"I think Nancy is getting a little impatient," Ted whispered. "Let's see if we can speed things up."

The three of them moved back to the interview table.

Nancy saw them and stood up. "We've had nothing but trouble since that woman opened that tacky store. She's the one you should be talking to. Where was she when all this was going on?"

"Yes," Liv said. "That's something we'd all like to know."

Chapter Five

....

Ted and Liv gave their statements and were released. As they left the Pyne Bough, they saw a crowd gathered on the far side of yellow tape that had been stretched across the end of the alley.

"Oh crud." Liv looked over the faces and tried to act normal.

"Look nonchalant," Ted said.

"Some kind of electrical problem?" Roscoe Jackson yelled from the crowd. Roscoe was the owner of the Celebration General Store and a member of the board of trustees who had hired Liv.

"That's what we heard," Ted said and motioned for the officer in charge to let them pass.

"Why's there an ambulance and no power company truck?"

Ted shook his head, yawned. "Roscoe, don't you have better sense than to stand out in the cold for no good reason? If anything of interest was happening, you'd hear it on the police band before you'd find out standing around getting frostbite."

Several people eased out of the crowd and began to walk away. They were soon joined by everyone else.

Roscoe scrunched down in his anorak, craned his neck to see down the alley, then nodded to Liv and Ted and walked away at a brisk pace.

The officer opened the tape and let them pass.

"A veritable stampede to their CB radios," Liv said. "Bill ordered police silence. You are good."

"I am that," Ted said with a grin. He took her elbow and maneuvered her around the line waiting for a table at the Corner Café. "Think you can come up with a Santa suit by nine a.m. tomorrow and find someone to go inside it?"

"I'm going to try."

"Good. You call around for a suit. I'll go out to the police station and try to get Santa back."

They split up at the steps of town hall; Ted headed for the employees parking lot around back. Liv reached for her keys and climbed the steps. She unlocked the Events Office door; reached for the light switch; and pulled off her gloves, hat, and coat as she went through to her office. She tossed them on the chair; booted up her laptop; and scrolled through her contact lists for costume shops, party stores, and everything rental.

Twelve calls later, she'd left seven messages, gotten three no-can-do's, and had found two suits. One size small in New Jersey, which would be totally useless. And a large one that could be overnighted from a theatrical costume shop in NYC . . . as soon as it was returned on Monday.

"This was not supposed to happen," she said to the walls. She'd triple- and quadruple-checked every aspect of the night's festivities. She was way ahead on the coming events.

She was a seasoned event planner. She knew that she had to be on top of everything. She also knew you didn't last long if you didn't learn to delegate. She would never try to make hors d'oeuvres or direct traffic. She hired professionals to do it. Of course, she only hired the best. Occasionally they screwed up, but not very often.

As soon as she heard they'd had the same Santa for a

decade, and he had his own suit and was ready to ride into town, she'd relaxed. Dexter Kent drove his own wagon and he was in charge of the two reindeer, which they imported from a nearby breeder and which would be housed at Dexter's nursery for the next three weekends.

Liv had even driven out to the nursery to check on the reindeer accommodations. The last thing they needed was to have PETA picketers stopping traffic before they even made it into town.

She'd made sure that the people who'd be serving the cider and donuts were licensed food handlers. She'd listened to reports of safety standards, porta potties, emergency medical services. She had ambulances standing by, inconspicuous but readily available.

She'd sent out memos and reminders with instructions for the Celebration of Lights. She'd made sure Chaz, the uninterested, would run the ads for each week's festivities without them being bumped for fishing news.

But she hadn't made sure there was a backup Santa suit.

She could kick herself. She stood, started to pace. There had to be a Santa suit out there. Even if she had to drive all night to get it.

She stopped at the window that overlooked the green. She hadn't even taken the time to look at the town in all its twinkling magic. In the center of the park the town tree was lit with thousands of lights. It was encircled by a gleaming square of sparkling lights, like a giant diamond necklace. Every store, restaurant, house, business—even unoccupied ones—were all lit, joining in the spirit of the community, the excitement of the season . . . except for the one dark gap where Trim a Tree had been the scene of murder.

And where was Grace Thornsby? No one seemed to know. She'd called Penny to say she couldn't make it in to work. Where was she? Did she sabotage her lights because they had insisted she get rid of Santa?

An icy tendril crept up Liv's neck. Had she taken them seriously and gotten rid of him? Permanently? Liv shuddered.

Absurd. She was getting off topic. The man was dead. An awful thing. She stopped. *The man was dead.*

She grimaced at the idea that had suddenly sprung to mind. He wouldn't be needing his Santa suit, not now or ever again. He wasn't wearing it when he died, so the police wouldn't need it as evidence.

Especially if Liv got to it before they did.

She grabbed her coat and keys. It wouldn't hurt to just take a look. She wouldn't remove anything without checking with Bill first. They could have it back as soon as the other one arrived.

It was a bizarre thing to do. She knew it. But if she didn't tell anyone where it came from, no one would feel squeamish about it. It wouldn't hurt just to check and see if it was still in the TAT store.

She locked the door to the outer office and hurried out to the street.

She wasn't sure if they would let her back across the caution tape, so she headed for the bakery. First she wanted to see if Miss Ida and Miss Edna were still there with Whiskey and to ask them to take him home with them. Then she'd ask Dolly if she could use her back door to get back into TAT.

Neither Dolly nor the sisters were in the bakery, but the girls at the counter said they were in Dolly's office and told her to go back.

Whiskey let out a bark and started dancing when she entered the room. The three women were sitting in the tiny room around Dolly's old rolltop desk, listening to the police band.

Liv knelt down to scratch Whiskey's ears. "Hey, buddy. Did you miss me?"

"They've taken someone into custody," Dolly said. "Do you know who it is?"

"Custody?" Liv stopped scratching, and Whiskey wiggled under her hand. What had happened to "radio silence"?

Ida pursed her lips. "Please don't tell me it's that nice young Newland girl. Fred said they kept her behind when you went down to the Pyne Bough. That poor family has suffered enough."

"They have," Edna agreed.

"I really need to get going," Liv said.

"Just because Penny made one little mistake, it doesn't give people a right to be mean," Ida added, looking stern.

"Nor accuse her of murder," Edna added. "The whole idea is absurd."

Liv wondered if Penny's little mistake had resulted in her little boy. "Are you sure they said Penny is in custody?" Liv tried to quell the surge of relief that it wasn't the town Santa. But time was passing and she needed to get to that suit before it was too late. She started inching toward the door.

"They said it was a ten-fifteen," Edna said.

Ida nodded, looking worried.

Dolly shook her head. "I don't think they meant Penny. Fred called to say they'd finished with him but he had to hurry over to a traffic jam on Delice Street. That he would talk to me later, and that Bill had sent Penny home."

"So if it wasn't Penny, who was it?" asked Edna, eying Liv speculatively.

Liv deliberated. She needed to get to TAT and collect that Santa suit before the police sealed the store. But her three friends would wheedle her for information until she told, and she didn't have the time.

She needed that Santa suit now. And then she would have to beg Bill not to put crime scene tape across the front of the store.

"While we were at Nancy's, Hank came in. There was blood on his Santa suit. They thought that maybe whoever stole it and left it in the Dumpster might have—well, they didn't actually say that, but the fact that there was blood on the suit, they needed to take Hank in to give his statement. Dolly, can I—"

"Hank Ousterhout?" asked Edna.

"Yes," Liv said. "Listen, there's something I have to do.

Could you please take Whiskey home with you? You can just put him in the carriage house. I shouldn't be too long."

"Of course, dear," Miss Ida said. "But we'll keep him with us. Just knock on the door when you get home."

"I might be late."

"Oh that's all right. With all the excitement we won't be able to sleep a wink."

"What she means," Edna said, "is we'll want to know the whole story when you get home."

Liv smiled tightly. This was the hard part of her new job. The public didn't need to know a lot of stuff. And yet the line between the public and her friends was blurry. She decided to skirt the issue for the time being.

"Dolly, do you mind if I use your back door?"

"Of course not, but what are you going to do?"

"I'm going to try to get back into TAT—"

"You're going to investigate," Miss Ida declared.

"No-o-o," Liv said. "I'm hoping the police are still there, and if it isn't needed in the investigation, they'll let me borrow the TAT Santa suit."

"I didn't think about that." Miss Ida pressed her fingers to her lips. "What's Hank going to wear if his suit is ruined?"

"Heck, what are we going to do for a Santa if Hank is in jail?" countered her sister.

"Come on." Dolly pulled herself up from her chair and shooed Liv out the door.

Whiskey tried to follow.

"Stay," Liv commanded.

Whiskey stopped but he whined piteously and gave her the nobody-loves-me look.

"I'm sorry," Liv said guiltily. "Soon we're going to have a treat day—all day long."

Whiskey yipped.

Edna managed to clip on his leash before he tried to follow. "Go on. We'll be fine."

"Thanks." Liv took off after Dolly, who was already halfway across the kitchen.

"Do you need help, dear?" Miss Ida called after her.

Edna let out a gruff laugh. "Yeah, we can distract the police, while you sneak in and steal the suit."

"Edna, you are not helping with that attitude."

"*Do* you need help?" Dolly asked seriously as she unlocked the back door of the bakery.

"Thanks, but I'm not going to do anything devious. I'll just ask politely and hope for the best."

"Well, just say the word." Dolly opened the door. "We've got your back."

"Thanks."

"I'll just watch to make sure you get there okay."

"I appreciate it." And she did. Though TAT was only a few stores away, and the alley was mostly well lit, tonight Liv felt eerily alone, even with Dolly watching from the bakery door.

Her cell phone rang. She fished it out of her pocket. Looked at caller ID.

"Ted, what's up? Are you at the station?"

"No, I'm in the car with Hank."

"They let him go?"

"Yes. Where are you?"

"Uh . . ." *In the alley about to remove something from an active crime scene.* "Well . . ."

"Liv?"

"I've called everywhere. I can't get anything until Monday. Though I'll start calling in the morning again. But it won't be in time for Breakfast with Santa."

The door to the Trim a Tree shop opened and a policeman stepped out. "Ms. Montgomery, is that you?"

She nodded, smiled, waved.

"You really can't be back here, ma'am."

"Liv, who was that? Where are you?"

The officer was headed her way.

"Ted, hang on for a minute." She covered the phone with her hand. Just as the officer met her.

"Ma'am, you know better than to be out here alone, especially after—" He jerked his head toward TAT.

"I know," Liv said. "I was hoping Bill was still there. I wanted to borrow the Santa suit. They confiscated Hank Ousterhout's."

"Yes ma'am, I heard. Darn shame. What's he gonna wear for breakfast tomorrow?"

"That's what I was hoping to see Bill about."

"Liv, where are you? Who are you talking to?" Ted's voiced squawked into her palm.

"I'll call you back." She hung up.

"I was hoping to borrow the one that Mr. uh, the TAT Santa wore. Just for a couple of days," she added quickly. "I have one arriving on Monday."

The officer bit his lip, looked back at the store. "I sure wish I could help you. But it's a"—he lowered his voice—"crime scene."

"Can you just tell me this? Is it still there?"

He shrugged. "I'm just stationed outside the door, making sure nobody tries to get in. I haven't even been inside."

Her cell phone rang.

"Well, thanks."

"Maybe if you called the sheriff . . ."

"I'll do that. Thanks for your help. Good night." She started back toward the bakery and answered her phone.

"What is going on?"

"Nothing, unfortunately. I was hoping to borrow the TAT Santa suit for tomorrow, but unless Bill okays it—"

There was an explosion on the other end of the line. Ted was laughing. "You were going to steal a Santa suit from a crime scene? Liv, I think that's probably some kind of felony."

"Of course I wasn't going to steal it." *Unless I had to*, she added silently. "I thought maybe Bill would still be there and give me a dispensation."

"Well, he isn't, he took Hank to the station, but I'm glad you're still in town. We have a plan of sorts."

"I'm listening."

"While I was waiting for Hank, I called A Stitch in Time to see if they had enough red velveteen to make a new costume. They're rustling up what they can and setting up their crafts room as a sewing room. I'm bringing Hank there. They'll need him for the fittings."

"Ted, I can't sew, can you?"

"Needs must—"

"Yeah, where the devil drives. I hope they catch this devil and throw the book at him . . . or her. I'm on my way. I'll meet you at the fabric store."

Dolly was waiting at the bakery door.

"Change of plan," Liv said. "They're going to make a suit down at A Stitch in Time."

"Bless Miriam Krause. I'll send over whatever pastries are left when we close up. It's going to be a long night. Good luck."

Liv hurried up the street to A Stitch in Time. She passed the dark Trim a Tree store and was thankful there was no crime tape across the front, though someone had installed a lockbox on the door. And the windows were covered over with brown paper.

Next door, A Stitch in Time seemed all the more festive. Small and narrow, the store was crammed with bolts of fabric and was decorated in swags of red and green calico ribbons. There were still quite a few shoppers in the store, carrying wicker baskets filled with fabric, notions, and gifts made by Miriam's sewing and crafts classes.

Liv hurried down the narrow aisle to the back where a quilting frame displayed the work of the quilting club. Opposite it was a cutting counter and cash register. Liv knew the shop also held sewing, knitting, and quilting classes. She didn't know how they could squeeze it all in. She didn't see any sewing space.

Several women had formed a line at the cash register, and Miriam Krause, the proprietress, called out over their heads, "We're setting up in back, go on through."

Liv had to sashay between the line and a shelf of shiny satins to get to the back of the shop.

A narrow hallway led to a back door and the alley, just as in all the other stores on the block. Liv couldn't help but wonder if the murderer had picked one store at random and it happened to be Trim a Tree. That would make sense: a robbery gone bad.

A door was open on her right and she looked in. It was a small square, maybe ten by ten. The entire space was taken up by a rectangular table covered with a cardboard cutting surface. A length of red material was spread across it, and two women were pinning tissue pattern pieces to it.

Liv didn't sew, but she understood the mechanics of it, and it looked like this project would take more than a few hours.

"Do you think you can finish that tonight?"

"Don't you worry," said one of the middle-aged women; she was wearing a green handmade sweater with a spring of holly pinned to the front.

"The Stitch in Time Sewing Club won't let you or Hank down."

The other lady nodded her agreement. She had a row of pins held between her lips.

Liv didn't want to take up what little space there was in the room, but she didn't want to leave. So she paced in the narrow hallway outside while she waited for Ted and Hank to arrive.

After an interminable few minutes, Miriam showed the last customer out and turned over the Closed sign. She walked briskly to the back of the store and began clicking light switches until only the spotlight over the quilting frame was left on. The front of the store was plunged into darkness.

Liv started. There was an uncanny resemblance to the way she and Ted had found the Trim a Tree shop only a few hours before.

"Give me a hand, can you, Liv?"

"Sure." Liv jumped to attention.

"We need to swing this quilting frame out of the way so we can set up the extra sewing machines in here. I have two in back, but we may need more. If you can just take that other side."

Liv positioned herself on the far side of the frame.

"You just hold that side steady." Miriam disappeared under the other side of the frame, the frame shifted, and Miriam's head popped up. "Now lift up your end."

Liv lifted. The frame came away from the legs.

"Now, we're just going to carry it into the main aisle and prop it against the shelves." In a matter of minutes, the frame was dismantled and moved out of the way and two sewing machines and a machine Miriam called a serger had been installed in its place.

"Wow," said Liv. "You really have this down."

"Yes, though sometimes it gets awfully tiresome always juggling for space."

Liv thought of the Trim a Tree shop next door. It had to be twice the size of the fabric store. She said so.

"Oh, it is," Miriam said. "Also twice the rent. I actually considered moving for a while, but with the economy the way it is, I was afraid to take the chance. Now I wish I had. Struggling to make rent would be better than having to put up with that . . . that . . ."

Woman, Liv finished for her.

"I don't know why Jeremiah Atkins leased the space to those people. He should know better."

"Jeremiah owns the building?" Jeremiah Atkins was president of First Celebration Bank.

"Oh, he owns a whole row of stores along this side of the square and a few rental houses in town. I don't know what he was thinking to let them take over the lease. That tacky window display, the cheap ornaments. It's just a crime."

And a crime scene, thought Liv morosely.

Chapter Six

....

Ted and Hank arrived at the front door about ten minutes later, along with two other women, who nodded to Liv and went straight back to the sewing area.

Miriam came out to greet them.

"I sure appreciate this." Hank nodded, docile as a kitten and sounding very depressed. Liv just hoped he'd bounce back to his jolly self by tomorrow's breakfast.

"Now, Hank, you don't worry about a thing. Here's the plan. We've got most everything cut out, but we're going to need to fit it on you a few times. I took the liberty of calling Nancy Pyne to see if we could use her back room. That way you could rest up for tomorrow morning in between fittings. This might take most of the night."

"Good thinking." Ted lifted his eyebrows at Liv and pushed Hank toward the back of the store. "We'll just cut across the alley. I'll call over to Buddy's and have them send over some sandwiches and things."

Now that he had mentioned food, Liv was ravenous. "Can I do anything here? Or should I go over with Ted and Hank?"

Miriam looked surprised. "Well, why don't you go over

with the men. Or you can go on home and get some sleep. I bet you could use it."

She could, but no way was she going to leave before that suit was finished and under lock and key.

"I'll stick around for a while." When Liv caught up with them, Ted was scooping out de-icer from a plastic tub and tossing it out the door. "We don't need anyone slipping and breaking an arm or anything. Come on, just be careful."

As soon as they stepped outside, they were hailed by the same police officer who had stopped Liv.

"Just going to the Pyne Bough," Ted called. "Making a new Santa suit. Lots of folks going to be coming back and forth all night, but we won't get too close."

"Thank you, Ted." The officer disappeared into the shadow of the building.

Nancy met them at the back door. "Come on in. Make yourselves at home." She didn't sound nearly as welcoming as she had the last time. And who could blame her? She probably just wanted to go home to bed, not have to put up with witnesses and seamstresses and a suitless Santa.

Liv could sympathize. This wasn't even déjà vu. It was more like being stuck in the same loop, like those people in the old French movie who could never leave the party, or Bill Murray in *Groundhog Day* reliving the same day over and over. This was one day Liv would be glad to see behind her.

"Nancy, thanks so much for doing this," Liv said. "You deserve a medal for all the disruption this day has caused you."

Nancy threw up a hand. "The least I could do. I just hope whoever robbed the Trim a Tree and killed that man isn't going to come back to murder us all."

"I'm meeting with the head of Bayside Security tomorrow and asking for additional guards. And I'm sure Bill will post more men around town."

"Great idea. Come spend your family holiday under the watchful eye of armed guards." Nancy's voice held an edge of bitterness.

"Why don't you close up and go home?" Ted said gently.

"You look beat. If you'll just show me where your de-icer is, I'll salt your steps. We don't want any seamstresses taking a tumble."

"Thank you. It's in the corner by the door."

While Ted broadcast the crystals out the back door, Liv and Hank took off their outerwear. There were new hangers on the clothes rack. The police had taken in the original hangers along with the suit. Nancy must have replaced them.

Ted came back inside and shed his coat. He had to reach around Hank for a hanger, because after hanging up his coat, Hank seemed to run out of steam.

"Sit down, Hank. I'm calling Buddy's. What would you like?"

"Huh? Oh, I'm not hungry."

"Well, you will be," Ted said. "It's going to be a long night. And the pancake breakfast is a long ways away."

Hank sat down on the edge of the cot. "Whatever."

"Liv?"

"Whatever, but lots of it, I'm starving."

Ted pulled out his cell.

"I'll make coffee." Liv grabbed the coffeepot and filled it at the water dispenser. She made a mental note to reimburse Nancy for all the coffee and water they'd been through.

As she went through the routine of pouring water and measuring coffee, her mind began to spar, one side saying, *Please let the murderer be someone passing through, a stranger, a random act of violence by an outsider,* while the other argued it would be better if it were a crime of passion, a personal vendetta; that way the visitors who flocked to Celebration Bay wouldn't be at risk.

Neither side was winning. While they were waiting for the coffee to brew, Liv said, "Why don't you fill me in on what happened at the station?"

Hank shuddered. "I'd like to forget."

"True," said Ted. "But we need to bring Liv up to speed so she can make contingency plans." He got three mugs out of the cabinet, searched for sugar, found milk in the fridge. Stared at the coffee as it began to drip.

Liv resisted tapping her foot in impatience. That would just egg him on.

The three of them watched the pot as it filled with coffee. When it was done, Ted poured out three cups, handed a cup each to Liv and Hank, pulled a chair up near the cot so Liv could sit, and got another one for himself.

"Now, what do you want to know?"

"For crying out loud. Did they arrest Hank or not?"

"They did not," Hank boomed so loud, Liv bobbled her coffee cup.

"So what did happen?"

Hank shifted his weight and the cot creaked. "They asked me a bunch of questions, I answered them. They let me go."

Liv looked to the ceiling. "Men and their idea of 'what happened.'"

"I think Liv wants a blow-by-blow," Ted said. "After all, she has to do triage on Celebration Bay's image."

"This is going to ruin Christmas," Hank said. "You know how this town is. When it gets out that they took me in for questioning about a murder, no one will let their kids come near me. Everybody will lose money. Then everybody will blame me, and I didn't do anything."

"No they won't," Liv said optimistically. "Because first thing tomorrow morning I'm going over to the *Clarion* and get Chaz Bristow to run a front-page article."

Hank bolted from the couch. "No, you can't."

"Sit down, Hank. Liv knows what she's doing."

"Thank you, Ted. You said yourself that the news will get out. There's no way to prevent that. We just have to spin it in our favor."

"How?"

"A human interest story on how you, Hank Ousterhout, have given up your time and energy for how many, ten years?"

"Twelve."

"Twelve Christmases to be the town Santa, the most beloved Santa on the East Coast or maybe 'on the lake' will suffice. Anyway, how someone broke into the Pyne Bough

and stole your Santa suit—maybe we could call it a prank?"
She looked at Ted for confirmation.

Ted grimaced.

"Anyway, someone stole the suit and stuffed it in a Dumpster. A piece of un-holiday-like mischief. But that didn't stop you. You looked high and low and found it in time for the parade. But it was stained . . . from the Dumpster . . . and there were no other suits to be found . . . anywhere."

Liv smiled at her story. "So the ladies from A Stitch in Time went to work to create a new suit so the children wouldn't be disappointed. I'll get Chaz to name them all, how the members of the sewing club stayed up all night constructing. How Nancy volunteered her store, how Dolly sent baked goods to sustain them through the night. Buddy's sent sandwiches to fuel the seamstresses. The whole town pulled together to make this the best Christmas ever."

Ted was grinning.

Liv huffed out air. "Well, I'm going to get Chaz to say something like that. Hopefully something that will downplay any suspicion that might fall on you—or anyone else. And give the police time to find the real culprit and arrest him."

"That sounds real good, Liv," Hank said, looking marginally calmer. "And it's just like it happened."

"Good. But I need to know a few more details. Chaz will want to know so he can add a little local color. Why, he was just talking about local color not a few hours ago." But not exactly in the way she meant.

"Okay. Where do you want me to start?"

"From when you brought the suit here. But hang on a second." She reached in her pocket for her cell phone. Brought up her notes. "Okay."

"I picked it up from Ivy Cleaners yesterday morning. I walked over here and hung it up on the rack there."

"What time was that?"

Hank frowned at her.

"For Chaz's story."

"Around nine o'clock."

Ted gave her a look. He knew just what she was doing.

Liv ignored him. "Did you come in the back or front door?" she asked, typing as fast as her thumbs would move.

"Back."

"Nancy let you in?"

"Yes. Then she gave me a key to use and went back out front." Hank licked his lips and smoothed his moustache. "I took off the plastic to let it air out and hung it up, checked it to make sure all the buttons were there. You know how sometimes they get broken at the cleaner's."

Ted and Liv nodded.

"Then I left."

"And you didn't return until time for the Santa Parade?"

"Right."

"Did you go out the back when you left?"

"Uh-huh."

"And did you lock the door?"

Hank's white brows dipped. "No. There was a delivery and they were moving boxes in. And these are practically the same questions Bill asked me downtown."

Ted suppressed a snort. Reached for his handkerchief.

"I don't mean to be nosey, but . . ."

"That'll be a first," Ted said under his breath.

"Are you typing all this into your phone?" Hank asked, craning his neck to see.

"Yes. I know Chaz won't be able to interview you himself, since you'll be busy all day." *And Chaz will be sleeping, if he gets his way. Which he won't.* "So I'm kind of interviewing you for him."

There was a knock at the door.

"Food's here," Ted said and went to answer it.

"When was the next time you saw the suit?"

"I didn't. When I came in to get dressed for the parade, it was gone. I asked Nancy, but she hadn't seen it. She was real upset, said if someone had come in because she'd left the door open, she'd never forgive herself."

"But she doesn't usually leave the door unlocked, does she?"

"No, but it's her busy season. I know she's had a lot of deliveries lately. Someone might have sneaked in while they were unloading one of the trucks, but they'd have to be mighty fast and sneaky to do that."

Which someone contemplating murder might be, Liv thought, but she kept it to herself.

Ted had finished arranging containers of food on the counter. He stopped and looked around, frowning.

"What?" Liv asked. "Did you think of something?"

"Just looking for a . . . ah, there it is." Ted strode across the floor and pulled a folded card table from behind a stack of boxes. "I don't mind having lunch at your desk, but I'm not going to have dinner in my lap."

He opened the table and placed it in front of Hank, drew up his chair, motioned Liv to do the same, and went to get the food.

Liv continued to ask questions, which Hank answered between bites of a hot roast beef sandwich.

They'd just finished eating when there was a knock at the door. Ted opened it to Miriam Krause and another lady from A Stitch in Time, carrying two large cardboard boxes. They dropped them on the floor next to the clothes rack. Miriam lifted the top from the first box and pulled out a plastic bag filled with red velvet.

"You'll have to try these on now, Hank, and let us get it fitted."

Hank pushed himself off the cot, smoothed out his beard, and went to wash his hands, then took the bag and disappeared behind the madras curtain. They listened to rummaging and muffled oaths, and finally Miriam called out. "Hank, just put 'em on over your BVDs and come on out. We don't have time for modesty tonight."

There was a gruff response and Hank plowed through the curtain holding his Santa pants up with one fist. His jacket hung from one shoulder, but finally his cheeks were back to rosy.

Miriam cast her eyes to the ceiling, and hurried toward him. "Don't wrinkle that velvet, I didn't have any velveteen."

"Heck, Miriam, they'll fall down if I let go."

Miriam lifted her chin toward the other seamstress. "Elsbeth, you take the right side and I'll take the left. Now, Hank, let go. And don't move."

Reluctantly Hank let go of his pants. The women caught each side of the waistband and began pinning fabric at an alarming rate, somehow communicating without speaking as one tightened and the other loosened, and vice versa.

Liv watched in amazement as the shapeless fabric turned into a pair of trousers in front of her eyes.

Miriam and Elsbeth moved on to the jacket, and within minutes, Hank was encased in red velvet, held together with shiny metal pins, including one that somehow had become stuck in his beard. He looked like an advertisement for Punk My Santa.

"Okay, just let me measure the trim." Miriam pulled over the second unopened box. "This just came in today, perfect timing." She rummaged in the pockets of her work smock. "Darn, I forgot my utility knife. Elsbeth, look over there and find something to open this box with."

Elsbeth went over to the shipping table, rummaged through the drawers, and brought a box cutter back to Miriam, who sliced through the tape with quick efficiency.

Real efficiency, thought Liv, thinking of the ugly red slash across the TAT Santa's neck. She looked away.

"There," Miriam said, opening the box and pulling out a roll of white fur. She and Elsbeth began tacking it to the edges of the Santa suit.

Then as quickly as they'd pinned him into the suit, they unpinned him. The jacket opened, and they slipped it off, carefully folding it into the plastic bag. But when Hank attempted to go into the dressing room to remove the pants, Miriam grabbed him by the back of his long johns.

"Nobody's looking and we're going to have to go through this routine several more times tonight. Drop those trou now."

Hank glowered at her but turned his back and let the ladies pull them off. Then he scuttled, as quickly as a man his size could scuttle, behind the curtain.

"Think we'd never seen a man in his long johns before." Miriam picked up the bag. "Don't get too comfy, Hank. We'll be back."

While they waited in between fittings, Hank paced like a caged bear. Ted found a tattered copy of *Forever Amber* and sat down to read. Nancy closed the store, stopped to say good night, and went home. Liv began writing a press release that would be the basis, she hoped, of Chaz's human interest story. Hopefully front page center.

It was after two o'clock and several more fittings that Miriam was satisfied the suit fit properly. They'd been through several pots of coffee and made short work of the platter of sandwiches. Several seamstresses surrounded Hank, admiring their handiwork and looking for flaws.

Liv looked up bleary eyed. *Red suit.* She stifled a yawn. "What about his hat?"

"Hat's finished. We can do the buttons and the rest of the finishing ourselves. You and Ted can go on home and try to get a few hours' sleep. Hank, you, too. You just lie down now and stop worrying. You're going to have the finest Santa suit in the state come tomorrow morning. Or I guess I should say later this morning."

"You're sure?" Liv asked.

"Everything is under control," Miriam assured her.

"Take my card, just in case. Call me if you need anything."

Ted hid a yawn behind his hand and closed his book. "Come on. I'll give you a ride home."

Liv gladly accepted. She lived only two blocks west of the park, but she was in no mood to brave the cold or the dark. Or lurking murderers.

The big Victorian was dark; her landladies must have given her up and gone to bed. But they had left the back floodlight on, for which she was grateful.

Whiskey didn't rush to meet her when she let herself in the carriage house. He barely looked up from his plaid doggie bed when she looked into the bedroom to make sure Miss Edna and Miss Ida had brought him home. He yawned and put his head back down on his paws. He was fast asleep when she climbed into bed a few minutes later.

Liv didn't feel slighted. Between Christmas festivities, too many treats, and an unexpected cat to chase, Whiskey was tuckered out. Between Christmas festivities, a missing Santa suit, and a murder, Liv was pretty tired herself.

She was still tired when her alarm went off at six. She let Whiskey out, waiting with her head resting against the door until he reappeared. She put down food and water for Whiskey and staggered into the shower. She felt somewhat revived when she stepped out again . . . until the steam cleared and she was faced with the Ghost of Christmas Past in the mirror. Like several days *past* its prime.

She was pale, her eyes were puffy, and her hair that Dolly said was the color of burnt sugar looked dull and was headed for a ponytail. With Breakfast with Santa, a trip to the Clarion office, and a meeting with the head of Bayside Security on her to-do list, she didn't have time for a prolonged poof and coif.

She pulled a pair of slacks out of the closet, topped them with a greenish sweater, threw a pair of loafers in a bag, and went to fortify herself with snow boots and winter outerwear.

Whiskey met her at the front door, bow tie in his mouth.

"You know," she said, as she knelt down to clip the tie around his neck, "for a dog—yes, that's you, a *dog*," she emphasized, "who won't wear a thing I buy him, who refuses all bows and furbelows from the best groomers in New York City, who has suddenly taken to wearing a red bow tie—" She stood up. "You've definitely been spending too much time with Ted."

"Ar-roo-roo-roo," Whiskey said.

"He's really a bad influence." She clipped on his leash and they went outside.

It was cold. Really cold. She just hoped it didn't deter people from coming out for the festivities and the shopping. This was her first winter in Celebration Bay. Ted assured her the cold wouldn't make a difference as long as the roads were clear.

But she wondered. She was certainly inclined to crawl back into bed and wait for spring. And it wasn't like people could hop on a bus or a taxi and be let out at their destination. They had to warm their cars, find a parking space, and walk, sometimes several blocks. Like she was doing. She could have taken her car and parked behind town hall, but by the time it was defrosted and warm, she could already be at work.

She ducked her chin against the wind and speed-walked her way down the sidewalk where patches of ice waited to knock her on her butt.

Fred Hunnicutt and his crew were already out de-icing sidewalks and curbs when she reached the village square. Businesses and residents would be out clearing their own sidewalks long before the stores opened. As she waited to cross the street into the park, the town's salt truck rattled past. The driver waved a salute.

Liv loved Celebration Bay. She loved almost everything about her new town, the fact that she could walk to work, and Whiskey had open spaces to run in and two sitters who loved him and would take him any time of the day. She even loved the nosey town busybodies. Most of them anyway.

The locals could be fiercely territorial. They held deeply ingrained opinions. And they were perfectly happy to duke out an argument when words failed. They were taciturn. More than a few were set in their ways . . . just like any town, large or small.

But they sure knew how to pull together when it counted. She just hoped this latest murder wouldn't put a damper on their tourist business.

Liv's nose began to grow numb from the cold. Time to hit the bakery and then BeBe's for coffee. As she crossed the street, her cell rang. She considered waiting until she was inside to answer it. But phone calls this early in the morning were generally bad news, and she knew this one would be no exception.

She didn't even have to look at caller ID to know who was trying to reach her. Across the way, BeBe Ford stood on the sidewalk in her barista's apron, waving her arms to get Liv's attention.

"Come on, boy, looks like our day has begun."

Chapter Seven

....

BeBe grabbed Liv as soon as she reached the sidewalk. A brief scuffle ensued while Whiskey headed toward the bakery, their normal first morning stop and where Dolly kept doggie treats, and Liv and BeBe headed for the Buttercup.

For a change, Liv won the test of wills.

"Grace Thornsby is at the back door of TAT arguing with the policeman in charge. Come on." BeBe propelled Liv through the coffee bar and to the back door, which, like the back doors of all the stores, opened onto the delivery alley.

Liv and BeBe both stuck their heads cautiously out the door only to see Grace Thornsby marching toward them. They ducked back inside.

"Whew," BeBe said. "Do you think she saw us?"

"I don't know." Liv opened the door just enough to look out. Grace had disappeared. "She's not there."

"The pedestrian walkway," they said together and hurried back to the front of the bar just as Fred Hunnicutt walked in.

"Whoa, where's the fire?"

"About to take place on the sidewalk." Liv opened the

door, and Whiskey, having caught on to the new game, trotted outside, pulling Liv with him.

BeBe and Fred followed them out.

They reached the sidewalk just as Grace came out of the walkway between the Bookworm and Bay-Berry Candles and turned left toward TAT.

She stopped at the door, tried to open it. She scowled at it, then grabbed the knob with both hands and shook it to no avail.

"Bill changed the locks," Fred said. "So he wouldn't have to use tape and start tongues wagging any more than they were already. Somebody oughta stop her before she tries to break a window."

"Looks like she doesn't know about what happened," BeBe said.

"Doesn't seem like it," Liv said.

"'Cause if she knew, she'd also know that she couldn't get back in the store until the crime scene people are finished with it," BeBe said.

"You've been watching *CSI*," Fred said. He turned to Liv. "Maybe someone should tell her what happened."

Liv huffed out a cloud of air. "I suppose someone should. Better get it over with." She started down the sidewalk, Whiskey trotting ahead of her and her entourage of two.

"Grace," she called when she was a few feet away. She didn't want to take her by surprise. The woman was in a fury.

Grace swung around. "You! You said get rid of the Santa, I got rid of him, now I'll thank you to unlock my store before I sue."

Whiskey growled, or his version of a growl.

Liv hushed him. "You must not have heard. Your store is a crime scene. The police sealed the premises, not me."

"Crime scene? What kind of crime? Have I been vandalized? Robbed?"

"You'll have to talk to the sheriff."

The door to A Stitch in Time opened, and Miriam stepped out wearing her coat and carrying a bucket of de-icer. She quickly broadcast the pellets on the sidewalk in front of her store and came over to join the growing crowd around the door to TAT.

Grace turned on the newcomer. "And I suppose you did nothing to stop them?"

"Me?" Miriam said indignantly. Her hand tightened on the handle of the bucket, and Liv rushed to intercede before de-icer pellets flew.

She angled herself between the two women. "Everyone was busy with the Celebration of Lights."

"Everyone but you, Grace," Miriam said.

"Ladies," Fred said, stepping into the fray, "let's not lose our tempers. There's been enough violence already."

"Would someone please tell me what happened to my store?"

"Someone broke in during the Celebration of Lights," Fred told her. "And unfortunately, your Santa must have interrupted him and was killed."

Liv frowned at Fred. Did he know this for real? Or was he just guessing.

Grace's dark eyes changed from full of anger to wide-eyed disbelief.

"Killed? Not possible."

"It is possible," said a new voice. And in spite of its softness, everyone turned toward it. Penny Newland clutched a lunch bag and a plaid thermos in front of her tattered down jacket. Her cheeks were splotched pink from the cold, and Liv wondered how far she'd had to walk to get here.

Grace practically pushed Fred out of the way to get to the girl. "What was he even doing here? And where were you? You were supposed to turn on the lights, not Phil."

"I—" The girl's lip trembled.

Liv was getting tired of Grace's bullying and Penny's subservience.

"He came for his paycheck," Liv said.

"I told him I would send it."

"Well, he came anyway."

Grace glowered at Penny. "So what happened?"

Penny shrugged.

"Well, you must have seen something."

"He said he'd stay and turn on the lights since I was supposed to sing in the choir. If you remember, I asked if I could take the afternoon off. You said you would mind the store."

"And if *you* remember, I called to tell you I couldn't make it and you'd have to stay."

Penny cowed back. Really the girl was too timid for the twenty-first century. But Liv had seen it before. Women so beaten down by parents, husbands, life, they were practically comatose.

"I couldn't let everyone down."

"But it was okay to let your employer down, and I suppose you expect me to pay you anyway."

"Grace, it's academic at this point," Liv said. "The man was killed. You should be glad that at least Penny was out of harm's way."

Grace snorted. "And if she had been there—"

"She might have been killed, too," Fred said.

"And if the ole witch had been there, maybe we wouldn't have to listen to her now," BeBe mumbled under her breath. Then looked shocked at her words. She covered her mouth belatedly. "I can't believe I just said that."

"I heard that."

"Well, I'm sorry," BeBe countered. "But you make it awfully hard to care what happens to you or your store."

"Grace, why weren't you at the store?" Liv asked. "Besides promising to give Penny the afternoon off, you also promised Ted that you would be there to make sure everything ran smoothly."

"None of your business."

"Perhaps not, but I'm sure Bill Gunnison will want to know."

"It's none of his business, either. And he can't just keep my store closed. It's Christmas. I run a Christmas store. What am I supposed to do?"

Fred stepped forward, took her by the arm. "I'm sure the

sooner you talk to Bill, the sooner you'll know what to do. Why don't you let me walk you to your car?"

"But where's Tinkerbell?"

There was dead silence as everyone turned to look at her.

"Come again?" Fred managed.

"My cat. What have they done with Tinkerbell?"

Fred's mouth went through a series of twitches. "I'm sure the sheriff has not forgotten the cat." He took her arm and propelled her down the street to the pedestrian walkway that would take them to the parking lot.

"Can things get any weirder?" BeBe asked. "Grace Thornsby has a cat named Tinkerbell?"

Miriam shook her head. "Wonders never cease."

"A misnomer if there ever was one," said Liv. "That's the unfriendliest cat I think I've ever seen."

"Took a page from its mistress, if you ask me." Miriam hunched her shoulders inside her coat. "Brr. I hadn't planned to be out here this long. I'd better get back inside."

"Oh, Miriam," Liv said. "I was going to come by to ask if you'd seen Hank."

"Yes, he was dressed and looking fabulously Santa, if I do say so. The ladies really pulled it out of a hat. Dexter picked him up and drove him over to the community center in the wagon."

"I don't know how to thank you. Please add up the cost of materials and the hours and I'll have the Events Office reimburse you."

Miriam waved her off. "I'll take the reimbursement for the fabric, but as far as the time goes, don't worry about it. It was time well spent and for a good cause."

Miriam hurried back into her store, leaving BeBe and Liv standing with Penny.

"What should I do now?" Penny said, tears starting to spill from her eyes.

You should start looking for another job, thought Liv. She glanced at BeBe.

"Maybe by tomorrow TAT will reopen," BeBe said.

"Maybe." Penny didn't look too happy about the prospect, and Liv couldn't blame her. "But I'm afraid she won't—I needed that job."

"I'm sure somebody will be looking for extra Christmas help," Liv said.

"I already tried. I've been looking for something on weekends to supplement what I make at TAT, but no one's hiring. At least not hiring me." Penny hung her head.

BeBe glanced at Liv. "Uh, I don't have need for a full-time employee, but I was intending to hire someone to clean the back room and sometimes help out at the counter during the rush. It would only be for the weekends, but you're welcome to it, if you want."

"I could use the extra hours even if I still have a job at TAT. I can start right now if you like."

BeBe glanced at Liv. "Great. I'll show you what to do."

Liv followed them into the Buttercup.

"But first we're all going to sit down for a cup of coffee before I open officially. All that standing around in the cold. And Liv hasn't had her coffee yet." BeBe stepped behind the counter. "How do you like yours, Penny?"

"Milk and sugar? Please?"

"It's been an awful couple of days, hasn't it?" Liv said.

Penny nodded. "Poor Phil, he wasn't so bad. Just watched everybody kinda funny. But he wasn't a sicko or anything. It was just like he was interested in people, you know?"

BeBe brought a tray with three cups to the table.

Penny smiled at her. "You're so kind. It hasn't been a very good Christmas so far, with Daddy sick and all, and now Jason's car broke down and he doesn't have the money to get it fixed. And I wanted to get Bobby something special from Santa."

Liv and BeBe exchanged looks. Liv wondered if Penny would qualify for Toys for Tykes. She'd have to ask the sisters when she got home.

"I just can't believe it," Penny said before they even had to prompt her. "When I left, Phil waved, told me to take my time. He would take care of everything."

"Was that right before you got to the ceremony?" Liv asked.

Penny sniffed. "No. It was around four o'clock. Ms. Thornsby was supposed to come in then so I could go home and change and get back in time to meet the choir at the church."

"That must have been so disappointing."

Penny nodded.

"But Phil came in time for you to get home?"

"Yes." Penny shook her head. "No, uh, I didn't have time after all."

Liv was dying to ask where she'd been instead, and why she'd had to rush to join the choir at the last minute if she didn't go home. Liv let it go; surely Bill had already done the questioning.

"And the worst thing is she waited until the last minute. Only said that something had come up." Penny cast her eyes to the ceiling. "I called home to see what I should do. Mama said she knew what that meant. That Ms. Thornsby was—well, I guess Ms. Thornsby has a reputation."

"For being mean?" BeBe asked innocently, but neither she nor Liv had missed the innuendo in that statement.

"For being, you know, man crazy. I guess she was married to Hank for a while, dumped him for Mr. Thornsby. She's a horrible woman. And Hank is so nice. He knew Jason couldn't afford to get his brakes fixed, so he's letting him help out in the machine shop while he's busy being Santa, and after Jason's hours at the diner. He's letting him stay over his garage, too. Hank's real generous that way. I just can't imagine why he would marry Grace Thornsby. I don't see what any man would see in her."

"Neither can I," BeBe agreed.

"But they did. At least they used to. Lots of them, according to Mama."

Maybe they still did, Liv thought. She wondered if a man had kept Grace away from the store while a murder was being committed. An assignation? Or had someone kept her away on purpose? Outside of the overturned tree, nothing in the store had looked ransacked. Liv tried to recall the room as they'd found it last evening. What had happened in the time between Penny's leaving and her returning to find Phil dead beneath the tree?

"Liv?"

"What?"

"You were frowning. Is something wrong with your latte?"

"No, I was just thinking. Penny, you said you left at four."

"Yes, Phil knew Grace was supposed to come at four, so he came in to get his paycheck. He was pretty unhappy about getting fired. I told him it wasn't his fault, that it was a town rule. He said it didn't matter, just made his job harder—I guess it's kind of late to find another Santa job. Then he told me to go on, he'd mind the store until I got back. I showed him how and when to turn on the lights and left."

"And you didn't come back until after the tree lighting?"

"Just before you came." Penny cocked her head. "It's funny, but those are the same questions Mr. Gunnison asked me." She sighed. "Except he asked me how well I knew Phil. And—and if *I* had any enemies."

"You?" asked Liv incredulously as her mind began fitting the pieces together. Not robbery, then. There must have been another motive.

The front door opened, bringing a gust of frigid air and putting an end to their conversation.

"Let me take care of this customer, and then I'll show you the ropes."

Liv ordered a tea for Ted and said good-bye.

She stepped outside just as Dolly Hunnicutt came out of the bakery, carrying two bakery bags.

"I was just on my way over," Liv said.

"I couldn't wait. Fred just got back from seeing Grace Thornsby off to the police station. He said you were getting coffee, so I brought these over. You're already leaving?" She sounded disappointed.

"I have to get to work."

"Well, here are two cranberry orange muffins."

Whiskey sat at attention.

"I'd never forget you." Dolly rattled the second bag and said to Liv, "They're candy canes. Well, I won't keep you. I think I'll just get Fred some coffee from BeBe."

And a bit of up-to-date gossip, thought Liv. She picked her way back down the sidewalk balancing drinks, bags, and leash while she attempted to avoid the melting ice.

Several people had stopped in front of TAT and were looking at the covered windows.

They nodded as Liv passed and went back to their conversation. "I heard it was some electrical problem."

"It's a wonder it didn't go up in smoke with all those flammable trees inside."

"Amazing the whole row of buildings didn't burn down."

"Yep. It coulda been a whole lot worse."

Actually it was worse. A man was dead. And it was just a matter of time until everyone knew it. Now Liv had to figure out a way to get the town through Christmas without further mishap, and then she would banish Grace Thornsby and her ratty TAT from the future.

Ratty TAT. Liv smiled. It was Christmas. And it was going to be the best Christmas Celebration Bay had ever seen. Come hell or high water.

The mayor was waiting for Liv when she reached town hall. So while Ted and Whiskey went through their morning yodeling, Liv set the bakery goods and cardboard cups down on Ted's desk and took the mayor back to her office.

Gilbert Worley had been mayor of Celebration Bay for the last eight years. He was planning to run for a third term, which made him a little nervous when things didn't run smoothly. And a murder was enough to send him into a tailspin.

He was short, stocky, and friendly—except when he was worried about reelection, which was most of the time. Today, his graying brilliantined hair seemed a little grayer and there were more lines across his forehead. Politics could do that. Today, Liv didn't think the trials of the office were making him old.

But murder was definitely taking a toll.

"This is just terrible," he said before the door closed on "Jingle-Bells-Aar-roo-roo-roo."

Liv didn't think he was referring to the man-and-dog racket that was occurring in the outer office.

"How could something like this happen? And in the middle of the tree lighting with over a thousand people in attendance."

"Have a seat, Mayor Worley," Liv said in her calmest voice.

But the mayor just stood in the center of the office, wringing his hands.

"I'm sure this was an isolated incident. As far as I know, there was no robbery and no fear that it will happen again."

"Again?" The word was a soprano squeak. "What about that crackerjack security firm you hired?"

"A.K. Pierce, the head of Bayside Security, is meeting with me later today to discuss what measures will be taken in—"

"A little late when the horse is out of the barn, so to speak."

"A terrible thing to have happened. But at no time were any of the citizens or visitors in jeopardy." At least she didn't think so. It had happened when everyone was gathered in the square, except the store owners or their proxies who were inside waiting for their cue.

The mayor continued to wring his hands. "Did you talk to Bill yet? Does he have any suspects?"

"No I haven't, and I don't think he'll be sharing any news with the rest of us until he has something definite."

"Maybe not, but you always seem to know what's going on. If you hear anything that might jeopardize—"

The door opened. Ted came in carrying a tray of muffins and cups. Whiskey trotted by his side, a red-and-white dog biscuit in his mouth. Liv did a double take at the red color, but knew Dolly would never use anything but vegetable dyes in any of her doggie products. People products? Liv was sure red dye number two was good enough for them.

Ted eased past the mayor, placed the tray on the table, and began arranging their morning meeting breakfast.

The mayor eyed the pastries suspiciously. "Do you two do this every morning?"

"Every morning," said Ted, passing Liv her latte. "Have to keep on top of those financial reports. We call it Munch and Crunch."

Liv had to bite her lip to keep from grinning.

"Humph," the mayor said. "There won't be any financial reports to crunch if people keep getting murdered."

"Which might not happen if outsiders were properly vetted in all areas, like Liv suggested." Ted pulled up his chair, sat down, and reached for the butter dish he kept in the portable fridge in the supply closet.

"What do you mean?"

"Well, think about it," Ted said, slicing his muffin and slathering it with butter. "Somebody is responsible for not insisting the Thornsbys conform to the one-Santa rule. Liv had to go tell them to cease and desist. They didn't. If they had, there would be no dead Santa, now would there?"

"Oh." The mayor stopped wringing his hands long enough to pull his palm across his mouth. "This is just terrible. I've called a trustees meeting for tonight. And I've invited a few local businessmen—businesspeople—to attend. I'd like you both to be there."

Ted stopped with the butter knife poised in midair. "For the purpose of?"

The mayor flinched and eyed the knife. "Tonight, seven o'clock. Now, I really have to run. Busy day." He scooted past Ted and hurried out of the office. They heard the outer door close.

"Oh, Gilbert, Gilbert, Gilbert," Ted said and finished buttering his muffin. He handed Liv the butter.

"Did you do that on purpose?"

"What?"

"Brandish that butter knife at the mayor?"

Ted smiled. "Would I do that? Now, let's eat and pretend

like it's a Merry Christmas before the accusations start flying."

Liv reached for her latte, which was quickly growing cold. "This isn't like you."

"I get cranky when people start calling useless meetings during my favorite holiday."

"He's concerned about safety."

"My dear Pollyanna, he's worried about the next election. And we can be sure Janine will be there to stir the hysteria. Same old, same old—and to make matters worse . . ." He stopped.

"What?" Liv asked, bracing for the worst.

"I'll have to miss choir practice."

Chapter Eight

....

"Really? Choir practice?"

"Really."

"So all the nonsense about the *Messiah* sing-along wasn't a joke?"

Ted shook his head.

"I can go to the meeting by myself."

"And let you face a boring two hours by your lonesome? What kind of assistant would I be?"

"A happy one?"

Ted grinned. "Oh, I plan on being happy with both barrels. I'm not going to let you have all the fun. Now, didn't you say something about writing an article for the *Clarion*?"

"Yes and the sooner the better."

Ted cleared the breakfast things and went back to his office. Whiskey curled up on his doggie bed and was soon snoring peacefully. Liv opened a new document on her computer and began to write.

An hour later she had a nice succinct article about how the town all came together for Christmas. Chaz would laugh, but surely he would run it. His livelihood depended on the success of the town, too. It took money to run a newspaper, even a weekly rag like the *Clarion*. The paper didn't have a wide distribution, and his secondary job as fishing guide could hardly support Chaz and the newspaper, both. Liv guessed that advertising must go a long way toward keeping him in ink and night crawlers.

She downloaded the article onto a flash drive and dropped it into her canvas bag.

Whiskey roused himself, yawned a yawn big enough to belong to a larger dog, and got to his feet. "You're going to stay with Ted for a bit. I have a lot of running around to do."

True to form, at the word "running," Whiskey shot across the room and hid beneath her desk.

Liv stopped by Ted's desk. "I may be gone for an hour or two."

"Not to worry, we'll amuse ourselves."

Liv had no doubt they would. "No feeding the d-o-g."

Ted toodled his fingers at her.

"I mean it."

"No feeding. Got it. We'll bring something back for you."

She had to be content with that. One of the hardest parts of her life in Celebration Bay was preventing everyone from feeding Whiskey and feeding her. It was a show of affection, she knew, but with these winters, it was hard to get any exercise in at all, for either of them.

She put on her coat and scarf and pulled her hat down over her ears, something she would have scorned to do in Manhattan. Fortunately, in Celebration Bay hat hair was a fait accompli. The winds off the lake could be fierce.

Chaz Bristow couldn't even claim hat hair for the way he looked when he opened the door of the *Clarion* office, which Liv knew was also his home. He was wearing a ratty T-shirt and checked flannel pants that Liv assumed were his idea of pajamas.

"Oh God, it's you," he said and pushed his fingers through hair that was already standing on end.

"Are you busy?" She'd thought about calling first, but she didn't want to give him time to escape. He was one of the least cooperative people in town. Fortunately for Chaz, he seemed to get away with it on good looks and occasional charm.

His height, his build, his blond hair—he could have been a beach bum in another life. Instead, he was a former investigative reporter who was content to fish and churn out a few pages of local news each week.

She didn't get him, and for some reason it just made her angry every time she got near him.

"If you can spare the time, I have something for you."

He grinned at her, white teeth flashing from a day-old growth of blond beard.

"An article I want you to run."

His face fell ludicrously.

She shook her head and pushed past him into the dim, neglected foyer. It was too bad. At one time, the *Clarion* office had been a charming clapboard bungalow. The rooms were square and still had the original details. But the inside was a pigsty.

Liv resisted making an analogy between the house and its owner.

Liv groped her way through the murky parlor to the "newsroom," once a bedroom or second parlor. She went straight to the window and raised the venetian blinds. Light washed over piles of paper, books, computers, and printers that littered several fairly flat surfaces.

Liv sat down at the nearest computer, pulled off her hat, unbuttoned her coat, and inserted her flash drive, while Chaz rummaged for the coffeepot, then took it into the bathroom for water. When he returned, she had the article on his screen.

He measured coffee and started the machine, then came to stand behind her, one hand resting on the back of her chair, the other on the desk.

"Huh," he grunted.

"I need you to run this on the front page. Not too splashy but big enough to catch the eye. You can change the wording as long as you keep the goodwill of Celebration Bay paramount, and do not under any circumstance mention what happened at TAT."

"Huh."

She would have spun around to glare at him to drive her point home, but he held her trapped in her chair.

"What happened to *Good morning, Chaz. Here's the coffee and bagel I thought to bring you when I have a favor to ask?*"

"Good morning, I have a favor to ask."

"You're getting closer." He leaned over her, ostensibly to read the article. Liv suspected he was just trying to crowd her space.

He rubbed a hand over his face. "It's a good thing you decided to go into party planning."

"Event planning."

"Because your journalistic skills are less than—"

"Chaz, will you please just do it?"

He lifted one shoulder and began looking for a clean cup.

Liv held on to her temper. "I don't suppose you were sleeping in this morning because you were up late surfing the Internet for Phil the Santa and the Thornsbys and have come up with a theory of why someone killed the man?"

"Nope."

"Well, do you have any theories?"

"Nope."

"Aargh. How can you just walk away from all the good you did as a reporter and be content with fishing news? You could help Bill if you wanted to."

"Well, there's the rub. I don't want to. But I'll print your article. Now go away."

"Thanks. I appreciate it. I'll let myself out."

She'd reached the door when he called out. "The sooner you give up on me being a productive citizen, the sooner we can be friends."

She didn't want to be friends. She wanted someone who cared enough to help catch a murderer.

The cold caught her off guard and she had to stop at the corner to button her coat. She yanked on her knit hat and marched toward the town green. Breakfast with Santa would be over by now. She'd meant to look in on it, just to see that everything was okay. Since she hadn't received any emergency calls, she would assume it went as planned.

Which meant Hank should be at Santa Village. She had time to make a quick visit before she prepared for her meeting with A.K. Pierce and then came up with a strategy to calm people at the meeting that night.

She turned right at the First Presbyterian Church and hurried toward the square.

Kids and their parents were already lined up along the sidewalk that cut through the park, waiting for Santa to open the doors for Christmas in Celebration Bay. The tree lighting and the Pancake Breakfast had just been preludes to Hank's real work. From now until Christmas Eve, he'd be ensconced in Santa Village taking Christmas wishes, hearing Christmas secrets, being sneezed and coughed on, having his beard pulled, and who knew what else.

The man could demand hazard pay, and yet he volunteered each year.

Santa was housed at the end of a row of colorful alpine chalets. One was a Santa-themed gift shop with inexpensive pencils, puzzles, and other things that might catch children's eyes as they waited in the cold.

Next to the shop was the North Pole Canteen where Donnie and Roseanne Waterbury were helping their father dispense hot cider and donut holes. The line entered the third chalet and cut through the next to Santa's throne, offering some respite from the cold. Two sides were lined with benches for weary parents and sleeping tots as they waited their turn to sit on Santa's lap.

Behind the chalets, porta potties were camouflaged as reindeer stables. Liv had to hand it to the residents; they knew how to carry out a theme. What they had needed help with was coordination and organization, and how to actualize germinating ideas in a creative and cost-efficient way.

It was the perfect job for Liv. And she really resented people killing each other on her turf.

She stopped at the North Pole Canteen to say hello to the Waterburys. Roseanne handed her a cup of cider. "Hey, Liv."

Joss Waterbury, tall, broad, and barrel-chested, said, "That's Ms. Montgomery to you, miss."

"She said I could call her Liv, didn't you?"

"Yes," Liv said. "If it's okay with your dad. We kind of bonded over the last few months," Liv explained. Because the girl had come to her, a stranger, for help. She'd thought that since Liv was from Manhattan, she would know how to solve a murder.

It was flattering but totally off base. Liv had never even been close to a murder before moving to this peaceful country community. Go figure.

"Well, I guess it's okay. My little girl's growing up." Joss tugged at the braid that ran down his daughter's back.

Roseanne rolled her eyes. "Da-a-ad."

Joss grinned at Liv. "She's my last. Donnie here's graduating from high school in June and going over to the aggie school in Cobleskill." He smiled proudly at his son, standing next to him, a spitting image of a younger Joss. "Though I spec he'll be back to get a good home-cooked meal and do his laundry."

"Which is why he's gonna ask Santa for a car," Roseanne said.

"Am not," Donnie said. "I already got some money saved."

"Then *I'll* ask Santa for a car."

Joss wagged his finger at her. "You won't be driving for real for another couple of years, Rosie."

"Yeah," Donnie said. "You better ask Santa for some help with your algebra."

She stuck out her tongue.

Joss shook his head, but he was smiling affectionately. "Better watch that or you're liable to bite it off."

"Thanks for the cider," Liv said and tossed her empty cup in the trash can. "Just what I needed. Is Santa here yet?"

"Been here since ten. He don't ever stay for the whole breakfast. Talks with the folks a bit, then comes on over here to set up. In fact, it's almost time for his break. Donnie, go put up that sign."

Donnie disappeared from the counter and came out to pull two posts, connected by a red velvet cord, across the sidewalk. A sign hung in the center. *Santa is feeding the reindeer, back at—*A clock with movable hands was affixed to the right, and Donnie checked his watch and changed the hands to two o'clock.

Liv looked at her own watch. It was past noon. Where had the morning gone?

She said good-bye and went to see Hank. She'd wait for his break and then would ask him a few more questions of her own. She stood just inside the door watching him chat with the child on his knee, then pose for a picture taken by a local photographer dressed as an elf.

Hank handed the kid a candy cane and then welcomed the next. He moved through the next few children efficiently without seeming to hurry. Some cried before they reached him, but they all seemed to leave happy.

He was a gentle giant, pleasant, friendly, and he seemed to genuinely like the children. He even laughed a big-belly "Ho, ho, ho" when one of them pulled his beard. And Liv just couldn't imagine him killing someone, even in anger. Of course, she'd only seen him mad in her office. His temper might be a lot worse than she knew.

It was only a few minutes before the last family left, and Hank stood and stretched. "Ms. Montgomery."

"Liv, please."

Hank nodded. "What can I do for you? The ladies did a good job, didn't they?" He spread his arms and gave Liv a full view of the suit. It was pretty impressive. The velvet, which would be a cleaning nightmare, was beautiful. Just like you'd imagine the real Santa would wear. The fur trim looked real, though Liv had seen it up close the night before and knew it was some kind of poly-something. The hat was jaunty and sported a huge white pom-pom at the point.

"I'm on my way over to the Pyne Bough for a couple of hours. Can I walk you somewhere?"

"Actually I wanted to ask you a few things . . . on our way."

But Liv didn't have much success on the walk over. Everyone waved or yelled hello at Santa, and Hank nodded and waved and "ho, ho, ho'ed" his way across the park, around the corner, where he stopped to hand out candy canes to families leaving the Corner Café, and into the alley and to the back door of Pyne Bough Gifts.

A truck was parked outside. The back gate was open and so was the door to the Pyne Bough. Not wide open but ajar, as if someone had swung the door closed but the latch hadn't caught.

Liv glanced at Hank to see if he'd noticed. He had and he returned Liv's look before holding the door and following Liv inside.

"Nancy?" he called out.

The stockroom was empty. Hank's street clothes were hanging on the rack where he'd left them. Several new stacks of boxes rose in the center of the floor.

Liv was beginning to think that the business of locked doors was more good intention than truth. And if that was the case, anyone could have slipped in, nabbed the Santa suit, and gotten away. They could be stealing inventory right now.

"Nancy?" Hank called in his rumbling voice. He passed Liv, pulled aside the madras curtain, and opened the door. Liv followed him into the store.

Nancy Pyne stood at the counter with the deliveryman, running down the items of the packing list. "See. Here's the discrepancy. There should have been two boxes of one hundred twig bird nests each. There's only one."

She was frowning when she looked up and saw Liv and Hank; she stiffened in surprise and a momentary unease, then pushed the packing slip at the deliveryman.

"Would you mind taking another look for the second one

on the truck? They're usually very good about shipping everything at once."

The man grumbled but took the slip and returned to the stockroom. As soon as he'd left, she turned to Hank. "Is everything okay?"

"Back door was open," Hank said. "You oughta be more careful, especially since . . . you know." He nodded his head so strongly that it set his pom-pom to swaying.

"Oh dear." Nancy started to move.

"It's okay. We closed it."

Nancy sighed. "It doesn't close sometimes. I try to keep the hinges oiled, but it's an old house. Thank you both, anybody could have come in and—" She broke off as she realized the implication. "Oh, Hank, I'm so sorry. This business is all my fault."

"No, no. Now, don't you feel like that. I'll take a look at the hinges, maybe get some replacements. And as far as that other business goes, it'll all be cleared up soon enough."

Not soon enough for Liv.

"Some burglar saw an opportunity and took it. Bill Gunnison will catch him, and when he does, he'll throw the book at him."

Nancy flinched. "I should have checked to make sure the door caught, but I get flustered when the trucks come, trying to watch the front while overseeing the deliveries." She smiled self-deprecatingly. "I can't seem to be in two places at once."

"Now, now," Hank said. And Liv suddenly wondered if there was a little mutual liking going on between the two of them.

"Why don't you hire someone to help you?" Liv asked, dragging her mind from the possible relationship between Santa and Earth Mother.

"At these rents, I just can't afford to."

Liv remembered Miriam saying the same thing. Were rents too high, or was the economy still faltering? The town certainly looked like it was doing a healthy business; the number of visitors was up according to Ted and the board, but maybe sales were still flat. She'd have to check into it.

A loud thump sounded from the back room. Nancy jumped, and Hank rushed out to see what it was. Liv and Nancy were right behind him. The door was open. One of the stacked boxes had fallen to the floor.

They all looked wildly around.

A blur of orange streaked past their feet and slinked through the crack in the door to the outside.

Liv's breath whooshed in relief. "It's Grace Thornsby's cat. I wondered if it would show up again."

"She came to the door last night as I was leaving. I fed her and let her stay. I always keep a bag of sand in my car for traction. It's perfect for kitty litter, and much healthier for the environment than chemicals. I figured it was better to keep her inside than take a chance of her freezing during the night."

"Thanks for that," Liv said. "I was feeling a little responsible for letting her escape last night. And Grace was asking about her this morning."

"As if she cares about the poor creature," Nancy said.

The deliveryman shouldered his way through the back door carrying a large cardboard box. "You were right. I found this in the back with the shipment to Nature's Nurture over in Plattsburg." He put the box down and pulled out his signature pad for Nancy to sign.

She followed him to the door, looked out before shutting it firmly behind him. "I guess the cat will be okay," Nancy said. "I hate to leave it out in the cold."

"I'm sure she knows where to come if she needs a friend," Hank said.

Nancy gave him a look that dispelled any question Liv might have about the woman's feelings for Hank.

"I brought a thermos of vegetable soup that I made last night. Would you like some for lunch, Hank?"

"Thanks, I would."

"How about you, Liv? Would you like to join us?" She was being polite, but Liv could tell she'd rather have a soup tête-à-tête with Hank. And that would put a bit of a damper on Liv's ability to ask Hank the questions she had in mind.

"Thanks, but I can't stay. I want to drop by A Stitch in Time and compliment them on their sewing skills. It's a great suit, Hank."

"Yep, we're real lucky to have all these folks who'll pull together to see each other through times like this."

Liv nodded. Like BeBe helping Penny out with a few weekend hours, and Hank hiring Jason and giving him a place to live. And Nancy opening her store, and possibly her heart, to the town Santa.

It was enough to give a person a little holiday glow.

Liv let herself out. Made sure the door was latched, then stepped out into the alley. The truck was gone, and she had a clear view all the way down to the other end of the block. Her holiday glow withered into a bit of holiday speculation.

There were clusters of trash cans at the doors of several stores. There were two Dumpsters, one at the far end and one between Nancy's and the Trim a Tree store; and two openings to the parking lot, one by the pedestrian walk and the other across from the Pyne Bough. Either one making for an easy getaway.

As Liv pondered this idea, several people came from the parking lot. They stopped at the pedestrian walk and looked down the alley, pointed at the door of TAT. They huddled together talking and looking and pointing, then continued between the buildings to the street.

Word was out.

"Well, Liv," she told herself. "It is Celebration Bay."

Most thieves waited until late at night to break in, when no one would be about. Though maybe this one had thought it would be safe to attack when the stores were empty except for a skeleton crew waiting for the light cue, and everyone else's attention would be on the tree lighting.

It would take guts, or desperation, she guessed, to steal a Santa suit and march down the alley to Trim a Tree when latecomers rushing to the tree lighting might see them. The murder had taken place somewhere between four o'clock when Penny left and around seven o'clock when they'd discovered Phil's body.

Liv looked around. It had been dark by four o'clock, but even so, the alley was fairly well lit, as was the parking lot. She could see the tops of the floodlights over the stockade fence that lined the alley. Anyone could have seen the killer walking down the alley. But he would be just another pedestrian. And if he were wearing the Santa suit before he entered TAT, everyone would assume it was Hank.

And maybe it was.

He might hold a grudge against his ex-wife, but why murder the fake Santa? Hank had been angry in Liv's office the day he told her about the second Santa, but his anger had been aimed more at Grace than the poor guy who now lay dead, just for doing a good deed and letting Penny go to sing at the tree lighting.

That was so not right—to die for a good deed. Especially to die violently. And it was hard for Liv not to feel responsible. She knew she wasn't, but she also knew the town was looking toward her, not only for their livelihoods, but also for their safety.

So far she was failing miserably.

She looked back at the alleyway. She walked over to the first Dumpster, wondering if a person could have stolen the suit, then changed in and out of it without being seen. She turned around and had a clear view from the Dumpster to the street.

Something rolled beneath Liv's feet; she looked down. Cigarette butts. Lots of them. Several were crushed beneath her boot; more littered the packed snow around the Dumpster. Several packs' worth. All with the same filter. Someone had either missed the Dumpster or stood smoking cigarette after cigarette, not more than twenty feet from the delivery door of the Pyne Bough. Nancy must have really hated that.

Liv walked down the alley toward the pedestrian walkway, finding the occasional cigarette butt, but not so many as at the other end of the alley. But she noticed that most of them were the same brand or at least had the same filter.

She slowed as she passed the Trim a Tree store. The door was still sealed. There was no sign of the cat. When she got to the pass-through, she turned back to look down the alley. No one could move from store to store without risking being seen when it was daylight. But what about when it was dark? There were lights, yes, but how many shadows? Could some-one sneak from store to store avoiding the light?

Unfortunately, there was only one way to find out.

She'd have to come back at night just to satisfy her curios-ity. But for now she had to be content to peruse the alley in daylight. Liv knew she wouldn't find any clues the sheriff and his team had missed. But she couldn't just ignore the fact that while she'd been waiting expectantly for her first Christmas success, someone was sneaking down the alley to commit murder.

And she didn't like it one bit.

Chapter Nine

....

There was a note on Liv's desk. *We had a few errands to run, your lunch is in the fridge.* Liv wondered what errands but knew Whiskey would be happy as a clam to explore new vistas with his pal and fellow yodeler.

She was deep into lunch and paperwork when she heard the outer door open and the tapping of doggie paws on the hardwood floor. Whiskey shot through the open door to her office and skidded to a stop at Liv's feet.

He had a Christmas tree biscuit between his teeth. Liv sighed. People just couldn't stop feeding him. "Because you're just so cute," she said.

Whiskey danced in a circle.

"And wait until you hear this," said Ted. He lifted his arms like a conductor.

Whiskey dropped the tree and sat.

"For we like sheep," Ted sang in a clear tenor.

"Aar-roo-roo-roo," Whiskey sang back.

Liv groaned. For a monosyllabic vocabulary, Whiskey did a pretty good job of mimicking whatever Ted taught him. But no way was he taking her dog to the *Messiah* sing-along.

"Do you know what the reaction will be if you show up to the *Messiah* with a singing dog?"

Ted grinned wickedly. "We'd probably get a solo."

"You'd probably be shown the door, punctuated by a swift kick, and followed by you being blackballed from the community choir."

"Nah. We just need a little more practice."

Liv spent the next hour listing security questions to ask A.K. Pierce. By the time he arrived, precisely at three o'clock, she was ready.

Ted ushered him in, or followed in his wake, it was hard to tell. The man had a presence.

He strode across the room, emanating authority. He was in his late thirties or early forties, tall, wide-shouldered, strong. Straight nose, firm jaw, shaved head. Not unpleasant to look at. But it was the don't-mess-with-the-ex-marine demeanor that would make someone think twice about causing trouble. It was part of the reason Liv had hired him.

But only part. She was savvy enough to know that looks and charisma were only part of success. The services his firm offered were the ones that most closely meshed with the town's needs. He was precise and ran a tight organization; he was a perfect blend of intimidation and approachability. His team of twenty were instructed to be friendly but firm. Just what she had envisioned for a security hire: a deterrent to anyone planning mayhem, but friendly enough that children wouldn't be afraid to go to them for help.

Bayside Security cost a bit more than some of the others she had vetted, but the expense would be worth it if A.K. Pierce turned out to be what he promised. The fact that a murder had been committed on his watch was troublesome, but she hadn't hired him to prevent murder, just to protect the crowd.

He stopped at her desk.

Whiskey jumped up, stood stiff legged, ears pricked, on the alert.

Pierce slowly turned his head to look at him, but before

Liv could command Whiskey to stay, Whiskey trotted over to be petted, which the security head did before returning his attention to Liv.

"Good afternoon," she said, standing to meet him.

He nodded brusquely and handed her a brown accordion folder. "The preliminary report for the first twenty-four-hour period," he said by way of explanation and stood at ease.

"Please have a seat, Mr. Pierce."

A.K. Pierce sat down, feet planted on the floor, forearms resting on his knees.

"Ted?"

Ted lifted an eyebrow and sat.

Liv untied the closure and pulled out several copies of the report. She handed one to Ted. It was clear and detailed, with color-enhanced graphs and charts.

She was impressed. The trustees should be pleased. On the surface of this report she would be inclined to hire his firm on a regular basis. She wished she had the funds to keep them year-round.

"Excellent," she said. "I must say you and your men and women covered a lot of ground."

"Any time you have a crowd of this size—we estimated upward of a thousand—you invariably attract pickpockets and petty thieves, underage drinking, standard drugs, mainly marijuana. Some rowdiness. All in all it was a pretty standard night—except for the murder."

Liv winced. *Except for the murder.* That was pretty major.

"I don't think my crew, or any crew, could have prevented it, unless maybe by chance."

"Why is that?"

He hesitated. "I've already discussed this with your sheriff."

"I realize, and I don't expect you to divulge any classified information. However, I would like your professional assessment."

She saw Ted cover a grin behind his hand.

"I told the sheriff that I was contracted to perform certain duties for the town, and since Bayside Security was hired by you, I was bound by that contract to apprise you of certain information."

Liv nodded seriously, though in the back of her mind she was thinking of what Chaz Bristow would think of the conversation. Each sentence more formal than the last. But formality worked for her, and evidently it worked for A.K. Pierce, too.

"I identified your Santa."

Liv forgot about Chaz.

Ted scooted his chair closer.

"At the crime scene," he clarified. "I didn't see him before he was found. Didn't know he was here until he was dead. But I knew him—well, was acquainted with him. He's an area private investigator."

Liv tried to keep her mouth from dropping open.

"Moonlighting for Christmas money?" Ted asked.

Pierce switched his attention from Liv to Ted. "Possibly. He's not, shall we say, the best nor the most efficient investigator. He may be tight for cash. I don't keep tabs on most of these guys; the fringe PIs, who spy on spouses, search for missing relatives whether they want to be found or not, and chase money, two-bit stuff.

"Phil Cosgrove was one of them. His cases were hit or miss with a lot of miss. And we don't necessarily work the same circuit, if you know what I mean."

At least now they knew his full name. Cosgrove. Phil Cosgrove. "Working as a Santa at Trim a Tree seems like an odd choice of jobs even if he were strapped for money," Liv said.

"I agree. It would be more likely, as I told Bill Gunnison, that he'd been hired to keep an eye on someone. Maybe they caught on to him and decided to eliminate the problem."

"So you've ruled out robbery?" She had, but she could always hope.

"It hasn't been ruled out, but at this juncture, it's unlikely. From what we saw initially, though I wasn't in on the official CSI, it didn't appear to be robbery. It's possible Cosgrove interrupted the thief before he got that far."

"Do you think that's what happened?"

"Possibly."

"But not probably," Liv said.

Pierce shook his head slowly. "I think Cosgrove got too close to whatever he was looking for. He wasn't very smart. He might have tipped his hand."

"Do the police know who hired him?" Ted asked.

"Not yet, as far as I know."

"Someone who wanted to watch Grace. Her husband?" Liv asked.

"That would be the most obvious conclusion but not necessarily the right one. Cosgrove could have been investigating anyone who frequented the store, or one of the nearby stores."

Liv's mind began to race. *Penny, Miriam Krause, BeBe—*

"Or a regular customer."

Did Grace have any regular customers?

"Actually the Santa gig gave Phil a reason to hang around town without being conspicuously out of place. It might not have had anything to do with the store itself. Or as your assistant here said, he could have just been moonlighting."

"How did you show up so quickly? I mean, I'm glad you did, but I was surprised."

"I just happened to be standing by when the sheriff got the call, and he asked me to ride shotgun."

"Did they find the murder weapon?"

"That's classified."

"His throat was cut."

A.K. Pierce's eyes opened marginally wider. "I'm not a cop. I'm not privy to classified information."

"But it had to be a knife or something like that."

"I'm not at liberty to say." He shot her a smile that was so fleeting, Liv was sure she had imagined it. "Bill said you would try to pump me for information."

"I—"

Pierce's back straightened a millimeter. "I know my job, Ms. Montgomery. Don't bother trying."

Chagrined, Liv didn't even bother to deny the accusation.

She'd have to find out more from Bill, who wasn't nearly as good at keeping his mouth shut as A.K. Pierce.

"So . . . in your experience, if this doesn't look like a robbery gone bad, was it a random act, or was Phil Cosgrove killed because of what he was, or at least might have been, investigating?"

"As far as the investigation goes, it could be any of those situations. Then again, it might have been something else entirely."

"Like what?"

"Name something. People get killed every day over things most of us wouldn't think twice about."

Liv sighed. "So I don't guess that we can ensure that it won't happen again."

"Ma'am, you put enough people together in a small space and you're bound to have trouble. It's just the nature of the beast. People get drunk, get angry, get stupid, do stupid things. Do god-awful things. Best thing you can do is to be prepared for it. Which you did by hiring Bayside Security.

"You read my report. All in all it was a successful night. Now, if you'll excuse me, I have assignments to detail." He reached across the desk and shook her hand. His hand was big, with fingers that could crush hers if he'd wanted. Fortunately, he just smiled and let go.

"Ms. Montgomery." He let Ted show him out.

"Well, that was one smooth sales pitch," Ted said when he returned.

"I know. He made it sound like if we hadn't hired Bayside Security, there would have been riots in the street, drunken orgies on every corner, and Celebration Bay would become a den of drug-addicted thieves." Liv slumped in her chair. "They did do a great job, but I wish he could have managed to stop just one killer."

"There is that." Ted sat down and crossed one foot over his knee. "A private investigator. Who would have thought it?"

"That puts a whole new spin on things, doesn't it?"

Chapter Ten

....

The meeting room was packed by the time Liv and Ted arrived for the mayor's hastily called gathering. They'd waited on purpose so they wouldn't have to answer the same questions over and over again. People in Celebration Bay had already begun to turn to Liv to solve not only event problems but town problems in general.

Murder was definitely problematic—not to mention tragic, Liv thought as she and Ted walked down the hallway to the meeting room. And she had a moment of contrition.

"What?" Ted asked. "Did you forget something?"

"Yeah. Actually I did."

"I'll run back and get it."

"Not that kind. I've just been so busy doing triage that I hadn't thought that there's someone somewhere mourning the death of a loved one."

"Yeah, but save it for after the meeting. You'll need your total attention to avert a panic."

"You think they'll panic?"

"We can hear them all the way down the hall. They're ready to blow. You can't have a murder on Main Street without everyone's life being thrown into confusion and fear."

Liv knew that was true. And the "trustees and a few businesspeople" who attended sounded like an angry lynch mob.

Liv adjusted the strap on her computer case. Ted opened the door and they stepped into bedlam.

There must have been twenty in all. Just a sampling of the local business and community leaders. The noise didn't diminish as she and Ted entered, just switched its focus to one individual. Liv.

She nodded and started to take her normal seat in the first row, where a projector had been set up for her presentation. She didn't make it two feet before she was engulfed by questions.

"Liv, do they know who killed that man?"

"What's going to happen to TAT?"

"You shouldn't have let them move in. I knew they'd be trouble from the get-go."

"And where was that expensive security service that we hired?"

"Yeah."

"Big waste of town funds, if you ask me."

"And where are the Thornsbys? They're probably ashamed to show their faces in town."

"Well, they should be."

"Roger Newland shoulda never sold out to Clarence Thornsby."

"That oily son of a—"

"Ain't Clarence's fault."

"Well, whose fault is it then?"

Once again everyone looked at Liv.

Liv turned to Ted. "They don't think it's my fault, do they?"

"Not likely. They're looking to you to solve the situation."

"They can't."

"Before you came, when something went wrong, it just

went wrong and we either muddled through or things came to a screeching halt. You actually fix things. It didn't take much to convince them you could do it again."

Fortunately, the mayor came in and the crowd redirected their barrage of questions at him. He held up one hand for quiet, which everyone ignored. Under his other arm was a copy of the report Liv had shot over to his office just an hour ago. She wondered if he'd had time to read it.

He was followed closely by Janine Tudor, who had been the event coordinator before Liv. It had been a volunteer position, and she'd been way out of her abilities. That didn't stop her from blaming Liv for taking her job.

She was one of those tall, lettuce-and-rice-cakes-thin women who had their hair streaked and their nails done and who bought their clothes in a town larger than Celebration Bay and called it sophistication. She'd gone back to selling real estate with some success. But what she held over the mayor was anybody's guess.

"Maybe she'll be on the hot seat for a change," Liv said. "She did broker the Thornsbys' lease renewal on the store."

Ted smiled a Cheshire-cat grin. "Wouldn't that be lovely?"

The mayor took his place at the podium on the raised dais at the front of the meeting room. Janine sat in one of the empty chairs that formed a row across the dais.

Janine had no official reason for being there, but she was like a bad penny: no one could figure out how to lose her.

"Wonder what Janine's up to tonight," Liv mused with little interest. She and Ted both knew that whatever it was, it would be designed to make Liv look bad.

Mayor Worley lifted the gavel from the podium and whacked it several times. The trustees emerged from the pack like sinners at a revival meeting and took their places in the other chairs on the dais.

Roscoe Jackson, owner of the local general store; Rufus Cobb from Cobb's B and B; and Jeremiah Atkins, banker and landlord, sat side by side in three chairs. Janine sat in the fourth. One chair and one trustee were missing. Chaz

Bristow, unwilling trustee and uninterested bystander, had once again failed to make an appearance.

The rest of the invited guests settled into seats behind Liv and Ted. Liv didn't like having her back to the others. Hard to read your crowd or be persuasive when you couldn't look them in the eye.

"The meeting will come to order," the mayor said.

Everyone settled down, more or less.

"I've asked all of you to attend this trustee meeting to apprise you of our current situation. As you know, there was an unfortunate incident during the tree lighting ceremony last night. I'm sure you all have questions."

"If you can answer them," said Quincy Hinks, owner of the Bookworm.

"We'll answer what we can. I've asked the sheriff to come a little later, and he may have some answers that I don't have. But before we do any of that, I've asked Liv Montgomery to give an update on last night's activities."

"You find the killer yet, Liv?" came a voice from the crowd.

Liv's face heated. They weren't being fair. She hadn't found the last one. It was rather the other way around.

She thought the mayor would intervene. If there was ever a time to wield his gavel, it was now. But he remained mute; he just joined the others and looked at her.

"I have a question." Janine's voice broke through the charged silence.

The mayor jumped as if she'd goosed him. "Why yes, Janine. The chair recognizes Janine Tudor."

Janine stood. Nodded to Mayor Worley and turned to Liv. "What I and I'm sure a lot of others would like to know, is what that security service Liv just had to have was doing while someone was murdering that poor man." She paused to touch her hand to her chest. "It could have been any of us."

"Yeah."

"I'd like to know that, too."

"We'd all like to know."

The mayor banged on the podium.

"That's actually a good question," Liv said. "Mr. Mayor, if I may." As she started to stand, she caught sight of the door opening and a man sauntering in. Oh great. The editor of the *Celebration Clarion* had deigned to make an appearance and just in time to hear her make her most officious speech. Liv gritted her teeth.

Chaz grinned at her and slid into a seat behind hers. She slowly turned her head. "Why are you sitting down here instead of up there?" she said under her breath.

"Better view." Chaz Bristow gave her the blandest look she'd seen on a face since she'd last seen him. She was sure he did it on purpose. "Come on, Manhattan, give 'em your old party of the first part."

Liv gave him a bland look of her own and turned around. He might kid her about the way she talked, but it worked. On most people. Certainly not on Chaz Bristow, probably because he'd gotten used to using only a smidgeon of his brain.

All eyes turned to Liv.

She'd asked herself the same questions as they had, and she'd prepared the answer. "Bayside Security was hired to patrol the streets, supervise the crowds, ensure orderly behavior, and investigate suspicious activities."

"What about the murder?" asked Jeremiah.

"Phil Cosgrove died inside the store, outside the normal jurisdiction of the security team."

"Party of the second part . . ." mumbled Chaz.

Liv cleared her throat. "They saw nothing suspicious as far as I've been told. I'm sure they are cooperating with Bill Gunnison in the investigation."

"I think we paid a lot of money for nothing," Janine said.

"Like she paid for that dress she's wearing," Chaz mumbled.

Liv shot Chaz a stern look. "As I was saying, the security service did exactly what they were paid to do: keep the peace and protect the tourists in public places. I have here the initial report from A.K. Pierce, the head of Bayside Security."

She plugged her laptop into the projector and the first page of the security report appeared on the screen behind the trustees. They all twisted around to see it.

"As you can see here, twenty guards, ten in plainclothes, were stationed in five areas. On foot, in radio contact, patrolling solo unless backup was required. And backup was never more than two minutes away.

"That left the controlling of traffic, including streets and parking lots, to the county police force." She forwarded to the next page. "The blue represents the police, and the red, Bayside Security. As you can see, all areas where crowd control was needed were covered at all times.

"In this next view, you'll see the preliminary statistics of crime thwarted or miscreants apprehended in a safe and quiet way." She brought up Pierce's chart. "As you can see, as compared to last year's incident report, there were fewer fights, fewer pickpockets, fewer falls and accidents. All in all, they did a very good job."

"That is impressive," said Jeremiah.

"Yes, and I didn't notice any major skirmishes like we had last year with those kids and beer and fireworks." Dolly Hunnicutt smiled at Liv from her seat next to her husband, Fred.

Janine's mouth tightened. "But still some thief was allowed to enter one of our stores and commit a tragic crime and no one noticed. All of our stores are at risk."

Liv took a breath and stepped out on a limb. "Even the most assiduous patrol can't always prevent a determined criminal."

"Determined? You mean it was premeditated?" asked Rufus Cobb, chewing on his mustache. "I need to be assured of the safety of my guests."

"I don't know if it was planned or not. The point is, no matter how much *we* plan and how many people *we* hire—"

"Stuff happens."

Liv acknowledged Chaz as formally as she could, and she had to admit, gratefully. "Well, yes, Mr. Bristow. Stuff does happen." She addressed the others. "Last night's festivities drew over a thousand people. Over fifty people made use of the first aid stations, mainly minor injuries and upset stomachs. The ambulance service reported two sprained ankles, a broken arm, several dizzy spells, and two possible heart attacks that necessitated the use of the ambulance. I'm happy to say, all with a positive outcome."

"What did she say?" asked a voice from the back.

"Except for the murder, there were no casualties."

"Shoulda never rented the place to Clarence Thornsby."

"That wife of his would be enough to drive any man to murder."

There was a smattering of laughter.

The mayor banged his gavel. "Now, folks, this is not time for talk like that."

"Well, that part's all water under the bridge," Roscoe Jackson, the third trustee said. "What we should be talking about is what we're going to do about the future. That Trim a Tree place is a nuisance. They mighta just brought their problems with them."

"Yeah. And where is Clarence Thornsby? He sure seems to be taking a jaded lack of interest in what's going on at his store."

"And where is his wife?" Quincy Hinks asked. "If you ask me, there's something havey-cavey going on over there."

"Quincy is absolutely right." Miriam Krause stood and gestured to the mayor. "We do need to deal with this. Putting paper over the windows is okay for a day or two. But we need a viable business in there and quick."

Roscoe Jackson rose from his chair to his full five foot six. "Miriam's right. An empty store front at the height of the shopping year makes all of us look bad. And I have to admit that so far, business at my general store has been better than it has been in years." He nodded to Liv.

"Thank you, Roscoe," the mayor said. "When Bill Gunnison gets here, you can ask him about how soon they can get back in."

"Not them," Roscoe said. "Something more in keeping with our town image."

"You tell them, Roscoe," someone shouted from the back of the room, setting off an avalanche of opinions.

"We can't let them open back up with all that folderol in the window."

"Well, we can't let the business lie idle. A Christmas store at the peak of the Christmas season?"

Roscoe jumped to his feet. "I think Jeremiah should evict them and let someone put a new business in there pronto."

"And just who do you suggest? Yourself?" Jeremiah shot back.

"Not me, I'm doing just fine at my present location. But hell, if you hadn't raised the rents, we might still have the Newlands' gift store in there instead of some hoochie-koo business."

The room erupted in opinions.

"Order," Mayor Worley cried over the din. "Jeremiah, do you want to address that question?"

Jeremiah Atkins stood and leaned over Rufus to glower at Roscoe. "Thank you, Mayor Worley. That particular property had sat vacant since the Newlands closed down last summer. The current enterprise would not have been my first choice as a tenant. I would gladly welcome a new business on the site. However, I don't see how I can legally evict the present tenants."

"Easy," someone called out. "A murder was committed there. It's bad for the community."

"And they didn't abide by the town's ordinances."

"I really don't have control over that as a property owner," Jeremiah said. "Any business wishing to do business in Celebration Bay signs a separate document agreeing to certain terms. It is a town ordinance."

"We've never had more than one Santa."

"And they didn't abide by it."

"No, they didn't."

"There's your out."

Ted leaned over to whisper in Liv's ear. "Except Jeremiah doesn't want to lose out on the income."

"I don't think it would really hold up in a court of law,"

Jeremiah said unhappily. "It's more of a good-faith document."

"But they signed it, didn't they?"

All eyes turned from Jeremiah to Janine Tudor, who had been uncharacteristically quiet during the last few questions.

"Well, I gave it to them," she said haughtily.

"Oh boy," Liv said under her breath.

"Yeah, but did they sign it?"

"Really," she said. "It's my busy season. How can I be expected to remember every little piece of paper that comes across my desk?"

"Well, did they or didn't they?" Roscoe craned to see Janine at the end of the table.

The mayor banged his gavel. "Whether they did or not, it's beside the point."

"And the translation of that is," Ted whispered, *"Get Janine off the hot seat."*

"I don't know why he's always sticking up for her," Liv said.

"Lack of backbone I suspect, but you didn't hear it from me," Chaz said in her ear. His breath sent shivers down *her* backbone, but not in a fun way.

Miriam Krause stood. "Well, what are we gonna do until this gets straightened out? We'll be overrun by morbid gawkers and news folks when this gets out. It'll scare away the shoppers."

"Don't know how you're going to keep the curious away."

"That's right."

"We just gotta make sure they're buying and not just gawking."

Rufus stood, smoothed his mustache. "I for one am impressed with the job Bayside Security performed. Liv, do we have funds for hiring this team of yours for a few more days until things settle down?"

"They should do it for free, useless waste of money if you ask me."

"Nobody asked you."

"They diffused a fight in the pub before anybody had a chance to break anything, including their heads. I say we hire them."

"Right and they helped out with crowd control at the end of the ceremony," Fred Hunnicutt added. "I say if we can, we should consider keeping them at least for the next two weeks through the *Messiah* sing-along and the Christmas pageant."

"Now, let's not get carried away," the mayor said.

"He's looking a little apoplectic," Liv said.

"Probably worrying how the expenses will look in the next election," said Chaz.

She turned her back on him. "Mr. Mayor, in my initial study of the efficacy of hiring a security firm . . ."

"The party of the first part, the hambone connected to the—"

"Shush," she said and stood to look at the audience, all owners or managers of local stores.

All the businesses on the west side of the park where Trim a Tree was located were represented except for BeBe, who didn't have anyone to watch the coffee bar while she was gone. Dolly and Fred were sitting together next to Quincy Hinks from the Bookworm. Nancy Pyne sat with her hands held in her lap. She smiled slightly as Liv caught her eye. Miriam Krause gave Liv a nod of encouragement.

"When I first began vetting companies for the job of security, I ran a comparative spreadsheet of the various packages the firms offered and their costs. I also prepared a specialized package for Celebration Bay's security needs, one for intensive high-traffic events and one for daily main-tenance in case we decided to go that route. I'd be happy to present that data to the committee. If I may?"

"Certainly," the mayor said, but he looked apprehensive.

Beside him, Janine rolled her eyes and began to study her nails.

Liv clicked on the spreadsheet, which appeared projected on the wall behind the trustees. "On this first page are the basic proposals." She waited for a minute to give them time to study it, then continued. "This second page breaks these down further to show individual a la carte services."

"To be served with a dry burgundy," Chaz said under his breath.

Liv refused to be baited. "I also have a comparison of incidents per capita from the last three tree lightings with this year's preliminary reports, if the council is interested."

"Of course we are," Jeremiah said.

Liv pulled up the next graph, color coded. It drove her point home. Crime and accidents were down across the grid.

"I say we just let Liv do what she needs to do," Roscoe said. "She obviously knows how to do it."

Janine cut him a look but kept her mouth shut.

"Thank you for your input, Liv," Mayor Worley said. "The trustees will take this into consideration when making a decision about continuing to use Bayside Security in the future."

Janine shot Liv a smug look. Would she really leave the town underprotected just to get back at Liv? Maybe it was time to have a little talk with the woman.

"Well, I say we vote to keep them," said Roscoe.

"At a later, closed meeting," the mayor said.

"And I second Roscoe's motion," Rufus said.

"Not now," the mayor urged.

"Chaz?" Roscoe asked.

"Sure."

"So do I," said Jeremiah. "And since Janine doesn't have a vote, I say the vote carries."

"Here, here."

The room broke into a noisy gaggle of voices. Mayor Worley pounded his gavel to no avail. Only the door opening and Bill Gunnison walking in brought the room back to relative quiet. Two people were with him. One was Grace Thornsby; the other one had to be her husband, Clarence.

"Now maybe we'll get some real answers," Rufus said, and began chewing his mustache in anticipation.

"Sheriff," the mayor said, his voice dropping half an octave.

"Thank you for coming. Now, if you'll all sit down, Sheriff Gunnison will apprise us of this ignominious occurrence."

"Oh God, it's catching," said the voice behind Liv.

She didn't bother to turn around. The mayor *was* sounding a little silly all of a sudden. Did she sound like that? She didn't think so. She knew what she was doing. She fit her language to the situation. She knew how to persuade and it worked, she reminded herself. Chaz was just a . . . jerk who took delight in baiting her.

Bill motioned the Thornsbys to chairs at the side of the room. And Liv took the opportunity to get a good look at Grace's husband. Middle-aged, wearing a suede jacket over a checked shirt, open at the collar. Tallish with a stomach that hung over his belt. He nodded his way to his chair and sat. Liv could imagine him doing his own boat commercials.

Bill stepped up to the podium, displacing the mayor, who moved down to occupy Chaz's empty seat.

"Let me first thank everyone for keeping clear heads and cooperating with the investigation." Bill gave the room the gist of what had happened, the barest details on the status of the case, and asked anyone who might have seen or heard something to please come forward, anonymously if they preferred. All information would be confidential.

He didn't say anything that Liv hadn't heard or seen before. And he left one big detail out altogether. The fact that Phillip Cosgrove was a private investigator.

One that followed cheating spouses. Liv glanced at Grace. Did she have a lover? Was that where she was when Cosgrove was being killed? Or had she found out about him and decided to kill him?

Don't be absurd. But who? And why?

"The police have finished their preliminary investigation, and the Trim a Tree space has been cleared to reopen."

The room erupted with angry voices.

"No. Haven't they caused enough trouble?"

"Close down the Trim a Tree."

"Quiet, let's have some order here." Bill looked at the

mayor, who threw up his hands. Bill picked up the gavel and whacked it on the table once.

Everybody shut up.

Damn, thought Liv. He might be slow, he might have sciatica, but people listened to him.

"The Thornsbys did not come here to be badgered by your questions. Clarence asked to come and make a statement."

Clarence nodded to the sheriff and stood. "I just want to let the people of Celebration Bay know how sorry both my wife and I are about the events of last night."

"A man was murdered in your store."

"I realize that. And it is unfortunate. But I don't see that there was a way that I could have prevented it."

Liv watched him speculatively. Where was he going with this? He should have given his goodwill speech *before* tragedy struck. Now he was in danger of throwing gasoline on the fire.

Several questions flew at once.

"Please let him finish," Bill commanded.

There was some grumbling, but they quieted down.

"Thank you, Sheriff. That's all I really have to say. Except, for everyone's inconvenience, I'm offering a ten percent discount on all boating goods at any of my stores through the end of the month."

There was a stunned silence.

It was the first time Liv had witnessed the entirety of the Celebration Bay business community at a loss for words.

Liv glanced at Ted, whose mouth had gone slack, and said, "I can't believe he just used this tragedy as a promo op for his business."

"What an ass," Ted said.

Clarence gave the attendees a satisfied smile. "Thank you." He turned toward his wife as if to leave.

"I have one question."

The room stilled.

Liv couldn't believe her ears. The laziest newspaperman in the state wanted to ask a question.

"Where was Ms. Thornsby during the tree lighting?"

Clarence glared at Chaz, glanced at his wife, and back to Chaz. "She was with me."

A sigh of disappointment seemed to go out of the room. Celebration Bay liked their intrigue. But a wife spending an evening with her husband was nothing to get excited about.

The only person who looked shocked was Grace Thornsby.

Chapter Eleven

....

"He's lying," Chaz said under his breath but loud enough for Liv to hear him.

She slowly turned her head. Of course he was slouched in his chair with his eyes closed.

"No kidding," she said. "Did you see Grace's expression?"

A faint brief smile followed by a deep, slow breath. Liv didn't get him at all. He was lazy, apathetic, and refused to get involved. So what was the point of dropping her a tidbit if he wasn't going to follow up?

"Okay, everyone," said Bill. "I didn't bring the Thornsbys here to be chastised or questioned. Clarence asked to come to show his goodwill."

Taking his cue, the mayor jumped up. "Thank you all for coming. And Merry Christmas."

Merry Christmas? A man was dead. His murder was unsolved, and Clarence Thornsby had turned the meeting into a sales pitch.

The Thornsbys were the first to leave. Grace's hand was tucked in Clarence's. The room began to empty while Liv put away her laptop and shut off the projector. She was hoping to wait around until everyone was gone and talk to Bill. But the mayor and Bill left together.

Ted carried the projector back to the office. Liv slipped her computer bag over her shoulder and went to the door.

Only Chaz Bristow was left, snoring gently in his chair.

Liv gritted her teeth. "Good night," she said and flicked off the lights.

The hallway was empty as Liv made her way back to her office. Usually after a meeting people stood outside chatting or complaining or planning trips to the pub, but not tonight. Liv yawned. They were probably already home getting ready for bed.

The majority of them would go to church the next morning, then head for their various businesses. Not even on Sunday did they get a day of rest when it was festival season, though the stores didn't open until after noon.

Ted was putting on his coat when Liv got to the office. Whiskey was sitting at his feet. Considering he'd been sleeping most of the day, he was ready for adventure.

"Want a ride?" Ted asked.

"Thanks, but no. It's not late. I thought I'd drop by the Buttercup and see if BeBe wanted to go out for a drink or something."

"Well, you girls have fun." Ted threw his scarf around his neck with a flourish, setting off the jingle bells attached to the fringed ends.

Whiskey jumped up and wagged his tail.

"Sorry, fella, you're stuck with the girls tonight. You want me to wait for you to finish here?"

"No, I'm just getting my coat and leaving, too."

"Good night, then. Good night, dawg." Ted left and closed the door. Whiskey barked. Ted stuck his head back in. "For we like sheep . . ."

"Aar-roo-roo-roo."

Ted grinned at Liv. "I think we're almost ready to start on the 'Hallelujah Chorus.'"

Liv rolled her eyes; Ted closed the door. She could hear him humming as he walked down the hall to the front door.

Liv grabbed her coat and clipped on Whiskey's leash, then slid her laptop case over her shoulder—she probably wouldn't be doing any work at home that night, but you never knew.

The cold hit her with a vengeance, and Liv shivered in spite of her coat. She pulled up the collar, pulled down her hat, and looked down at Whiskey. "Aren't you the least little bit cold?"

He yipped and started down the steps.

She crossed the street and had to pull him past the Corner Café, which was just closing for the night. He was hungry and so was she, but she needed to satisfy one question. How dark was the alley?

Okay, two questions. Was it really dark enough for someone to steal the Santa suit, change into it, and go into TAT without being seen? Unless they had stolen the suit earlier and sneaked back through the parking lot after dark. Either way, she rationalized, she would need to do something about enhancing the lighting. And the only way she would know was to look.

This would be a perfect time, while things were still open and people were about. She wouldn't walk down it alone, just stand at the entrance and take a recce.

She walked to the alley entrance. As she stood there, the lights in the Pyne Bough went dark. Nancy had been at the meeting; maybe she had come back to finish locking up. There was still light coming from the two side windows of the storeroom where Hank changed.

Liv looked down the rest of the alley. The lampposts were set at intervals of about fifty feet, bright enough to cast cones of light over most of the area. She could see the brighter lights of the walk-through two-thirds of the way down. Though the middle of the alley was fairly well lit, the sides were not. There were plenty of places to hide in the shadows against the fence and the buildings.

The front of the Dumpster where Hank had found his Santa suit was lit. Liv could see it quite clearly, but the back half was cloaked in total darkness. Enough so that someone could dress and undress quickly without being seen.

A shiver prickled up her spine. She would assign an extra security guard to the area to supplement the police patrol. She didn't think the trustees would begrudge her spending a little extra on something that might prevent further crime.

But they really needed to make a concerted effort to upgrade safety. The festivals were growing exponentially, and they didn't have enough permanent security measures in place. She'd prob—

There was movement ahead. Liv peered down the alley. Whiskey stood at attention. Legs set, head erect, ears pitched forward.

The Trim a Tree delivery door opened and cast a rectangle of light on the pavement.

Liv was inclined to run, but her feet wouldn't move. She dropped to a crouch, fumbled in her bag, pulled out a dog biscuit, and gave it to Whiskey. She put her finger to her lips. "Shh."

She eased forward.

Clarence Thornsby stepped into the alley. Was Grace still inside? Clarence hadn't bothered to turn out the lights.

Liv couldn't seem to move away. Curiosity, nosiness. Call it whatever, Liv had known without Chaz having to tell her, that Clarence was lying about Grace being with him during the time of the murder. Why would he do that?

And what were they up to?

Maybe neither of them had hired Phil Cosgrove. Maybe someone had hired him to investigate the Thornsbys. And if that was the case, they might have conspired to murder him.

Liv took a deep breath, slowly let it out, watching the puff of fog it caused. Too much imagination. There was nothing at all—not much anyway—that made their actions suspicious. If they were planning to open the next day, they of course would want to check out the condition of their store. She should mind her own business.

Clarence strode away from the door. He was carrying a folded newspaper under his arm.

"Wait just a minute." Grace's voice shot out of the shadows and sliced through the clear night air.

Clarence stopped, turned. Grace came out of the store, and they faced each other in the rectangle of light, silhouetted like an old Victorian Christmas card.

An old, menacing Christmas card, Liv amended silently.

"Don't"—Clarence poked his finger at Grace's nose—"start with me again. You've made me look like a fool. These people are my potential customers, their friends are my potential customers. They want to deal with someone they can trust. And look what you've done."

"Me? I haven't done anything."

"Ha." The sound cracked like a gun, making Liv jump. Whiskey yipped in return, and Liv reached over and scooped him up into her arms as she ducked into the shadows.

She held Whiskey close to her, whispered in his ear. "Quiet." His ear twitched and tickled her nose. She had to quell the urge to laugh. It was absurd, skulking in the shadows with her dog, listening to a husband and wife argue.

A husband and wife who may have committed murder, she reminded herself.

In which case you should get the heck away.

Keeping to the shadows, she maneuvered to the back of the Dumpster. She squatted down, put Whiskey on the ground next to her. Keeping a restraining hand on his back, Liv crab-walked to the edge of the Dumpster and peered out.

"If you had been at the store, none of this would have happened."

"What you mean is, he might have killed me instead," she cried hysterically. "You wish I were dead."

"You're crazy. I just want to know why you weren't here for the tree lighting. It's the biggest night of the season. And you took the night off? Where were you, Grace?"

"I was busy. Penny Newland was supposed to do it. The Newlands have been doing it for years. She knew exactly what to do. But she cut out on me. You can't trust anybody these days. And I'm not hiring her back."

"Where were you?"

"None of your business."

Liv shifted position, trying to ease a cramp in her hamstring.

"The hell it isn't." His voice dropped. "I lied for you. Tell me, or I'll—" He grabbed her arm.

Liv leaned forward to hear better. Her hamstring spasmed and she pushed to her feet, standing with her weight on one leg while trying to relax the cramp in the other.

"What? Kill me? Do you think anybody will buy any of your stupid boats if they think you tried to kill your wife?"

"Dammit, keep your voice down. Do you want the whole town to hear?"

"That you tried to kill your wife?"

"You're insane." Clarence turned away.

Grace grabbed at his sleeve. Clarence jerked his arm away; the folded newspaper he'd been holding under his arm fell to the ground. He stepped over it and crowded Grace until she stumbled backward.

Liv hoped to hell they didn't start hitting each other or she'd feel compelled to intervene. And what good could she do? And she would blow her cover.

She balanced on one leg, and holding her computer case behind her, Liv leaned farther out from behind the Dumpster to get a better look. She never made it. A hand clamped over her mouth and yanked her back.

Liv froze. She'd survived how long in Manhattan without being mugged? This couldn't be happening.

"Do not stomp on my foot," a voice whispered in her ear.

Liv's breath came out in a whoosh, or it would have if he hadn't covered her nose with his palm.

She pushed the hand away. "Dammit, Chaz. Shh."

She peered around the Dumpster. Chaz came with her, looking over her shoulder, so close that it was distracting.

"What are we watching?" he whispered in her ear. It sent vibrations all the way down to her toes.

"The Thornsbys."

"Oh." He moved closer until her back was molded to his front.

"You're trying to distract me."

"Is it working?"

"This is serious."

"I'm feeling a little serious. What are they doing?"

Liv leaned out just in time to see Grace stalk into the store. As soon as she was gone, Clarence bent over to scoop up the newspaper and something else. A rectangular something, a book or a bag of some sort, maybe a bank deposit bag. He slipped it into the folded newspaper, looked quickly around, and shoved it inside his coat.

Liv didn't blame him. Even though most of the locals refused to patronize the store and it had been closed on the first big shopping night because of the murder, it had still been open for a week or so. He could be carrying a substantial amount of cash and checks.

"I think the show is over," Chaz whispered and pulled her even closer.

"Stop it."

Grace reappeared in the alley and turned to lock the door. The Pyne Bough door opened, and Nancy Pyne stepped out.

Chaz yanked Liv behind the Dumpster. Liv nearly tripped over Whiskey as Chaz pulled her into the shadows.

"Did she see us?" Liv whispered.

"I don't know, are we hiding from her, too?"

Liv growled, so did Whiskey. "No, shh, shh, I was just kidding." Liv clamped her hand over Whiskey's mouth.

She could see Chaz grinning in the half light.

"Shit, she's coming to take out the garbage." He pulled Liv down, where they crouched against the side of the Dumpster. Hopefully out of sight.

Liv held her breath. Feeling stupid. And wishing Nancy would hurry and get back inside before the Thornsbys left.

She heard the squeak of the Dumpster lid, the sound of a bag being shoved in and the lid closing. Then nothing. Nancy didn't move away or move at all. What was she doing? Why wasn't she going back to the Pyne Bough? Liv cut her eyes toward Chaz. He shrugged.

It seemed like eons with Liv, Chaz, Whiskey, and Nancy

suspended in time. Nancy must have been watching the Thornsbys, too. But what were they doing? Liv strained her ears but heard nothing; then finally Nancy's footsteps moved away.

Liv and Chaz let out their collective breaths. Whiskey licked both their faces. Liv started to stand, but Chaz pulled her back. "Wait."

Liv watched Nancy start back across the alley. She was taking her time. Finally she opened the door, but before she got inside, something orange streaked past her feet and into the alley.

"Oh no," said Liv. She grabbed for Whiskey, but he shot out from behind the Dumpster and took off after Grace Thornsby's cat.

"Why did you let go of his leash?" Chaz asked.

"I thought you had him." Liv used Chaz's shoulders to push to her feet. She stepped into the open.

"Liv?" Nancy Pyne stood at the open door.

Chaz stepped behind Liv.

"Chaz? What are you two doing?"

"Busted," Chaz said and squeezed past Liv into the light.

Liv didn't wait for the explanation. She didn't even want to know how Chaz would spin it. She took off after Whiskey and caught up with him, and an angry Grace Thornsby, at the TAT door.

Clarence was gone.

Grace had scooped up her cat and was holding him out of reach of the jumping, frisking Westie. "Get that dog out of here!"

"Sorry," Liv said. "He just wants to play." She grabbed at Whiskey's leash and slipped it over her wrist. She pulled him behind her. As much to protect her dog as to appease Grace Thornsby.

Grace dropped the cat. It sidled away to stand behind her, back arched and fur standing on end. Grace glowered at Liv. "Just how did my cat get out of the store?"

Liv shrugged as Chaz sauntered up beside her.

"Probably got out during the investigation," Chaz said,

almost purring himself. "Cats are such resilient creatures; he probably saw his chance and took it."

"She," Grace said.

"She—nice kitty." He reached to stroke the cat.

Liv could have told him, but she didn't get the chance. The cat swiped at Chaz's outstretched hand.

"Ow." Chaz snatched his hand away.

Grace scooped up the cat, tossed it inside the store, and slammed the door shut.

"Ow," Chaz repeated as they watched Grace storm away.

"A salutary reminder to wear your gloves and hat in this weather. At least it didn't go for those baby blues."

Chaz's face went from hurt feelings to a grin. "She." He batted his lashes at her.

"Ugh."

Liv just caught sight of Grace's back as she hurried to the parking lot. Liv's spying had turned into a three-ring circus. At least she knew for sure what they'd already guessed. Grace had not been with her husband the night of Phil Cosgrove's murder.

She huffed out a sigh. "Come on, buddy, let's go home."

Chaz fell in beside her as she backtracked her way up the alley. "Do you have any food at your house?"

"I meant Whiskey, not you."

"Hey, I'm your buddy. And if you weren't so bossy—"

"Do not say something snarky or off-color. You are responsible for me missing the end of the Thornsbys' fight."

"Yeah. Do you make a habit of skulking in alleys spying on people?"

"No, and I wasn't skulking . . . exactly."

"Uh-huh, and you were so caught up in whatever they were saying that I could have crept up behind you and slit your throat. Jesus, how lamebrained can you be?"

From her feet, Whiskey growled.

"I should sic him on you," Liv said.

"Oh please, don't say this ferocious little powder puff would save you." Chaz addressed his sentence to Whiskey in a sing-song voice. And while Liv boiled, Whiskey wiggled and preened and placed both paws on Chaz's knees to be petted.

"Traitor."

"Come on, I'll walk you to your car."

"I don't have my car, I'm walking home."

"Then I'll walk you to my car, 'cause I'm not walking you home in this weather."

"Thanks, but I'll be fine." She kept walking.

Nancy Pyne was standing in the open doorway to her store.

"'Night, Nancy. Sorry we disturbed you."

"No bother. But it's a crime the way she treats that cat. Did you see the way she threw him into the store?"

Liv had, but she had to admit she might have been tempted to give the cat a gentle toss herself. Didn't cats always land on their feet?

"People like that shouldn't be allowed to have animals. Well, good night." Nancy closed the door.

Liv picked up her pace. That ridiculous excursion hadn't been a total waste. She'd learned that a person could have stolen the Santa suit, changed into it, killed Phil Cosgrove, and changed out of it again without being seen, even by pedestrians crossing the alley or store owners taking out the trash.

She knew that the Thornsbys were not getting along. And that Clarence didn't trust his wife, which added credence to the idea that Clarence might have hired the detective to follow her. Could Grace have found out and killed the detective? Seemed far-fetched.

Liv wondered whether Bill had any theories, and would he share them with her if he did.

"Hey, wait up." Chaz strode after her, sucking on the back of his hand. "How about a beer?"

She ignored him and kept walking.

"A Band-Aid?"

Chapter Twelve

....

Liv fisted a hand on her hip, which didn't have nearly the effect she was after, since Whiskey was tugging at the leash, making up for lost sniffing time.

"You look like a powder puff to go with your powder-puff dog."

"Okay. That does it." Liv tugged at Whiskey's leash. "Let's go."

"Where are we going?" Chaz asked, striding after her.

"Whiskey and I are going home. You can go to—"

"Come on, Liv. Have a heart. I'm bleeding and I need a beer."

She slowed, gave him a look, known as "the look" in Manhattan event-planning circles. It went right over Chaz's head.

She gave it up. "Why do you think the Thornsbys were lying?"

"That's easy. Didn't you see Grace's face?"

Of course she had. Liv gritted her teeth. "Let me rephrase that. Why do you think they needed to lie about being together?"

"That's easy, too."

"How?" she asked, nearly at the end of patience.

"I'll tell you after the Band-Aid and over the beer."

"Forget it."

Whiskey barked and stiffened all fours.

"Good dog," Chaz said, and Whiskey, fickle friend that he was, pattered across the asphalt to paw at Chaz's knees.

"I don't have any beer at home, and I can't take Whiskey into a bar and I won't leave him out in the cold. So you're out of luck."

"Sure you can, you're local, sort of—getting there anyway."

"Gee, Chaz, that's the nicest thing you've ever said to me."

He grinned at her. "And if you get drunk, I'll be there to drive you home."

"I never get drunk."

"Why am I not surprised." He took her by the elbow. "Hey, it's just a beer. And then I'll drive you home, drunk or not. Besides, you never can tell who might be there or what news you might pick up over your Virgin Mary." His eyes glinted in the streetlight.

Liv couldn't tell if it was from amusement or challenge. She went with the challenge. "Okay. But just one. And you're buying."

He trundled her across the alley to the parking lot. Liv couldn't help but look around to see if one of the Thornsbys was still there.

"We're driving?"

"No, we're cutting through the parking lot."

"Where are we going?" asked Liv, hurrying to keep up and practically sliding right past him.

Chaz grabbed her and kept her on her feet. "Watch out for the icy patch."

"Funny, but thanks for the save."

"You're welcome."

"So where are we going?"

"To Buddy's. Not very romantic, I realize, but then,

neither are we. And the dinner crowd will be gone. Genny won't have closed down the cash register yet, and she won't mind us sneaking Whiskey in."

Buddy's Place, known to the locals as Buddy's or the Place or just plain Genny's, was a cross between a Jersey diner and a luncheonette. Genny Parsons was owner, manager, and sometimes waitress. No one seemed to remember Buddy.

It was Liv and Ted's go-to take-out place, and Liv ate dinner there at least once a week. It was a popular hangout, especially because it had a liquor license and a better-than-average wine and beer list.

Genny had already locked the door, but Chaz being Chaz, knocked on the glass.

Genny appeared on the other side and peered out, saw who it was, and unlocked the door.

"Come on in. It's cold as you know what out there. Whiskey, you, too. No health department rules after hours. Bill's in that back booth if you want to join him."

Liv's eyes widened. Did Chaz know Bill would be here? And why on earth would Mr. I-Won't-Get-Involved get involved now?

She was about to find out, because Chaz had gone ahead. Genny and Liv exchanged looks.

"I'll be right there," said Genny and took off to the kitchen. Liv hurried after Chaz.

He was standing over Bill, who was cutting into a thick steak. A bottle of locally produced micro beer sat at his elbow.

Chaz pushed Liv into the banquette, gave Whiskey a boost up, and slid in beside them.

Bill put his fork down and wiped his mouth. "Something happen?"

"Liv has a confession to make."

"What?" said Liv.

"What?" said Bill.

Whiskey, who had just settled down next to Liv, stuck his head over the table's edge.

"This is gonna be good," said Genny, who put a Corona and a glass of pinot grigio on the table, then slid in beside the sheriff.

"Mind if I keep eating while you confess?" Bill asked. "Or is it gonna take my appetite away?"

"I don't have anything—" Liv stopped. She had been spying on the Thornsbys in the alley. There might be something in their fight that would be helpful to Bill's investigation. Though she couldn't imagine what.

"Actually."

Bill groaned, put down his fork, and speared his fingers through his salt-and-pepper hair.

"Keep eating," Liv said. "It isn't anything bad."

Chaz snorted. Whiskey gave a big doggie yawn, then stretched out with his head on Liv's lap.

Liv took a deep breath, fortified herself with a sip of wine. "I was on my way home from the meeting when I remembered that I wanted to take a look at the alley."

Bill groaned again. Genny patted his shoulder, then gave Liv her full attention.

"I just needed to see how dark the alley was and if I needed to requisition additional lighting to ensure the safety of our visitors and ourselves. It was an innocent recce."

"Ha," Chaz cracked.

"I was just going to look. I wasn't going to go *into* the alley. Just stand on the sidewalk and check out the light. I'm not that dumb."

"Ha," repeated Chaz.

Liv glared at him.

Resigned, Bill said, "Go on."

"Most of the alley is decently lit, but the edges are really dark. Then I thought, it would have been almost that dark during the tree lighting. Dark enough for someone to steal the suit, change into it, then get into Trim a Tree, kill the PI—"

"What?" said Chaz.

"What PI?" Genny asked.

Liv clapped her hand to her mouth. "Sorry."

"Don't matter much," Bill said. He wiped his napkin across his mouth and tossed it on the table.

"The fake Santa was a private investigator?" Chaz asked.

Bill nodded. "But I'll thank you to keep it to yourselves."

"Sure thing. Who hired him?"

"Don't know. The only reason I found out so quickly is because Liv's security head recognized him."

Chaz whistled. Turned to Liv. "And I suppose he told you?"

"It was part of his report. How am I supposed to stay on top of things if I don't know what's going on?"

Chaz put down his beer. "You think Clarence Thornsby hired him to keep tabs on his wife?"

"I didn't get a chance to ask," Bill said. "He roared into town like a crazy man. I ran into the both of them on my way into town hall. I asked him to come to the station, he said he would. But while I was reassuring the mayor, he ran off again."

"Did you put out an APB on him?" Genny asked.

"No, as far as I know he hasn't done anything. But I will get him to come in and tell us what he knows about Phil Cosgrove."

"The dead Santa?" Chaz asked.

"Oh, Chaz, that sounds so awful." Genny shook her head. "What is this town coming to?"

Liv's face grew hot.

Genny reached across the table and patted Liv's arm. "Don't you look like that, Liv, it's not your fault that some crazy person came in and killed that man."

"Or someone who found out he was a private tec decided to take him off the case, permanently," Chaz said.

"Do you think Grace did it?" Genny asked, wide-eyed.

Bill huffed out a sigh. "Let's just keep an open mind and stop conjecturing. If something like this gets out, they'll draw and quarter Grace before she can say, 'Bah humbug.'"

"So where was Grace when he was killed?" Liv asked.

Bill frowned at her. "Didn't say. I heard she was back in

town, and I thought she'd come out to the station. But she didn't. Maybe she was with her husband like she said."

"No, she wasn't."

"And you know this how?"

"While I was looking at the lighting, Grace and Clarence came out of TAT. I guess that means it really will reopen tomorrow?"

Bill shrugged. "I gave them the key. Crime scene finished up this afternoon. So I guess it's back to business as usual."

There was nothing usual about Grace Thornsby or her tacky Christmas store. "I didn't want it to look like I followed them." Liv glanced at Chaz. "Which I didn't, if you're wondering. So I stepped into the shadows."

"Hid behind the Dumpster," Chaz corrected.

"Anyway, they were arguing, and he asked her where she was last night and why she wasn't in the store. Then carped on about his reputation. Then Batman here grabbed me from behind and shoved me on the ground where I couldn't hear any more."

Bill turned his frown on Chaz. "And what were *you* doing there?"

"Following her. I swear, the woman's a walking self-destruct button."

"I am not. I would have waited for them to leave, which they did—Clarence to the parking lot and Grace into the store—and then calmly walked away."

She laughed, ruefully. "Except Nancy came out to empty the trash. She's been keeping the TAT cat—which, by the way, is named Tinkerbell—and it ran out of the Pyne Bough and Whiskey chased after it."

Whiskey lifted his head, ears twitching.

"It's all right, buddy, you showed that cat. I had to go after Whiskey, and Chaz and Nancy followed. Then I was apologizing, and we would have gotten out of there, but Chaz tried to pet the devil cat and it scratched him."

She suddenly remembered. "How's your hand?"

Chaz rolled his eyes to the ceiling. "Gangrene could have set in for all you care."

"A big guy like you getting scratched by a cat named Tinkerbell. Give it here." She took his hand and wet a napkin in Bill's untouched water glass. "And that's all I—we know," she said as she patted the scratch clean and Chaz winced.

Bill dropped his head to one side and the other, cracking his neck. "Well, I'll just have to see what Grace Thornsby has to say about that. So, can a person get from Nancy's to TAT and back without being seen?"

Liv shrugged. "Possible, if they were lucky. Even this late, several groups of people crossed the alley." Liv frowned.

"What?"

"Well, did it have to happen in order? Couldn't someone have taken the suit, put it in a bag, and dressed somewhere else, then . . . no, that doesn't make sense."

"And hiding behind a Dumpster, eavesdropping on possible suspects does?"

"Come on, Bill. It wasn't exactly like that. I didn't even know they would be there."

"No, but you being there might just be a lucky break for us." He nudged Genny out of the booth. "I'd best be getting home. I think tomorrow might be a busy day."

Chaz stood. "We'll get going, too, so Genny can close up. You okay here by yourself?"

"Oh, the boys are still washing down the kitchen, I'll be fine. Night, Bill. Chaz, you and Liv have a good time."

"I'm going straight home," Liv said, in case there was any question in anyone's mind, including Chaz's.

"Well sleep tight," Genny said, but her grin said something else entirely.

They parted on the sidewalk. Bill's car was parked at the diner. Chaz's Jeep was in the town parking lot.

"You knew Bill was going to be there, didn't you?" Liv said, her breath making puffs in the air with each word.

"No idea."

"I've never known you to take an interest in the police blotter."

"You've only known me for four months."

"So, are you?"

"Am I what?"

Liv suppressed an urge to smack him. "Are you interested in this case?"

"Nope."

While Chaz drove her home, Liv tried to get him to admit he was intrigued by the latest murder. God forbid he actually felt something like compassion or outrage. But she soon gave up and just looked out the window. The streets were dark except for the streetlights. The homes had turned off their decorations; the wagon and carriage rides had stopped hours ago.

Celebration Bay seemed like any other small town asleep for the night. Except for the murder. A man was dead. While they had all been celebrating the start of the Christmas season, someone had sneaked in and taken his life.

"What's wrong now?" Chaz asked, without taking his eyes from the street.

"Nothing."

"Then why were you sighing?"

"I was just thinking about Phil Cosgrove. He probably had a family." A family whose Christmas would be ruined this year and for years to come.

"That's the thing about murder. It screws over a lot more people than just the victim."

"Is that why you quit reporting and came back to Celebration Bay?"

"I came back here to take over the paper I inherited."

"A weekly paper with local news."

"That's what's important to the local people," he said, concentrating on the street ahead.

She looked at his profile. His hair looked dark, only hinting at its true color when they passed under a streetlamp. He had one of those leading-man noses, straight, not too cute, not too big. A face with good bones. He was almost too good-looking. The first time she'd met him, she'd immediately pegged him as a misplaced airhead surfer dude.

Most of the time he acted like a rube. But sometimes, when he wasn't holding up that façade, she thought she glimpsed something deeper, someone who might care about injustice, someone who had—at least from her Internet search—cared enough at one time to put himself in harm's way to uncover a story.

She had to respect that person even if the one now sitting beside her in an old, battered Jeep cared only about fishing and sleeping and seemed as shallow as a birdbath.

Against her protests, he drove her all the way up the driveway to the carriage house. But when he cut the engine, she put her foot down.

"I was just going to see you to the door like a perfect gentleman."

"Thanks, but Whiskey and I can take it from here."

"Suit yourself. I'll just wait until you get inside."

Liv smiled. "Thanks. Good night and thanks for the glass of wine."

He gave her a two-finger salute and winked.

"That is so annoying." She closed the door on his laugh.

Liv didn't go to bed but booted up her laptop. She still had a lot of work to do, which only partially included stemming the fallout from the murder. She pulled up her calendar. Added notes to the "scheduled events" column. Wondered if she should give it up and just add another column for murders.

"You're being morbid," she said out loud. Whiskey, who was sleeping on her feet, twitched and lifted his head.

Liv looked beneath her desk. "Sorry, buddy. Don't get up. You're comfier than a pair of Uggs."

Whiskey gave her a look, yawned, and stretched out over her ankles.

She reached down and scratched his ears, then pulled up the next day's schedule.

Sunday. She had to make an appearance in church. The sisters expected her, and it was something she should do to become a part of the community. Besides, she had to admit, she liked going.

Then after that she would swing by the Trim a Tree store

to see if Grace had reopened. Make an appearance at Santa Village, go to the office, make a few calls.

Then she should really drive out to Dexter's Nursery to check on the reindeer. Later that afternoon she had to meet with Fred for an opening-night traffic-flow report, and maybe get to bed early for a change. Her list was two pages long when she finally closed her laptop.

And remembered that Chaz had never told her the other reason he'd known the Thornsbys were lying.

The First Presbyterian Church was packed with worshippers.

The organ was playing a quiet hymn. The front of the church was overflowing in color. Two huge arrangements of red carnations and white roses sat on the altar. Pots of red and white poinsettias lined the communion rail. They would be taken to shut-ins and nursing homes in the week before Christmas.

"Look, there's Roger Newland," Miss Ida said. "Let's say a quick hello."

Liv followed them to where several people stood around a man in a wheelchair. Roger Newland was all bones and flaccid skin, ravaged by illness. Next to him at the end of the pew, his wife kept a brave smile as people nodded and stopped to talk. She'd once been a pretty woman, Liv guessed, though now she was gaunt and sallow looking. Illness didn't just strike the victim, but the whole family.

Sort of like murder, Liv thought.

The organ swelled to a new tune, interrupting her morbid thoughts. Miss Edna hurried them to their pew and stared at the family that was sitting there until they scooted over to make room.

"They only come on holidays," Edna said and sat down, giving an extra nudge to the child sitting next to her. The kid climbed into his mother's lap.

"Edna," Ida scolded.

Liv sat between them feeling a little dowdy in her dark green slacks and sweater. The sisters were dressed in red and green from head to toe: hats, dresses, shoes. Like traffic lights, thought Liv. But they went all out for holidays, even though they were long-retired schoolteachers and didn't make a dime off the tourist season.

They volunteered for a multitude of tasks. They practically ran the local Toys for Tykes, including collecting, wrapping, and delivering presents out of their old Buick.

"Lo, How a Rose E'er Blooming" filled the sanctuary and could probably be heard out on the street. It gave Liv a rush to think of the four Celebration Bay churches all pouring out their hymns at the same time.

The congregation rose, picking up their hymnals as the choir, dressed in white and purple, processed up the aisle. Edna opened her hymnal and pointed to the place. As the choir passed, Liv caught sight of Penny walking with the sopranos, her face uplifted, her hair shining and falling past her shoulders. At least Grace hadn't demanded that she work instead of going to church.

At the end of the hymn, the Reverend Schorr, a young man with a flair for dynamic sermons, climbed to the pulpit.

"Behold the days are coming . . . ."

In view of recent events it would have sounded like a threat coming from anyone else. But the words were offered in a melodious tenor, and the pastor spread his beneficent smile over his flock as he spoke.

At the end of the sermon, the choir rose and began to sing "O Come, O Come, Emmanuel." On the second verse, Penny Newland stepped away from the choir and sang solo. She was looking at her father, her love so readable that it hurt to watch.

Liv wondered if this would be Roger Newland's last Christmas and the last time he would hear his daughter's lovely voice. And it brought an unexpected tightness to her throat and a sting to her eyes.

At the end of the service, BeBe met them at the back of

the church. "I was running late and had to sit in the last pew. Wasn't Penny's voice glorious?"

"The whole service was just beautiful," Ida agreed. She had a little sparkle to her eye, and Liv wondered what Christmas would be like for two elderly sisters, who lived alone and had no family. They had gone to friends for Thanksgiving. Liv had grabbed a turkey sandwich leftover from the cast-of-thousands Pilgrims' Feast and worked at her desk.

That had been necessary with Christmas following so closely on the heels of Thanksgiving, but she didn't want to do that for Christmas. She'd spent her last several Christmases and Thanksgivings sitting at a computer planning for the next holiday she wouldn't have time to celebrate. But this year she was determined to do something festive.

"Are you coming with me to the Tour of Homes this afternoon?" BeBe asked.

Liv deliberated. She'd just been thinking she should enjoy the holidays more, but there was so much work. . . .

"You really should. Just to make sure everything is running smoothly and keep your finger on the pulse of Celebration Bay."

"And we're the last house on the stop unless you go on to the inn for dinner," Ida said. She lowered her voice. "Edna made mulled wine. You're both invited."

"How can I resist?" Liv said.

"Good." BeBe buttoned up her coat. "Gotta run. Meet me at the trolley stop at five to three. We don't want to miss it. That's the last tour of the day." She hurried out the door.

"You young girls work too hard," Ida told Liv as they stopped at the cloakroom to retrieve their coats.

"Does seem that way. But it would be even worse if I didn't have Ted."

"And Penny Newland is another one," Edna said. "Now, there's a burden on slim shoulders."

Ida sighed. "When bad things happen to good people, Edna."

"Seems to be a theme these days." Edna flourished her scarf around her neck. "And I refuse to let it interfere with my Christmas spirit. Life is short. Come along."

They'd almost reached the door when Liv saw Roscoe Jackson and Rufus Cobb cutting through the crowd, practically pulling another man along between them. And they were headed straight toward Liv.

Liv recognized Frank Salvatini Sr., who ran the Corner Café. He was a friendly, talkative older gentleman with an eye for news and an ear for gossip.

"Frank has something he wants to tell you," Rufus said.

Frank's lips were clamped so tight, Liv doubted if he could speak even if he wanted to. And it didn't look like he wanted to.

"Go on," Roscoe urged. He turned to Liv. "I know we put a spanner in the works back in October, but now we aim to help."

Great, thought Liv. *What are they up to now?* "What's this all about?"

Rufus drew himself up to his full five foot six. "Frank saw the murderer going into TAT."

Chapter Thirteen

....

Liv's head swiveled so fast—checking to see if anybody had overheard them—she felt like Linda Blair in *The Exorcist.*

"Shh," Edna said, and she and Ida and BeBe leaned closer.

Liv moved closer, too. "Don't you think you should go to the sheriff with any information you have?"

"We jumped the gun last time," Roscoe said. "So we wanted to come to you first. Then if you think—"

"No." Frank shook his head so violently that his glasses nearly flew off his face. He wrenched his arm loose from Roscoe and pushed them back up the bridge of his nose. "I told Roscoe and Rufus I wouldn't rat on a friend."

Oh Lord, thought Liv. *Please don't let it be Hank.*

"And you better not tell Bill, either."

This was not the first time Liv had run into people determined to protect their own. It was one of the good and bad things of small-town life. Frank wanted to do what was right, but he was torn between loyalty and honesty.

Liv knew how he felt. "I really think—"

"Ida, Edna, yoo-hoo. So good to see you." Ruth Benedict, a holier-than-thou busybody whom no one liked, waved. The sisters waved back. Liv and BeBe just smiled.

Frank Salvatini took advantage of the interruption to try to ease away, but Roscoe and Rufus held him tight.

"See you this afternoon," Edna called out.

The woman nodded and waved and looked like she was dying to join the conversation, but Edna turned her back on her. "Insufferable old gossip." She herded the little group farther into the hallway. "Now, keep your voices down."

Roscoe, Rufus, and Frank nodded dutifully.

Liv marveled at how easily Edna had managed that sleight of hand.

"Now, tell us what you saw."

Frank glanced over his shoulder. Grimaced. Shifted from one foot to the other, like a guilty man.

"Frank," Miss Ida said.

"I can't be sure. I only saw the suit."

Everybody by now knew Hank had been taken in for questioning. It was written all over Frank's face. He thought Hank was the killer and he didn't want to be the one who sealed his fate.

Liv felt for him. She'd lived here only a few months, hardly knew Hank at all, and she wouldn't want to be the one to accuse him. "The sheriff needs to know. It might help clear, um, any suspects, just as well as convict him—them."

"Well, I'm not sure if it really was—"

Rufus jabbed him in the arm. "Aw, just go on and tell her."

"It was his suit."

"Which suit?" Liv asked, wondering if she was going to have to drag every half statement from him. And would it be worth it.

"The Santa suit. He was wearing a Santa suit."

"And what time was this?"

"I don't know exactly. It was getting toward the tree lighting. About five thirty, maybe? My kitchen staff was busy, and I wanted to see the tree lighting. I decided I might as well take out a trash bag on my way to the square. So I did and that's when I saw him."

Here it comes, thought Liv.

"And you're sure it was a Santa suit, not just a red coat or parka?" Edna interjected. "It was dark, wasn't it?"

"Yeah, but the alley was pretty lit up."

"What did he do?" Liv asked.

"Well, like I said, I was putting out the trash. He had his back to me, walking toward the Trim a Tree store. I didn't think anything of it, just dumped the bag in the Dumpster and headed for the square."

Liv's mouth felt suddenly dry. "Did you see who was wearing the suit?"

"I only saw his back. And I wasn't really paying attention. Figured it was just that fella over at TAT, going back after a break. He was always out by the Dumpster talking on his phone and smoking. But then I heard he wasn't wearing it when they found him—you know—dead. Now I'm thinking maybe it wasn't him. Maybe it was the killer."

Liv's mind was racing ahead, making contingency plans in case they arrested Hank for good. She should insist he go to the sheriff. And yet . . .

Ida beat her to the punch. "It had to be whoever stole Hank's suit, doesn't it?"

Or Hank himself, thought Liv. It was not her job to ferret out the truth, thank God. "You should tell the sheriff. It might be helpful."

"I don't know."

"You do what Liv told you to do," Ida said.

Frank hung his head. "I really don't like having to do this." He slumped off like a chastised schoolboy.

"Happy holidays," Roscoe said.

Rufus nodded, clearly relieved that their duty was done. They hurried away.

"Well," Edna said, "we'd best get home and get ready for the first house tour. There're two today."

Liv climbed in the back seat of the Zimmermans' old Buick, wondering if Frank Salvatini's testimony could do any good at all. Or if it would be the thing that nailed the Closed sign on Santa Village.

Whiskey shot out of the carriage house as soon as Liv opened the front door. He sped around her feet, then took off toward the sisters' back porch, where he looked back at her, his tail beating an arc in the air.

"Sorry, buddy. You're banned from inside today. They're getting ready for the holiday house tour. Come on. Treat," she called.

Whiskey hesitated. Looked back at the Zimmermans' door, then back to Liv.

Probably sensing a trick, thought Liv. "Really, treat."

Whiskey raced back and into the house.

Liv adjusted her new wreath, compliments of her land-ladies, and followed him inside.

She found Whiskey in the kitchen, sitting expectantly at the counter right beneath the red-ribboned jar of Dolly's Doggie Treats.

Liv looked in the fridge. A carton of past-its-prime yogurt. Some limp celery and a container of something Liv was afraid to open. She tossed it, container and all, into the trash and gave Whiskey a dog biscuit in the shape of a candy cane.

She got out peanut butter and a spoon for herself and carried them into the living room. She sat on the couch, and Whiskey climbed up beside her. There were a little over two hours before she had to meet BeBe. She had a list of things to do a mile long. She could get some work done or . . . she could do them tomorrow. She reached for the remote, ran through the channels, found a music channel playing Christ-mas carols.

"Be right back." She eased Whiskey over and went to get her laptop. When she sat down again, Whiskey snuggled closer. She opened her laptop, balanced it on her knees, and logged on to the Internet.

As "Santa Claus Is Coming to Town" played in the

background, Liv typed in "Phillip Cosgrove, private investigator."

And there he was: Cosgrove Investigations. A photo of him on the bio page. Why would a private investigator have a photo of himself? Wasn't he afraid of being recognized? Maybe the Santa suit was his disguise. Which was stupid because he'd had his beard pulled under his chin the first day she saw him.

She read down the page: *Domestic Investigation, Surveillance, Pre-litigation.*

Had Clarence hired him to inform on Grace? Was he planning a divorce?

Background Checks, Missing Persons, People Finder, Asset Searches.

None of those made any sense. You didn't have to play Santa Claus to do a background check or search for missing persons.

Asset searches? Maybe Clarence thought Grace was dipping into the till. Maybe that's why he'd come to town yesterday, to make sure the receipts got to the bank. Or maybe they were both dipping into the till.

But if Phil wasn't hired by Clarence, who else would need him to play Santa? Or could Phillip Cosgrove really have been moonlighting as Santa just for the extra money? A.K. Pierce had said that he wasn't all that great at investigating.

She bookmarked him and started a separate e-file for TAT.

Her next search was for Clarence Thornsby. He owned four boat dealerships between Plattsburgh and Saratoga Springs. The man owned a lot of boats. His website called him "the Boat King." So why did he decide to go into Christmas ornaments? Grace seemed to hate the job, so it couldn't be to please her. Actually, she didn't seem to like her husband very much. But it was hard to tell about couples. Sometimes the ones who fought the most were the happiest. Go figure.

Liv wouldn't know, since the only long-term relationship she'd had was with event planning. There just wasn't enough time to build a lasting partnership while planning other people's fun and games. Her longest "serious" relationship had lasted nearly eight months, probably a record in her profession and in his, financial planning.

Thank God she hadn't let him plan hers. He bit it big time in the Madoff scam. Close call. "Anyway," she said out loud, pulling Whiskey's ear, "you're the only man I love."

Whiskey cocked his head.

"Really." Sort of. For now, anyway. But thinking about her ex sent her mind in a new direction. Probably because of some of her former clients. Ones who opened all sorts of businesses for one purpose. Laundering money. But really how much money could you launder with Christmas decorations?

Grace Thornsby had a Facebook profile. Her information was available only to her friends. All thirty-seven of them. Not that Liv really wanted to know all about her. But she was mildly curious. Did they have kids? Liv couldn't imagine it, but that wasn't being fair.

Maybe Grace loved children. Then Liv remembered her attitude toward Bobby Newland when her cat scratched him. Okay, not kids. Maybe Grace was an animal lover. Except she'd tossed her lost cat into the shop without so much as a "kitty, kitty."

She loaded up another spoonful of peanut butter and stared at the screen. Gave up and pulled up solitaire, but that didn't hold her interest. It was hard to concentrate on anything with murder hanging like a black cloud over her town. A cloud that had come to Celebration Bay with Trim a Tree.

She just hoped the storm had passed with the murder of Phillip Cosgrove.

This was not helping her Christmas spirit at all. She turned up the television. "Jingle Bells," blared into the room.

Whiskey sat up. "Ar-roo-roo-roooo."

BeBe was waiting for her at the trolley stand. She was standing near the front of a line of people waiting for the house tour to begin.

"I already got the tickets," BeBe said. "My treat."

"Thanks. I'll buy you dinner if you're free tonight."

"It's a deal." A knit cloche of blue heather was pulled down over one of BeBe's ears. She was wearing a matching scarf and mittens.

"Let me guess. You bought those at the Yarn Barn."

"Of course. Support local businesses." BeBe laughed. "I just wanted the scarf, but those knitters can be very persua-sive. And I do feel rather française in the hat, but I put my foot down at the matching sweater."

"Well, it's very pretty."

"I suppose you bought yours at Bloomingdale's."

"Actually, I never wore a hat when I lived in Manhattan. Hat hair is a definite no-no in event planning. And I didn't need one just to step out of a building and yell 'Taxi!' I ordered this from an online catalogue when I decided to take this job. Though I guess I'd better get over to the Yarn Barn and make amends."

The trolley doors opened and the driver climbed down to the street. He was dressed in a navy blue uniform with brass buttons and gold braid. His conductor's hat had a sprig of holly tucked in the band.

"Welcome to the Annual Celebration Bay Holiday Tour of Homes." He took their tickets, and Liv and BeBe climbed inside.

Most of the passengers were tourists, but there were a few locals that Liv recognized. Ruth Benedict was sitting a few rows back. Two ladies from the Garden Club, whom Liv suspected of taking the tour to get ideas for the spring Tour of Gardens, sat across the aisle from Ruth. Liv pulled BeBe down into a seat near the front; she had no intention of getting within earshot of the town's worst gossip.

The doors closed and the conductor slid behind the wheel. "Welcome. The trolley will take you to your first stop where our hostess, Maeve Kingston, will guide you through some of Celebration Bay's loveliest homes. The trolley will pick you up at the last stop and return here or continue to the inn for those of you with tickets to the Dickens Dinner."

He chuckled. "And you won't want to miss the inn's roast beef and Yorkshire pudding or their Christmas trifle or flaming plum pudding.

"Now I'll turn the show over to Maeve."

Maeve waved from her seat at the front. The conductor clanged the bell and the trolley pulled into the street.

"Our first stop is the historic Chapman House. Built in 1874, it has been accurately and lovingly restored by the Charles Chapman family."

The trolley came to a stop in front of a white clapboard cottage decorated with a multitude of white lights. The façade was trisected by three pitched roofs of varying sizes. Icicles hung from the eaves and wreaths hung in every window; a lit candle, which for safety's sake were actually electric, sat on every sill.

They all descended from the trolley.

"This was a good idea," Liv said. "I can get an idea of how it comes together."

"And if you can make it more efficient and bring more people in, and keep things moving, and—"

"Stop, stop. I'm not always working."

BeBe raised her eyebrows.

"Am I?"

Her eyebrows disappeared into the blue yarn of her hat.

They walked beneath a swag of pine and twinkling lights onto a wide porch surrounded by a wrought-iron rail, festooned with pine swags that were tied up with bows and decorated with red-and-silver ornaments.

It was charming. The foyer table was country antique, and held a huge glass bowl of oranges and cinnamon sticks. The smell was heavenly. A fat white pine tree sat in the corner of the living room.

That was when Liv realized she didn't have a Christmas tree in her little house. But it wasn't too late. She'd go buy one . . . soon. In the meantime, she'd enjoy the ones on the tour.

They spent several minutes all crowded into the living room while Maeve pointed out several family quilts, a display of vintage Christmas cards, and the row of wooden nutcrackers across the mantel of the stone fireplace. A needlepoint fire screen depicted an image of Thomas Nast's Santa. There was a lot of Christmas stuffed into that room.

People oohed and aahed and remarked on the cute fabric dolls that sat in a wicker chair beneath the tree. And in a few minutes they were walking down the sidewalk to the next house.

The whole street was decorated; each house seemed more festive and beautiful than the last. There were Craftsman cottages, Cape Cods, a carriage house three times the size of Liv's, all cheerful, welcoming, and joyous. And by the time they reached the next-to-the-last stop, a larger white colonial with pine-wrapped columns, Liv was totally in the Christmas spirit. Here, everything was on a grander, yet simple scale, which Maeve explained was the Federal style.

Liv and BeBe went inside on the heels of Ruth Benedict and her two friends, who had spent most of the tour commenting and gossiping instead of actually listening to the tour guide.

A decorative Yule log filled the white marble fireplace. Two topiary trees sat at opposite ends of the mantel, flanking a dark wooden mantel clock. The Christmas tree was decorated in real candles, which were unlit but haloed by white lights hidden among the branches.

Liv took a quick look into the dining room where a long rectangular table was covered by a white damask tablecloth topped with a red-and-green table runner and set with gold-rimmed china.

"I'm thinking a cup of good cheer would do nicely right now," BeBe said after another half hour. "Miss Ida and Miss Edna's house is next."

"And they invited us for mulled wine. We'll just lag behind when the tour ends."

Liv hardly recognized her landladies' Victorian, even though she passed it every morning and every night when she came home. But mornings she was in a hurry and walking away from the house, and by the time she got home it was always too late to stop inside.

Two weeks before, men had come to do the outside lights, and it had taken them several days. Now Liv saw why. The eaves, the porch rail, the turret, and even the attic gables were lit in white. Not with the strips of icicles that were so popular but with lights intertwined in pine boughs—real pine boughs. Liv caught wafts of scent as she walked up the steps to the porch.

There were two spruce, cedar, and holly wreaths encircled with oranges, lemons, and kumquats, on the front door. Miss Edna and Miss Ida, looking every bit the ladies of the manor, greeted them at the door before discreetly withdrawing.

Maeve gathered them into the dark wainscoted foyer to show them a festooned tree that was at least ten feet high. Stairs, swagged with pine and red ribbon, curved to the second floor.

In the parlor, another tall tree stood in the window and an antique train ran on a track beneath it. Little houses, people, and cars dotted the white felt tree skirt. There was a fur teddy bear with movable arms and legs, a porcelain doll in an elaborate ball gown. There was a little table with a child's puzzle in progress. A Victorian feather tree on the bookshelf. A row of needlepoint stockings hung on the mantel from painted cast-iron figures of Santa and his reindeer.

"Wow," BeBe said. "This is beautiful. Did they do all this themselves?"

Liv shrugged. "I don't know. I've been so busy. . . ." It was a lame excuse. And she resolved not to let her job make her neglect her friends. She'd had enough of that in Manhattan.

They moved from the fireplace to the piano in the far corner where old sepia photographs were interspersed with an old wooden top, a game of jacks, and a cylinder of pickup sticks.

Christmas was for children. It seemed natural that two retired schoolteachers would have children in their minds when they decorated. But it might also be in the minds and hearts of two spinster sisters, who had lost their fiancés to war and who had never married or had the families that they had once dreamed of.

"Well, that's what happens when people get too uppity." Ruth Benedict's voice crashed in on Liv's reflections. Was Ruth talking about the Zimmerman sisters? Nothing could be further from the truth.

"Well, she managed to ruin the tree lighting, that's for sure."

The three women were standing by the fireplace, ostensibly looking at the stockings.

"Said she was with her husband," the third woman snorted. "That's a laugh."

The three women didn't move from the fireplace. "Do tell."

Ruth Benedict picked up a delicate angel from the mantel and held it up to the light. "Geraldine Madison was at the Blue Boar not long ago, and she saw her with a man young enough to be her son."

The other two tittered.

"Maybe it was her son."

Ruth slowly shook her head and put down the angel. "No children. Too selfish. And besides, Geraldine said that by the way they were acting, they were something more than just friends. And where there's smoke . . ."

"She was trash from the get-go. Some things never change."

Liv became very interested in a copy of *'Twas the Night Before Christmas* placed on a round table near the window, which put her in a better position to hear the women's conversation.

"You think there's some hanky-panky going on there?"

"Geraldine said the way he was fawning on her, there was no mistaking what he had in mind."

Maeve began to gather them together for departure. "The trolley's outside."

People began moving toward the archway, where Edna and Ida were handing out little mesh bags of Christmas potpourri.

The three women began to move slowly toward the door. "Disgusting."

"If you ask me, he's just looking for a rich sugar mama."

"Well, he's in for a surprise," Ruth said.

"What do you mean?"

"Ladies, the trolley is ready to leave." Maeve motioned for them to step it up.

BeBe came back to where Liv was standing. "I told Maeve we weren't coming."

Liv grabbed her by the elbow, put her finger to her lips, and eased in behind the three women.

"Well, my Jonathon said that Clarence Thornsby is in financial trouble."

"No."

BeBe's eyes widened at Liv.

"That's what Jonathon said. He heard it at the Rotary last month."

"Lord, do you think Grace knows?"

"That young stud might be in for a rude awakening."

"Ladies, please hurry." Maeve hustled them out the door, throwing a wave over her shoulder to Liv and BeBe and saying a hasty thank-you to the sisters.

The door closed on the women's laughter.

"Now, what was that all about?" asked Edna.

Chapter Fourteen

....

"We thought they'd never leave," Miss Ida said, placing the tea tray on the coffee table in front of the Queen Anne couch. The sisters always served tea in china cups and saucers edged in pink roses. Today those were replaced by a big plaid thermos and thick lead-glass mugs with pewter handles. A Spode Christmas plate was piled high with cookies and tortes and was accompanied by four smaller plates and cocktail napkins in a holly and ivy pattern.

Ida sat at her usual place, a spoon-back armchair upholstered in gold-and-white stripes.

"You've decorated for the holidays so beautifully," Liv said.

"It's like a fairy tale," BeBe said. "Especially the tree."

Ida passed the plate of sweets. "We just love the season, don't we, Edna?"

"The best holiday of the year." Edna leaned forward from her spot on the sofa and lifted the thermos. As she poured, a heady mixture of steam and spices filled the parlor.

"That smells divine," Liv said as she took a mug from Edna.

"We always had mulled wine for Christmas," Ida said. "Even as children we were allowed Mama's nonalcoholic version. It made us feel so grown-up." She looked fondly around the room.

Liv was a little surprised. The sisters didn't really reminisce about the past too much. Maybe Christmas was a little sad for them. "What are you doing for Christmas this year?"

"We're thinking about staying home this year," Edna said as she finished handing the mugs around. She lifted hers in a toast. "Merry Christmas. May God bless us, every one."

Liv smiled and raised her mug to the others. Leave it to an ex-schoolteacher to quote Dickens.

Silence fell over the little group as they took their first sips of the potent wine.

"We had Thanksgiving dinner with Dolly and Fred," Ida said. "They invited us for Christmas, but we didn't want Dolly to have to go to all that trouble. Between the bakery and home, she hardly ever gets out of the kitchen." She sighed. "We used to have Christmas dinner here, but our old friends moved away or went to visit their children and grandchildren and we just stopped doing it."

"We got lazy," Edna interjected in her usual no-nonsense way.

"I'm staying at home for Christmas, too," BeBe said. "I drove down to Jersey for Christmas last year. Left after I closed up the Buttercup Christmas Eve. Got in about two o'clock. Woke up to help with turkey at six, opened presents, ate, and drove back late that night. Never again. I may just sleep in this year. What about you, Liv?"

Liv laughed. "I haven't gotten that far. I thought about going to the city. I mean Manhattan. But I may take your cue and just sleep."

"Nonsense." Miss Ida held out her mug. "Everyone should celebrate Christmas with friends and family."

"True," said Edna and poured more wine into Ida's glass.

Ida sighed. "We're just getting to be a couple of old humbugs."

Edna barked a laugh. "I'm not."

"Well, maybe we should make Christmas dinner for everyone like we used to."

"Fine by me. I never wanted to stop."

"It's settled, then. Liv and BeBe, would you like to have Christmas with us?"

"That would be great," BeBe said. "We could all bring something. Liv?"

"Are you sure it wouldn't be too much trouble?"

"None at all," Ida said, flushed with anticipation. Or maybe with mulled wine.

Liv hoped Ida didn't regret her generosity once the wine wore off. "Why don't you think about it later and let us know."

"We don't need to discuss it," Edna said.

"No we don't," agreed her sister. "We'll ask Ted. I don't know what he usually does for holidays. And Nancy Pyne. I don't think she has any family nearby. And Chaz Bristow, unless he's going to LA for the holidays. I know he has friends there. And . . ."

"Well, that settles that," Edna said and topped off the mugs with more wine. "But in the meantime, what have you learned about the murder?"

Well, that was one way to dispel her Christmas spirit, thought Liv, and pushed her mentally conjured list of food and Christmas gifts aside.

"You know about Frank Salvatini seeing the Santa in the alley. And while we were on the house tour . . ." Liv brought the sisters up to speed on the gossip they'd overheard while visiting the decorated houses.

"Interesting," Edna said when Liv had finished. "But, if it's true that Clarence is broke, why would he keep adding businesses instead of retrenching?"

"We were wondering the same thing," Liv said.

"And Grace Thornsby having an affair with a young man." Ida reached for a pecan torte. "It boggles the mind. She used to be such a pretty girl."

"She was," Edna and. "And she used it to her advantage, if you know what I mean."

"She certainly did. Now she just looks like a sour old broad." Ida tittered. The wine was certainly having an effect on her. On all of them, Liv thought, feeling a little buzz herself.

"How old is she?" Liv asked.

"Let me think. I had her in class in . . ." Edna frowned. "Sixty-three or maybe sixty-four. Ida, go get those yearbooks and let's have a look. Might be a photo of Hank in there, too. You know they were married once."

"I heard," Liv said while Ida went to the other room for the yearbooks. "Not happily I take it." She winced at her own blatant curiosity. She was becoming something of a gossip herself since moving to Celebration Bay.

Though if she were honest, it was a skill she'd learned working in Manhattan. It was just called something else. You had to keep your edge to stay on top and not become a victim. Gossip in Celebration Bay could be malicious, but mostly it just passed the time and was often the best source of entertainment as well as information. It also had been pivotal in solving one murder. It might just help solve this one.

Ida returned with a stack of books. "I brought several years. You know Hank and Grace were prom queen and king one year."

"Did Clarence go to school here, too?"

"Oh no. Don't know where his people are from, but she met him when she was away staying with a sick friend. I guess things hadn't been going so well between her and Hank at that point."

"That's an understatement," Edna said, reaching for the top yearbook. "With her sense of entitlement and Hank's temper, it was bound to blow up sooner or later."

"Hank?" asked Liv incredulously. "He seems so kind and even tempered." Except for that day in her office, but even then he'd been in control.

"He is, most of the time," Ida said.

"Most of the time when he's not around Grace."

"That girl knew how to push his buttons," Edna said.

"She did," Ida agreed. "Even in high school."

"Pfft. Even in grammar school. But Hank wasn't her only victim. She teased the boys mercilessly. Made up to one, then flitted off to another."

"I had no idea," Liv said.

"Me neither," said BeBe. "I didn't even know they'd been married."

"Ted told me," Liv said. "You don't think that Hank would do anything crazy, do you?"

"Hank? Only to Grace. And I don't think anybody could mistake that ersatz Santa for her. Now, if it had been Grace . . ."

"Edna, you hush. You'll give Liv and BeBe the wrong impression. Don't you worry, Liv. Hank is as mild mannered as they come. Except when it comes to Grace. And nobody but nobody could blame him for that."

"Maybe not," Edna said. "But you know how people talk. They might start asking questions about Hank's involvement."

Especially with that bloody Santa suit, thought Liv.

"Why?" asked BeBe, putting her mug down and giving the sisters her full attention. "He didn't do anything."

"That we know of," Edna said.

"Hmmph," Ida said. "You'd best be careful what you say, or you might be guilty of starting rumors you didn't mean."

"That Grace could drive anybody crazy, not just Hank. And the way she flaunts all that bling. Someone should hang her from a Christmas tree."

"It's shameful," Ida agreed. "And her from a family poor as dirt. Always put on airs, though. Always had to make people think they were better than they were."

"Maybe buying her all that jewelry took its toll on Clarence's finances. Or do you think it's fake?" BeBe turned to Liv. "Does it look like what your rich clients in New York City wore?"

Liv laughed. "I'll let you in on a little secret. A lot of their jewels were paste."

"Really?"

"Really. And I never really learned to tell the difference. I guess because it didn't matter to me."

"I sure wouldn't know the difference," Edna said.

"Maybe someone came in to steal her jewels and that poor man tried to stop him and he got killed."

"That would be a great theory. Only Grace wasn't there," Liv said.

"That's what she says."

"Hmm. That's a good point. She could have come in after Penny left," Liv said. "I wonder if Bill is checking out her alibi."

Edna snorted. "Bill's got too much to do, policing the county for fender benders and shoplifters. They'll end up sending in the state like they did last time, and then where will we be?"

"Heaven forbid." Ida's hand went to her chest. It landed right on the angel appliqué of her sweater.

Liv had already thought about that possibility. She'd been hoping Bill would sew up the case before then. It was bad enough having hired security people running around.

She wondered what A.K. Pierce was doing. Did he sit at home trying to solve the murder? Or did he leave his work at his office. A quality that Liv had never mastered.

"Liv, did you think of something?"

"I'm sorry, Miss Ida. I can't think of a thing."

"I guess it being an accident has been ruled out," BeBe said.

"Pretty much."

"Maybe someone did it in self-defense," said BeBe. "And is afraid to come forward."

"Like who?"

"Maybe he was taking liberties with Grace and she had to fight him off."

"I can't imagine anyone taking liberties with Grace."

"Or with Penny?"

"What?" asked Liv. "She kills him, runs out to sing 'O Tannenbaum,' and comes back to discover him dead?"

"Pfft," Edna said. "And why would she go to the trouble of implicating Hank when he's been very generous with her and Jason?"

BeBe frowned. "Maybe Hank and Grace were arguing and he tried to stop him. So he . . . he . . ." She turned to Liv. "How did he die?"

"Slit his throat," said Edna. "We were there right after Liv found him."

BeBe's eyes widened.

"I didn't actually find him," Liv protested. "It was Ted."

"And his throat was slit?"

"That's what it looked like. I didn't really look that closely." Except she had. The bane of the conscientious event planner, the devil was in the details. And those details would live with her for a long time. And were totally useless except for freaking her out.

"Have another cookie, Liv?" Miss Ida asked.

"Thanks, but I think I've reached my limit. They were delicious."

Liv had noticed Edna flipping through one of the dark green yearbooks. Now she handed it to Liv.

There was no mistaking Grace Thornsby, nee Gilstrap. The younger Grace had a wickedly mischievous smile even in her yearbook picture; on the older Grace it just looked sour. That jet-black hair was real enough, or at least had been at one time. Liv passed the book to BeBe.

Edna handed Liv the second book and pointed to a photo.

"That's Hank? I can't imagine him without that big white beard. He's so . . . skinny."

"Yes, but rawboned," Ida said. "You could tell even then that he'd fill out."

Edna laughed. "I think he's gone a bit further than filled out."

Ida pursed her lips. "Hefty, then."

Liv passed the yearbook on to BeBe. There was nothing much to be learned about the present-day people from their old pictures.

BeBe handed the book back to Edna. "Do you and Miss Ida have all your old yearbooks?"

"Oh yes, dear," Ida said. "They still send us one every year. Isn't that thoughtful?"

"So you have one with Penny Newland in it?"

Edna and Ida exchanged looks.

Edna rose and left the room. She returned with another yearbook. "This is her junior year. She wasn't in the yearbook her senior year."

"She didn't finish school," Ida said. "She was expecting by then."

"Oh," Liv said.

"Too much fun at the junior prom," Edna said.

"Edna."

"Well, it's true. And a shame. She was a bright girl. Planned to go on to study business. Never even got her GED." Edna shook her head. "At least Jason Tully is planning to do right by her."

"Such a sweet boy," Ida said.

"Is he the father?" asked Liv.

Edna shrugged. "That's what people say. But I'm not convinced. She has always refused to tell who it was. But I think it was because she wasn't sure of Jason. He was a year ahead of her, and he left for the navy the day after graduation.

"But now he's back and they're getting married?" Liv asked.

"That's the plan," Edna said. "But she won't leave home until her father gets better."

Both sisters sighed and shook their heads.

"Roger's not going to get better, poor soul," Ida said quietly.

"And Jason is too proud to live with the Newlands. He's determined to support his family. So everything is at a standstill."

"Well, we'll just have to wait and see." Ida took the yearbook from Liv. "Have you ever had English trifle? I have my mother's recipe. Maybe I'll make it for Christmas dinner."

BeBe and Liv left a few minutes later. Ida and Edna stood at the front door to see them out.

"Well, that was an eye-opener," BeBe said, weaving slightly as they walked down the frosty driveway to Liv's cottage. "Are you going to tell Bill Gunnison all you learned today?" Ida asked.

"Yes. Though it's really only gossip."

"Gossip isn't always wrong, you know."

"True," Liv said. "What do you say we order in tonight? That mulled wine went down way too easily."

"Boy, did it. How about Chinese?"

Liv unlocked the door and Whiskey bolted out.

"You'd think I'd been gone a week instead of a couple of hours. Do you want to go inside while I wait for him to come back?"

"I'll stay out here; the cold is doing wonders to clear my head."

Liv laughed. Whiskey checked out a few bushes, looked back at Liv, and headed inside. "Guess he's hungry."

While Liv opened a can of dog food and put down fresh water, BeBe called the China Sun and they went out to the living room to wait for the delivery.

Liv pulled out her laptop.

"Are you going to do work now?"

"No. I'm just jotting down some notes about what we learned today." She turned her laptop screen so BeBe could see.

"Spreadsheet?"

"Lesson plan."

"What?"

"Something Miss Ida and Miss Edna suggested during the last, you know. See, there's a column for information. One for the purpose of said info. One for action. One for outcome."

"And you said you weren't investigating."

"I'm not. Just keeping the facts straight, so I stay on top of everything. You wouldn't believe, the tiniest thing can unravel an entire event. Can turn a sure thing into a flop. So imagine what a murder could do."

"Oh, I see what you mean. Sort of."

"I just like to be prepared for any contingency."

"Even murder."

"Even murder."

Over pork dumplings, beef with broccoli, and shrimp lo mein, they reviewed what they'd overheard during the house tour. Liv entered it all into her spreadsheet/lesson plan document with one hand while she ate with the other. Whiskey sat on the floor between them waiting for a wayward morsel to drop. Which happened quite often when you were using chopsticks and typing at the same time.

Once they'd closed up the leftovers and taken out the trash, Liv insisted on driving BeBe back to the Buttercup to get her car. "Since the sisters cleared a space in the garage, life has gotten a lot easier."

"But you always walk to work."

"I need the exercise and so does Whiskey. Plus it's invigorating."

"Especially when the temperature is single digits."

"I'm prepared for the cold. I did some serious online shopping when I got the job. Besides, I'm totally paranoid about it snowing while I'm at work and having to shovel my way out of the parking lot at the end of the day."

They bundled up in outerwear, and Whiskey trotted over to be put on the leash.

"I'm coming right back, buddy. Stay."

BeBe waited until Liv backed out far enough to close the garage door, then they both got in.

"This was a really long day; it's a good thing I close early on Sundays," BeBe said as they drove toward the Buttercup.

"It was long, but fun. I'm glad you suggested the tour. Work and pleasure, but mostly pleasure." Liv turned into the parking lot at the back of the row of stores.

"Oh, I forgot to tell you, I saw the lights on at TAT when I closed up this afternoon. Grace's car is still here. That silver Mercedes under the light post. Do you think they're going to try to open tomorrow?"

"I have no idea. I'm sure the crime scene was cleared before they let Grace back in, but it still has to be a big cleanup job. All those broken decorations and . . ."

"Euww. Maybe that's what they were doing all afternoon."

"Let's just do a little reconnaissance, shall we?" Liv pulled into an empty parking place near the pedestrian walkway.

"You mean spy on Trim a Tree?"

"We'll just take a look. I'd like to see for myself what Grace Thornsby is up to." And if they saw anything, anything at all, that looked suspicious, Liv would call the sheriff. She was getting tired of the Thornsbys and their theatrics.

Chapter Fifteen

....

"Right," BeBe said. "A reconnaissance."

They stopped to look down the alley toward the Trim a Tree store. The alley was empty and dark except for the security lights.

A short detour through the pedestrian way to the street brought them in front of TAT. The brown paper was still covering the windows, but there was a sliver of light coming from inside.

Liv and BeBe exchanged looks.

"Should we knock on the door?" BeBe asked.

"And say what, *Are you meeting your lover later tonight? Oh, and by the way, what's his name again?*"

BeBe spluttered a laugh. Clapped her hand over her mouth. "So what should we do?" she whispered.

"Well, we could go home to bed, or we could wait for a while and see where she goes."

"You mean to the Blue Boar?"

Liv shrugged. "I don't see Bill out here following her, do you?"

BeBe's eyes lit up.

"We will not engage. Just check it out and tell Bill if we find out anything."

"Fine by me. I wouldn't know what to say if we did catch her in flagrante."

"Oh, please—I wonder."

"What?"

"I wonder if that's what Phillip Cosgrove was investigating."

BeBe's eyes rounded. "I bet it is. And if Grace found out . . . Oh Lord."

Liv shivered. "It's unlikely. It's freezing out here. Maybe we should call it a night."

"No way," BeBe said. "We can watch from the Buttercup where it's warm."

They took turns looking out the delivery door of the coffee bar. BeBe made them decaf tea. They shared an almond biscotti. An hour passed and Liv was yawning, when a rectangle of light appeared on the alley pavement.

"BeBe." Liv motioned her to the door and they both peered out as three women carrying buckets, vacuums, and other cleaning paraphernalia came out of TAT. The door closed behind them.

"Grace must still be in there," BeBe whispered.

Liv checked her phone for the time. Almost nine and she was exhausted. She yawned again. "Twenty more minutes and I'm off to bed."

It was seventeen minutes before the door to TAT opened again and Grace Thornsby came out wearing a midlength fur coat.

"So not PC," BeBe whispered.

Grace locked the door, then walked cautiously toward the opening to the parking lot.

"It's amazing that she doesn't fall on her skinny butt wearing those boots in the ice and snow. I bet those heels are four inches high."

"Seems like an odd choice of clothing for scrubbing floors," Liv said.

"She probably just watched to make sure they didn't miss

anything." BeBe shivered. "Do you think . . . ? No never mind, I don't want to think about what they were cleaning up."

They watched until she'd disappeared through the parking lot opening.

"Now what?"

Liv shrugged. "We could go home, or we could just take a little look-see to find out where she's going . . . dressed so fine."

They scrambled into their coats. While BeBe locked up, Liv crept to the opening in the fence. She'd been skulking around in alleys a lot this month, and she automatically glanced around to make sure no one—Chaz Bristow in particular—was going to jump out at her. She pressed up against the security fence and eased her head out in time to see the Mercedes backing out of a parking place. She windmilled her arm to hurry BeBe along.

"All right, let's go." BeBe shoved her keys into her coat pocket, and they took off at a trot to Liv's car.

They caught up to the Mercedes as it turned onto Third Street.

"I'm feeling a little silly," Liv said, her eyes glued to the car in front of them.

"Oh no. We're aiding the investigation."

"We're probably breaking the law. But what the hey, we're here, we might as well try to move things along."

Ten minutes later, the Mercedes pulled into a parking lot of a rectangular one-storied building. Liv slowed and parked at the curb where she could see the Mercedes and the sign.

"Rock Road Fitness Center? Are you kidding me?" Liv heaved a frustrated sigh. "Who besides Grace Thornsby would come to a gym in a fur coat and stiletto boots?"

As she spoke, the side door opened and a man came out. He was midheight, extremely buff, and midthirties, max.

"Guess she isn't planning to do her sweating at the gym tonight," BeBe said.

"Guess not," said Liv. "Though let's not jump to conclusions. It could be her son. No, someone said she didn't have children. Her nephew or . . ."

The man opened the door, and Grace stepped out of the car and into his arms. And into a major tongue-wrestling kiss. "Okay, not her nephew. Looks like we just confirmed the rumor we heard today. Grace Thornsby is having an affair."

"Euww," BeBe said.

"Yeah, I'm getting a pretty icky visual myself. Not that I have anything against cougars, but imagining Grace with anybody skeeves me out."

The man walked Grace over to the passenger side and held the door for her. Then he got into the driver's seat.

"You know," Liv said, "if it was this easy for us to find out where she was going, Phil Cosgrove probably already knew. So what was he doing sticking around playing Santa?"

"Maybe he wasn't investigating *her*."

"Hmm," Liv said. "It's possible. Clarence, maybe? Or anyone on that side of the green. Or an employee? Penny Newland?"

"Oh no. That would be terrible."

It would indeed, thought Liv. Penny did have a couple of hours unaccounted for before the tree lighting, and she wouldn't say where she'd been. What was she hiding?

The Mercedes turned right out of the parking lot.

"Now what? Do we keep following them?"

Liv deliberated. "It's tempting, but I think I have a better use for our time." She turned off the engine and opened the car door.

"What are you doing?"

"Going into the gym, want to come? With all this weather, I haven't been able to keep up my daily runs, and here we are at a fitness center. Maybe I'll sign up."

"Uh-huh," said BeBe and got out the other side.

The first thing that Liv noticed when she walked through the doors of Rock Road Fitness was the steam and the smell. Not your average Upper East Side health club.

The gym was small and minimal, painted a nondescript beige and finished in linoleum and industrial carpet. A few desultory Christmas decorations hung haphazardly around the sign-in desk. Rap music played through overhead speakers.

Several weight lifters were groaning under their barbells. And a few women in tiny color-coordinated workout suits ran on treadmills or went through circuit training with their personal trainers.

Liv walked up to the desk.

A young woman, buff and spray tanned, looked up and smiled her close-this-deal smile. "Can I help you?"

Liv smiled back. "I've been thinking about joining, and I think I just saw my old trainer leave as I was coming in. It would be great if I could work with him again."

"Let's see, would that be . . . She looked over a clipboard. "Jerry Esposito just left."

"Jerry. So it *was* him."

"Yeah, you probably had him at Jake's Gym. He was there before he came here. Unfortunately, he's already leaving, though I can set you up with Geordie. He's really good."

"I'm sure he is, but I was really hoping to get Jerry again. Do you know where he's going?"

"He's getting out of the business. Said his ship just came in, whatever that means."

Liv thought she knew exactly what he meant.

"I'll have to think about it."

"Well, don't wait too long. You want to get rid of those extra pounds before the holidays. And we're running a special this week."

Extra pounds? Liv was wearing a down coat. "Do you have a handout?"

The girl, sensing she'd lost a sale, reluctantly handed Liv a printed paper. "This lists our different programs. Just give us a call or come in and I can sign you up."

"Thank you," Liv said and hustled BeBe out the door.

"How did you learn to do that?" BeBe asked on a giggle.

"Many years of staying one step ahead of clients who tried to stiff me. Forensic event planning."

They walked back across the street to the car.

"So now we know who Grace is seeing. I wonder if Bill knows."

"You could ask him," BeBe suggested.

"No way. I'll mention it to Ted. He'll do the rest. In the meantime, why don't we swing by the Blue Boar on our way home and see if Grace's Mercedes is there."

Grace's Mercedes was not at the Blue Boar. And neither was anyone else. It seems the Blue Boar was closed Sunday nights.

Sunday. It was still Sunday, Liv thought and stifled a yawn. "I'm beat. We did what we could. Let's call it a day."

She drove BeBe back to the parking lot, waited until she started her Subaru, and then drove home as big fat flakes of snow began to fall.

Snow. At least five new inches of it. Liv leaned her forehead against the kitchen door. Snow. Monday. She was already exhausted. Not a good sign. Must be the letdown after all that planning for Santa's arrival and the Celebration of Lights. Not to mention the house tour, the mulled wine, and her late-night investigation of Grace Thornsby.

Liv was learning to love freshly fallen snow. In the city it stayed beautiful for about as long as it took to hit the ground. Before taxis, trucks, and traffic jams left the black of their exhaust fumes blanketing the surface.

Here, there was traffic, but it seemed the snow stayed fresh longer, especially off the main roads. Like in front of her carriage house. Neither she nor the sisters would take their cars out until after the plows came.

At least they'd gotten through the weekend before this latest accumulation, and if it moved through fast, the town could be ploughed out by the next weekend rush.

Liv was actually looking forward to Christmas. Especially if the Zimmerman sisters were going to cook. She hadn't spent Christmas with her family in years, but with her job, her parents enjoying retirement by nonstop traveling, and her siblings spread out over the country, it was impossible. She'd even considered trying to get back to the city, but since moving here, she'd always been too busy to leave, even for a weekend. Besides, most of her friends who could get time off headed for the islands. Which brought her mind squarely back to TAT and its tacky swimsuit-wearing Santas.

Something had to be done. They could survive one Christmas with plastic hula dancers, but come this time next year, Liv planned to have a tasteful store in its stead. One that stayed open all year.

Whiskey padded into the kitchen, gave her an accusing look, and crossed to the door. "I know it's early. But we have things to do. People to see. Snooping to report. And . . . you at least will be very happy."

She opened the kitchen door. "Ta-da."

Whiskey stopped at the open door, looked out at the drifts that covered the kitchen stoop, took a couple of warm-up prances, and shot out the door.

Liv watched, shivering as he tunneled through the snow, nose to the ground, like a fluffy white mole, creating crazy eights and dead ends across the backyard. Then he popped up, shook, looked back at her with the snow caked on his muzzle, and took off again for a tour of the Zimmerman's shrubs.

The snow was still cloaked in early-morning shadows. But soon it would be sparkly on the trees and softening the lights of the Christmas decorations. Liv made a mental note to contact the photographer to do some new "Christmas in the Snow" shots of the town for next year's brochure.

Her cell phone beeped. Somebody was pinging her already and it was hardly seven o'clock. Whiskey was still frolicking, so she picked it up on her way to the closet to get towels for cleanup duty once he came in again. She'd leave any outside cleanup until she was fully dressed.

The message was from a Manhattan costume shop. She read the text. *Sorry. Suits all out. May have one coming in Wed. Good Luck.*

Thanks to the Stitch in Time ladies, an appropriate name

if ever there was one, they had a Santa suit, and a very beautiful one. But it wouldn't hurt to have a backup—and not a rental one.

She might be able to afford one out of miscellaneous expenditures. Maybe Grace would be interested in selling the TAT suit. Since she wouldn't be needing it, she might sell it cheap.

Whiskey came to the back door. Barked. But when Liv opened the door, he ran off again.

"Sorry, bud. We don't have time to play today. Come on."

Whiskey stopped, facedown, rump up, tail in the air. He watched her until she stepped toward him, then took off again.

"Don't make me come after you." Of course that's just what he wanted. She was glad one of them was bright eyed and energetic this morning.

She crossed her arms over her nightshirt and frowned at him. He stopped, watching her. She felt her lips quiver. She fought the smile. It was so ridiculous. You couldn't make a Westie feel guilty. They were the princes of dogs. In their minds at least. She gave it up.

"Please?"

Whiskey bounded around another circle in the snow. Liv stepped back and started to close the door. Whiskey shot past her into the kitchen and proceeded to shake globs of caked snow from his body.

Liv jumped back but not before her feet and ankles were covered in pellets of packed snow.

She reached for one of the towels.

Whiskey immediately sat down and waited to be dried off.

"It's a good thing you're so cute and faithful, because that was not fun."

She left him with dry fur, a bowl of kibble and vegetables, and fresh water, while she went to the take a hot, hot shower.

He was waiting by the front door with his red bow tie when she emerged from her room a half hour later.

They walked down the driveway, Whiskey in his plaid doggie coat and bow tie, Liv in a new sweater, covered by a down jacket that came to her knees and snow boots that came to the top of her calves. She'd ordered a Tibetan hat with ear flaps, but she would be sure to stop by the Yarn Barn and purchase something for herself and for a few friends.

She wanted to get Ted and BeBe and Ida and Edna something special for Christmas. And a few things to send to her family. She should probably buy something at each of the stores. Well, as many as possible. She didn't want to show favoritism. Fortunately, Dolly's was the only bakery on the square, and the Buttercup the only specialty coffee store. But that still left a lot of stores to be patronized.

Actually, she'd have to take a day off soon and do some serious shopping.

She had just reached the street when Miss Edna stepped onto her front porch. "Liv, I hate to ask, but if you have time, could you or Ted drop by the library for me? Lola Bangs is holding a book for me. But only if you have time."

"Of course I will. It's only a block from town hall."

"Thank you. I'll get it when you come home tonight."

"See you then."

Liv and Whiskey walked down the middle of the street toward town. The sun was just peeking through the bare branches of the trees, turning them into confection. In the distance, snowplows began to rumble their way through the town. But here, everything was quiet except for the occasional plop of heavy snow from a tree limb as it hit the ground.

Within a few minutes they had reached the square, which sat like a big white iridescent blanket in the middle of town. Only a few solitary footsteps marred the untouched beauty of it. Around its perimeter, businesses were getting ready for the day, shoveling and de-icing the nearby sidewalks. A few people waved to Liv as she passed.

The Apple of My Eye was open for business. Dolly

always said her first duty was to get everybody going with something sweet every morning.

And Dolly was certainly succeeding with Liv. She hadn't been totally kidding last night about joining a gym.

She wasn't the first customer this morning. Quincy Hinks from the Bookworm was drinking a cup of coffee from the Buttercup and talking to Dolly while she filled a bakery box with Christmas cookies.

"Morning, Liv," Dolly said. "Quincy here was just telling me that he saw Grace Thornsby going into her store this morning. She's planning on opening today. You'd think they would at least close for a decent period of mourning, even if that poor man was just an employee."

"Ha." The bookstore owner lifted his hand in a theatrical gesture, a copy of *The Pickwick Papers* sticking out of his tweed jacket. "Neither rain nor sleet nor a murder in our midst will stop the intrepid tasteless, and generally greedy, Thornsbys."

"Shh," Liv warned and looked around to make sure no one had come into the bakery to overhear murder mentioned.

"Liv, my dear, the whole town is talking about the murder. Isn't there anything we can do to rid ourselves of that unholy terror? It's a blemish on the block. I'll have to line my windows with the classics to counteract the effects of her kitsch."

"We're working on it. Unfortunately, it might not be until after Christmas before we can act."

"We'll see about that," Dolly said. "Janine stopped by this morning to get breakfast rolls for her real estate meeting. I don't have any use for people who call themselves locals then ignore our rules just to make money. And I told her so." Dolly smiled what Liv assumed was supposed to be a malicious grin, but Dolly just looked like Mrs. Claus. "I also charged her the tourist rate. Let her think about that for a while." She nodded and a wisp of hair fell out of her bun.

Quincy chuckled. "Maybe if we make Janine's life

miserable, she'll figure out a way to get rid of them. They must be in violation of some code. Lord knows we have enough of them."

"Even so, they would probably be given a grace period in which to rectify the infraction," Liv said. "But that's a good idea. I'll have someone look at the zoning codes."

Liv chose two gingerbread muffins. Dolly added a gingerbread man biscuit for Whiskey. "No sugar, no wheat. Let me know how he likes them."

Whiskey barked a thank-you, and they went next door to the Buttercup.

There were several people standing at the coffee bar, glued to their smart phones and laptops.

Sprawled at the only table, and looking like the kiss of death, was Chaz Bristow.

"You're up early," Liv said, surprised.

"Haven't been to bed yet."

"Ice fishing?"

"As a matter of fact . . . no. Here's your article." He held up a crumpled piece of newsprint.

Liv took it. Read. He had tweaked it a bit. Actually it was a lot better than her original one. The guy could write. There he was, slumped in his chair, rumpled and unshaven and looking like a Bowery bum, and the man could write.

"What?"

"Nothing. Thank you. This is really good."

"Spare my blushes." His tone was dry, ironic, maybe a little flattered? Nah. He was half-asleep.

"Can't you just say thanks?"

"Thanks." He went back to drinking his coffee.

Liv went up to the bar to get her order.

BeBe rolled her eyes.

"How long has he been here?" Liv whispered.

"Twenty minutes." BeBe leaned even closer. "I think maybe he was waiting for you." She pulled a face and batted her eyelashes.

"Uh-huh."

BeBe started the steamer and for a minute, screeching

blocked out all other sounds. She filled the cup and leaned closer. "I thought you'd never get here. The paper is off the windows of TAT. I think they plan to open today."

"I heard."

"I can't believe all the stuff we found out yesterday. Are you going to tell Bill?"

Liv nodded and surreptitiously slipped a finger to her lips.

BeBe nodded, lowered her voice. "But I want to hear everything that happens today."

Liv nodded but didn't promise anything. She had no idea what new craziness might be waiting for her in the next twenty-four hours. The last twenty-four had been wild enough.

"Call me."

"I will, but don't say anything."

BeBe shook her head. "My lips are sealed."

Liv took her drinks and turned to go—right into Chaz Bristow.

Chapter Sixteen

....

Liv stepped to the side and headed to the door.

Chaz was there to open the door for her.

She narrowed her eyes. "Thank you." And stepped out into the frigid air, practically having to drag Whiskey away from his newest favorite person.

"You look like a lovable yeti in that parka, or Admiral Barbie Byrd in the Arctic," he said, falling into step beside her.

She smiled. "You look terribly underdressed." He was wearing some kind of canvas car coat.

This earned her a full-blown Chaz grin. "So what were you and BeBe whispering about?"

"Girl talk."

"Right. Girly stuff that the sheriff would be interested in."

"I thought you gave up being nosey when you gave up investigative reporting."

"I'm not nosey. Just curious."

"No you're not. Remember? You're not interested in helping."

"True. But I don't want to have to run to the rescue if you do anything stupid."

"Excuse me?" She turned on him, and her foot slipped.

Chaz grabbed her and put her back on her feet, wrestled with a smile. "See? Maybe you need some spikes on those alpine boots you're wearing."

He was wearing running shoes; the right one had a hole in the toe.

"Sticks and stones." She slid to a stop. They were in front of the Trim a Tree store. The windows had been denuded of all paper and even the wreaths that had tried to make the obvious less so. Too bad, because they might have gone a long way in camouflaging what was now on display. Hanging behind the surfing Santas was a row of tasteless T-shirts alternating red, green, and white.

"Are you kidding me?"

"And we thought Janine was baiting you. Grace is going to give you a coronary."

"Not if I get to her first."

"Easy."

"I'll easy her. Does she think this is Coney Island? Those are totally inappropriate. We're a G-rated town. And those T-shirts are pushing the boundaries. Hold this." Liv shoved her bakery bag, coffee tray, and Whiskey's leash at him and knocked on the door.

No one answered. She knocked again. Whiskey growled impatiently.

"Not there," Chaz said. "You'll have to come back later— with reinforcements." He laughed, tried to stop, couldn't do it.

Liv knew it was an act to annoy her, and she *was* annoyed.

She lifted her chin, wrestled her food and leash from him, and hurried toward town hall.

"Okay, okay, I'm sorry. But you're so—"

"So help me, if you say 'cute,' I'll—"

"I won't say it."

"Fine." Liv started walking again.

Chaz caught up and again matched his stride to hers. "But you are."

She marched up the steps of town hall despite Whiskey's insistence on exploring a torn paper bag that had frozen in the snow.

Chaz opened the door for her.

"Don't you have a nap to take or something?"

"Yep. Once I listen to you tell Ted what you and BeBe did yesterday."

"What makes you think I'm going to tell Ted?" She stopped on the mat to stomp the snow off her shoes.

"Because he'll find out anyway."

"I know you're not going to help solve the murder, even though you have skills that Bill could use. So why take the time and energy to listen to me gossip?"

She reached for the door to the outer office.

"I told you why. I meant it."

It took a moment for his words to sink in, then she dismissed them and opened the office door, dropping Whiskey's leash at the same time. Whiskey dashed between their feet and into the office, where Ted was waiting for their morning solfege.

Today he was wearing a green V-neck sweater with a reindeer head in the center, its two big antlers spread against his chest. Above the sweater, a white shirt collar was finished off by a red bow tie.

Liv groaned. *Matching outfits.*

"For we like sheep," Ted sang.

Whiskey skidded to a stop and sat at Ted's feet. "Ar-roo-oo-oo."

"What the—?" Chaz said.

"Welcome to my world," Liv said as she put down food and drinks and began shedding her coat.

"Like sheep," Ted crooned.

"Aroo-oo-oo," Whiskey sang.

"We need to do something about the TAT window," Liv yelled above them.

Ted saw Chaz. "Oh, good. This choir needs a baritone."

Chaz looked at Liv, then opened his mouth. "For we like . . ."

Ted joined in. "For we like."

"Ar-roo-roo-roo," sang Whiskey.

"Oh my Lord." Liv clapped her hands over her ears and yelled, "In case anyone is wondering, I know who Grace Thornsby's lover is."

She marched into her office and slammed the door.

The caterwauling in the outer office stopped abruptly.

Her door opened, and two human heads appeared in the opening, followed by one shaggy white one at knee level. The three of them came inside.

Ted brought in the coffee and muffins and put them on the desk. Chaz pulled up a chair, and Whiskey retreated to his doggie bed.

"I'm flattered," Chaz said and nodded toward the clean, folded *Clarion* that Ted had put on the tray.

"Have to keep you honest," Liv said, but her heart wasn't in it. She needed to do some damage control, not be sitting here fencing with the reprehensible newspaper editor.

"It's a good article," Ted said.

"I already thanked him." Liv reached for her coffee.

"Now, what's this about the TAT windows?" Ted asked.

"Forget the damn T-shirts," Chaz said. "Who is the lover?"

Liv glared at him. "You are such a girl."

Ted chuckled.

Chaz lifted one eyebrow, and Liv could read his thoughts as sure as if he'd said them aloud. She wouldn't be taking his challenge. She had enough problems to deal with.

"Liv, doll, you've gotta learn to go with the flow a little bit. I bet Ted saw those shirts on his way to work."

"Actually I did. I left a message for the mayor for when he comes in. I figured you'd want it taken care of."

Liv stared at her assistant. "Thanks." She tried not to

smile but couldn't stop it. "You might want to consider trading in that reindeer sweater for a red cape."

"And tights," Chaz added.

"I'll keep the sweater, thank you. And the tie. I'm thinking about working up an act." Ted sat back, complacently eying his muffin.

Chaz yawned.

"Don't you want to go home to bed?" Liv prompted. She really needed to discuss things with Ted, and she didn't need a running commentary from Chaz.

"A tempting proposition." Chaz leered at her.

Ted suppressed a smile.

Liv silently fumed but didn't rise to the bait.

"I'm going, but not until you tell me what you and BeBe found out. Or more to the point, how?"

"Why?"

"You both sound like journalism students," Ted said. "Who, where, when, and why. So, Chaz, stop goading Liv and let her tell it her way."

"Who, where, when, and why," Liv repeated almost to herself. "We know who or at least half the who, and the where, and pretty much when. We just need the why, and that will lead us to the other who."

"To Cindy Lou Who down in Whoville," Chaz said in a deadpan delivery.

"Grr," Liv said.

"Grr," echoed Whiskey from his doggie bed and scrambled up to come stand guard at Liv's feet.

"Good dog."

Ted and Chaz burst out laughing, and Whiskey raced around the desk several times before returning to his bed and going back to sleep.

"Good to know you have protection," Chaz said.

"Stop it, both of you," said Ted. "It's Christmas, and neither you two spatting nor Grace Thornsby and her tasteless decorations are going to dampen my Christmas spirit." He bit into a muffin. "Hmmm, good."

"And murder?"

"Well, there is that. But I refuse to be kept down."

"Good for you." Chaz settled in his chair like he was planning to stay.

What did he want? She didn't have time to bother with him; there were problems trying to derail her Christmas events.

"That store has been nothing but trouble." Liv took a sip of her latte, savoring its warmth as it went down. "You know, at first it didn't seem so bad. Are we making too much out of it? You see that stuff all over the streets of Manhattan—well, on some of the streets. But that's just the point. It doesn't fit the reputation we want."

"There is the little thing of free enterprise," Chaz pointed out.

"It cheapens everything we try to provide. You can go to the mall and buy that kind of stuff."

"Hmmm."

"Am I being closed minded?"

Ted wiped his mouth with a napkin. "In the scheme of anything goes, maybe. But when it comes to how we want our town portrayed? Not so much."

"Maybe we could help them relocate. Somewhere like Atlantic City or Las Vegas."

"Yeah. Well, don't let it ruin your day," said Chaz behind sleepy eyes. "It will all work out."

"Can I quote you on that?"

His eyes opened and a flash of appreciation lit them before he punctuated it with a jaw-cracking yawn.

Liv heaved a sigh. "If I tell you what I found out this weekend, will you leave so Ted and I can get some work done?"

"Sure."

Ted polished off his muffin, brushed his fingers over the tray. "Hit us with it."

Liv narrowed her eyes at him. Ted was always the first with any gossip. Did he already know about Clarence's financial woes and Grace's man candy?

"First of all, Frank Salvatini saw a person dressed as

Santa going down the alley Friday night before the . . . murder."

Ted nodded. "Roscoe called me."

Of course.

"And Clarence Thornsby is going belly-up."

"Uh-huh."

"And Grace Thornsby is having an affair."

Ted nodded.

Chaz snorted a laugh.

"With a guy named Jerry Esposito from the Rock Road Fitness Center."

At last she had their full attention.

"You have been busy," Ted said.

"Are you sure you didn't know about Grace already?"

Ted shook his head. "Figured she was up to something. She rented a holiday cabin down by the lake. She isn't sharing it with Clarence, so it stands to reason. But no, are you sure about this Esposito fellow?"

"Yes. Well, at least from his greeting I'd say more was to follow." She carefully avoided Chaz's eyes, which were suddenly wide awake, not with interest so much as amusement.

"And you found this all out how?" Ted asked.

"BeBe and I overheard some women talking when we went on the house tour yesterday. They knew someone who had seen Grace at the Blue Boar, with a man who wasn't Clarence. A much younger man."

"And?"

"We left the tour at my house, and later I drove BeBe over to get her car and we saw lights in TAT. Then a little later"—*like an hour or so of peeking out the back door*— "Grace got in her car and we decided to follow her."

Chaz groaned.

"To the Blue Boar?" Ted asked.

"We thought it was worth a try, I mean since we were there. It could be helpful." She gave Chaz a look that dared him to interrupt. "She didn't go to the Blue Boar, but picked him up at the gym."

"And then you followed them to the Blue Boar?" Ted asked.

"They never went to the Blue Boar."

"Then how did you find out the guy's name?" Chaz asked.

Liv swallowed. "I went into the gym and asked."

Ted clapped his hand to his forehead. "Oh my God."

"You idiot," echoed Chaz.

"Liv, you've got to stop putting yourself in harm's way," Ted said.

"Leave it to the damn experts," Chaz said.

"One of the experts is sitting on his butt in my office. And as far as it being dangerous, I had backup."

"Who?" asked Ted.

"BeBe."

"Oh God, this is more hilarity than I can take this early on a Monday. I'm going home to bed." Chaz heaved himself out of the chair, hooked his jacket with one finger, and walked out of the room laughing and mumbling to himself.

"He did that on purpose," Liv complained as Ted began cleaning up.

He put the plate with Liv's muffin in front of her. "Eat."

"He acts like everything is one big joke."

"Coping mechanism, is my guess."

"Why? What do you know?"

"About Chaz? Nothing more than you do. He came a couple of years ago to run the family paper. He was an investigative reporter in LA before that. From all reports he was a damn good one."

"So what happened?"

Ted shrugged. "He came back to run the paper."

Liv was sure there was more to the story than that. At least she hoped there was.

"He refuses to use his experience and skills to help Bill, and yet he keeps hanging around."

Ted grinned, shook his head. "I think he's more concerned for your safety than helping Bill catch a murderer."

"Mine? Oh please, he doesn't strike me as the Sir Gala-had type."

"Oh God, no. I was thinking of the courting ritual of the—" He broke off, smiling.

"Of what?"

"Nothing. I'm glad you went on the house tour yesterday. Not just for the info but to show your support and be a presence." He picked up the tray. "And, that means I don't have to go.

"But one of us does need to drive out to Dexter's Nursery to meet the SPCA guy who's coming to check on the reindeer and make sure everything is to code, though I'm sure it will be. Dexter's has housed these reindeer for the last four years. He knows what he's doing, but all we need is some PETA person picketing because we didn't do enough inspections. I've got my car, so I can do that if you want to go over to Santa Village when Hank goes on duty, just to keep tabs."

"Works for me. I have to pick up a book for Miss Edna at the library, then I'll go check on Hank. I'm holding my breath that nothing happens to him or his Santa suit. I'm still planning to buy an extra suit. Now, if I just had a backup Santa."

"That's my girl, plan for every contingency. I'll take Whiskey with me, if that's okay."

"So you can get more practicing in? Fine, but don't feed him."

"Call me if you need anything. Come along partner." He picked up the tray. Whiskey looked at Liv.

"Go ahead."

Ted left the office chuckling; Whiskey trotted after him.

The Celebration Bay Public Library was a one-story brick building dating from the fifties. Its windows and eaves were framed with white wood in need of a coat of paint. Liv knew from the sisters the budget had been stripped to the bare bones like at so many libraries, and it stayed open only three days a week, with shorter hours.

Liv walked into a large room with stacks and stacks of books. There were already a number of people reading in the easy chairs or sitting at one of the four computers.

A woman about the same age as the Zimmerman sisters sat behind the circulation desk, a shawl draped over her cardigan sweater. Tortoiseshell glasses attached by a black cord magnified her blue eyes. It had to be Lola Bangs, the head, and Liv was guessing only, librarian.

Liv introduced herself, and Lola got the book from under the counter. "It's already checked out," she said. "It's such a shame about that poor Mr. Cosgrove."

"Yes, it is."

"It's hard to believe. He came in several times just last week. Nice man."

Liv, who was reaching for the book, stopped.

"He was here?"

"Oh yes. Sat at that computer right over there. Number four." Lola Bangs looked sadly at the one unused computer. "You know I'm seventy-six years old and I knew more about the Internet than he did. Had to have help accessing it. Can you imagine?"

Liv shook her head. Phil Cosgrove here at the library. On the Internet. It could be totally unrelated. "And you had to help him?"

"Oh, I didn't mind. I like to be able to help people who come here."

"I'm sure he was appreciative."

"Oh yes, he was trying to access the *Chicago Tribune* archives from years ago, but the poor man didn't have a clue."

"Sounds interesting."

"He certainly thought so. Three days in a row he read that paper, took notes, and made some copies. I asked him if he was writing a book. Thought he might be a history buff.

"He said he might one day. And I said if he did, we'd have a book signing right here because this is where it all started."

"That would be exciting," Liv said, thinking fast. Was Phil Cosgrove just passing the time between Santa shifts, was he a history buff? "What was his . . . topic?"

"He didn't say, but he was looking at articles from nineteen sixty-nine when we had all that unrest in the country over the Vietnam War. And that terrible man who killed the president. And we landed on the moon. So much happened that year. But I remember he was looking at April, because it was around Arbor Day and the library always does a special Arbor Day presentation.

"All those terrible riots, such a depressing topic. But men like those kinds of things, history and war and such."

"I guess," said Liv. "When was he last in?"

"Last Friday morning." The librarian sighed. "He seemed awfully pleased with whatever he'd been reading. I told him that we were closed on the weekends, but he said that didn't matter, he'd found what he wanted. I guess it was a good thing he left happy. Didn't know it was going to be his last day on earth, poor soul."

"Did you tell Bill Gunnison about this?"

"No, do you think he would be interested? I heard that Mr. Cosgrove was killed in an attempted robbery."

"Well, it might not hurt. At least that would give the sheriff an idea of what he did that day."

"Oh dear, I suppose I should call over to the station." She handed Liv the book. "Merry Christmas, dear."

"Merry Christmas, Ms. Bangs."

Liv didn't stop by the office. Since Ted's parking slot was vacant, she headed to the square. She needed to mull over the new information about Phil Cosgrove. It was out of her hands as long as Ms. Bangs actually called the sheriff. Maybe she should just mention it. But she just couldn't figure how something that happened in 1969 could be linked to Cosgrove's murder. Maybe he *was* just a history buff. She'd have to look it up later. She was kind of vague on American history, and she didn't like reading about war any more than Lola Bangs.

There was a line waiting to see Santa. But there was no Santa. The sign said he'd gone to feed his reindeer.

"What's going on?" she asked Joss Waterbury. "Where's Hank? He should have been here twenty minutes ago."

"He was," Joss said from behind the cider counter, where a toasty heat emanated from a space heater. Liv made a mental note to have Fred get someone to check all the wiring in Santa Village.

"Please tell me he isn't sick." Please don't let her have to start looking for a replacement Santa now. Though she would first thing tomorrow, just in case.

"He got a phone call from Jason Tully."

"Jason Tully?"

"The young man who's seeing Penny Newland."

"Right. Why did he call Hank?"

"He's staying out at Hank's, saving money so he and Penny can get married. Which everyone is hoping will happen soon." Joss gave her meaningful look. "Anyway, he said there was some flak over at that darn Trim a Tree place. Jason's dad and Hank were in 'Nam together. Hank's always kept an eye out for the boy. He got the call and off he went."

Liv blinked. That was the second time today someone had mentioned Vietnam. "Do you know what the flak was about?"

"I didn't hear. That's all I got from Hank before he told me to put up the sign and he marched over to the store. I called Bill Gunnison. I didn't like the look on Hank's face."

Joss's brows dipped into a frown. "That place has been nothing but trouble since it opened. We should've found a way to save the Newlands."

It wasn't the first time she'd heard that. They couldn't afford to let businesses keep failing. Liv had already begun formulating a merchant's assist plan. She just had to find funds to support it and someone to run it.

"Thanks. Hold down the fort."

Liv cut through the park toward TAT. She might be

poking her nose into police business, not leaving it to the experts, and she might be putting herself in harm's way, but this situation was wrecking her event. And Liv had had just about enough.

She opened the door to TAT, marched inside. And stopped.

Oh Lord. Déjà vu.

Chapter Seventeen

Bobby Newland was howling, face red, nose running. He was clinging to the leg of a lanky young man whom Liv recognized as Jason Tully, who had an arm protectively around Penny's shoulders. Penny's face was as colorless as her son's was red. She leaned into Jason as if he could hold her on her feet.

"You leave her alone," Jason said between clenched teeth. His cheeks were slashed with heat.

"She's a thief," Grace yelled back, gesticulating with both hands. The glass in her heavy bracelet flashed like Christmas, and Liv had to fight the urge to duck when Grace's arm flailed in her direction.

"I'm not. I didn't," Penny wailed, and covered her face with both hands and sobbed.

Jason squeezed her tighter.

"You're a nasty old . . . witch," Hank roared. "The way you traipse around town doing God knows what instead of watching the store, anyone could have come in and helped himself to the cash register. Hell, he could have helped himself to everything." He snatched a golf-club-wielding nutcracker from the counter. "And he would be doing us a favor!"

Grace grabbed for the nutcracker. "Put that down. You were probably in on it with them. I'll see the three of you in jail."

"Wait just a minute," Jason cried. He pushed Penny toward Liv and stepped toward Grace, knocking Bobby on his little butt. The child let out a fresh round of wails, and Penny scooped him up.

Grace stepped back. "Don't you threaten me, you piece of white trash. You neither, Hank Ousterhout. You big bag of air."

"What did you call me?" Hank lunged at her, knocking Jason aside. "I oughta ring your neck." Hank reached for her.

"Stop it!" Liv yelled in her shrillest voice.

Four faces turned toward her. Even little Bobby stopped crying and sniffed.

No one had even noticed Liv entering the store.

"Stay out of this, Ms. Montgomery."

"I have no intention of getting involved, Hank. This is a peaceful town with a lot of tourists, and you will not, any of you, disrupt this holiday season. Is that understood? Now, will you all calm down, or do I have to call the sheriff?"

"I already called him," Grace said. "Taking his sweet time about getting here, too."

"You can't prove Penny stole anything," Jason said defiantly.

"Why? Because you did it for her? I'll see both of you in jail."

"Over my dead body," Hank roared.

Liv slipped her computer case off her shoulder and put it out of harm's way. Then she fished her cell phone out of her purse. It wouldn't hurt to give Bill Gunnison a follow-up call. She left a voice mail; then she called Ted.

"Just got back, I'm on my way," he said.

Good. Between Bill, Ted, and her, they should at least be able to restore the peace. She didn't want to believe Grace's accusations. The Newlands had enough problems without their daughter being arrested for theft. Was she so desperate for money that she'd resorted to that?

"Now, nobody talk, just stay where you are until Bill gets here."

As Liv returned her phone to her coat pocket, the front door opened and Bill Gunnison walked in. He stopped just inside the room and gave the group an appraising look.

No one but Liv even acknowledged his entrance, just continued to stare daggers at each other.

Bill came to stand next to Liv. "What's all this about?" he asked.

The question galvanized Grace into renewed fury. "Those two pieces of white trash stole money from me."

"We did not."

"She's just causing trouble like she always does," Hank said.

Bobby began to cry again.

Bill rolled his eyes and pulled Liv aside. "Do *you* know what's going on?"

"Grace is missing some money. She's accusing Penny and Jason of stealing it. That's all I know."

"Hell, then I'm waiting for backup, because I'm not even going to attempt to question these people in the state they're in."

"I called Ted. He's on his way."

"He'll do. Actually, he'll probably fare better than my young officers will. But I have a feeling I'm going to need another squad car. That woman. I wish she'd just leave well enough alone."

Liv wished Grace would just leave. Period.

"She did it," Grace said, waving that tacky bracelet at Penny. "I told Clarence we couldn't trust her. And after all we've done for her and her family."

"What?" demanded Hank. "You cheated them out of their business, and you're paying their daughter slave wages as if that will make up for it. What's wrong with you? What did they ever do to you?"

"We were doing our Christian duty toward the family by helping them out financially."

"By *pretending* to help them while you were finishing them off. Thank God I don't have family like you and Clarence."

"Why is everyone blaming me?" Penny sobbed. "I didn't hurt Phil and I didn't steal anything. I didn't do any of it."

"Hush," Bill said. "No one's accusing you of killing Phil Cosgrove."

"Maybe not," said Grace, "but I'm missing a lot of money. Maybe she tried to steal it when everyone was at the tree lighting and Phil caught her at it."

"You shut your mouth, you vindictive witch." Hank took a menacing step toward her. Grace cowered back, but Liv was pretty sure it was an act. Pretty sure. Hoped it was.

At that moment the front door opened. *Thank God*, thought Liv. Ted must have run the whole way. She turned to bring him up to speed. But it wasn't Ted. Two middle-aged women stopped on the threshold, their conversation arrested as they took in the group.

Liv sprang into action. "I'm so sorry," she said, easing them backward. "They're not quite open. If you could come back this afternoon? Thank you." She managed to back them out of the door and saw Ted striding down the sidewalk.

Liv smiled at the ladies. Nodded. "Come back after twelve. Happy holidays."

Ted slipped past them into the store.

The ladies exchanged looks and scurried into the next store, no doubt to spread the word that all hell had broken loose at Trim a Tree.

Liv shut the door and turned the Open sign over to "Closed." If she could find the wrapping paper, she would tape it over the windows and start eviction proceedings. And worry about the consequences later.

"Thank God you're here."

"World War Three?" Ted asked, slightly out of breath, and surveying the scene.

"More like the revenge of the Harridan."

"Ooooh, that bad, huh?"

"Possibly. She's accusing Penny of stealing money."

"Oh dear."

Liv hesitated. "You are the only person besides Bill who isn't quick to defend her."

"Well, I hope she didn't do it. But you don't know when a perfectly nice, peaceful person will break and do something desperate."

Liv thought about it. Is that what had happened to the person who killed Phil Cosgrove? Had they panicked and lashed out? Or had the murder been premeditated, the killer waiting until everyone would be in the square before slitting the man's throat.

Liv looked at the floor where Grace was standing. The exact spot where they'd found Phil Cosgrove's body. Liv imagined she could still see bloodstains in the wood.

Liv shivered.

"You okay?"

She nodded. "Just not happy."

Grace turned on the sheriff. "I demand you arrest them."

"I'm not a thief. I didn't take anything," Penny sobbed.

Bobby let out a wail and wiped his nose on Jason's pants leg. Jason lifted the child and bounced him on his hip. "You leave her alone, you old—"

Bill stepped into the middle of the combatants. "Calm down, everyone. It's Monday morning. People don't want to start their workweek with a bunch of hollering."

Hank roared. "Bill, you're not going to take the word of that—"

Bill held up both hands, almost as if he were fending off a physical attack, which was definitely a possibility, judging from the red face of the town Santa and the savage expression of his ex-wife.

"One person at a time. Grace, tell me what happened."

"She's a thief and she probably killed Phil Cosgrove." Grace pointed a finger like the Ghost of Christmas Yet To Come at Penny.

Penny shook her head. "It wasn't me, it wasn't me!"

"You leave her alone," Jason repeated. Bobby wailed.

"She's innocent," Hank yelled over the child's crying.

"Egad," said Ted. "It's mass hysteria."

Bill held up his hand again, trying to restore order. "I think we best continue this down at the station." Everyone moved at once. "Grace and Penny will be sufficient. I'll call the rest of you as I need information."

"Dang it, Bill. . . ."

"Hank, let's all stay calm. I'll talk to the two ladies and see where we go from there. Grace, can I trust you to drive to the station? Now?"

"Of all the—I can't leave the store. I have a business to run."

"Or you can ride in a squad car. Your choice."

"You can't—"

Bill reached for his radio.

"Oh all right, but I should send the town a bill for the inconvenience and business lost."

"Penny, you come with me."

She nodded, a disjointed movement that was heartrending. "Jason?"

"I'll come, too."

"Can you take Bobby home first?"

"Sure, honey."

"I'll drive them," Hank began, then looked down at his Santa suit.

"I can give them a lift," Ted said.

"Thanks, but I have my car," Jason said.

Hank looked surprised. "Fixed?"

Bill looked back and forth between the two. "What was wrong with it?"

"Brakes, back and front. But I had to get it done." Jason squeezed Penny and jostled Bobby. "I got some precious cargo."

"Musta cost a bit."

"Yeah, it did. That's why I haven't had wheels."

Liv shut her eyes. The boy seemed to have no idea where Bill was leading him.

Bill gave him a considering look. "I have to ask you, and don't take this the wrong way, but where did you get the money to pay for it?"

Jason's face flooded with color.

"Dang it, Bill."

"Sorry, Hank, but I have to ask. Where did you get the money, son?"

Jason shrugged. "I didn't want to take it. But—"

"There, you see, he's confessing," Grace said triumphantly. "It was the pair of them, together. And I insist you arrest them."

"Shut up, Grace." This from Bill and not Hank. "What do you mean, son?"

"Someone left an envelope with the money in Hank's mailbox. It had my name on it. It was just enough to pay off the garage and get my car back."

"Ha. A likely story," Grace said. "You can see he's lying."

Beside her, Ted stiffened. "That's enough, Grace."

Liv started. She'd seen her even-tempered assistant angry only once before, and that hadn't ended well.

Bill looked at Hank; Hank averted his eyes. Liv was sure this was the first he'd heard of the envelope or the money.

"Do you still have the envelope?"

Jason stuck his hands in his pants pockets.

Grace shrieked. "He's got a gun."

Liv was ready to smack the woman herself.

Jason's hands came up empty. "No sir, I guess I tossed it at the garage. Yeah, I chucked it in the trash can at the garage."

Bill pulled out his radio, talked quietly into it, sending a man to check Jason's story.

"What about the rest of the money?" Grace demanded. "There was over four thousand dollars."

"There wasn't that much. Just enough to get my car. I swear. I thought maybe it was from Hank, and he didn't want to let on he was helping."

Hank shook his head. "Musta been the Good Samaritans."

Liv glanced at Ted.

"A group of folks from the local churches who like to help out their neighbors. Anonymously."

"I didn't want to take it. I don't like being beholden, but at that point I would have taken any handout if it would help Penny and the Newlands out." Jason let go of Penny and hung his head. "I just can't seem to get anything right."

"That's not true," Penny said. "You're a good man, it's not your fault."

Hank stepped in front of the two. "They're not saying anything more without a lawyer present."

Grace sneered. It destroyed whatever residual beauty might have been hiding beneath her hard features and mean disposition. "That's practically a confession. I demand you arrest them both."

Bill let out a long suffering sigh. "No, it isn't Grace. You've done nothing but cause trouble since you returned to town. I suggest you go over the facts—and only the facts—before you make your statement."

"Huh. I suppose you're going to let those two off scot-free."

"No, I'm going to take them both with me."

"Bill, they've done—"

"Hank, stay out of this. I'm just going to take their statements and remove them from this environment. No need to worry any of the Newlands. There will be someone down at the station to see to Bobby."

He said it calmly, but Liv didn't doubt that she wasn't the only one who had added a silent "toxic" to the "environment" he was talking about. She knew she couldn't wait to get away.

Bill gave Grace a pointed look. "And, Grace, do not start spreading rumors that may or may not be true. You wouldn't want a lawsuit on your hands."

Grace sniffed. Crossed her arms.

Bill led the two young people and baby out the front door.

Ted grabbed Hank as he headed after them, motioned to Liv, and they went outside together, without giving Grace another look.

They stood on the sidewalk as Bill helped Penny and the baby into his cruiser. A crowd was forming, watching and wondering. Bill took one look and opened the front passenger door and motioned Jason in.

"Nothing serious, folks, baby just needs a ride home." He nodded to the group on the sidewalk and got into the car and drove away.

"The baby's not sick, is he, Hank?" asked a lady in a hunting cap and jacket.

"Just a little under the weather. Nothing to worry about."

"That new pediatrician in town is real good I hear. I hope Penny takes him over there and not to the clinic." The woman shook her head. "I wonder if she has insurance."

"We'll take care of him, don't you worry. Thank you for asking, though."

Liv looked at Hank. He'd gone from fiery bull to mild-mannered Santa in a heartbeat. Were these lightning-quick Jekyll-and-Hyde changes his normal behavior, or was it really just Grace that set him off?

The crowd dispersed. As soon as they were out of earshot, Hank said, "I don't care how much the Newlands need Penny. She is not going back to that store, if I have to hire them both myself."

Ted placed a sympathetic hand on the larger man's arm. "No, I don't think she should go back. But that could make things tight for the Newlands. I know they're depending on her income."

Hank shook his head. "Penny couldn't possibly steal. I don't care what Grace says, she's a good girl and shouldn't be subjected to that vile creature."

"Penny's just started working at the Buttercup," Liv said. "BeBe gave her a couple of shifts when she's not at TAT. Maybe we could piecemeal a salary for Penny from several merchants. Not ideal, but better than nothing."

"Anything to keep Penny out of that place," Hank said, watching the police car turn the corner.

"I couldn't agree more," Liv said. And as soon as they got Penny out, she'd start working on a way to get Grace out. "I know Nancy could use some help, she was just saying so, though I'm not sure how much she can afford. I'm sure there are others."

"I really appreciate it, and I know Penny will, too. You don't mind asking?"

"Not at all," Liv said, surprised. "But I think it would be better if we both go. Do you have time to stop for just a second on your way back to Santa Village?"

"Sure. I could do that. Do you think that might help sway Nancy to take Penny on?"

Liv thought Nancy would do anything Hank Ousterhout asked her to do. Liv was counting on it.

Chapter Eighteen

....

"Poor girl," Nancy Pyne said, looking with concern at Hank.

"So *Hank*," Liv stressed, "and I thought that you might be able to use her just for the Christmas rush."

Nancy looked around the store where two customers were burrowing through a pile of organic hand-dyed scarves.

"She already has a few weekend hours with BeBe at the Buttercup," Liv continued. "If you can use her a few hours somewhere, I'll see if any of the other merchants can add to it. That way, maybe she won't have to go back to TAT."

"She can't go back," Hank said. "Even if Grace would let her. She accused Penny of stealing this morning."

"She didn't do it, of course," Liv said quickly, and hoped she was telling the truth.

"Of course not," Nancy said.

Hank rumbled his agreement. "The Newlands and I would be real beholden if you could help Penny out, Nancy. Though not if you can't afford it. We completely understand. Don't want to put a hardship on anybody."

Nancy caved. "Of course I want to help. What are friends

for?" The look she gave Hank was a little pathetic. Hank didn't even notice.

"I might be able to use her for a few hours toward the end of the week, when traffic picks up." She cast a quick glance over to the young women who had totally wrecked her display. "Not an eight-hour shift, but something."

"That's great, Nancy, thank you," Liv said, already calculating whom to see next.

"Yeah, Nancy, that's awfully kind of you. But I knew you'd do what you could." Hank heaved a satisfied sigh. "Well, I'd best be getting back to the kiddies. Joss Waterbury's probably wondering where the heck I got off to."

He smiled quickly and headed to the back room.

"Thanks, Nancy," Liv said.

Nancy nodded slowly, but she was watching Hank's retreating back. "I just want to do my part. A girl in trouble needs friends. Penny's a lucky girl." She looked so wistful that Liv was moved to commiserate.

"You sound like you're speaking from experience."

Nancy sighed, only half aware of Liv's question. "I was pregnant once, when I was in college in Wisconsin. I lost the baby. Lost the boy. I lost a lot that year."

She watched until the door closed behind Hank, then turned back to Liv with a slight shake of her head as if dispelling a sad memory. "It was a long, long time ago. Water over the dam. I'll do what I can to help Penny. Let me know how things go."

"I will, and I'll be back in to do some shopping myself. I haven't even started my Christmas shopping."

The women came to the counter. They each had a scarf in hand. At least they were buying and not just being a nuisance.

"I think I'll catch up with Hank before he leaves." Liv went through to the back room, where Hank was standing in front of the mirror adjusting the Santa hat.

"Okay, that's a start. You go be Santa. I'll ask Miriam and some of the others and start working out a schedule."

"Thank you, Ms. Montgomery. Not everybody would take time out of their busy schedule to help out a poor girl."

"I'm glad to do it. It will help Penny and the Newlands, and it will make my job easier not having to deal with Trim a Tree every other minute."

Hank regarded himself in the cloudy mirror. "You know, Grace was something else when she was younger. Always had a malicious streak, though. None of us saw it. None of us boys, I mean. Not till it was too late, anyhow."

"Well," Liv said and stopped, at a loss for how to continue. *She sure fooled you?* Or, *She's made up for it now?* "I'm going down to A Stitch in Time to see if Miriam needs help. I'll let you know."

She left him still standing there. She felt a little guilty. She'd jumped at the chance to get Penny other work, not just to help the girl, but to clear the way for getting rid of TAT once and for all. Liv had her own motives, but why was Hank so intent on taking care of the girl? Maybe he was just a good soul like everyone said. Or maybe he had other reasons?

Miriam was de-icing the sidewalk in front of the fabric and quilt store. She broadcast a handful of pellets and waved at Liv as she came down the sidewalk.

There was a pile of de-icer at her feet.

"Aren't you getting a little carried away?" Liv asked, indicating the pile.

"Oh." Miriam hurriedly spread them out with the edge of her boot and moved closer to Liv. "Just between us, I'm standing out here waiting for the sheriff's men to leave. I just couldn't bear to watch. I hope they don't make a mess."

"They're in your store?"

Miriam nodded.

"Doing what?"

"Looking for box cutters. Which is ridiculous if you ask me. Of course I have box cutters, a whole drawer full. And I told them so."

"I would think that most merchants have them."

"They do. You need them to open stock and cut string,

break down boxes . . . a lot of things. But they've gone store to store looking for a murder weapon, I guess. The news has traveled like wildfire. No one is happy. They even emptied the Dumpsters and trash cans out back. We're all ready to lynch Grace Thornsby."

"Do people think she had something to do with Phil Cosgrove's murder?"

"I have no idea. I just know everybody would be glad to blame her for all our troubles. And I'm inclined to agree with them. I don't know what she has against this town."

Or against someone in particular? Liv wondered.

"Miriam. Did you know her when she was married to Hank?"

"Oh yeah. I've known her or at least about her since I was in school. Nobody liked her then. Well, she came from a poor family, and to our discredit we might not have been real nice to her—us girls anyway. But not because she was poor. She was always acting like she was better than us. Even dressed better than some of us, though no one knew how her parents could afford to buy her those things. Just plain spoiled and selfish and vindictive, even back then. And boy crazy. If you started seeing someone, she made it her business to steal him.

"Finally got her claws into Hank Ousterhout, made his life a misery. Such a kind, loving man. He would have been a great father, but she couldn't be bothered with children. Wrecked his life in that department."

Was that why he took such an interest in Penny and Jason, so he could at least be a surrogate grandfather? "Well, he's Santa to a lot of kids," Liv said, knowing that it sounded lame.

"I suppose that's some consolation. Listen to me carry on." Miriam glanced back at the door of A Stitch in Time. "I wish they'd hurry."

Liv did, too; she's almost forgotten her reason for talking to Miriam, and she didn't want to conduct business on the street with a distracted store owner.

"Thank goodness I didn't have any customers. Can you

imagine what they would have thought? But I can't stand out here forever. I think I'll go see if I can hurry them along."

She hoisted her de-icer bucket and went to the door. "Nice to see you, Liv. Or did you need something from the store? The Santa suit is holding up okay, isn't it?"

"Oh yes, it's wonderful. Actually, I came to talk to you about something else."

"Well, come on inside and let's see what's what. When you see these things on television, they really toss a place. But I told Officer Meese that if he left a mess I was going to complain to Bill, and then I was going to tell his mother. That did the trick."

Liv smiled. "I bet it did." Small-town life, where even the policemen have to answer to their mothers. She followed Miriam into the shop.

"So, is it true they arrested Penny Newland for theft? Well, I'll tell you right here and now, she wouldn't do such a thing, and if Bill Gunnison thinks she did, he ought to be run out of town."

Liv could hear police moving around in the back of the store. "Grace accused her, but I don't think anyone believes it's true." Liv was beginning to think that this wasn't the best time to be asking people to help out Penny Newland. What if she was a thief? Or worse, a murderer?

"Well, I hope she doesn't go back to that horrid store. Clarence was supposed to be helping the Newlands out. I heard he bought them out lock, stock, and barrel. And I ask you, where are those beautiful decorations they used to sell? Certainly not in Grace Thornsby's store."

"That is weird. I wonder what happened to them." And if they were collecting dust in someone's shed, Liv might be able to jump-start their business again.

"No telling. We all thought Clarence was going to keep the family business going, but, poof"—Miriam gestured with her fingers—"he sold them down the river."

"Do you know why? Did he think he could make more money with his current merchandise?"

"I don't know, and I don't care how much money he's

making, we won't put up with it, I'll tell you right now."
Miriam began straightening bolts of fabric. "You know, I
should ask Penny if she has time to make more of these
pretty Moravian stars she used to make for their shop."
Miriam indicated the counter where a plastic tree was hung
with glittering, three-dimensional paper stars.

"They're lovely," Liv said. "I would definitely buy some.
Penny made these?"

"Yes. I bought a bunch last Christmas, but people keep
trying to buy them. She folds strips of paper, I don't know
how, then dips them in wax and sprinkles them with glitter.
They're the prettiest things, aren't they?

"I could sell all she made, but I don't suppose she'd have
the time between working, and taking care of her father and
the little boy."

"Well, actually . . ." Liv told Miriam about what had happened at Trim a Tree. And how Hank was determined that
she not go back.

"I'm inclined to agree with him," Liv said. "Nothing
good can come of it."

Miriam sighed. "That's for sure."

"I told him I'd see if I could get some of the merchants to
take her on part-time and patch together a job for her. I suppose
we should wait to see how this accusation pans out. Penny is
already working a few hours for BeBe at the Buttercup, and
Nancy at the Pyne Bough said she could give her a few hours
a week. I'm not even sure if Penny would want something like
this, but I thought she should have an option."

"That's very thoughtful of you, Liv. Let me think. If she
can do nights, I can have her help out with the craft classes.
Then if that works out, I might be able to give her some
more hours closer to Christmas."

"It's a start." Liv rummaged in her bag for her phone and
wrote down Miriam's offer in the notes section.

"That's clever. You keep all your notes in your phone?"

"Yes, it makes life a lot easier and my bag a lot lighter."

"Too complicated for me. I can barely text my
grandchildren."

Liv clicked out of notes and shut down her phone.

A shout from the back made them both jump. Miriam nearly dropped the fabric she was adjusting. "What on earth has happened now?" Miriam took off toward the stockroom. Liv followed.

Two officers were bent over the shipping table; Sergeant Meese was on his radio, but he shut it off when he saw Liv and Miriam.

"Uh, Ms. Krause. Do you recognize this?" He motioned her in, and the two men stepped aside. Lying on the table was a box cutter. It looked like all the other box cutters Liv had ever seen. But he wouldn't be asking unless there was something different about this one.

"It's a box cutter," Miriam said. "I have a whole drawer full of them, which I showed you when you came looking for them."

"Yes ma'am. But do you recognize this particular box cutter?"

"Oh for heavens' sake." Miriam reached for it.

Meese stepped in front of her. "Please don't touch anything."

A siren sounded in the distance, getting closer.

Miriam stared at the policeman, then turned to Liv.

The siren rose in pitch and volume, then warbled to silence.

"That sounded like it was right out front," Miriam said and ran from the room, followed by Liv and Officer Meese.

The front door opened and two more policemen stepped into the store. They strode straight toward the back.

"Didn't I tell you to come around back?" Meese asked.

"Sorry, but there was a truck in the way. Where's the perp?"

Meese groaned. "Man, this is so uncool." He turned on his heel and strode back to the stockroom, the two officers following behind.

Miriam turned to Liv, her eyes filled with confusion and dawning fear. "What's going on?"

"I'm not sure." But it didn't look good.

"Mrs. Krause?" Meese blushed, cleared his throat. "I'm afraid I'll have to take this in as evidence. And, um, ask you if you'd mind coming down to the station to talk to the sheriff?"

Miriam sucked in air. "Me? But why?"

The two newcomers stepped forward to flank the fabric store proprietress.

"These two officers will give you a ride."

One of the two officers in question pulled out a pair of handcuffs.

Miriam squeaked and began to shake her head.

Meese groaned. "Jeez, put those away. She's just a person of interest."

Miriam shot an anguished look at Liv.

"I'll call Bill Gunnison and tell him what's happened and to keep Silas Lark there," Liv told her.

"Silas Lark? Do I need a lawyer?"

"Don't worry," Liv said. "It's a party down there this morning. He's probably already at the station representing Penny Newland and Jason Tully."

They led Miriam toward the front of the store.

Liv gave Meese her hardest are-you-kidding-me look and speed-dialed the police station. While she waited for someone to answer, she followed the officers and Miriam to the front, where Miriam had stopped to give instructions to her assistant, who had just come in.

Bill was just as perturbed as Liv when she told him what had happened and promised to keep Lark there until Miriam arrived.

"Damned fool boys. Hauling her off like a common criminal." He rang off.

Liv went outside where Miriam was climbing into the backseat of the squad car. A crowd was forming on the sidewalk. Some were wearing outerwear, but just as many were in shirtsleeves, the siren having drawn them from work and coffee breaks. Liv saw BeBe and Dolly among the onlookers.

Liv went to meet them.

"What on earth is going on?" Dolly asked, vigorously chafing her bare arms below her puffed gingham sleeves.

Liv pulled them away from the crowd. "They found a suspicious-looking box cutter in Miriam's store."

"What's suspicious about a box cutter?" Dolly said. "We all have them. I have a drawer full at the bakery. I guess I'm lucky they didn't arrest me."

"I don't get it," BeBe said. "They've searched every store on the block. I figure they've probably found several dozen by now."

"I bet it's a false alarm," BeBe said. "If I were going to hide a box cutter, I'd dismantle it and spread the pieces to kingdom come."

"Well, don't say that out loud," Liv told her.

"It's just stupid," Dolly added. "First they accused Penny Newland, then Hank, now Miriam Krause. What next? Are they going to arrest everyone in the whole town until they run out of people? A silly waste of time. The killer's probably in another state by now."

Liv certainly hoped so, but she didn't place any great credence on it being true. But that wasn't what really worried her. Suspicions and concern were already making the rounds of the townsfolk, and now with this very public action by the police, the rumors would churn up to a new level.

She could imagine tourists leaving in droves. More stores closing instead of opening. She had no doubt that when the murder became public knowledge—public outside of Celebration Bay—people would not let their children visit Santa—a possible homicide suspect—much less sit on Santa's lap.

They had to stop this now, before it got any worse.

"I'll walk you guys back and pick up some fortifications for the afternoon," Liv said and pulled out her phone. She hit speed dial for the Events Office as they picked their way down the slushy sidewalk.

Ted answered.

"Hi, it's Liv. I'm on my way to the Buttercup. Did you order lunch? No? Well don't. I need you to do two things.

Pack up my laptop and pick me up at the Buttercup. Yes, in your car. I'll tell you when you get here."

Liv hung up as they reached the pedestrian passage, and she paused to look down the narrow walkway. Reimagined the day she and Ted saw Phil Cosgrove standing in the alley, talking on his cell, holding a cigarette while he read something from a little black book into his phone. Reporting his findings to the person who hired him?

And what had happened to his notebook? Did Bill have it? Did Bill even know about it?

"What's up?" BeBe asked, narrowing her eyes at Liv.

"Nothing. I just can't get a handle on this."

"Maybe because you're an event planner and not a detective?"

"Could be. But no one else seems to be having any better luck."

"True," BeBe said.

As they passed the Bookworm, Quincy Hinks came out. "What the heck is going on now? I just heard they took Miriam Krause away in a police car."

"They think they found the murder weapon," Dolly said.

"At Miriam's? Absurd. They're never going to solve this case if they keep arresting the wrong people." He pointed to his temple. "Little gray cells. That's what we need."

"Bill Gunnison is doing the best he can," Dolly said.

"I'm not saying he isn't. It's just with the new surge of tourists, for which we're grateful, I might add, we need better security."

"I'm working on it," Liv said.

"We can't expect Liv to do it all," BeBe said.

"Not saying she should. Just that we need the manpower to solve this before they send in the state again."

"Heaven forbid," Dolly said, holding herself tighter.

Liv knew he was right. What they needed was more investigators with experience—but not ones from the state. And she intended to enlist one in the next few minutes.

Chapter Nineteen

....

When Ted pulled his SUV up to the curb, Liv was holding a large paper bag and a tray of three steaming paper cups.

Ted reached over and took them from her as she climbed inside.

"Is my favorite dawg taking up coffee drinking?"

"No. I brought one for our host."

"And who would that be?"

"The editor of the *Clarion*."

"Ooh-kay. Does he know we're coming?"

"No. I want to catch him unawares."

Ted handed the tray back and pulled away from the curb.

"Where's Whiskey?"

"Sleeping it off in the office."

"Oh Lord, what did you feed him?"

"Nothing, Scout's honor, but we had a busy morning." Ted chuckled.

"Ted?"

"He thought the reindeer needed some exercise."

Liv closed her eyes. "And?"

"And nothing. A good time was had by all."

"And is Dexter Kent still talking to me?"

"Dexter laughed himself silly."

Ted found a place to park across the street from the *Clarion* office. Liv jumped out and walked ahead while Ted carried the provisions.

She knocked on the door. As expected, there was no answer. There was also no sign that read *Gone Fishing*. She knocked again, then tried the knob. The door opened. She stepped inside and motioned Ted in.

"You could get shot walking into people's houses unannounced," Ted said.

Liv stopped. "Chaz owns a gun?"

"I don't know, but lots of people around here do. Chaz!" he called. "You've got visitors."

"Tell her to go away," came a muffled voice from the back room.

Ted grinned, Liv didn't.

"Chaz, dammit, we need your help."

A groan.

"We're coming in."

Another groan.

Liv strode through the house, turning on lights as she went.

Chaz was sitting up on the sagging couch that took up a good portion of his "office."

He ran both hands through his hair, leaving it sticking up in all directions. "It must have been something I did in a former life. Do I smell coffee?"

Liv took a cup from Ted and stuck it under his nose.

He took it, flipped up the top, and took a cautious sip. "Yummm, thanks. It was nice of you to drop by. See you in the spring maybe."

Liv kicked his shoe, which he hadn't bothered to take off before going to sleep. "We need your help."

Chaz finally raised his head to squint at her. "Maybe it was something I did in this life. Or both."

"Oh stop it. They just found the murder weapon in A

Stitch in Time and took Miriam Krause to the police station to be questioned."

His eyes finally opened all the way. "Miriam Krause? Are you serious?"

Liv nodded.

"Numbskulls. Bill must've been dipping into the eggnog."

"It was Officer Meese. They've been searching each store for box cutters."

Chaz sputtered into his coffee. "Bet they only found, what, five hundred?"

"Well, they found one that looked suspicious."

Chaz held the cardboard cup in both hands and stared at the lid as if it were an ancient rune.

Liv held her breath, waiting to see if he'd respond with a quip or actually have something intelligent to say.

"You should really let Bill handle this."

Nothing she didn't already know. "I will. But he's taking too long and it's going to wreck Christmas."

Chaz nodded to himself. "You know, if you ever decide to give up event planning, you could work for the Hallmark Channel. *The Year They Wrecked Christmas.* A real tearjerker."

"Ugh. You're the most—I'm not giving up until you say something useful." She turned to the desk, which she barely recognized under the stacks of precariously balanced books and papers.

Chaz sank back on the couch and yawned.

In one motion, Liv swept her arm across the desk. Papers slid to the floor; a few sailed across the room to scatter at Chaz's feet. She was aware of Ted's mouth opening in surprise, and Chaz rearing up off the couch.

"Hey, what the f—"

She looked at him and smiled sweetly. "I needed a place to put my laptop."

"You made a huge mess."

"It was already a huge mess. Now, are you going to help, or am I going to have to clean off the rest of the desk."

"One day . . ."

"Promises, promises," Liv shot back, using one of Chaz's default answers, while she searched for a wall outlet. She found it by following the lamp cord through several stacks of newspapers and a tackle box.

When she stood up again, Ted had placed her cup by her computer and was holding the open bakery bag. Chaz reached inside, brought out a cookie shaped like a star. He held it up and batted seriously long eyelashes at Liv. "I don't know whether to put it on my chest or on the sidewalk outside." He bit off two of the points.

Liv looked to heaven, rolled an ancient desk chair over, sat down, and began shrugging out of her coat. Ted offered her the bakery bag, fighting a grin. She glared at him and took a cookie.

Chaz wandered over to stand behind her and look over her shoulder as she scrolled to the bottom of her spreadsheet. She typed in the date in the Date column, moved to the Event column and typed, "Murd. Weap. Fnd. ASIT." And underneath, "M. KR > Pol ST." Next to it, under "People," she typed in all the people pertinent to the event. She moved the cursor to the To Do column. She'd have to have Ted call Silas Lark and find out what he could from the lawyer. She moved the cursor to the Outcome column, which was fairly empty.

"What's that?" Chaz asked, leaning so close she could smell cookies and coffee on his breath.

"It's Miss Ida and Miss Edna's lesson plan for solving a murder."

"They're not involved in this nonsense, are they? Just shoot me now."

"No. But they show more interest in helping than certain people who are in a position to expedite the investigation but refuse to cooperate."

"The leg bone connected to the—"

Liv clenched both fists, beginning to wonder if she'd come on a fool's errand. He just refused to do anything useful. But he could—if only he would. When she'd first met

him and found out he'd been an investigative reporter—and
a good one—she'd asked for his help. He'd blown her off
and had continued to do so ever since.

He was stubborn, but so was she. And she usually got
her way. Chaz Bristow didn't hold a candle to some of the
executive hosts or the mothers of the bride she'd had to deal
with.

"So," she said, "this is what we have so far."

She heard his breath quicken as he read. Finally he
reached past her and scrolled to the top of the document.
She had a brief moment of panic that he was going to delete
it, but he merely scrolled through the timeline: Finding the
body; Hank's bloodied Santa suit; Grace and Clarence's
argument in the alley.

Then he reached over Liv and he began to type. When
he moved away, she saw that under "Who Hired the PI?"
he'd written "Clarence Thornsby."

"Are you sure or just speculating?" Liv asked.

Ted moved to her other side and peered at the computer
screen. He let out a low whistle.

Liv gave the sleepy editor a speculative look. Was he
jerking them around or telling them the truth? "And you
know this how?"

Chaz sighed dramatically. "If you must know, I was up
in Plattsburgh the other day picking up supplies. And I happened to be in the neighborhood of Phil Cosgrove's office,
such that it is."

"I thought he was a one-man show?"

"He is—was. But his 'secretary'"—Chaz made air
quotes with his long fingers—"was there packing up his
files. She let me have a peek."

"Isn't that confidential?"

"It is, but I guess she figured since he wouldn't be working any more cases, it didn't really matter. Besides, I have
a certain je ne sais quoi."

"Right," said Liv. "How much did you pay her?"

Chaz sighed. "Fifty bucks."

"Why?" Liv didn't think he had two pennies to rub

together. Why had he paid that much for a little information he didn't care about?

"Why what?"

"Oh never mind. Did you learn anything else?"

"Only that Clarence suspected Grace of having an affair and wanted proof."

"Do you think Clarence was looking for excuses to divorce her? Why not just declare irreconcilable differences and call it a day?"

"Maybe she doesn't want a divorce," Ted said.

"Wants to have her cake and eat it, too," Chaz said as he reached into the bag for another cookie.

"Hmm," Ted said, frowning at the screen. "So Clarence sets her up in business close to where her lover works and hires Cosgrove to play Santa. But surely the lover didn't come into the store. Why not just have him follow her after work?"

"Good question," said Chaz.

"If the gossip is true that he's in financial trouble, maybe he was afraid Grace was going to shortchange him," Liv said.

Ted rubbed his chin. "Keeping the profits for herself? Possible. In which case, that scene about Penny and Jimmy stealing money could have been a ruse to divert suspicion. Interesting."

"It makes more sense than Cosgrove catching Penny stealing from the till and her killing him." Liv shuddered. "That just seems far-fetched."

"That's the problem with murder. It's often a crime of passion; people who are normally perfectly docile will suddenly snap, go berserk, and kill." Chaz glanced down at Liv. "Something you might want to remember."

"Me?"

"People also get killed for sticking their noses where they don't belong."

"But I don't."

"You don't mean to, maybe, but there's no guarantee that the killer knows the difference."

"Who do you think it is?"

"I have no idea."

"Did you tell Bill what you found out?"

"Of course. Did you?"

"Of course."

They both turned to Ted.

"What?"

"We've both told Bill what we know," Liv said. "What has Bill told you?"

Ted tried to look innocent, but he enjoyed knowing secrets as much as anyone. "You know Bill can't discuss the case."

"But that doesn't mean he didn't find a way to clue you in," Liv said.

Chaz laughed. "She's got you there."

"Well, not much. Actually, they don't seem to have a real lead, if I'm reading between the lines correctly. They sent Hank's Santa suit off for analysis where I'm sure it sits languishing in an evidence bag on a back shelf. The murder of an ersatz Santa in a small town is not a high priority." Ted paused. "Let's see. They've ruled out Grace for the moment, since the boyfriend says she was with him."

"So Bill guessed Clarence was lying about her being with him?" Liv asked.

"Bill is slow and methodical, not stupid. Clarence didn't fool him any more than you, me, or Chaz. He called Clarence, and Clarence confessed. Says he was just trying to save face. Didn't want people to know she was cheating on him." Ted heaved a sigh. "As if anyone could give two hoots. Then Bill questioned the boyfriend."

"Maybe she wasn't with the boyfriend, either. He could be lying," Liv said.

"They usually are," said Chaz.

"Which leaves us with zip." Liv went back to studying her spreadsheet. "I remember A.K. Pierce saying—"

"The beefy security guy?" Chaz asked.

Liv gave him a look. "*He* recognized Cosgrove at the scene and later told me that Cosgrove made his living mostly by spying on people in divorce or money cases. Nothing big time."

"So divorce and money. Grace fits both those categories," Ted said.

"And Clarence," Liv added. "Has anyone asked Clarence where he was on the night of the murder?"

"What? You think he hired the guy and then offed him?"

Liv glared at Chaz. "It's possible. Maybe he found out something he wasn't supposed to."

"He was at a boat show," Ted said.

"And Bill checked his alibi?"

"Hell, Liv, I don't know."

"You know, Liv, the sheriff is not the only working stiff hired by the county police department. There are other people working on the case." Chaz gave her a condescending look meant to piss her off.

"I know that. I didn't necessarily mean Bill specifically, but generally, that is, as representative of the entire department."

Chaz looked at Ted. "Gotta love her when she gets all fancy on you."

Liv glowered at him. "I meant did anyone, *anyone at all*, check his alibi?"

"Don't look at me, I didn't."

"Ugh. You are so counterproductive."

Chaz burst out laughing. "See what I mean?"

Ted fought not to smile.

Liv closed her laptop.

"Fine. I knew this was a waste of time, but hope springs eternal. But not anymore. I'll just ask Bill myself."

"Aw c'mon, Liv. Don't get all pissy. We were just having some fun."

"A man was murdered. No one has assured me it won't happen again. And you sit there laughing." She struggled back into her coat, slipped her laptop into the case with trembling fingers. She was so angry she could hardly see. How could someone who was supposed to be good at what he does—did—be so uninterested?

She stopped in front of him where he'd returned to slouch

on the sofa. "So, Mr. Editor, if you wake up from one of your many naps and are bored, maybe you could look at some back issues of the *Tribune*, around Arbor Day nineteen sixty-nine. Maybe you can figure out what Phil Cosgrove was researching the day he was killed."

Chaz's eyes sparked momentarily.

She didn't give him time to come up with something snipey to say, but flounced out of the room. Immature and girly as it was, she didn't care. She needed to get away from this hyena before she burst from suppressed anger.

Ted caught up with her on the front porch. "What an exit."

"Don't," she said. "You may think he's funny, but I think he's selfish and coldhearted and—"

"And has seen things you've never dreamed of. Cut the guy a break, Liv."

Liv's anger dissipated like a leaky balloon. "You mean he's lost his nerve?"

"I mean he came here to fish and run a local paper. I think we should respect that."

Liv flushed. "I just wanted his expertise."

"You're not responsible for the investigation. That's why we have a police force. Bill is slow but he's thorough and he and his detectives will figure it out."

"I know. I know. I don't even want to think about the investigation." She and Chaz weren't that far apart in their feelings about that. "But the weekend is coming. Thousands more people will come pouring into town during the next few weeks. I—we need to be able to guarantee their safety."

"And the police and the security agency will."

"I still want to talk to Bill."

"Fine." Ted reached for his cell. "And then you can tell us both about Phil Cosgrove and Arbor Day nineteen sixty-nine."

Bill arrived at the Events Office thirty minutes after Ted and Liv. He looked tired, and Liv reminded herself not to be impatient. There were people at work on the case that she didn't know about. Fine. She got that. She just wanted to know . . .

How much longer it would take? *Fat chance of getting an estimate.*

If the town was safe from further attacks? *No one could promise that.*

If they'd hired enough extra security or if the extra presence was even doing any good? She could start there and hope Bill had some good news. Even if just a little.

She did.

He didn't.

"Not much to tell," he said. He leaned forward and rubbed his lower back.

Liv sent a silent prayer to the chiropractic fairies that he'd catch the murderer before his sciatica returned.

"I'm keeping Penny and Jason at the station until someone can corroborate Jason's story. I've got a call in to the Good Samaritans' office."

"You don't think Penny and Jason really stole Grace's money?" Ted asked.

Bill shrugged.

"Unbelievable," Ted said. "Grace just noticed this morning that her register had been cleaned out? Any normal proprietor would put the till in a safe overnight."

"Well, it wasn't the register," Bill admitted.

"Not the cash register?" Liv half stood from her chair. "Oh no."

Both men turned their attention to her.

"What is it?" Ted asked, looking concerned.

"We all just assumed. I am such an idiot."

"What?" Bill asked.

"When I got to the store that morning, Hank was carrying on about the cash register. But she was talking about one of those canvas money envelopes that the banks use, wasn't she?"

"Yes."

"I can't believe I missed that. Clarence Thornsby took it. I saw him drop it in the alley after the meeting."

"Why didn't you say so then?"

"I didn't think about it. It was dark. At first I thought it was a book, but it was soft like a bag. I even thought at the time he was taking money to the bank. It would be a perfectly normal thing to do: close the store, take the money to the night deposit. Besides, I was sort of caught up in the domestic drama."

Bill pulled out a notebook from the police jacket he'd hung over the back of his chair. "Go on. Tell me to the best of your recollection, everything you saw and heard. Everything."

Liv thought back. "I was checking the lighting in the alley, like I told you. Then Clarence and Grace came out of the shop, and I ducked behind the Dumpster. Well, I didn't want it to look like I was spying on them."

Ted made a noise in his throat and covered his mouth.

"I wasn't spying on them . . . not at first anyway.

"They were arguing." Liv closed her eyes, tried to bring back the scene: hunched behind the Dumpster, holding Whiskey close so he wouldn't give them away. "She accused him of trying to kill her. But more like she was pushing his buttons than being afraid.

"Then . . . she grabbed his arm and a folded newspaper he'd been carrying fell to the ground. He stepped toward Grace so that she had to step back. And he—I was afraid he was going to hit her, but that wasn't it. Now I realize he just didn't want her to see whatever had fallen to the ground."

Liv took a long breath while she conjured the scene. "When she turned her back to lock the door, he picked up the newspaper and the money pouch. Then he quickly slipped both of them inside his coat." She glanced at her laptop open on her desk. She'd just told Chaz and Ted about Cosgrove and the *Trib*. "Or maybe there was something in the newspaper he didn't want Grace to see?"

"Possibly both." Bill sat up suddenly alert. "Grace didn't see it?"

Liv thought back. "No, and I was so caught up in their argument; the implications of his actions just didn't register."

"Not your job. Then what happened?"

"Then Chaz grabbed me from behind and scared the bejeezus out of me. And I didn't see what happened next."

"Did Chaz see?"

"I doubt it. He was too busy being obnoxious."

This time Ted chuckled out loud. Bill shook his head and kept writing, but it didn't totally hide his smile.

Liv shot Ted a warning look.

"Sorry, but really, the two of you could be a stand-up comedy act."

"That was not my fault. If Nancy hadn't come out with that stupid cat, we might have learned a lot more. No. It is my fault. I know the importance of details and I missed them. Events have floundered on less inattention."

"Don't blame yourself. You shouldn't even have put yourself in possible danger."

"I didn't mean to. Do you really think he was taking the money without telling Grace?"

Bill shut his notebook. "I'll certainly be asking him."

"Why would he do something like that?" Liv asked.

He pushed himself up from the chair. "Possibly because he needed the cash. Clarence Thornsby just declared bankruptcy."

Chapter Twenty

·····································

"So why did he buy out the Newlands and open this store if he was in that much financial trouble?" Liv asked. "Hank said he cheated them, but it doesn't make sense."

"I think he genuinely wanted to help them," Bill said. "He's only a cousin, but around here family is everything."

Liv was learning that the locals stuck together, protected their families and their property. It took years and years before a newcomer was accepted totally. BeBe had lived here twelve years or so, and she was accepted. Nancy Pyne had been here only eight or nine years, and she was a member of the merchants' commission, though Liv suspected that if that bond was ever tested, blood and longevity would win out.

Liv liked it here. People seemed to like her; she had helped to rejuvenate the economy. But she wasn't so smug as to think they wouldn't turn on her if she didn't live up to their expectations or if she became a threat to one of them.

"Uh, Liv?"

"Sorry, Bill, my mind was off on a tangent."

"Did you think of something?"

"Nothing valid. But there is one thing, probably unrelated."

"Just tell me and I'll decide."

"Did you talk to Lola Bangs?"

"The librarian? Yes, she called to tell me that Cosgrove had been looking up things in the library."

"Newspapers," Liv said. "From nineteen sixty-nine. Maybe Cosgrove had left the newspaper for Clarence and he was trying to hide that as well as the money."

"A paper from nineteen sixty-nine?" Ted asked.

"No, of course not. But maybe there was something in a recent newspaper that made him look up those dates."

"More likely there was an announcement of his bankruptcy." Bill scratched his head. "I don't suppose that you were able to see which newspaper?"

"No. Sorry."

"Not to worry. I'll call Clarence then put someone on the newspaper angle. Well, I'd best be going." Bill lifted his police jacket off the back of the chair. "Sometimes this job gets to me, you know? Here it is Christmas and we should be full of good cheer, and I got a murder on my hands. And the worst part of it is, the victim had done all his Christmas shopping. His trunk was full of bags. He'd bought something from A Stitch in Time, the Bookworm, Bay-Berry Candles, the Pyne Bough, and a bunch of other places."

"An equal-opportunity shopper," said Ted.

Bill frowned. "Either way. He bought them for someone. And we don't even know who he was planning to give them to. Kind of depressing."

"That is sad. His family maybe?"

"Doesn't have any—not that he's in touch with, anyways."

"Girlfriend?"

"Not according to the secretary."

"So what are you going to do with them? Are they evidence?"

"Nope, but we can't release them until any potential heirs come forward. So they'll go into storage."

Liv tapped her pen on the desk blotter. "I don't suppose you can tell us what was in Cosgrove's notebook?"

Bill had been shrugging into his police jacket, but he stopped. "We didn't find a notebook."

Liv and Ted exchanged looks.

"Maybe he left it in his apartment or office," Ted offered.

"They were searched."

"TAT?"

"Thoroughly. What do you know about this notebook?"

"Ted and I saw him after we told Grace she had to deep-six the Santa. He was out in the alley smoking a cigarette and talking on his cell. He seemed to be reading out of this little black notebook."

Ted nodded. "I figured he was already looking for a new job. Of course, we didn't know he already had a job. Hmm. Maybe he was reporting in to Clarence."

"I'm telling you there was no notebook. I'll have to call Clarence and ask him if he knows anything about it."

"Maybe the killer took it," Liv said.

"I wasn't going to mention that," Bill said. "I should know better than to try to keep anything from you. You're always thinking, aren't you?"

Liv wasn't offended. "It's part of my job."

"You sound like you're not liking it much right now."

"I do. It's just, well, this looked like a holiday that after the Celebration of Lights would run itself. Now it feels more like a game of dominoes."

"Everything is running smoothly," Ted assured her.

Liv was barely listening. "Bill, did you book Miriam Krause for murder?"

"Of course not. Anyone could have put that box cutter in her store; there was a drawer full of them. There were traces of blood, which I figure you've already guessed, but one of her employees may have cut a finger. She's probably already back at work." A reminiscent smile passed over his face. "She was mad as all get-out, though, once the shock of riding in the back of a police cruiser wore off.

"I apologized and gave her a ride back to town. Don't worry about Miriam."

"I'm not worried, I was just thinking about dominoes."

"What?"

"Liv's mind works in mysterious ways," Ted intoned. "What about dominoes?"

"Well, think about it. Someone kills the private investigator. Penny was supposedly the last person to see him alive and the first person to see him dead. She's taken down for questioning. Hank's missing Santa suit is found in the Dumpster, covered in blood. He's taken down to the station. It's all circumstantial—isn't that what they call it?"

"Uh-huh."

"Then money goes missing from the Trim A Tree store. Grace accuses Penny and Jason. They're taken in for questioning.

"Then the possible murder weapon shows up in A Stitch in Time's stockroom. And Miriam gets taken in."

The tips of Bill's ears turned pink. "For questioning. Nobody got arrested. It's what the police do in an investigation."

"I know, Bill. I didn't mean to insult anybody. But doesn't it seem there are almost too many clues in too many places?"

Ted moved to the desk and propped one hip on the edge. "Something's not adding up here."

Bill sat down again, rubbed his temples. "Or too much is adding up. And the bitch of it is—oh, sorry, Liv."

She waved away his apology. "What I mean is, there are too many clues. Some of them might be coincidence, like the money. The suit and the box cutter may be involved in the crime. Cosgrove's notebook could be either. Which we won't know unless we—you—find it.

"If Grace found out he was paid to spy on her, she might have lashed out—" *Literally, with a utility knife.* Liv couldn't suppress a shiver.

"She might," Bill agreed. "But she has an alibi. Though I wonder if the boyfriend will change his story when he discovers that his cash cow just went dry."

"But how would she have gotten the suit and had the time

and the opportunity to plant the box cutter in Miriam's store? Someone was bound to see her."

"I don't know yet. But I'm beginning to think this wasn't just an unplanned act of passion or a robbery gone wrong. We might just have a cunning killer on our hands. Now, I'd better get going. I have a few more questions that I need to ask."

Bill left, and Ted and Liv spent a long moment staring at the door. Then Ted turned to her and said quietly, "I don't envy him."

"Me neither. Do you think he can find the killer?"

"I do. Like I've told you before: slow and steady. But he'll get the job done. Now, back to priorities. We missed lunch."

"Did we?" Liv checked her cell.

"And we're about to miss dinner. It's almost five. Let's call it a day."

Always alert, even in sleep, Whiskey jumped up and trotted to the door.

Ted chuckled. "How does he understand these things?"

"Just smart, I guess."

"Like his mistress. Come on, let's get out of here."

They packed up. Liv clipped on Whiskey's leash. Ted turned off the lights and locked the office door.

They stopped on the steps of town hall and looked out over the square. White lights twinkled in the trees. The shops and restaurants were open, and the warm yellow light coming from their greenery-framed windows was cheery, a soft glow of welcome in the middle of a black night. It looked like a peaceful Victorian town enjoying an old-fashioned Christmas.

Marred only by an old-fashioned murder.

"You all right?" Ted asked.

"Yes, just thinking."

"Well, stop it. Do you want a ride?"

"Thanks, but we'll walk. I could use the exercise. Maybe I *should* join the gym."

"Not until this murder has been solved, you don't. I'd rather you fat and out of shape than stalked by some steroid-pumped potential killer."

"Am I?"

"Not even close."

Liv sighed. "You know what the saddest part of this is?"

"What?"

"That poor man's presents left in the trunk of his car. He was planning to have a nice Christmas with someone, friends or family, or both. They won't even know what's happened to him. They'll never know he'd thought of them." Her voice cracked. She shook herself. "Maudlin."

"'Tis the season. Go home. Have some eggnog. Play some carols. Maybe Whiskey will sing along with you." Ted gave her a quick, one-armed hug.

"Thanks. See you tomorrow."

Ted touched the brim of his hunter's hat and took off toward the employee parking lot behind the building.

Whiskey tugged at his leash.

"Are you cold? I told you, you should wear those cute little booties I bought you." She stepped off the curb. "My feet are perfectly warm in my boots." Even if Chaz made fun of them.

Which sent her mind on a different path of what had happened to Chaz Bristow that made him so—she couldn't even think of a word. He was smart, good-looking, if a bit scruffy. He'd had what looked like a brilliant career. And he'd given it all up to come back to a little country town to run the family paper and report on 4-H fairs and fishing conditions.

Whiskey wasn't cold. He just wanted to climb a mound of hardened snow left by the snowplow and anoint the edge of a parking meter. Then he was ready to cut through the park toward home.

It was still early in spite of the dark. And as Liv passed the houses along her way, she thought of the families who lived in them. Some still at work, some retired, children and parents and pets, all getting ready for the holidays. Some grieving but carrying on for the sake of others, some giving in to despair—the loneliest time of the year for some.

She was feeling pretty down by the time she came to the

Zimmermans' Victorian, lit up like there was no tomorrow. She could see the big spruce through the front window.

Liv had a wreath, but the rest of her house was bare of decorations. And she'd forgotten to get a tree—again. No matter what happened during the night, first thing tomorrow morning she was going to do some Christmas shopping, then drive out to Dexter's to get a tree.

She unlocked the door, and Whiskey shot in, stopped on the mat to dry his feet, then trotted to the little kitchen at the back of the house. Liv fed him and changed into sweats and a sweatshirt that Miss Ida had bought for her at the Baptist Christmas Bazaar. Actually, Miss Ida had bought three—one for herself, one for her sister, and one for Liv. Liv's had angels on hers.

She hadn't worn it outside her own house yet. It was festive, but more like something Ted would wear.

She heated a can of tomato soup, poured it into a mug, and took it into the living room, where she curled up on the couch and reached for the remote. At least she had cable. Hearing the television, Whiskey trotted into the room and made a couple of attempted leaps to the couch.

Liv put down her soup and lifted him up. He waited for her to pull a throw rug over her feet and retrieve her soup before he burrowed a place next to her and settled down for a long winter's nap.

It only took once through the stations to find three holiday movies. The first sounded too sappy, the second, too sad, but the third seemed safe. A movie with Whoopi Goldberg as Santa Claus. That should lift her spirits and make her laugh. She was crying in the first three minutes.

Whiskey snuggled closer. He was used to her blubbering over movies. But tonight he must have sensed more than Liv's compassion for a fictional child who had stopped believing in Santa.

But she was soon rooting for Santa to make the adult believe again. Whoopi had just discovered that the Santa hat lit up when she wore it and was dancing around her apartment, when Liv saw a light of her own. The headlights of someone pulling into the driveway and stopping near her door.

Whiskey slid off the couch and raced to the window to peer out. A car door slammed; there was a knock at the door.

Whiskey ran to the door. His tail was wagging, but since he was Mr. Congeniality, Liv was taking no chances. She wiped her eyes, smoothed her angel sweatshirt, and peeked out the window. A Jeep. Just about everybody in town had a Jeep, truck, or SUV. But she recognized this one. It belonged to Chaz Bristow. What was he doing here?

Another knock.

She padded over to the door, running fingers through her hair.

"Who is it?" she called.

"Chaz."

"What do you want?"

"I've come a-wassailing," he said through the door.

Liv tried not to laugh; she was angry with him and a little depressed. But she was also curious.

She opened the door.

Chaz had struck a pose like the caricature of an Italian waiter, a pizza box held in his palm, a wine bottle in the crook of his other arm. The only incongruous part of the picture was the laptop case slung over his shoulder.

"And I brought pizza. No anchovies. No onions . . . in case I get lucky." He waggled his eyebrows at her.

She stepped aside to let him in.

"Did you eat already?" he asked, crossing the foyer, Whiskey gamboling at his feet. He put the pizza box on the coffee table, shed his canvas jacket and tossed it on a chair, and placed his laptop on her desk. He picked up her mug of congealed soup and made a face. "Please tell me this wasn't your dinner."

Liv shrugged. It did look pitiful, but she was just too tired to explain that she'd been too tired to make anything else.

He carried it into the kitchen, where he put it in the sink and began rummaging through the utensil drawer.

"Make yourself at home."

"Thanks. You do have a corkscrew, don't you?"

"Second drawer."

While he continued to rummage, Liv got down two wine-glasses, a couple of plates, and a roll of paper towels.

She put them on the table. "Sorry, I don't have any napkins."

Chaz was grinning at her.

Liv took quick stock of what he was seeing. Her hair was okay, though it tended to go really straight in cold weather. Then she remembered the movie; her makeup was probably smeared, her eyes swollen and no doubt red. He'd either feel sorry for her that she was taking the murder so badly or laugh at her if she told him she'd been watching a movie.

Better to be laughed at, she decided. "I was watching a Christmas movie."

"Is that why you look like Rudolph?"

She rubbed her nose and sniffed. "I guess."

He pried the cork out of the wine, slipped the glasses between two fingers, and carried them back to the living room. Liv grabbed the plates and a dog treat to save their pizza from greedy Westies and followed Chaz to the living room.

Whiskey was waiting expectantly by the pizza box.

"Not happening, buddy. It's bad for you. But look, I brought you a treat." She held out one of Dolly's gourmet dog biscuits.

Whiskey cocked his head and looked at her hand.

"Suit yourself." She took back the treat.

Whiskey eyed the pizza box, clearly torn. Then came to sit in front of her. "Arf."

"Good choice," she said and handed him the treat, which he took to the other side of the room where he was still within easy reach of raining pepperoni.

Chaz poured out two glasses and handed one to her.

"You know, I'd never have figured you as a red-nosed, angel-sweatshirt-wearing kind of girl."

Liv cheeks heated. She'd forgotten about the angel sweat-shirt. "I'm just full of surprises."

His playful expression turned to one of quick interest.

"Stop it and open the pizza."

A wonderful aroma wafted straight to her nose as he lifted the lid. He slid a piece onto one of the plates and handed it to Liv, just as music from the television swelled and Whoopi and her eight tiny reindeer swooped into the air.

"And they all lived happily ever after." Chaz picked up the remote. "Do you mind?"

Liv shook her head. Her mouth was filled with a big bite of cheese, pepperoni, and olives.

The screen went black, and the room suddenly seemed very quiet. Liv swallowed and took a sip of wine. "Dare I ask if this is a social call?"

"That's up to you," he said, at his smarmiest.

"Do you hit on every woman that moves to town?"

"Hmm." Chaz scratched his head. "Let me think."

"Did you put up a Christmas tree?"

"What?"

"I said—"

"I heard you. How did we go from seduction to Christmas trees?"

"Just curious."

"Your mind is an amazing contraption. The answer would be . . . no. And no."

"Oh."

"But in your case, I might make an exception."

"Thanks, but if this isn't social, why are you here?"

"Well, I just got curious about Arbor Day."

Chapter Twenty-one

....

Liv gave him a speculative look. "That's what the computer is for?"

"Yeah, in case we got bored with whatever."

Liv gave him a sardonic smile, but she couldn't keep it from morphing into genuine humor. He was so ridiculous, it had to be an act. Didn't it? "So what did you learn?"

"Well, a lot of shit happened that year. I'm just wondering what you know about it."

"Why didn't you ask me earlier?"

"I wasn't interested earlier."

Liv helped herself to another slice of pizza. "It might not have anything to do with Cosgrove's death. Maybe he was just passing the time."

"Or he might have stumbled onto something that would hasten his demise."

"Something that happened in nineteen sixty-nine could come back now?"

"*You're* asking *me*? After this past fall? I think we both know that it can, and might—and did. So tell me everything."

"You're helping with the investigation."

"No. I'm just passing the time."

"Liar."

"Yeah, well, I told you before, curiosity is a curse."

Liv gave him a look. "What you said was that investigative reporting was a curse."

"That, too. And don't ask me again why I moved back here."

"All right, then, let's look at nineteen sixty-nine." Liv put down her plate and carried her pizza crust to her desk, where she opened her laptop with one hand.

"This is what I have." She punched in some keys and the front page of the *Chicago Tribune* came up.

Chaz followed her over and opened his computer. A search engine displayed several archive sites, some that dated back to the eighteen hundreds.

"Serious search engines. For some reason I didn't take you as a history buff."

"You know me, a little of this, a little of that."

"You're just a whichever-way-the-wind-blows kind of guy."

"I guess you could say that."

"Whichever way the wind blows," Liv repeated. "David Bowie? Right? Never mind, it isn't important."

"It wasn't Bowie. He wrote 'When the Wind Blows.' Have I said before, your brain—"

"Is detailed and eclectic."

Chaz laughed. "I wasn't going to put it quite like that, but okay. Anyway you're probably thinking of Bob Dylan. 'You don't need a weatherman to know which way the wind blows.'"

Liv gave him a look. "And you think my mind is eclectic?" She frowned, moved him over, and sat down at her desk. Scrolled through the newspaper archive.

"What are you thinking?"

Liv shrugged. "I don't know, talking about the weather made me think of being in the library."

"Something that Cosgrove was reading about?"

"I don't know. It's gone now."

"Did Ms. Bangs say what papers he was reading?"

"I asked her. She helped him log on to the *Trib*. But after that he could have been looking at anything.

"Though I can't imagine that something happening in Chicago could have anything to do with Celebration Bay, New York. Maybe you could look at the back issues of the *Clarion* and see if something correlates." She managed to say it with a straight face. The *Clarion* had never been put on microfilm or on the Internet, and all the back issues were stored in boxes in the musty, dust-covered basement of the *Clarion* office.

"Hmm. You're just getting back at me for making you look through all those back issues. But hell, you're probably right. I wonder if the police found the copies Cosgrove made. That would cut down on a lot of reading."

And sneezing, Liv thought.

"I don't suppose you wheedled any information out of Bill?" he asked her.

"I do not wheedle."

"Whatever. Did he say anything?"

Liv thought back. Stifled a yawn. She was tired. She'd been going nonstop since she'd arrived in September. Her brain was not at its best. She didn't tell Chaz that.

"He said that he'd talked to Lola Bangs. I told him about seeing Clarence with a folded newspaper—Saturday night at the Dumpster."

"One of my fonder memories."

"I told him about Cosgrove's little black book."

"It just keeps getting better."

She scowled at Chaz's smarmy expression.

"He didn't find a book. And why do you do that?"

"What?"

"Act like a bonehead surfer dude all the time."

His expression froze, then dropped away to no expression at all. "Surfer dude? I don't know how to surf."

"Okay, maybe I'm exaggerating. It's just when I first saw you, that's what I thought. Blond, suntanned." *Lethargic*, but she didn't say that.

"I fish. That puts me in the sun a lot. I need more wine."

He refilled their glasses, then pulled up a chair to sit next to her.

They started with Chicago. The *Tribune* was filled with articles concerning the war raging in Vietnam, sit-ins at colleges, and riots in the street.

"It sounds horrible," Liv said.

"It does." Chaz kept reading.

"What about that? The Chicago Eight?" Liv leaned closer to read a headline.

"They caused a riot at the Democratic convention a year before. Old news."

"Oh."

"Look for something less newsworthy. Like a mass murder or arson."

Liv stared at him.

"I wasn't kidding. Keep looking."

She kept looking. "A murder of a farm family? Four children, a woman, and a man."

"That looks promising. Write it down. We'll make a list. Here's something. Arson at a shopping center."

Liv wrote it down. "But how does any of this relate to us?"

"You have to follow a lot of trails—many of them false— before you get to the truth."

"We don't have time."

Chaz gave her a look. "Write. Bombing at a chemical factory in Wisconsin. One apprehended, three at large."

"I thought they made cheese." Liv wrote it down, but her eyes were getting heavier by the second. Even Chaz grew quiet. After a while she leaned over to see what he'd discovered. He was reading the sports page.

"Really? Sports? At a time like this?"

"It's Lou Piniella."

"Never heard of him."

"Sacrilege. How about this? . . ."

They gave it up at one o'clock. Liv could barely keep her eyes open. She pushed herself out of her chair and handed him his jacket.

"Are you really sending me out into the cold, dark night?"

"Yes. Do you really want to stay here?"

"Well, yeah. I'm a guy."

"Thanks, but I need a little more incentive than that." Especially if she had to put up with gossip and innuendo.

"You're right. It's probably not a good idea. Maybe after you've been here longer. Say fifteen years."

"You're so weird."

"Not normally, just with you. I really don't get it." He put on his jacket and went to the door. Liv let him and Whiskey out. Chaz left; Whiskey came back after two minutes.

"Too cold for you, buddy?"

Whiskey raced inside and into the bedroom. Chaz backed out of the driveway and drove away. Liv closed the door.

"Oh the weather outside is frightful," she sang, only slightly maliciously, as she carried the pizza box and glasses to the kitchen. It wasn't that cold. It wouldn't hurt Chaz to be a little uncomfortable on his ride home. Though he had spent hours doing research, even if it was fruitless. And she could use a little fun.

But not with Chaz. The less she thought about him, the better. They were oil and water. "A" type and no type. Over-achiever and slob. The odd couple.

And even though nothing had happened, Liv had no doubt the sisters had seen his car and would have questions in the morning. She sighed. *All the suspicion and none of the fun.*

Morning came all too soon. Despite sleeping late, Liv woke feeling dragged out. She'd spent the night dreaming about wars, explosions, and Bob Dylan songs. Definitely an extra-vitamin-C-and-zinc day.

She found some Christmas music on the radio and put in

a call to Ted, who told her to take the whole day off. But that was way too much free time for Liv. When Christmas was over . . . no, when New Year's was over, she'd take a week off to regroup and start planning the next events.

When she let Whiskey out, she saw there were ominous clouds hovering low in the sky. Snow was expected. She always kept up to date on the weather forecast, but this looked like more than the promised accumulation of three to four inches. This looked like it held the potential for several feet.

She quickly went down her mental list of the week's events. She'd better check that they would be able to keep the venues open.

She called Ted.

"Inches," he said to her first question.

"What about—"

"I double-checked. There's plenty of de-icer on hand, and the county has assured me that all roads leading to Celebration Bay will be a priority. Now go shopping."

"What about—"

"Shop till you drop."

"What about you? Don't you have any shopping to do?" Ted never talked about his personal life, but surely he must have someone to buy for.

"Finished weeks ago. Now, don't call unless you need help carrying your packages."

A day off. She two-stepped across her bedroom to the bath singing along to "Winter Wonderland." And hoped it would be a wonderland and not the worst blizzard in fifty years.

A hot shower went a considerable way toward making her feel human again. And when she'd dried off, she felt absolutely optimistic, enough so that she sang along with "Let It Snow."

She got out Whiskey's food. "Oh the weather outside—"

"Aroo-roo," Whiskey finished.

"Da de da dee da dee dee."

"Aroo-roo."

"You are the smartest dog in the world," she told him and spooned food into his bowl. For the next minute or so, all doggie singing stopped while Whiskey scarfed his breakfast, then ran to the bedroom for his bow tie.

It was looking a little ratty. Okay, a lot ratty. She'd have to stop by the Woofery and buy another one. Who knew he'd turn out to love bow ties?

She clipped it around his neck, zipped up her parka, and pushed her feet into snow boots. She probably should drive if she wanted to get all her presents home, but by the time she got her car out of the garage, warmed it up, and drove around looking for parking, she could be halfway finished with her shopping.

She could just store stuff at the Events Office, wrap them there, take the ones for her Celebration Bay friends home all at once, and walk across the street to the post office when the packages for her family were ready to be mailed. Totally efficient, if a little late.

She turned down the heat, clipped on Whiskey's leash, and locked the door behind them. She wasn't surprised to see Miss Ida out salting the sidewalk.

"Morning, Liv. Morning, Whiskey." Whiskey sat and waited for a treat she always kept in her pocket. "You good dog," Miss Ida said and slipped him a little piece of biscuit.

"You're up early," Liv said while she waited for Miss Ida to start questioning her about Chaz's visit.

"Have you gotten any further in solving the murder?"

Liv blinked. Did Miss Ida mean her specifically? Surely not. "I talked to Bill yesterday, but he didn't have much to tell me or that he could tell me. I don't think they've got a real suspect yet, unfortunately."

"Well, I'm not worried. I saw Chaz Bristow's car here last night. The two of you will get to the bottom of things. And who knows?" Miss Ida looked mischievous.

"I think we'll just let the police handle it," Liv said hurriedly.

"Such a nice young man, especially when he cleans

himself up. So kind. And he used to have a big job on some newspaper in Los Angeles. We've all been expecting him to get bored and leave us high and dry. It can't be too exciting after the big city. I'm glad to see he's found an interest that might keep him here." She absolutely twinkled at Liv.

Liv didn't think she meant solving murders. She considered trying the usual protest of "We're just friends," but they weren't even that. And not colleagues, because Chaz wouldn't cooperate. Even though he kept coming back in spite of himself.

A curse, he'd said. Maybe she wasn't being fair to ask him. Maybe he had a good reason for staying aloof.

A gust of wind whipped past them.

Miss Ida looked up at the clouds. "Feels like another storm coming in. Sure don't want to have bad weather for the ice-carving exhibition out at Andy Miller's this Saturday. Always dicey. Too cold, people stay away. Too hot or too rainy, just makes a mess."

"Well, I just hope it holds off until tomorrow. I need to get my Christmas shopping done."

"Do you have much left to do?"

"I haven't started yet."

"Oh dear. Not at all?"

Liv shook her head. "Been too busy. And I have to mail a bunch to my family. At this rate they won't get them before Christmas." Actually they never got their presents at Christmas. It had become a family joke. "Liv always sends her presents in January when the rush is over and the bills come in and you really need some Christmas cheer."

"Ted said I could have the day off."

"Why don't you leave Whiskey with us? Then you won't have to leave him outside or carry him when you're in the stores."

Liv had planned to drop him by the office, but this would be even better.

"Thanks, I'm sure he'd love to spend the morning with his two favorite ladies."

Miss Ida leaned over and slipped him another piece

of biscuit. "We know how men hate to shop, don't we, sweetums?"

Whiskey happily followed Miss Ida into the house. Liv wrapped her scarf over her chin to ward off the wind and set off to town. She stopped by Dolly's and explained that she needed only one pastry since she was going shopping.

"Ted told me." Dolly handed her a bag containing a cranberry orange muffin that was large enough for at least two people.

She went next door to the Buttercup.

"Ted came by and said you'd be in late. Sit down for a minute." BeBe made Liv's usual latte, poured herself a cup, then joined Liv at one of the small tables. "Are you really going Christmas shopping?"

"I am."

"Have you made a list?"

"And checked it twice. And don't ask me what's on it. Just know that I correlated the gifts with a list of local stores and I plan to buy something at all of them."

"That could take forever."

"I don't have forever. I'll drive over to the Yarn Barn this afternoon and hope they have some of those cute hats and scarves left. Perfect for the aunts and uncles. And Miriam had these wonderful three-dimensional paper stars at A Stitch in Time. She's saving me a few for my sister, the Christmas nut.

"I'll hit the two dress shops on the other side of the square for my mother and grandmother. The Bookworm for my father."

"Are you going to Trim a Tree?"

"Not a chance, but I do plan on loading up with some natural products from the Pyne Bough. Let's see, did I miss anyone?"

"The newsstand?"

"Okay, I'll pick up a few magazines. I wonder . . ."

"What?"

"I just thought about all those cigarette butts Phil Cosgrove left in the alley. I wonder if he went into the newsstand. And if Mr. Valenski talked to him."

"I knew you couldn't keep your mind off that topic for very long."

Liv sighed. "I just want this all to really work. To be the best Harvest Festival, the best Thanksgiving, Christmas, and New Year's Eve Celebration Bay ever had. And I can't do that," she lowered her voice, "if people keep getting murdered."

"True. At least not if it happens right downtown and the killer is still at large."

The door opened, bringing in a frigid gust of wind and Janine Tudor. She was wearing a fitted camel coat and a stylish cloche hat. Her platinum-frosted hair fell straight to her shoulder as if it had never seen a breeze much less the winter gusts that were blowing outside. At least she'd exchanged her usual stilettos for fur-trimmed high-heeled boots.

"There goes my Christmas cheer," Liv said in an undertone.

BeBe grimaced and stood. "Good morning, Janine. Can I get you something?"

Janine huffed. "If I wanted a four-dollar cup of coffee, I'd drive to Albany to get it."

Four dollars? Liv mouthed.

BeBe shrugged and managed to get back to the counter before snorting out a giggle.

Janine zeroed in on Liv. "I need to speak to you."

"And there goes my lovely shopping day." Liv had known that expecting Janine to continue keeping a low profile over the TAT situation was a hope in a bucket. It was true that Liv saved her skinny butt not long ago, but it just seemed to have increased Janine's resentment. Though she had been giving Liv a wide berth lately—until now.

Janine sat down in BeBe's vacated seat. "You've got to do something."

"Want to give me a context?" Liv asked.

"Everyone is blaming me for that crazy woman in the Trim a Tree store."

"Well, Grace Thornsby said you told her the one-Santa rule was no big deal."

"I told her no such thing. I didn't talk to her. Clarence did all the negotiations." Janine's eyes rolled upward. "Tried to finagle a lower rent. Grace just stood in the background, flashing tacky jewelry. New money." Janine's mouth curled. "You can tell every time, if it's not the way they talk or walk, it's what they wear."

"Janine, I'm not the fashion police."

Janine gave Liv's L. L. Bean cable-knit sweater the once-over. "Obviously. But not even you would wear that tasteless bling. Bigger in some cases is not better. Just gaudy." She shook herself. Gold earrings flashed between the strands of perfectly styled hair. "I want you to get rid of her."

"Janine, you were responsible for renting the place to them. You figure out a way to evict them."

"I can't. Only Jeremiah Atkins can do that, he's the land-lord. But he refuses to do anything. I think he enjoys making my life miserable.

"I won't have a moment's peace until she and her horrid store are gone. Dolly Hunnicutt had the nerve to charge me the tourist rate at the bakery. And Rufus Cobb took my parking space when he has a perfectly good space at the B and B. And stayed there all day."

Janine hadn't worked at town hall for over four months but still somehow thought she should be allowed to keep her reserved space in the employees lot.

She seemed to run out of steam. "If you and Ted had just left well enough alone, she would have been out of here as soon as Christmas was over. Those kinds of stores always close after the holidays. But no. You had to give her a hard time. Now, she'll probably never leave, just to spite us, and it's all your fault. You have to do something."

Chapter Twenty-two

···

Liv nearly choked on her coffee. "Me? How do you figure that one?"

"Well, we never had any murders before you came."

"Oh please. Some people might say that we wouldn't have had this one if you hadn't rented the store to Trim a Tree and their illegal Santa." Liv could have kicked herself for that retort. She knew not to engage. You could never win an argument if you tried to reason with someone like Janine, or tried to outyell them. You had to act before they knew what you were doing. "In fact . . ."

Liv stood, grabbed her parka off the back of the chair, took Janine by the elbow, and muscled her toward the door.

"What do you think you're doing?"

"*We're* doing. You and I are going down the street to speak with Grace. *You're* going to explain to her that you misrepresented the rental space. *I'm* going to make sure this time you actually do it. Then *you're* going to tell her that you completely understand and will speak to the landlord about releasing her from her rental agreement."

"I will not."

"Or *I'll* make sure the next time you try to buy a coffee it will be ten dollars, not four."

"You can't do that."

"Oh yes she can," BeBe said from the espresso machine.

"That's extortion."

"That's life."

BeBe grinned and fist-pumped the air.

"I'll be back," Liv told BeBe as she guided Janine toward the door. "Don't let my latte get cold."

"I'll make you a fresh one—on the house."

Liv wrestled Janine through the door and out onto the sidewalk. "Would you like to do this is in a dignified manner, or do you want to give your neighbors even more to talk about?"

Janine stopped struggling, pulled her arm away, and straightened her coat. "One day, Liv Montgomery."

"Janine, give it up. I didn't take your job as coordinator. You were a volunteer. You could have applied for the job if you wanted it that bad."

Janine's lips tightened until they were bloodless and two slashes of pink that weren't makeup appeared on her cheekbones.

Oh crap, thought Liv. *She did apply and they passed over her to hire me.* "Can't we just call a truce and work on getting this embarrassment off Main Street and replace it with something that is profitable *and* appropriate? You'll be hailed as the one who reestablished harmony. And everyone will be so grateful." For about ten seconds, and Liv bet Janine knew it, but at least Liv was offering her a way to save face, at least in her own mind.

Janine huffed out a resigned sigh. "All right. I'll see what I can do. But I can't promise miracles."

Liv opened the door to the Trim a Tree, and they both stepped inside to the tinny ho-ho-ho'ing of the mechanical Santa.

Grace was sitting on a stool behind the cash register, thumbing through the pages of what appeared to be a travel magazine.

"What do you want now?" she asked Liv, and turned the page of her magazine.

"Ms. Tudor has something to say to you." Liv poked Janine for encouragement.

Janine begrudgingly took a step toward Grace. "There seems to have been some misunderstanding at the initial lease signing." She ran her tongue over her lips.

"There was no misunderstanding. You said they couldn't enforce the Santa rule. I heard you when Clarence signed the lease."

Janine glanced sideways at Liv. "I said that although it wasn't an actual law, that merchants have honored the . . . custom since it began. And that . . . the town—"

"Save your breath." Grace looked to her left as if she'd heard or seen someone, but there was only shelves of cartoon Santa statues. "You know what? You can have this dump back for all I care. I've got better things to do."

Liv wondered if she had managed to clean Clarence out, like people were saying. She might have once been a good-looking woman, but it would take more than her acerbic lack of charm to keep a younger man in the style he expected to become accustomed to.

"But you'll have to talk to Clarence. He signed the lease. Dumb fool." She snorted out a derisive laugh. "And speak of the devil. Here he is, and Sheriff Gunnison, too."

The door opened, the Santa ho-ho-ho'ed. Bill winced. Clarence Thornsby walked over to the Santa and yanked the plug out of the socket. He crossed his arms and turned to Grace.

Grace ignored him. "Well, Sheriff, did you come here for me to sign a complaint against that little thief and her boyfriend?"

"Penny Newland is no thief, and neither is Jason Tully. Your husband took that money."

Grace switched her scowl to Clarence.

"Well, you could have told me before I accused that poor Newland girl."

Liv stifled a groan. Grace's suddenly generous spirit was as fake as her jewelry.

"Don't you look at me like that," Clarence said. "I knew if I didn't take it you'd squander it on that muscleman you've been keeping."

For the briefest moment, Grace looked nonplused.

"But it stops now. I'm filing for divorce. You're a mean-spirited woman, Grace. I'll be glad to see the back of you. And don't bother countersuing. You've gotten all you're getting from me."

"We'll see about that."

"If you ever bothered to talk to me, your husband, you'd know that I had to declare bankruptcy. There's nothing left. You can pass that along to your boy toy and see how long he sticks around."

Clarence turned to leave, and Grace lunged at him. Bill grabbed her and held on.

"Loser," she cried. "After all I've put up with. Your dumb jokes. Your bad breath. Your fat belly. And you're lousy in bed."

"Euww, TMI," Janine said under her breath.

Clarence stopped at the door. "Hank warned me about marrying you. I should've listened. I'm on my way to see Jeremiah Atkins and try to talk him into letting me out of the lease. If you want to keep this store, you'll have to pay for it yourself."

Grace's anger changed immediately to something much calmer and more sinister. "Tell him I'll just stick around until the end of the month to keep an eye on things."

Keep an eye on what things? Liv wondered. After all the trouble she'd caused, not only would the locals not patronize her store, but they would encourage tourists to join the boycott.

Grace had relaxed slightly and there was a sly smile on her face. What the heck was she up to?

"Good-bye, Clarence."

He opened the door.

"And good riddance."

"The feeling's mutual." The door slammed behind him. For once there was no "Ho, ho, ho" to see him out.

Bill looked at Liv and nodded toward the door. Liv was more than ready to go, and so was Janine, who'd already started her escape.

"Oh by the way," Bill said. "Penny Newland won't be working here anymore. Under the circumstances, she decided it would be better to look for work elsewhere."

"Well, she can try. She was totally useless. I can't imagine who'd hire her. The only reason she was here was because Clarence insisted." Her eyes rolled to the back of her head. "Some outmoded sense of family. They were only third cousins or something." She sighed. Looked at her nails. "Though I suppose failing businesses might run in the family."

"Actually she's working at A Stitch in Time nights, and she starts at the Pyne Bough this afternoon," Bill said.

Grace flinched, clearly surprised, but she recovered quickly. "Well, I hope they don't regret it."

That was all Liv was willing to hear; she opened the door. Janine scuttled out, and Liv and Bill were right behind her.

"What a be-otch," Janine said.

Liv didn't point out that this might be a case of the pot calling the kettle be-otch.

Clarence was waiting on the sidewalk. Liv had trouble meeting his eye.

"I've been a fool," Clarence said. "I know that. I sure hope it wasn't my fault that someone killed Phil Cosgrove. I hired him. I got so sick of her talking about Hank this and Hank that, and how great he was. I thought for sure she wanted this store so she could reacquaint herself with him. I was so sick of her by then, I would have welcomed it."

"So why didn't you just divorce her?" Bill said, his voice vibrating with exasperation.

"I didn't know then that I couldn't work my way out of this financial hole, and I didn't want her to get half of my hard-earned money. She's wearing over half of my income on her neck. I thought if Phil could get evidence that she was committing adultery, I could get out of giving her anything."

"That tacky jewelry is real?"

"And did he get evidence?" Liv asked, ignoring Janine's outburst.

"He found out she was seeing this goon from some gym around here. I have his report at home. And also that she was skimming the till." Clarence frowned, his face was chalky white. "Then he said he was really onto something. I thought great, I could get rid of her sooner than later. But he said it wasn't about Grace."

"Did he say what it was?" Bill asked.

Clarence shook his head. "Just that he wanted to stay on an extra week without pay. Just to keep an eye on things."

Liv looked from Clarence to Bill. Janine had lost interest and was inching away from the group.

"Sorry if I caused trouble for you, Janine. It was a stupid idea."

Janine flicked the air with manicured nails. "Not at all." She looked at Liv. "It was all *Grace's* fault."

Okay, Liv thought. That might be progress. At least she was shifting blame from Liv to Grace. She doubted if Janine would ever take the responsibility for any of her own actions.

"Sorry for all the trouble we caused," said Clarence. He huffed out a sigh. "Well, I'd best catch Jeremiah. Then I have a meeting with my lawyers."

"Sorry about your bad luck," Liv said.

"I tried to expand too fast in an economy where people weren't buying boats." His eyes suddenly teared up. "It's been a pretty rotten few years."

Liv couldn't think of a thing to say. She couldn't see his life getting better any time soon.

Clarence shoved his hands in his pockets and walked off down the street.

"Whew," Bill said. "I'm with Clarence. I'll be glad to see the back of that woman."

"You and everyone else," Liv said.

"Maybe she killed that PI. I wouldn't put it past her," Janine said.

"She has an alibi."

"Too bad. If Grace had killed him, you could have

arrested her and we wouldn't be stuck with her for the next few weeks."

Liv winced. "She didn't seem at all upset by the news that Clarence had declared bankruptcy. Do you think she's been socking away money?"

"I wouldn't be at all surprised."

"I would have if I'd been married to him." Janine shuddered dramatically. "Did you see that beer gut? And he wears polyester. What?" Janine asked, seeing Bill's and Liv's expressions. "I mean if I were Grace. Which I'm not. Euww."

"Well, I'd best be going," Bill said. "I hope there's an end to it. I haven't been able to make one choir practice."

"Et tu, Bill?" Liv asked. "Does the whole town sing in the *Messiah* choir?"

"Not in the choir. There's only about thirty of us, though anybody who can even remotely carry a tune comes to the sing-along." His mouth drooped. "At the rate this investigation is going, I'll probably have to miss it this year."

"But Penny may actually get to sing," Liv said. "I heard her in church last Sunday. What a voice."

"Wait until you hear her solo. She sings like a real angel. Now, you ladies better get inside where it's warm."

Liv and Janine watched Bill stride up the street humming. Before he climbed into his police cruiser, Liv heard him singing. The car door closed on "He shall feed his flock."

Janine turned to Liv. "Now that that's over, we're even."

"What? How do you figure that?"

"Tit for tat."

Liv considered. "Maybe."

Janine lifted her chin, then minced and slid down the sidewalk. Liv watched her go. She'd never intended to use certain information against Janine, but it wouldn't hurt for Janine not to know that. It might just keep her in line in the future.

It was almost lunchtime and Liv hadn't even started her shopping. She wanted more coffee since she hadn't finished her last cup. But it occurred to her that if Grace was closing and still had the extra Santa suit, she might be willing to sell it to Liv . . . cheap. She would need every penny if she wasn't going to get alimony from the bankrupt Clarence. And Liv could hold on to the Santa suit in case of emergencies. It paid to have a backup, as they had learned just last week. And Nancy could burn sage over it, to chase away the evil spirits.

So casting a longing look down the street to the Buttercup, Liv steeled herself and stepped back into Trim a Tree. The tinny "Ho, ho, ho" greeted her, and Liv gritted her teeth. Was Grace just born belligerent?

Grace was back to reading her magazine. She looked up. "Now what?"

Liv pushed her mouth into some semblance of a smile. "I was just wondering if you still have the Santa suit? Or if you returned it to the rental store?"

"That was no rental. I paid good money for it, though for what? To let it sit in my trunk for the last five days?"

"Oh. Did the police look at it?"

"I showed it to them. Don't know why on earth they insisted on seeing it. He wasn't wearing it when he died. It's been in the trunk of my car since you created such a scene about it."

Before the murder. "And they gave it back?" Liv asked, surprised.

Grace gave her a how-stupid-are-you face. "Yes. And I put it back in the trunk. Do you want anything else, or did you just come back to chat?" She looked pointedly to her magazine. "I'm busy."

"I thought you might want to sell it," Liv said. "Since you won't be needing it."

Grace's eyes narrowed. It made her look perfectly malevolent. Liv couldn't imagine her being young and flirtatious. "Why?"

"After what happened this past weekend, I've decided to purchase a backup suit. But if you're not interested in selling, I'll just go to one of my normal suppliers." Liv started to turned away.

"Two hundred dollars."

Liv looked back over her shoulder. "Get real."

"It was an expensive suit."

"It didn't cost two hundred, it will have to be cleaned if there's any chance of getting the cigarette smell out of it, and for all I know, he could have dribbled food down the front." She stepped toward the door.

"One hundred."

Liv turned around to face her. "Fifty. That's my only offer."

Grace huffed and pushed herself off her stool. "It's in my car in the parking lot. I suppose you want it now."

"I have the cash right here." Liv patted her coat pocket.

Grace deliberated.

"I'll even go get it. Or I can stay and watch the store while you're gone."

"You're dressed. You get it. But don't touch anything in that car but the bag with the suit in it."

"Wouldn't dream of it," Liv told her. Much.

Grace handed her a ring of keys. "It's the silver Mercedes. This opens the trunk. Bring it right back."

"Of course. Can I go out the back?"

"Whatever. But it locks automatically. You'll have to come back in the front."

"No problem." It would give her a chance to take a quick peek at whatever else was inside.

Liv let herself out the back door and walked down to the entrance to the parking lot. Stopped to look at the Dumpster from where she'd watched Grace and Clarence fight. While she stood there, the back door to the Pyne Bough opened, and Penny Newland hurried out, carrying two black garbage bags. She threw the bags in the Dumpster, saw Liv, and waved.

"Thanks so much. Hank told me how you got me these jobs. I really appreciate it."

"It was nothing," Liv called back. "Go on inside before you freeze. I'm coming by to do some shopping later, but tell Nancy that we have a backup Santa suit."

Penny's mouth rounded in an "O." She pointed toward the back of TAT.

Liv gave her a thumbs-up.

"I'll tell her. See you later." She rushed across the alley to the Pyne Bough, and Liv stepped into the parking lot.

The Mercedes was parked by the fence several spaces down from the entrance. Instead of going directly to the trunk, Liv glanced to make sure she was alone and sauntered around the car, looking into the windows, which were only lightly tinted.

It was empty. Grace Thornsby must be one of those annoying people who kept their interiors spotless. Her cup holder had probably never seen a take-out latte. Liv looked anyway but didn't go so far as to open the doors.

Feeling mildly disappointed, she walked around to the back of the car, beeped the trunk open. It lifted to reveal a perfectly neat trunk with one clear plastic bag enclosing the Santa suit next to a plastic folder from an Albany travel agency. It appeared Grace was planning a trip.

Cautioning herself not to overstep the line, Liv took the Santa suit, jostling the folder as she did. Oops. Several brochures slid out. They were all ads for the Caribbean. She slid them back into the packet and closed the trunk.

She walked around to the front of the store and went inside. She dropped Grace's keys on the counter, took out fifty dollars from her wallet, and put it down next to the keys.

Grace took both without looking up from her magazine.

"I couldn't help but see your travel brochures. Going to the islands?"

"Not that it's your business, but yes. Tickets for two."

Poor Jerry Esposito. He was in for a big surprise. And so, Liv guessed, was Grace.

Chapter Twenty-three

··

Liv returned to the Buttercup, clutching the suit bag to her chest. And ran into A.K. Pierce just leaving.

"Mr. Pierce," Liv said too brightly.

"Ms. Montgomery." He glanced at the bag, then nodded and went out the door.

Liv watched him stride down the street, wondering if his shaved head ever got cold.

BeBe came up to her. "He's kind of intimidating, isn't he?"

"A bit," Liv agreed. But also a little interesting.

BeBe noticed the bag Liv was carrying. "Is that what I think it is?"

"Yep. I just bought it from Grace Thornsby for fifty bucks."

"God, she'd sell her soul. Did you open it?"

"Not yet. I thought we could do it now, but I'm warning you, it's going to smell."

"Take it to the back but stay by the door so I can watch the store while you search through the pockets."

"You know me so well."

They carried the suit to the back where Liv pulled open the plastic. She was hit by a miasma of stinky Santa suit.

"Whew. I can smell it all the way over here." BeBe left the doorway and moved closer. "Okay, quick, I'm dying to see if you find anything."

Liv dropped the plastic to the ground, shoved the coat at BeBe. "Look through this while I do the pants."

"Haven't the police already searched them?"

"Grace said so, but she also said the suit has been in her car trunk since last week, and that's before Phil Cosgrove was killed."

"If we can believe anything she says."

"Probably not, but the police don't have the notebook."

"Notebook?"

"Yeah, Cosgrove had one. I saw him put it in his pants pocket. It's probably not here, if the police actually searched it. But it won't hurt to look again."

BeBe began to rummage through the pockets. "Gum wrapper, crushed cigarette package, cheap pen . . . no notebook."

Liv stopped with her hand in one empty pants pocket. "Well, it was worth a try."

"Hold on." BeBe rifled the other pocket. Patted the whole coat. "Nope. That's all. How about you? Find anything?"

"Just the gum pack that your wrapper came from."

BeBe handed the coat back to her, and Liv stuffed the suit into the bag and resealed it. She joined BeBe at the sink where they scrubbed their hands.

"Well, that was disappointing. Not that I really expected to find anything. I would like to have a backup suit, but I'm not even sure dry cleaning will get rid of that smell."

"Well, come out front and have a latte on the house."

While Liv drank her latte, she called Ted, gave him a condensed version of the morning's events, updated him on the purchase of the Santa suit, and asked him if he needed her.

"Always, but shop. I'm leaving at four thirty. I'm not missing choir practice again."

Liv laughed. "Even Bill was singing today."

"Christmas is in the air."

"And chestnuts are roasting on an open fire. And I have to get going." But she leisurely finished her coffee.

Her first stop was the Bookworm. She stepped into the warmth and musty smell of the bookstore and immediately felt the weight of the last week slough from her shoulders. Quincy Hinks was standing on a stepladder dusting the bookshelves with a feather duster, which merely disturbed the dust motes until they settled back on the surfaces.

He was the perfect bookstore owner. Part tweed-jacket intellectual, part crusty New Yorker, part jolly elf for the children who came to the store for story time, and part cranky gnome for adults who were only interested in the latest best sellers.

He acknowledged Liv, made a final agitating sweep of the feather duster, and climbed down the ladder.

"So is it true? Are we getting rid of that eyesore?"

"Seems that way. I'm keeping my fingers crossed."

"Well, someone should put it to Janine Tudor about leasing to inappropriate businesses."

"I think, I hope, Janine understands that now."

"Got her good, did you? Well, bully for you. Now, what can I help you with?"

"I'm just starting my shopping. My father is a big American history buff. Do you have anything particularly interesting?"

"What period?"

"I know he reads a lot of Revolutionary stuff and also New Deal–era books."

"Sounds like an interesting man."

"He is."

Quincy thought for a second, nodded to himself. "I think I have just the thing."

After twenty minutes, Liv left the store with several books on the founding fathers, a historic map, and a set of Beatrix Potter books for her niece. She hauled her shopping bags next door to the Buttercup.

"Ha, he got you," BeBe said by way of welcome.

"Yeah, he's good," Liv agreed. "My dad's set for Christmas, Father's Day, and a couple of holidays in between. Can I please store these in back until I finish the rest of my shopping? I'll pick them up later today."

"Sure. Where are you going next?" BeBe asked as they lugged the heavy bags to a corner behind the coffee bar.

"Bay-Berry Candles. Then A Stitch in Time for those Moravian stars Penny Newland makes. I'm going to send some to my sister and save some for myself."

"But you don't have a Christmas tree."

"I will."

"When? For Valentine's Day?" BeBe laughed. "You should get one of those artificial ones with the lights. The people next door to me have one. When it's time to take down the tree, they just throw a sheet over the whole thing and carry it up to the attic."

"Still decorated?"

"Yep, and the sheet keeps the dust off."

"I think I'll go for small and real. In fact, I plan to run out to Dexter Kent's this afternoon. I'll see you before then."

Liv said good-bye and went to Bay-Berry Candles, where she bought a dozen candles scented in pine, cinnamon, and cranberry vanilla. Luanne Dietz, the candle lady, offered to box them and deliver them to the Events Office.

Liv thanked her and continued on to A Stitch in Time. The store was busy.

Miriam threaded her way through one particularly noisy group to get to Liv. "So I hear we'll be getting rid of that Thornsby woman, though I also hear she won't be a Thornsby for long. I'll never forgive her for giving me the scare of my life. The idea of me killing that poor man. It's downright heathen."

"I'm sure no one ever suspected you."

"Then they shouldn't have hauled me off like a common criminal." Miriam smiled suddenly. "Being arrested is not the way I would have chosen to get my fifteen minutes of fame, but I must admit it's been good for business." She gestured around the packed store.

"But not to worry. I put away ten Moravian stars for you. I kept three out in case other customers wanted to order them. Penny said she could start making more tonight after choir practice. She's working over at Nancy's this morning, she'll do another full day there tomorrow, and she'll come to me two nights a week to do the craft classes. She doesn't know much about quilting, but she makes the cutest raggedy dolls. I don't know why I didn't think to ask her sooner."

"I'm glad it's working out," Liv said. She ordered another ten stars and picked out a baby quilt for her newest niece, whom she'd only seen on Facebook.

She walked around the corner to the Pyne Bough. The tinkle of tiny brass bells greeted her when she opened the door, a far cry from the laughing Santa at TAT. Incense was burning from a brazier behind the counter. The room was a heady mix of crisp spice and mellow herb and exuded tranquility.

Penny Newland was rearranging figures on a wide shelf.

"Hi, Ms. Montgomery. Can I help you?"

"Hi, what are those?"

"Aren't they the cutest?" She picked up one of the figures. "They're little reindeer planters, made from slivers of driftwood. You put a little plant in the opening. Or lichen like the one here or . . . look at this." She put the planter back and reached for a larger one, which was planted with multicolored grass.

"They're really feathers," Penny told her. "Isn't this clever? They separate the barbs—that's the individual strands of the feather," she explained to Liv, the urbanite, "and surround it with down. I might have to try making one of these myself. Mom would love it. This one's too expensive for me." She immediately colored. "I mean . . ."

Liv took the feather planter and looked at the price tag.

"I know just what you mean."

The storeroom door opened and Nancy wielded a large box through the opening. She put the box down, stopped when she saw Liv, then hurried over.

"Morning, Liv. Penny said you bought the Santa suit from Grace."

"I did. It's not nearly as nice as the one he has now, but I'll feel better if there's a backup."

"Yes, that was just too much excitement. Is it in that bag?" She indicated Liv's Stitch in Time bag. "Shall I hang it up in back?"

"Actually, no, this is from Miriam's. I'm doing my Christmas shopping this morning. I left the suit at the Buttercup with some other packages. I'll pick it up tonight and drop it off at the cleaner's tomorrow. It reeks of cigarette smoke."

"I don't doubt it. If you change your mind, just bring it here. A little sage, baking soda, and fresh air, it will be good as new." She smiled. "I'm sure Hank will be relieved to have an extra one."

Liv smiled. Did Hank have any idea how eager Nancy was to please him? "You've already gone beyond the call of duty."

"I was glad to help out."

Penny's lip quivered. "They still haven't found the killer. I hope he's long gone from here. So far that they never find him."

"So do I," said Nancy.

"Well, I hope they catch him. I will sleep better at night," Liv said.

"Surely he won't strike again," Nancy said. "It must have something to do with that dreadful Grace Thornsby. Bad karma, that one."

"I've never met anyone so mean," Penny said.

"It's the bitterness. Sad really . . ." Nancy trailed off.

"Well, I hate her." Penny hung her head. "I shouldn't say that."

Nancy placed a hand on her shoulder. "Better to let it out than to let it fester inside you."

Penny shook her head.

This shopping expedition was getting a little too philosophical for Liv. She eased away to look at what turned out to be a votive candleholder made of shells. Clever and beautiful. But she couldn't think of a relative who would use it. BeBe didn't have any candles that she'd seen. She had no idea what Ted's house was like, since she'd never been invited. And it wouldn't fit in with the Victorian décor of her landladies.

"At first I thought maybe Grace killed him," Penny said. "What do you think, Liv?"

Reluctantly Liv turned back to the conversation. "I don't know what to think, Penny."

"It doesn't do any good for us to speculate," Nancy said. "Though it's beginning to look like they're going to question the whole town before they're satisfied."

"Doesn't it?" said Penny. "Miriam said they found the box cutter that killed him in her store. It had traces of blood on it. But she didn't do it. Miriam has been here forever. Everyone knows her."

Liv smiled slightly. As if longevity had anything to do with innocence or guilt.

"I wonder how it got there."

"I suppose anyone who had access to her store could have put it there," said Nancy.

"But that could be just about anybody."

"Just about." Nancy opened the box and began lifting out packages of ornaments.

"The quilters? Or someone in the sewing class? I can't believe it. Maybe someone sneaked in? But how? And why?" Penny's eyes grew larger with each thought. "Do you think somebody wanted to frame Miriam?"

"Oh good heavens," Nancy exclaimed. "You've been watching too much television."

"I'm sure no one wanted to frame Miriam," Liv told her. "They don't know yet if the box cutter they found was the murder weapon. It has to be sent out for tests before they can be sure. It might be as simple as someone in class cut their finger and didn't clean the knife very well.

"But I'm sure the police are working on finding out. They'll probably question everyone."

"Everyone?" asked Penny.

"Well, whoever might have been back there or . . ." Liv stopped.

"Or what?" asked Penny.

"Or whatever." All those seamstresses the night of the murder. Any one of them under the guise of helping Hank could have slipped the box cutter in the drawer at A Stitch in Time or even into one of the many bags and boxes that traveled back and forth between the two stores that night.

Nancy carefully lifted something from the box, laid it on the counter, and began to gently unfold the surrounding tissue paper.

"Well, it wasn't me," said Penny. "Or Jason."

"Not Hank," the two women said together.

Liv shrugged. "I don't think they can even be sure that it was somebody involved with the Thornsbys." Liv watched Nancy untangle a jumble of delicate seashells and hold them up to the light.

"Oh, Nancy, that's beautiful."

"It's a wind chime, handmade with brass and abalone."

"I'll take one. Miss Ida and Miss Edna will love it."

"You mean Phil might have been working on another case?" Penny asked.

"I guess. Do you have something like this but a little more masculine?" Maybe Ted would like a wind chime.

"Over here." Nancy walked over to a wooden rack of chimes.

"Hmm." Liv didn't see anything that screamed Ted at her. Maybe she'd get him something from the Yarn Barn. He seemed to like sweaters. Hanging at the very end of the row was a wind chime made of dangling primitive heads. Scary and comic at the same time. Perfect for a certain annoying newspaper editor. She lifted it off the hook and handed it to Nancy.

Nancy raised her eyebrows.

"It isn't anything weird, is it?"

"Not in this store. It's the artist's rendering of Kapua, the mischievous god of ancient Hawaii."

"Perfect," Liv said. "I think that just about does it." And she needed to hit a lot more stores so she didn't appear to be showing favoritism.

"Penny, can you ring Liv up while I wrap these?"

"Sure." She took the tags from Nancy, and Liv followed her to the cash register. "I heard he was working on more than one case."

"Hmm," Liv said noncommittally.

"So what kind of case do you think he was working on?" Penny chewed on her bottom lip.

"Nothing you need to worry about, I'm sure."

"How can you be sure?"

"Because I have it on good authority that he was just researching something that happened years ago somewhere in the Midwest. See, nothing to be worried about."

A tinkling noise made them both turn. Nancy was picking up Chaz's wind chime from the counter.

"Sorry, they get tangled so easily." She lifted it up and straightened the strings. The evil little heads grinned back at Liv.

Nancy returned it to the paper and folded it into a gift box; then she handed Liv her purchases and walked her to the door.

"Looks like snow," said Nancy, studying the sky. "How are you adjusting to all this cold weather?"

"As long as I don't have to shovel, I love it. Thanks again, Nancy, these are perfect gifts." *Especially the one for Chaz.* Liv grinned at the thought of those diabolical heads clattering in the wind, the snow, the rain, the least little breeze. *Try napping through that, Mr. Bristow.*

"Merry Christmas, you two." Very pleased with herself, Liv left the Pyne Bough singing. "You won't need a weatherman to do dee do dee do dee. 'Cause now you've got this wind chime, do dee do dee do doo." She did a little jig outside the door.

Her day was beginning to look up.

Chapter Twenty-four

··

It was almost four o'clock by the time Liv finished her shopping and hauled it all into the Events Office. Ted was back to wearing a suit, but his tie was red, dotted with little sprigs of holly. In the background, the little drummer boy rum-pum-pum-pummed.

Ted raised an eyebrow. "Well, I see you shop with the same efficiency as you do everything."

"I was on a time crunch. Any disasters while I was gone?"

"No. One of the trolleys broke down, but since it was a weekday, we just fudged the scheduled stops and it's working out. The garage said they can have it back to us before Friday."

He followed her into her office. Reached for a bag as she attempted to drop them on the table where they kept "works in progress," that is, unfinished tasks, tasks they wanted to ignore, a spare box of dog biscuits, and a stack of trade catalogues and data reports that no one had time to read.

Liv shouldered him out of the way. "Thanks, but I know

you're just trying to get a peek at what I bought. Don't. Do. It."

Ted looked hurt.

"Uh-uh. I know your sneaky ways. There *is* something in there for you." Actually there were several somethings. Once Liv got started, she couldn't stop. She smiled. She couldn't help herself.

"Holy cats, you look like you suddenly got the Christmas spirit."

"How about that, and it isn't even February. That's usually the first time I stop long enough to realize I missed it." Liv looked over her mountain of gift bags. "I'll still probably miss it this year. By the time I get all this to the post office, it will be too late to be delivered by the twenty-fifth. But my family is used to it."

"Do you ever get to go home for the holidays?" Ted's finger was creeping toward an open paper bag.

Liv slapped his hand away. "Any event planner who goes home for Christmas is either crazy or wants to fail. It's the biggest time of the year, not to mention the most lucrative."

"You're on salary."

"But I'm not crazy."

He chuckled.

"Do *you* ever go home for Christmas?"

"Celebration Bay is my home. Well, if you won't let me help wrap, I guess I'll go out to my desk and start working on the Memorial Day Picnic."

Liv laughed. "I do appreciate that we have to plan ahead, but you're welcome to leave early so you won't be late for choir practice."

"Heaven forfend. You *are* coming to the sing-along tomorrow, aren't you?"

"As long as I don't have to sing."

"Why not? Make a joyful noise. I assure you, not even all the choir sings on key. It's just really fun and beautiful in its own small-town way."

"Well, maybe. I did go to one once at Avery Fisher Hall,

but I got all tangled up in the 'ah-ah-ah amens' and started giggling, which earned me dirty looks from the people around me. Who, I might add, came with their own scores. Serious stuff."

Ted laughed. "We do have a few of those, but mainly we hand out the same dog-eared copies year after year. And there's no audition. Giggles welcome."

"In my defense I was sixteen."

"And you haven't been to one since?"

"No, but I listen to the Carnegie Hall live stream if I have the time." Though really, when did she ever have time at Christmas? She was always planning someone else's celebration and stayed backstage until the cleanup. But not this year. This year she was going to experience Christmas in December.

"Okay, I'll be there, and I promise not to giggle."

"I'm holding you to that." Ted left her office humming the "Hallelujah Chorus."

Liv sat at her desk and scanned down the To Be Dones, found that Ted had already done them. Even the plans for First Night were complete.

She leaned back in her chair. Looked up at the ceiling. Christmas, New Year's Eve. She sent a message skyward, *Please let Bill catch the killer before then.*

Ted left a few minutes later; Liv left shortly after and walked home. She stopped at the Zimmermans' to pick up Whiskey.

"We had a lovely time today," Miss Ida said as she hustled Liv inside. "And Edna made her signature beef burgundy. It's good stick-to-your bones food, though don't tell Edna I said so. It's French cuisine, but it still sticks to your bones. It's not quite ready. Would you like to sit down for a little glass of something?"

"Sounds delicious, thank you. And I would, but I did all my Christmas shopping today and I told BeBe I'd come by to pick up the stuff I stored at the Buttercup." Liv looked around. No welcoming excited dog to greet her? "Is Whiskey back at the carriage house?"

"No, Edna had to run out for a few supplies to see us through the snow. Whiskey loves to ride in the car, so she took him with her. I hope you don't mind."

"Of course not. I thought the snow was supposed to be days away."

"Just some showers, but better safe than sorry. So if you need to pick up packages, I think you should go now while the roads are clear. Dinner will be ready when you get back."

"Thank you. I feel like I've hardly seen you two or anyone else for ages. But I'm going to start making some time to visit with my friends."

"That sounds like an excellent plan."

Liv went directly to the old garage where the sisters had cleared a space for her car, bless them.

The air was clear and dark and Liv thought how like a fairy-tale village Celebration Bay looked when it was all lit up. She drove around to the alley entrance and down the alley to the Buttercup's back door.

She left the car running while she banged on the back door of the coffee bar. BeBe pulled the door open. "Do you need help?"

"No thanks. I'm just going to drop these off at the office where all the wrapping paper and mailing supplies are and then go home to have French cuisine with my landladies."

"*Mon dieu.* Have a good time."

Liv lugged her box of books outside. "It seems a lot heavier than it did this morning."

"Maybe they've spontaneously generated. Little *Life of Thomas Paine*s all over." BeBe held the door open, and Liv shuffled out to her car. She had to balance the box on her knee to beep the trunk open. She slid the box into the trunk.

"Hey, did you mean to leave this here?" BeBe held up the bag with the Santa suit.

"No, I'll take it and drop it off at the cleaner's tomorrow. Nancy suggested sage and baking soda. But I think I'll go for the hard stuff."

"Nancy thinks sage cures everything." BeBe tossed the bag to her. "See you tomorrow."

Liv dropped the bag into the trunk and drove the block and a half to town hall. There were a few cars in the employee parking lot, but none of them looked familiar. After six, the lot was opened to visitors. There was a free space right by the back door. Liv pulled in and popped the trunk.

She found the key to the employees' entrance—at least she hoped it was this one. She rarely used this entrance since she usually walked to work and entered through the front door. She was glad of it tonight, though, because it went straight into the building, unlike the front where you had to climb a hefty set of steps.

She slid the Santa suit off the box and left it behind. Better it stink up her trunk than her office. She hoisted up the box of books, then stretched to reach the hatch. The box nearly spilled out.

She grabbed again and pushed the trunk down. With the box sliding down her legs, she staggered to the door.

"Next Christmas, Dad, you're getting an e-reader and some downloads." Except the kinds of books her dad read were often primary sources; and besides, how festive was a download?

She pulled the door open and angled the box through. Five minutes later her books were sitting on the worktable waiting to be wrapped and sent. Her stomach growled. And she wouldn't even be late for dinner.

She turned out the lights, locked the door, and headed back to the parking lot. The first thing she saw was her open trunk. What the heck? She had shut it. It should have locked automatically. She ran to the back of the car. Looked in. The Santa suit was gone.

She turned around in a full three-sixty. No one in sight. She ran to the side street. No one. The post office parking lot across the street was almost as light as day. And nothing moved.

She walked slowly back to the car, looking for any sign

of a break-in. Fortunately, her car was fine, no broken windows. She unlocked the driver's door and the interior light came on. She looked in the front seat. Clear. Looked in the backseat. No one there.

She got in and locked the door. Someone had stolen the Santa suit. Kids? Delinquents who had taken the opportunity to burglarize the cars that were hidden from view by the building?

As she backed up, a man stepped out of the shadows. He walked toward her.

He waved. And she recognized A.K. Pierce.

With a sigh of relief, she lowered her window.

He looked inside. "Everything all right?"

"Yes. I was just dropping some stuff off at the office. You're out late."

"I like to stay in the field with my men. I'm taking the second shift this week."

She wondered if she should tell him to be on the lookout for a Santa-suit thief. But she was pretty sure this thief had been after one thing and had gotten it. Which meant the killer hadn't left town.

"You've got plenty of staff out there?" she asked.

"Yes. Three uniformed and three plainclothes. Between us and the county, we have the area covered."

Except for where it wasn't. "I'm concerned—"

He put his hand on the window frame and leaned in. "Don't be. We've got a handle on it."

She smiled, wanting to believe him but focused on the theft of the suit from her trunk. He was leaning awfully close. Solid. A man that could protect a town. And a woman.

"Well, good night," she said.

He moved away. Smiled in a disarming way that was totally at odds with the burly ex-marine body and the no-nonsense ex-marine mind. He watched as she drove away.

Interesting. She didn't know whether to be flattered or frightened.

* * *

Miss Edna was just setting the table when Liv arrived.

"Ah, there you are," Miss Ida said. Whiskey looked up from the huge bone he was gnawing and beat his tail on the floor to let her know he saw her.

"Something strange just happened," she told her landladies as Ida handed her a glass of wine.

"Strange?" asked Edna.

"Yes. And maybe something bad."

"Oh dear," Ida said. "Is there something we can do?"

She told them about the theft and about A.K. Pierce showing up two minutes too late.

"Did you tell him about the theft?"

"No, but I'm not sure why I didn't."

"Did you call Bill?"

"No. I think he finally might have made it to the *Messiah* rehearsal and I hated to bother him."

"That's what he's here for," Edna said. "You just call his cell and tell him to come on over after practice. We have dinner for him."

Bill showed up just as they were clearing the plates away.

"Sit down, I'll fix you a plate," Ida said.

"Why didn't you call me when it happened?" he asked Liv after she explained why she had called.

"I didn't want to drag you away from choir practice. I looked to see if there was anyone hanging around and acting suspicious. He was long gone."

"I suppose you messed up any fingerprints we might have gotten from your car."

"Do they really take fingerprints from a burglarized car?"

"Not usually, but this is different. There's still a killer on the loose and it sounds like he's too close for comfort."

"Oh dear," said Ida.

Miss Edna slid a steaming plate in front of him. "Well, the car is in the garage, and it's too late to go chasing off after a Santa-suit thief. So eat your dinner before it gets cold."

Bill dug in and for a few minutes there were only sighs and "umms" coming from the sheriff.

"I made decaf," Ida said when he was finished.

Everybody had coffee and little cookies that Edna called silver bells. They were shaped like little bells, covered in a white icing with three little silver dragées as the clappers. Beautiful and delicious.

"I don't want any of you ladies going out at night by yourselves," Bill said. "Especially you." Everyone looked at Liv.

"It was only six o'clock."

"But it was already dark."

"It was dark at four o'clock."

Bill's brows dipped.

"We'll be careful," Edna said. "But, Bill, is anything jumping out at you over this murder?"

"Oh yeah. Too much."

"Like what?" asked Ida.

"Miss Ida, you know I can't talk about an open case. Just be careful, please."

"We will," Edna assured him. "But you don't think the killer stole the suit out of Liv's car?"

"I don't mean to scare you, but yes, I think there's a good chance that he did."

Liv frowned. "Doesn't it seem like one more instance of evidence popping up all over the place and moving from place to place?"

"Liv," Bill warned.

"Please, just listen and then tell me I'm wrong so I can sleep tonight."

Ida nodded. "You should listen to her, Bill Gunnison. The girl has a head on her shoulders."

Resigned, Bill sat back. "Okay, shoot."

"The first Santa suit is stolen from Nancy's back room, worn to kill Phil Cosgrove. Found in the Dumpster and worn by Hank in the Santa Parade.

"Cosgrove was not wearing the second Santa suit when he was killed. According to Grace, it was in the back of her trunk the whole time."

Bill nodded. "Until tonight."

"Yes. Sorry about that, but BeBe and I searched it first. We didn't find anything but gum wrappers and cigarette packs. And you didn't find a notebook on his person or in his apartment."

Bill just scowled.

"I'll take that as a yes."

"Very nice, dear," Miss Ida said.

Miss Edna poured more coffee.

"I offered Grace fifty bucks for the suit to use as a backup. She sold it to me, and through my own negligence, within eight hours it's stolen out of my trunk. But how did they know it was in my trunk?"

Bill scratched his head. "Someone heard you say you were going to pick it up."

"I told BeBe this morning, but I didn't say what time, and I told Miss Ida right before I left."

"Well, I didn't do it," Miss Ida said indignantly.

Edna laughed. "She leads a double life, my sister."

Ida pursed her lips. "This is not a laughing matter."

"No. I apologize."

"And no one else knew?" Bill asked.

Liv thought back. She hadn't even told Ted, and there'd been no reason to mention it to anyone while she was shopping. "I did tell Penny Newland that I was going to buy it back if Grace would sell it. No wait. I saw her in the alley when I was going to get it out of Grace's car. I told her to tell Nancy that we had an extra. The two of them were concerned about having a backup. They both seem very attached to Hank."

Bill raised both eyebrows and reached for another cookie. "I'll let that pass for the moment. Could anyone have overheard you?"

"I don't think so, but they could have. About buying the suit, I mean. That still doesn't explain how they knew where I'd be. Unless they've been following me. Or unless . . ." For a second Liv saw stars, and not the beautiful Christmas decoration kind, but the please-don't-let me-pass-out kind.

"What?"

"When I came out and discovered the theft, A.K. Pierce stepped out of the shadows. He said he was on patrol. He was in BeBe's when I took the suit there. I think he noticed it."

"Did you tell him about the suit being stolen?"

"No. I—I don't know, I was kind of spooked, so I just left and called you." She swallowed. "You don't think . . . no." A.K. Pierce had recognized Cosgrove . . . but surely he wouldn't have volunteered that information if he'd killed the man, right?

Though now that she thought about it, who but a security person could move from place to place without raising suspicions? He'd certainly made himself visible during the last few days. And if he just happened to move evidence around . . .

Her stomach clenched. Where had A.K. Pierce been the night of the tree lighting? She'd seen him in the crowd, hadn't she? Surely . . . though he didn't seem at all surprised at finding a body in the store. He was probably used to finding bodies, right?

"Liv?"

She jumped. "What?"

Bill swallowed. "That's it. I'm assigning a squad car to sit outside tonight."

"Outside where?"

"Here."

"Good heavens," said Miss Ida.

"What on earth for?" Edna asked.

"Because," Bill said, looking intently at Liv, "if whoever stole the suit tonight didn't find what they were looking for, they may think Liv still has it."

Chapter Twenty-five

Liv slept well that night. Maybe it was knowing there was a squad car parked outside to scare away potential burglars or murderers. Or maybe she was just tired from running on adrenaline since October.

Whichever it was, she arrived at work the next morning wearing a red sweater and feeling optimistic. Whiskey was wearing his bow tie, though Liv hadn't made it to the Woofery and the bow was looking positively dog-eared.

It didn't deter Ted or Whiskey from bursting into song.

Liv just handed Ted the buns and tea and coffee and went into her office, smiling.

The yodeling duo came in a few minutes later, Whiskey with a Santa biscuit—Liv shuddered—and Ted carrying a tray of food to which had been added a miniature Christmas tree with battery-powered lights.

"You know," Liv said as he sat down and passed her a plate, "I could deal with your mysterious self, your love of sweets, and your penchant for drawing out a story, but this Christmas-cheer thing is a really big surprise."

Ted looked shocked. "Why, Liv, we are Celebration Bay. It's our duty to celebrate."

"Oh yeah? Well, celebrate this." She told him about the theft from her trunk. The squad car outside her house during the night.

"So that's where Bill went in such a hurry after rehearsal last night. You *are* coming tonight?"

"Wouldn't miss it, but I'm taking Whiskey home first."

"If you insist, but we could use another tenor."

"You'll have to find him elsewhere. Now, what about the arrangements for the ice sculpture exhibit on Saturday?"

"I talked to Andy Miller yesterday. He has the stations set up and cordoned off."

"Cordoned off? What about flying ice shards and escaping chain saws?"

"We're talking about Andy. He's on top of it. There are bleachers and plenty of local folks policing the area and making sure no tools are left unattended and no one gets too close."

Liv checked it off, reminding herself that she couldn't be everywhere at once. "The house tour?"

"Trolley will be back by tomorrow afternoon, latest. We're expecting a larger crowd than ever this weekend and up until the twenty-fifth. I ran it past Fred and he's got some extra folks on traffic, and he's coordinating with A.K. Pierce and company. We should be good there."

A.K. Pierce.

"What?"

"Hmm? Nothing. You're amazing."

"While the boss is out Christmas shopping, the drone makes the calls."

"You can take off early to get ready for the sing-along today."

"I was going to. We have a run-through before the performance just to get the pipes going and clean up a few ragged hallelujahs. Now, drink your coffee before it gets cold."

* * *

By afternoon both desks were clear, and Liv pulled out the folder for First Night.

"It's three o'clock."

"Good-bye. Break a leg. Or whatever you say to singers before a performance."

"See you tonight." Ted bundled up and went out the door humming. Whiskey padded after him but returned quickly, shot an accusing look at Liv, and went back to his doggie bed to sleep, no doubt to dream of a doggie Hallelujah Chorus to judge from the sounds that emanated from the snoring Westie.

It grew dark. Liv checked her watch. Four o'clock. Plenty of time to finish up here, walk Whiskey home, maybe even get a shower in before coming back for the *Messiah* sing-along.

Her cell phone rang.

"Hi, Liv, it's Dolly. I'm at the *Messiah* rehearsal and Penny hasn't arrived. I tried calling the Pyne Bough, but no one answers. I know they were planning on closing early like everyone else, but Penny isn't at home. I thought maybe she's gotten involved making those stars that Miriam ordered and lost track of the time.

"She may be on her way, but if you're going home soon, would you mind swinging by the Pyne Bough?"

"Sure. In fact, I was just about to close up. I'll call you when I get there and let you know."

"Thanks. I'll tell the choir director." Dolly hung up.

"We're packing it in, buddy." She shut down her computer, looked at it, decided she wouldn't need it until tomorrow at the earliest, and left it on her desk. Whiskey danced as he waited for her to clip on his leash. He was as anxious to get outside as she was.

It was getting late and she wanted to get home while there were still lots of shoppers on the street. She'd hardly ever felt unsafe in Manhattan, but then she'd spent a lot of her life there and knew the ropes. It was unnerving to move to a seemingly idyllic town and discover that things weren't always as peaceful as they appeared.

She waited for several cars to pass, then crossed the street.

Chaz was right. When you attract a lot of outsiders, they bring their problems, their misconceptions, and their anger with them. Usually when they left, their problems left with them. Of course, then new problems would arrive. Like this past month with the opening of TAT.

Somebody had that notebook and it had to be one of the Thornsbys or Penny Newland. And she just didn't see Penny as a killer. Just a naïve young woman who was now paying for one night of poor judgment.

Maybe whoever killed Cosgrove had the book. If Cosgrove had it on him when he was killed, surely the killer would have taken it. But what if Cosgrove didn't have it? Maybe he was at the store, not to get his paycheck, but to get his notebook out of the Santa suit. But the suit was already in Grace's car, or so she said. The police hadn't found a notebook and neither had Liv. So where was it?

Whiskey pulled at the leash, and Liv started toward the Pyne Bough again.

Cosgrove clearly had evidence on Grace Thornsby and her lover. But Grace didn't seem to care. She said she didn't need Clarence's money.

And what had Cosgrove been looking up at the library? Could it in any way have something to do with his murder?

The Pyne Bough was dark, and the door was locked. A sign read, *Closed Early for the Messiah Sing-along.* Most of the stores had similar signs, though many of them planned to reopen after the sing-along and stay open late.

Liv detoured down the alley to the delivery door and noticed that a car, packed to the top of the windows, was parked at the back door of TAT.

Liv's immediate reaction was "Yes." Maybe Grace was already packing up.

Except the car wasn't a Mercedes. It was old, really old.

Jason's maybe? Was Penny with him? Were they leaving? What about the sing-along?

Liv felt sick. She knocked on the back door of the Pyne Bough. The door swung open and Whiskey lurched inside.

Liv forgot about Grace, the car, and everything else. The lights were still on in the back, and Liv reminded herself that Nancy often left the door open during a delivery. And maybe other times, too.

She tightened Whiskey's leash and cautiously poked her head in. "Nancy? Penny?"

The storeroom appeared empty. Hank had left for the day. His Santa suit was hanging on the clothes rack. He must not have closed the door when he left.

"Nancy? Penny? Anyone here?"

Not a sound came from the store.

"Nancy?" *Okay, time to get out of this store.* Liv was no wuss. But there was a murderer on the loose.

Her heart kicked up. Lying in the middle of the floor was a coat, an old parka that Liv remembered seeing the first time she'd met Penny Newland.

Looking quickly around to make sure no one was creeping up behind her, she hurried over to the coat. She felt a little foolish, but better safe than sorry.

Whiskey immediately began to snuffle at the coat, uncovering Penny's purse, a crumpled piece of copy paper—and the extra Santa suit.

Liv snatched up the paper and reached for her cell. She didn't call Dolly, but speed-dialed Bill. It went directly to voice mail. She left a message.

She tried Ted. Same thing; Dolly, no answer. They must all be singing.

All this time Liv was walking toward the door to the alley, dragging a reluctant Whiskey with her.

Something was not right. Penny's coat and the Santa suit. Did that mean Penny had stolen it? Liv couldn't make herself imagine Penny breaking into the trunk of her car. But Jason could have. He helped out at Hank's machine shop, and though Liv wasn't really sure what a machinist did, she was pretty sure he could pop a trunk, especially if it hadn't closed properly.

Both coat and suit were lying on the floor as if they had been tossed there. Like they had fallen when someone forced Penny out of the store?

And where was Nancy? Hank had been here. His Santa suit was hanging on the rack. Had he taken both of them? She'd never seen Hank's car, had she?

Her mind recoiled from that possibility.

Liv stood in the alley, her back to the wall, and straightened out the paper. She recognized the article before she even read the words. She and Chaz had read it two nights before. Wisconsin. An explosion. The work of antiwar activists. A bombing that left a security guard dead.

Wisconsin. Someone had been talking about Wisconsin lately.

One person caught; three others escaped. Joss said that Hank knew Jason's father from 'Nam. Had they returned disenchanted, been part of that crime, the ones that had escaped? Grace and Hank? How long had they been married? Had they blown up a building before returning to Celebration Bay and getting married? Was Grace even old enough to be a radical activist?

She didn't want to jump the gun. There could be a simple explanation. . . . No there couldn't. Either Hank had kidnapped the women, or they had gone willingly. Or someone else had forced them to leave together once Hank was gone.

Liv pulled out her cell and started to call nine-one-one. Stopped, afraid that a siren barreling toward the Pyne Bough would panic whoever was holding them.

She looked down the alley, went over to the opening to the parking lot next to the Pyne Bough, and peered out. Cars were driving around searching for parking spaces, but there was no one she recognized. Not that she'd really expected to see them running across the asphalt.

She called Bill again. Left another message.

She looked back at the packed car at the door of TAT. Grace wasn't moving out. Someone was getting away. The car was facing west, the direction of the highway. But if it wasn't Grace, why stop at TAT?

Whiskey pulled at the leash.

"Okay, we'll just go take a quick peek at the car. But not too close." They skulked forward, Whiskey pulling at the leash, Liv holding tight with one hand and holding her cell in the other.

Keeping what she hoped was a safe distance from the car, she peered in the windows and saw faded quilts, a tattered suitcase, a box of natural soaps, two smaller boxes of incense. An empty dog crate. Dog crate? A bag of sand. And she remembered Nancy saying, *I always keep a bag of sand in my car for traction.* Nancy? Activist turned earth mother?

She had access to Hank's original Santa suit.

Her interest in the TAT Santa suit. It wasn't for Hank's sake, but for her own. Because she thought it held the notebook?

And Nancy had brought up Wisconsin. *When I was in college in Wisconsin.*

Liv pulled at Whiskey's leash, backing slowly away as other pieces fell into place. The box cutter. Miriam telling Elsbeth she'd forgotten hers the night they'd fit Hank for the new suit. And Elsbeth borrowing one from Nancy's packing table. She'd probably just returned it to Miriam's sewing box without thinking. Nancy didn't even have to get rid of it. The seamstresses had done it for her.

Where was Bill?

Before she'd gone ten feet, someone screamed. Whiskey went nuts; Liv nearly dropped her phone. To hell with causing a disturbance.

She punched in nine-one-one.

The door to TAT opened halfway. A hand appeared, then it was dragged back inside. The hand, looking incredibly small, grabbed the edge of the door. Grasped at the door until she was yanked back into the store. The door continued to swing open.

And it was at that moment the TAT cat slunk out from under the car and darted through the open door. Whiskey lunged, barked furiously, and tried to follow it inside.

Another scream.

Whiskey went wild.

Liv was in way over her head. She scooped Whiskey into her arms, and clutching the wriggling dog and her cell phone, she made a rush toward the street.

Before she'd gone two steps, a loud "Stop!" came from inside the store. Liv stopped. The point of a gun appeared in the doorway. A gun. A gun? A gun. Aimed at Liv.

Liv tried to swallow.

"Inside. Hurry."

Liv had no choice, she'd rather take her chances inside than be shot in the alley.

Whiskey fought to get down. Liv held him fast and reluctantly stepped through the door and into the gun-wielding Nancy Pyne.

"Drop the phone."

Liv dropped her phone.

"Now, go over there and sit down." Nancy motioned her inside where Grace and Penny were huddled in the corner of the storage room. Liv didn't see Hank anywhere.

Liv moved toward the other women, sat down, and held Whiskey in her lap, willing him to stay calm while her thoughts ran and she kept one eye on the earth mother's pistol.

Nancy looked almost as unhappy as the others. "I wish you hadn't figured it out, Liv. I really do."

"But I—" *didn't*, Liv thought. She hadn't had a clue until a few minutes before in the alley. And even as the pieces fell into place, she still couldn't wrap her mind around Nancy, the sage-burning, peacenik earth mother as a murderer.

"First I made that stupid slip about Wisconsin. I'm always so careful." Nancy sniffed. "I got too comfortable here. Started thinking I could have a life. A . . . a life. Then when I heard you humming that song when you left the store yesterday—were you trying to warn me or threaten me?"

What song? Liv remembered Nancy saying Penny was luckier in her love life than she had been. That she had been pregnant once, back in Wisconsin, and lost the baby. But that had been earlier in the week. What song had Liv been humming when she left the store yesterday?

She searched back to yesterday's shopping spree. She bought incense and wind chimes for her landladies and that funny one for Chaz. And left . . . she left.

And then she remembered. The one she and Chaz had been talking about the night before. Joked about even. She'd sung a parody of it as she left the store, Chaz wouldn't need a weatherman with those silly wind chimes proclaiming the weather.

Nancy must have thought she was talking about The Weathermen. And by then, Nancy had already killed to keep her secret safe. Not Hank or Jason or Grace or Penny. But Nancy Pyne.

"Oh, Nancy."

Nancy's lip quivered. She looked like a sad, broken woman, not a cold-blooded killer.

"He wasn't supposed to be there. It was a mistake. An awful, awful mistake. We didn't mean to hurt anyone."

Nancy was one of the bombers. And she'd been on the run ever since. Liv was so astounded and saddened that she forgot to be afraid for a second. Over forty years on the run. What a horrible, unhappy life.

Liv's phone vibrated. Nancy kicked it into the corner.

Next to Liv, Penny was trembling all over. And her eyes were so large they looked as if they might burst. Liv gave her a smile that was supposed to be reassuring. How would they ever get out of this alive?

Keep Nancy talking. That's what Jessica Fletcher would do. But Jessica always had the police waiting behind the door. Liv's police were all at choir practice.

Liv cleared her throat. It hurt. "Nancy, don't do this." Whatever this was. And Liv had a sickening idea what that might be.

"I don't want to. Why did you have to come? I wasn't going to hurt them. Just get the cat."

"What?"

"Even an old cat deserves better than her." She lifted her chin toward Grace.

On cue, the cat appeared to rub a figure eight around Nancy's ankles.

Kind to animals; a murderer of men. But hopefully not women.

Nancy bent down and scooped the cat into her arms.

Whiskey's headed snapped up. His ears pitched forward. Liv held him tighter. And held her breath.

"Nancy, go. We can't stop you. And you can't stay here. Just go while you have the chance."

Nancy's lip quivered; she held the cat close and rubbed her cheek along its fur.

"I liked it here. I felt like maybe it was finally home. But I'll never find a home, never find . . . " Her voice broke. It was pitiful.

Suddenly she straightened and turned toward Grace. "Give me the notebook and I'll leave."

Grace crossed her arms. "I don't have it here."

Of course. Grace must have found the notebook when she packed Cosgrove's Santa suit away and put it in her trunk. Before Nancy had even come after Cosgrove. And Grace had tried to blackmail Nancy. That's why she wasn't disturbed when Clarence announced his bankruptcy. She thought she had found another source of cash.

"Grace, give it to her and let her go."

Grace shrugged and sneered at the desperate woman. "You silly freak. You could have kept your stupid secret if you'd just paid up and left town. The notebook is at the bank."

Panic flashed in Nancy's eyes. She turned the gun on Grace. Her hand was shaking. Not a good sign.

"Nancy, go. Grace won't tell. I'll make her give it to me and I'll destroy it."

"I can't." The words came out in a wail. "I killed a man. I didn't mean to. I saw him outside smoking and writing in that notebook. He slipped it away when he saw me, but I knew. The look on his face. He knew. Then he started coming into the store. Asking questions. I panicked. I didn't mean to do it. I was happy here."

Nancy was at the breaking point; she might kill them all out of sheer terror.

"You can tell this to the—to Bill. He'll understand."

"No he won't. I don't understand. How did this happen to me? One stupid mistake forty years ago. We just wanted to destroy the chemical factory. What they made killed people. We wanted to stop the greed, the corruption. We didn't mean to kill anybody. The guard wasn't supposed to be there."

"What's she talking about?" Penny whispered. "Is she crazy?"

Liv was afraid the pressure had gotten to be too much for Nancy. To realize that Phil Cosgrove had decided to delve into the past, now of all times, after so many years. She must have felt like a cornered animal.

But she's a murderer, Liv reminded herself. The death of the guard may have been unintentional, but she'd known what she was doing when she killed Phil Cosgrove.

Liv heard something. Listened. Was someone coming up the alley? *Please let it be Bill.* Surely he would check his messages before the performance. What if there was an emergency? This definitely qualified as one.

"And Phil Cosgrove found out?"

Nancy nodded, rubbed her cheek against that mangy cat again. If Liv hadn't been so petrified, she would have felt sorry for her.

Definitely footsteps coming. The door banged open and in stormed Quincy Hinks. "Whoever's blocking the alley better move that car right now."

Nancy whirled around. The cat scratched her face. Nancy dropped the gun, which discharged, deafening everyone in the room. The cat took off. Whiskey yanked free of Liv's arms and ran after the cat.

"I—uh, well take your time." Quincy started to back away.

Nancy recovered quickly and knelt down to get the gun.

"Quincy, stop her," Liv yelled. But before she or Quincy could move, Grace lunged at Nancy. "You bitch. You stupid bitch. You could have been out of here and I could be on my way to the islands." She grabbed Nancy's hair.

Nancy elbowed her and tried to roll away, but Grace hung on. "You stupid—"

Liv jumped up and kicked the gun across the room where it joined her cell phone, just as A.K. Pierce burst into the room, pointing something that made Nancy's gun look like a toy.

He grabbed Grace with one hand and flicked her back toward Liv. Liv didn't even try to catch her, but let her hit the floor. Whatever Grace had been involved in, it wasn't nice.

He pulled Nancy to her feet just as more footsteps sounded in the alley; seconds later, four more men crowded in the doorway. Ted, Bill, Chaz, and Hank Ousterhout.

Liv burst out laughing.

"She's in shock," A.K. said. "Bill, call someone to pick this one up. You might as well take that one over there, too." He indicated Grace. "From what I heard, I think we have a case of blackmail against her."

Penny started to cry. Quincy sat beside her and patted her shoulder.

Liv stood there trying to figure out what had just happened. She watched Bill pull a pair of handcuffs from his belt and wondered if he'd worn them at choir practice. Somehow that made her want to laugh again.

Bill led Nancy gently toward the door, but she stopped when she reached Hank.

"It was all a mistake. A stupid, stupid mistake," Nancy said. And it wasn't an excuse Liv heard in her voice. Just regret.

"Nancy?" Hank said.

"I didn't mean to get you in trouble, Hank. I wasn't thinking clearly. I was desperate. I just wasn't thinking."

"Come on, Nancy. Time to go." Bill took Nancy away.

A.K. took note of the gun in the corner but didn't pick it up. "Whose phone is that?"

"Mine," Liv said, but it was barely a whisper.

A.K. picked it up and handed it to her. "You okay?"

She nodded. She didn't trust her voice. Now that it was over, she felt a little like Penny looked.

She was aware of Chaz walking toward them.

He glanced at A.K. before scowling at Liv. "Hey, I was going to come to the rescue. Only I didn't know you needed rescuing. Of all the stupid—"

"Leave her alone."

Chaz frowned at A.K. A.K. frowned back. They were about the same height. But A.K. had it in muscle over the newspaper editor. Across the room she saw Ted grimace, then the grimace turned to a grin.

Chaz lifted both hands in defeat, but his eyes were laughing, not with humor but with something that might be self-mockery.

Sirens sounded, A.K. nodded at Liv, shot Chaz another frown for good measure, and escorted Grace outside.

Her knees suddenly too weak to hold her, Liv sank onto the nearest shipping crate.

"Are you really okay?" Chaz asked.

"Yeah. I think. Don't tell me you were at the sing-along rehearsal, too."

"Me? Can't carry a tune in a bucket. No, I finally made the connection between the Wisconsin bombing and Phil Cosgrove's murder."

"That it was Nancy?"

Chaz nodded. "I was on my way to warn you. I tried calling, but when you didn't answer, I figured you were in trouble. Knew I was right when I saw the mess at the Pyne Bough and the car in the alley. Jesus. You're making me an old man."

"Sorry."

"You should be." He sat beside her. "But what I don't know is how Cosgrove stumbled onto it."

"Maybe Bill will find out when Nancy makes her statement."

Bill strode back in. "Okay, those two are on the way to the station. Looks like I'm going to miss the sing-along again this year."

"The sing-along," said Penny. "What time is it?"

Chaz looked at his watch. "Almost seven."

Penny cast an anxious look toward Bill.

"Aw hell, at this point I guess I can wait until after the sing-along to take your statement. Get going and don't forget anything that happened. Meese, get someone to drive her over. I'm not taking any chances on our lead soprano getting lost on the way. Ted, Hank, you go along, too."

Meese escorted Penny out the door. Ted and Hank followed.

"Are you going to the sing-along?" Chaz asked.

"I'm planning on it, though I have to find Whiskey first and take him home. Guess I won't be getting a shower or changing clothes, though."

Chaz lifted an eyebrow.

"Don't be smarmy. I was afraid we were all going to be killed."

"Yeah, okay. Let's go find the dog."

They found Whiskey and the cat at the door of the Bookworm. Whiskey's butt was up. He wanted to play. The cat's back was up, which didn't bode well for her dog.

"Whiskey, come." Reluctantly, he obeyed.

Quincy came up beside them. "What a night. Don't tell me what I just walked into. I don't want to know. At least not until tomorrow." He unlocked his door. The cat darted in before him.

"Looks like you just inherited yourself a cat," Chaz said.

Quincy shrugged. "Every bookstore should have a cat. But I won't be calling it Tinkerbell. Good night." He went into the bookstore and closed the door.

Whiskey whined.

"Sorry, buddy. The fun's over. And I need to get you home so I can go to the sing-along."

Chaz looked at his watch. "Not enough time if you want to be there from the beginning."

"I can't take him with me. Ted taught him to sing."

Chaz gave her a look. "This I gotta hear."

"But not during the *Messiah*."

"Come on. He can sit in the choir room until it's over."

Chapter Twenty-six

....

Liv and Chaz struck off across the park toward the church. Whiskey trotted along beside them.

"It's kind of sad," Liv said. "Make a mistake when you're young and pay for it for the rest of your life."

"She didn't."

Liv frowned at him.

"She's been free for forty years. Forty more than the guard got."

"I don't think she was really free. What a lonely existence. No real friends, no companion. And she finally got caught because she couldn't leave without saving the cat."

"Don't make her out to be better than she was. She came back for the notebook. She killed a man for it. She would have killed you and whoever else stood in her way."

It was a depressing thought. Nancy had always seemed so good-willed. Peaceful. Willing to help. Chaz was jaded, but he was right. She'd killed Phil Cosgrove, not forty years ago, but just last week. To protect herself. And for what? Had he threatened her? Was he blackmailing her like Grace had tried to do? What had Phil Cosgrove planned to do with the information he'd found?

"But Grace had the notebook. She must have found it and the papers Cosgrove had copied. With Clarence going belly-up, she saw her chance to clean up. Surely Nancy didn't have enough money saved to make blackmail worthwhile?"

"Who knows, Liv? We probably never will. Now, come on. We better move it if you want to be there for the opening notes."

Somewhere during their walk across the park, the full import of what had happened hit Liv, and her knees began to wobble.

"Maybe we should stop at McCready's first," Chaz said. "You look like you need a brandy more than a songfest."

Liv shook her head. What she and the whole town needed was beautiful music, shared together, the community of one another to wash away the violence and anger and fear of the last week. They needed an affirmation of life to be able to go into the season with hope and a sense of peace and a new beginning.

"Thanks, but I don't want to be late. You go ahead."

Chaz sighed, took her elbow, and steered her down the walk.

Light poured out of the church windows, creating a gold nimbus around the building. The doors were open, and people thronged up the steps. Several knots of people stood on the sidewalk, and as Liv and Chaz drew nearer, Liv realized that news of Nancy's arrest had preceded them.

"Is it true?" Miriam Krause asked. "Nancy Pyne is a murderer? I just can't believe it. She was such a nice person."

Chaz snorted. "Just like every psychopath ever arrested. He was such a nice, quiet person. Excuse us, we have to see a preacher about a dog." He steered Liv away from the group.

"You're sounding especially cynical tonight," Liv told him.

Chaz didn't answer, just continued to guide her past curious looks and up the front steps.

Liv stopped before they went in. "Thank you."

"For what?"

"For coming to the rescue and walking me over."

"I was late for the rescue, and I don't mind walking you over. You're growing on me."

Pastor Schorr was greeting people at the door. He took Liv's hand. "Thank God you're safe," he said. "Welcome."

He shook Chaz's hand. "Haven't seen you in a while."

"Fish don't wait."

The pastor clapped him on the back.

"Would it be okay if I left Whiskey somewhere? I didn't have time to go home after the . . . uh . . ."

"Of course. Leo?"

A young man serving as usher stepped over. "This is Ms. Montgomery, Leo. Leo helps me out at the community center."

"Ma'am."

They solemnly shook hands.

"And this is Mr. Bristow."

"Oh, I know Chaz. He takes us fishing." Leo grinned at Chaz, who gave him a quick thumbs-up.

"Indeed," the pastor said, giving Chaz an appraising look. "Could you show Ms. Montgomery to my office?" He leaned down to pat Whiskey. "I have a very comfy chair. But please don't eat my sermon."

"Maybe I shouldn't leave him," Liv said.

"I'll stay with him, Pastor. I like dogs and they like me."

"Well, that's excellent, Leo. But you don't want to sing?"

"No sir. I like to sing, but I can't remember the words."

"Well, all things solved."

Liv handed Whiskey over to Leo.

"I'll take real good care of him, miss."

"He will," Pastor Schorr said. "He's a gentle spirit, our Leo."

They took two scores from another usher and went inside.

"You take kids fishing?" Liv asked.

"When I get tired of them pestering me."

She nodded and smiled as people turned to look at them. They passed the Newlands and Jason. Mrs. Newland, whom Liv had never really met, gave her a heartfelt smile. Jason, with Bobby sitting quietly on his lap, smiled tentatively. Mr. Newland, looking even frailer than he had on Sunday, just stared into the half distance.

People whispered as they passed. Everyone was relieved and curious. "Maybe I should have just gone home and stayed."

"Too late now."

They passed the Waterbury pew. Joss and his wife, Amanda, both smiled and nodded. Donnie was leaning forward talking to a girl in the pew in front of them. Roseanne was sitting behind them with several other teenage girls. She waved when she saw Liv. Then she saw Chaz and gave Liv a thumbs-up.

Great. Roseanne thought she was on a date.

"You don't have to walk me down the aisle."

"I don't plan on it."

Liv frowned at him. "What? Oh. Don't worry. I just meant, you didn't have to stay."

"And miss the 'Hallelujah Chorus'?"

Miss Edna saw them, waved, and scooted over to make room. BeBe widened her eyes at Liv from the far side of Miss Edna. Miss Ida patted Liv's hand, a gesture that encompassed so many feelings that Liv felt an unnatural urge to burst into tears.

But the lights lowered. The choir took their place on the risers that had been placed across the front, and the sound of scores opening rustled across the room. Liv saw Ted standing between Jeremiah Atkins and Hank Ousterhout. Penny was a few rows down. Liv could tell she had been crying, but she stood tall and determined.

The music started, wafting over them in a pure melodic line, a soothing balm. It grew, swelled, gathered them in and lifted them up.

When they came to the first chorus, Liv sang with the

others. It was something she didn't do much anymore. But she would from now on. Next to her, Chaz's voice was a clear baritone. On key and he didn't miss a note.

She glanced over at him. He shrugged.

Penny's solo was spellbinding, singing her thanks, her faithfulness, her love, and, Liv guessed, her relief at being alive.

Bill slipped into the pew beside them just in time for the "Hallelujah Chorus." He leaned over Chaz to Liv and said, "Singing like birds, both of them. I think it was a relief for Nancy finally to be caught. Grace, however." He rolled his eyes. "She'll get off with a warning probably. A fine for withholding evidence. But she's finished here."

The introduction began, music swelled, and the singers all stood. The first "hallelujah" reverberated to the ceiling, followed by another, and another until the air vibrated with the sound. And if there were two extra voices, singing off-key but enthusiastically from the pastor's office, no one seemed to mind. They were part of the joyful noise that welcomed a peaceful Christmas to Celebration Bay.

Christmas Day

....

The Zimmermans' old kitchen was toasty warm. The windows were fogged up with steam, and aromas swirled around the room as Miss Edna opened the oven and stepped aside for Ted to pull out the roast and transfer it to the carving board. "Just a few more minutes for the roast to rest." He was wearing a red apron over a red-and-green jacquard sweater Liv had bought him at the Yarn Barn, and a candy-cane tie from Ida and Edna.

It was a perfect old-fashioned Christmas, Liv thought, not that she'd celebrated many Christmases lately. Most Christmases she was either working, winding up working, recovering from working, or organizing her next job.

Not a good way to live. She was really committed to not making that mistake again. And though this hadn't been the easiest holiday season, recent events made this day extra special.

They had all met earlier to open presents, Miss Ida, Miss Edna, BeBe, Ted, and Bill, sitting around the tall Victorian tree in the parlor. They opened their presents amid Christmas music and laughter and those wonderful aromas wafting from the kitchen. While Whiskey, wearing a new red bow tie, gamboled among the wrapping paper, the humans sipped a special Christmas blend coffee—a present from BeBe—and enjoyed a platter of holiday breads delivered the morning before by Fred and Dolly, who were spending their Christmas with their son in New York City.

The table had been set the night before with beautiful Spode Christmas china, crystal water- and wineglasses, and the "real" silver as BeBe called it. In the center of the Battenberg lace tablecloth was an elaborate silver candelabra filled with red tapered candles.

There were seven place settings, but so far, only six diners. The seventh guest had yet to make an appearance.

"He's probably sleeping," Liv said.

The back door opened and closed, bringing a gust of freezing air. Bill came in from where he'd been hanging the abalone wind chime Liv had bought the sisters at the Pyne Bough. "All set and tinkling away," he said.

"Thank you, Bill," Miss Ida said. "So beautiful . . . poor Nancy."

They all fell silent for a second remembering the woman who had been so kind and yet had killed not once but twice.

"Will someone take over the store? What will happen to all her merchandise?" BeBe asked. She was wearing the "I'm the Barista Boss" apron Liv had ordered for her Christmas present.

"That will make two stores empty in the new year," said Miss Edna. "Not that we'll miss that awful Trim a Tree. I hear Clarence Thornsby isn't even waiting for the after-Christmas sales, but returning what merchandise he can to the wholesaler and selling the rest bulk to another store."

Miss Ida clicked her tongue. "It's such a shame, the Newlands losing the store like that. We'll need them even more now that Nancy's gone." She sighed. "She did a terrible thing, but I just can't seem to make myself hate her."

"Well, Christmas is a time for forgiving," Edna said.

"There *is* good news," Liv said. "I hope it's not too early to divulge." She looked at Ted.

"Take it away."

"Miriam has decided to go into partnership and expand A Stitch in Time into the TAT space."

"Partnership?" Ida exclaimed.

"With whom?" Edna added.

"With Penny Newland and Jason. Hank is cosigning a loan for them, and they're reopening Newland's Gifts in conjunction with the crafts groups that Penny will be running for Miriam."

"And," Ted volunteered, "it turns out that Clarence hadn't had time to unload the stock from the old Newland store— it's been in his garage—and is selling it back cheap."

"He should give it back," Edna said.

"At this point, I think he needs the money as much as the Newlands."

"Well, I'm glad that something good came from all this nonsense," Miss Ida said. "Bill Gunnison, I see you picking at that roast. I'm going to get my ruler if you don't stop this instant.

Bill pulled back his hand. "Just testing to make sure it's ready."

Edna sighed. "Good for Hank. He never had children of his own, but I'm sure he's going to take care of his old friend's son and his wife. They've decided to get married right away . . . so Roger can see his youngest married. Bless him." Edna's eyes misted, and she pulled a handkerchief from her sleeve. "Then they'll live over his garage until they can afford a bigger place."

"Well," Ida said, breaking into the silence that had followed as they all remembered the ailing man. "It will be good for Hank to have young people around the rest of the year and not just at Christmas."

Edna tucked her handkerchief back in her sleeve. "I'm sure he'll spoil little Bobby rotten."

"And the ones that follow," Ida said. She looked up at the wall clock. The doorbell rang, long round tones that rolled through the foyer and hall to the kitchen. Miss Ida wiped her hands on her apron and with a command to Edna to put the rolls in the oven, she went to answer the door.

"Perfect timing," Liv said to BeBe.

They heard Ida's, "Oh, they're just beautiful," echo from the hall. "Edna, come take Chaz's coat."

"Good. Now, can I carve the roast?" Bill asked.

Ida returned carrying a huge bouquet of long-stemmed red roses, followed by Chaz sans coat.

"I wonder where he found roses on Christmas morning," BeBe said under her breath.

"Probably pestered Della Grimes to open the florist shop for him. He's such a—" Liv did a double take. There wasn't a speck of red or green anywhere on him, but he wore gray wool trousers with a navy blue sweater pulled over a light blue dress shirt and he looked almost preppy. Even his hair was spiked less than usual.

BeBe rounded her eyes at Liv and went back to mashing potatoes.

"Ted, you go out and keep Chaz company," Miss Ida said. "Bill, start carving, and us girls will take care of it from here."

The men retreated and in a few minutes, and several trips from the kitchen to the dining room, everything was ready, and BeBe, Ida, Edna, and Liv were all gathered in the dining room.

"Dinner's served," Ida said.

Chaz jumped up from his chair, followed by the two older men.

"First to the trough," Liv told BeBe under her breath.

"Chaz, you stop right there," Miss Ida said.

Chaz froze in the archway.

"Look up."

They all looked up.

Above his head, hanging from the top of the archway, was a bough of mistletoe. He looked down again right at Liv, who happened to be across from him.

She took an involuntary step back.

Looking his smarmiest, Chaz pointed upward, shrugged, and grabbed her by her shoulders and pulled her under the mistletoe. He let go but only long enough to capture her face in both hands. The last thing she saw before he planted a kiss on her mouth was his grin.

It seemed to last a really long time, and by the time he pulled away, she was a little breathless.

Chaz looked gob-smacked—for a nanosecond—before he recovered and became his normal cheeky self.

He looked around. "Come here, Miss Ida. Let's show them how it's really done."

Ida giggled but presented her cheek. Chaz kissed her, making silly growling noises, until she playfully pushed him away.

"Been dipping at the cooking sherry, if you ask me," Edna said before Chaz pulled her into a big hug and kissed her, too.

"Now, that's enough young man. If you need more kisses, here's BeBe."

"Hey, I'm saving the cutest for last." He pulled BeBe toward him and planted a quick, loud smack on her mouth.

"Anyone else? Ted, Bill?" Chaz asked.

"Food's getting cold," Bill said and headed toward the table.

Ted raised a hand. "Think I'll pass. Miss Ida, something dinged."

"Oh, my rolls." Miss Ida scurried past them into the kitchen.

"Sit down, everyone," Miss Edna said. "Bill, bring the decanter of wine from the sideboard."

When everyone was seated and the wine was poured, and after Bill blessed the food, Ted stood and raised his glass. "Here's to absent friends and those that are here among us. And especially to Miss Ida and Miss Edna for their wonderful hospitality."

The roast was served. Potatoes, beans, relishes, and rolls were passed. They all had seconds, and Bill and Chaz had thirds, before they all indulged in dessert, a rich English trifle in a thick cut-glass bowl, and coffee while both sisters beamed with delight.

Liv had to admit, it had been a pretty wonderful day. When the food was put away, and a container of bones was set aside for Whiskey, who'd been sent home after the present opening; after the china was hand washed and returned to the cabinet, and the silver had been carefully dried and laid in its wooden storage box, they all sat in the parlor, sated and quiet.

And were startled when the doorbell rang.

"I'll get it," Edna said and pushed herself off the sofa.

There were mumbled voices and Edna returned bringing A.K. Pierce.

"Why, A.K.," Miss Ida said, "we were hoping you'd stop by."

A.K. nodded to the room. "I can't stay long, but just wanted to drop this off before the day was over." He held out his hand to Miss Ida. "For you and Miss Edna." A square, wrapped package was dwarfed by his large hand.

"How sweet. Edna, take his coat. A.K., you know everyone here, I think."

A.K. nodded at the room again. Ted and Bill mumbled hello. Chaz nodded back, barely.

"What's his problem?" BeBe whispered.

"Beats me, he's been weird all day," Liv said.

"And BeBe, and of course you know Liv."

A.K. saw Liv and his face softened a fraction.

"Oh," breathed BeBe. "I get it. Want me to push you under the mistletoe?"

"Absolutely not," Liv said. "I've had enough of that for today. Besides, I have too much work to do. I don't have time for . . ."

"Dalliance?" BeBe laughed. "Surely you can juggle a couple of boyfriends along with all the other things you have to take care of."

"Don't get any ideas. Right now I'm stuffed and happy and I'm ready to sleep for a week. Valentine's Day is only a month and a half away . . . and then Saint Patrick's Day . . . and Easter . . . Heck, before we know it, it will be the Fourth of July."

Holiday time is party time in New York City, but after a sparkling winter bash ends with a murder, Village Blend coffeehouse manager Clare Cosi vows to put the killer on ice...

From New York Times Bestselling Author

CLEO COYLE

HOLIDAY BUZZ

A Coffeehouse Mystery

At the Great New York Cookie Swap, pastry chefs bake up their very best for charity. Clare is in charge of the beverage service, and her famous Fa-la-la-la lattes make the gathering even merrier. But her high spirits come crashing down to earth when she discovers the battered body of a hardworking baker's assistant.

Police suspect a serial attacker whose escalating crimes have become known as "the Christmas Stalkings." Clare's boyfriend, NYPD detective Mike Quinn, finds reason to believe even more sinister forces are involved. Clare isn't so sure—and when she finds a second bludgeoned baker, she becomes a target. Now Clare is spending the holiday season poring over clues, and she's not going to rest until justice is served.

INCLUDES HOLIDAY AND COOKIE RECIPES!

"Highly recommended for all mystery collections."
—*Library Journal* (starred review)

"[A] frothy cast of lovable eccentrics."
—*Publishers Weekly*

facebook.com/CleoCoyleAuthor
facebook.com/TheCrimeSceneBooks
penguin.com

M1288T0313